The Forged Prince

BOOKS BY MICHAEL LAIRD

The Chronicles of Tethera

The Forged Prince

The Torc of Tethera

The Queen of Deceit

The Gates of Annwyn (forthcoming)

The Forged Prince

Book One of the Chronicles of Tethera

MICHAEL LAIRD

The Forged Prince

By Michael Laird

ISBN: 978-0996650311

To my wonderful daughters, Caitlin and Elinore, who brought me back so many times to Narnia, Prydain, and Middle Earth and to my amazing wife, Linda, who got me here.

CONTENTS

Chapter I

A Desperate Pursuit

The attack was swift and brutal. Moriganna's men and shape-shifters had become scattered and strung out in their pursuit. Now each was an island as the enemy force surged against them from all sides. To Llew's eyes, their foes first appeared to be enormous numbers of armed men, but it took him only a moment to see his mistake. With a shock of horror he realized that, while they might once have been men, this was no longer the case. Although he had never seen one before, it was evident they could only be the macabre instruments of the Lord of Annwyn . . . his dreaded barrow warriors.

Llew saw, or thought he saw, half a dozen of his party pulled or knocked from their mounts in the first moments. One barrow warrior rose directly before him and Gower, without instruction, gave a ferocious growl and rose on his hind legs to meet it, while flailing with his forelegs. The barrow warrior went down and his mount came down upon it as well, stamping to finish the job. Whether the dead that walked could truly die or not, this one would do no further walking, certainly not with all of its bones broken.

Llew cast his gaze about desperately for Afaggdu. The chaos was nearly complete as battle swirled up and down the forest trail. He drove Gower through the heavy foliage, ducking low branches where he could, checking first one fight then another, and not lingering long enough for any of the undead to transfer their attentions to him. The eerie fight was worse, if anything, for the fact that while the living grunted and groaned, howled and shrieked, the barrow warriors made no sound at all save for the ringing clash of their weapons upon their foes.

The shape-shifters were quite a different matter. Dropping all semblance of humanity they had become screaming, snarling terrors of sinew and claw, speed and motion. No single barrow warrior could challenge them; the beasts were frenzied blurs as they ripped through the ranks of their undead foes. Nonetheless, as he searched, Llew saw at least one of Moriganna's clawed creatures go down beneath the press of its attackers.

Hearing a familiar bellow to his right, he pulled sharply on Gower's reins and plunged through a layer of undergrowth into a partial clearing. Afaggdu was there, dismounted and with his back to a large tree, ringed by perhaps a dozen barrow warriors. Although blood streamed down the left side of his face, he seemed otherwise uninjured and was holding his own. Shattered remains marked where at least two other barrow warriors had already fought, and lost, their last battle to him.

As Llew braced himself to charge into the fray Afaggdu spotted him and roared, "Do not waste your time, laddie. Ride east while none can stop you. Catch the ones with the prince!" His arms tutor stopped speaking then and, with a mace in one hand and an axe in the other, turned the rush of two barrow warriors at once, then counter-attacked and smashed a third down to a dismembered doom.

Llew hesitated, unsure whether to obey or assist. "By Cadafael's craven feet, do it!" Afaggdu swore, without taking his attention off his foes. "These are courtesy of Lord Arawen and we have lost already if they get him away! Ride!"

Still Llew stood, paralyzed by indecision. Then three of the barrow warriors took notice and moved to intercept him as several more came crashing into the clearing, already finished with their first antagonists. With a cry he turned Gower and together they plunged away towards the trail. Regaining it, they dodged a pair of shape-shifters surrounded by a thick clot of barrow warriors and then raced eastwards through the trees, easily outdistancing the many barrow warriors pursuing them. Thwarted, yet seemingly incapable of feeling disappointment, these then fell instead upon the beleaguered shape-shifters.

Following the eastern track, the sounds of battle behind Llew became fainter and faded out. The trees themselves became fewer, and farther apart, until it was clear to Llew that he had left the cover of the forest altogether. The land was now fairly open, the trees increasingly scarce and all of them stunted.

Unfortunately, the cloud cover was still impenetrable and a mist began falling, increasing the chill and limiting how far he could see ahead. It was then that a large black bird settled on his right shoulder. Cymri had found him at last.

There was no time for pleasantries. Striving to be as succinct as possible, he said, "They have taken the prince on ahead. Can you fly ahead and ensure we do not lose them? I would also like some idea of how many we pursue and how far and how fast they are moving if possible."

His answer was a loud caw near his ear. "Ack," exclaimed Llew. He shifted one hand to seize the amulet he was wearing about his neck. "Again, please?"

"I said I can do that, but do you have a plan for if you overtake them?" Cymri asked.

"Nay, but I will think of something. Afaggdu said they cannot truly be killed, but chopping them up works almost as well."

"That may not be easily done, Llew."

"It does not matter. It must be done or, as you once pointed out yourself, I may never find a place for myself in this world." With that, Cymri said no more and took wing, vanishing into the mists ahead of them.

Gower carried him eastward across the damp heath at a gallop while Llew attempted to glimpse his quarry in the mist ahead. A number of questions burdened his thoughts. How long a head start did the barrow warriors have? How many were there? He was caught by surprise when Cymri came winging in from above and suddenly spread her wings before them while she shrilly cried out: "Hold, hold!" Gower stopped abruptly, nearly sending Llew flying over the great horse's head even as he tried to rein in.

Llew's breath caught in his throat as he saw what had nearly befallen them. They were poised at the top of a stone bluff that was at least nine or ten feet high. It ran off both left and right as far as he could see. At its base was a very steep slope that ran down into the mists. Going over it at a gallop would likely have killed or severely injured both himself and Gower. He swiftly dismounted and moved up to the very edge. Looking down the rock face, he saw it was possible he could brace himself and drop down, but there was no way he was going to get Gower down from here.

Cymri had alighted on a nearby rock. Glancing at her, Llew could tell she was impatient to speak to him so he gripped his amulet again.

"There is but one barrow warrior carrying the prince. It just jumped down and kept on going," she told him.

Llew returned his gaze to the drop. "The dead are said to lie beyond pain and suffering so I suppose a barrow warrior can do that." He frowned, then said, "Although it is a pity it failed to break a leg in the process."

"Pity and barrow warrior are terms seldom heard in the same breath," remarked Cymri.

Llew frowned again but did not answer. Without Gower he would be sacrificing an advantage should he catch up to his quarry. He considered the situation again, but it already felt clear to him what he had to do. "Find a way down or around for Gower and bring him, please," he asked Cymri.

Without waiting for a response from her, Llew spoke to Gower, "Gower, follow Cymri. Be a good boy, follow Cymri." Trusting to Gower's keen canine-like mind, he grasped the lichen covered limestone of the ledge's top and lowered himself over. He kicked about for a toe hold beneath and found one, but he was only able to lower himself another foot before he had to drop the remaining four feet or so.

Unfortunately, the ground was uneven. Llew landed badly and lost his balance at once. He rolled down the grass and stone covered slope nearly twenty feet before twisting sideways and arresting his momentum. Although the slope was covered in tall, wet grass and small yellow flowers, it had many good-sized stones upon it as well and he keenly felt every bruise they inflicted.

His breath had been knocked from him. After lying still for a minute, Llew slowly managed to stand. The armor had helped somewhat; at least he was not bleeding and his head seemed okay. At the end of his roll he had lost his helmet, but it had already saved his skull from being cracked wide open. As he picked it up and put it back on he noted, with some surprise, that neither of the antlers had suffered so much as a broken prong. He would have expected both to have snapped off completely during the repeated impacts. He considered that for an instant. Moriganna was an enchantress and it was she that had insisted on him wearing it. Enchanted armor?

Limping a little, he began moving straight out from the wall. The land quickly returned to a relatively flat heath; it was covered in knee high grass with intermittent boulders and stones and, occasionally, a stunted tree or two. They might have been alders, but Llew did not stop to look. The pain faded somewhat as he moved, indicating nothing critical was broken in his mishap. Dropping the limp he was able to increase his speed.

The barrow warrior was carrying a heavy load. Llew could easily see where the wet grass had been crushed by its passage. If what little he had been told of them was correct, the thing he pursued was tireless, but there would not be much speed in its dead limbs. Llew hurried on, picking up his pace yet again.

After a time that seemed less than an hour, Llew could discern a shambling motion ahead of him. As he closed the distance between them it revealed itself as an armored figure carrying another such slung across its right shoulder. Llew passed the ruins of a herdsman's hut barely visible in the mist to his right; the partially collapsed thatch roof bore testimony to long years of disuse. Now he was coming up on the revenant fairly quickly. Sensing him, the creature abruptly turned, then let its human cargo drop heavily to the ground as it unthonged a heavy mace from its belt.

At close range Llew could see that its armor, although once perhaps of reasonable quality, was now badly damaged and corroded, as though it had been torn at by many weapons and then buried a long time in a damp place. The wearer was in no better condition. The face itself was a thing of pure horror. Llew tore his eyes away from it to focus on the creature's torso, glad he could do so. Afaggdu had taught him repeatedly that any warning of his opponent's next move would be seen there first, in any case.

Llew came to a halt well out of his foe's reach and drew his own sword. Somehow he had failed to come up with a clear idea on what to do next. Not only was the creature already dead, it must also be very strong to have carried the prince as easily as it had. The mace would likely have colossal force behind it were it to land a blow. He also recalled Afaggdu's words of warning concerning such; thrusting would be nearly worthless against it. That was only a potential way to bind and possibly lose his blade. Still, if it was as slow in swinging as it was at running, then perhaps he could strike while it attempted to recover. Possibly he could even sever the arm that held the mace. With that done he could surely then disable it completely.

He feinted towards it, hoping to get it to swing at him. Predictably, it did so and he leaped forward to catch it off guard as the swing passed. Not so predictably, it recovered far too quickly and Llew had to quickly check his rush and retreat to avoid getting brained by a back swing. His soreness from his earlier fall slowed him and, instead of a clean miss, the mace hit him for a grazing blow on the left shoulder. The pain sent stars through his vision and he was barely able to refocus in time to sidestep the next downward stroke of the barrow warrior.

Llew backed up quickly, suddenly realizing he might be outmatched and not sure what to do about it. The barrow warrior lunged after him, then the thing stopped short and inclined its head to look down and back at its left foot. With his peripheral vision, Llew noted that the prince had roused sufficiently to seize the creature's left ankle in both hands and was holding it fast. Evidently the barrow warrior was puzzling out how to extricate itself without overly damaging its captive. Llew wasted no time gaping; instead he stepped forward and, ignoring the pain in his shoulder, took the sword in a two-handed grip and swung with all his might.

The attack lacked any finesse but, with the barrow warrior's guard completely down, no finesse was required. Afaggdu had not exaggerated when he had told Llew he was a strong lad for his age. Llew's two-handed swing caught the barrow warrior just above its gorget and below its helmet in a flat arc. Head and helmet went flying into a nearby mound of boulders with a meaty smack and an awful clatter.

Llew's inelegant attack had him completely off balance so, rather than trying to catch himself, he instead spun completely around while raising and planting his boot in the middle of the barrow warrior's chest, amazed at his own grace even as he did so. The now headless monster flew away and landed heavily on its back, its mace spinning away from its outstretched hand. It did not move again.

With his balance regained and his sword still held high before him, Llew turned back to the prince. He was still sprawled flat on his stomach but had his head lifted just high enough to regard Llew in turn. "Well done," he remarked, and then collapsed utterly.

Much as he would have liked to do the same, Llew felt he did not have the luxury of resting yet. Dusk would soon be upon them and they would need shelter. Continuing on in the dark as tired as he was, while somehow dragging the injured prince, just did not seem a good option.

Unfortunately, the low boulders, high grass, and stunted

trees of the heath offered little in the way of protection. Recalling the ruined hut he had seen on the way he calculated how much effort it would take to get them there. Sighing ruefully at the thought, he let himself collapse to sit on the grass next to the prince.

The young man was clearly injured but, upon a cursory examination, his armor was not rent anywhere save high on one arm and that did not seem to be bleeding profusely. The dent in the left side of the prince's helmet, together with the blood trickling out across that side of the face, concerned Llew more.

What little medicinal gear he had was on Gower. He had not so much as a water skin with him at present. Given how fatigued he was, Llew realized he would also need the big horse's help in moving the prince. For both these reasons, it seemed the best thing to do was to wait. It also gave him time to reflect on what he had just done. Although what lay ahead might make this seem the easy part, he had never really expected to get even this far.

Chapter II

The Healing Hut

The light of day was fading from the lonely heath as Llew's reveries came to an end. The time from when he first rode into the ambush by barrow warriors and all the way through the subsequent battle in the forest still had a surreal feel to it. By this he knew he was not ready to even attempt to come fully to grips with it all. Could Afaggdu have died? Centuries of life, of constantly increasing skill and canniness . . . all of that coupled with a zest for life that was second to none . . . could a spark that strong have been extinguished by even the horrendous barrow warriors?

After checking the fallen prince to make sure he was still alive, even while feeling a bit silly for it, he checked to make sure the decapitated barrow warrior was still neither alive, nor dead, nor anything else.

There was a quick flapping of wings and a familiar weight settled on his right shoulder. He quickly reached to his neck and grasped the amulet again.

"Oh, Llew, nicely done," Cymri exclaimed appreciatively, as she cocked her head and flicked her gaze to the nearby remains of the barrow warrior.

"Thank you, Cymri, but had the prince not distracted it, the affair might have gone much differently."

"The prince? He saw you then?"

"Only for a moment," replied Llew, wondering what this was about. Oh. "And I had my helm on still. He could not see my features. We will deal with that later. Where is Gower?"

"He will be along in a few moments, Llew, he has your scent and is coming fast."

Sure enough, Gower came trotting up at a brisk clip. Ignoring the barrow warrior's corpse, he stopped near the unconscious prince and sniffed suspiciously. Then he moved to Llew and began licking him on the ear.

"Arggh! Leave off Gower! No, stop, you galoot, stop already," Llew cried, struggling to rise to his feet.

* * *

The hut Llew had noticed earlier was a sturdy, windowless structure of sod. He now noted that the thatched roof was only half gone so there would be some protection if it rained, maybe. He warily looked in through the open doorway, but the hut was pretty much as it appeared. It consisted of a single room, now floored with a mixture of bare earth and some grass, with a fire pit in the center. No trace of furniture remained if, indeed, there had ever been such.

He led Gower in and then unstrapped the prince from where he had been ignominiously tied across the saddle. As gently as was possible, Llew lowered him to the ground. It was getting darker rapidly so fire was the first order of business. It was essential that he and the prince have one. Hopefully it would not attract any survivors of the altercation that had occurred just a few miles to the east. All he could do would be to keep it small and shielded. Gathering fallen limbs from the trees nearest the hut, and some large branches from a dead tree just behind it, he was able to use his flint and steel, together with tinder from Gower's saddle bags, to get a small fire going. Cymri located a small spring nearby and Llew managed to get his water bags filled just before night closed upon them completely.

With a sigh, he regarded the prince. Llew knew his skill in healing was not great, although perhaps not so bad by the rough and ready standards of a battlefield. Treat the most serious first, he reasoned. He unbuckled the prince's helmet and carefully removed it. After seeing the great dent in it he was not surprised by the raw goose egg on the prince's scalp. Gently, using only his fingertips, he could feel no softness, which he presumed to be a good sign. There was not much he could do with a head injury save pray there was no concussion or permanent damage. Accordingly, he cleansed the wound and then, with advice from Cymri, applied a poultice and bandaged it.

As he worked in the firelight, he could not help but take notice of the resemblance that had so captivated Moriganna. The prince's features were very nearly his own, perhaps appearing a tiny bit younger than his own fourteen summers. They seemed slightly finer too, more evidence of royal breeding, no doubt. Still, a substitution could well have worked, particularly if some weeks or months had separated the observer's viewing of the prince and himself. The hair was certainly a perfect match, the straw color and fine texture feeling identical to his, even to his own experienced fingers.

The arm injury, while larger and uglier than the scalp wound, was one Llew found much less alarming. He had frequently had occasion to treat such wounds on horses, even to sewing them up once the stable master had developed some confidence in him. While the prince would likely bear a substantial scar upon his upper left arm, the wound would heal neatly . . . or would if it did not become infected. There was no telling what vileness might have been on the blade of a barrow warrior.

"You will need to wake him up when you finish there, Llew," Cymri had remarked, when he consulted with her on proper treatment.

"Kinder, I think, to let him sleep. This will hurt a great deal and I have no wine to ease his pain."

"Nonetheless", Cymri insisted, "with a head injury they must be woken up occasionally, or risk never waking again."

Llew had just tied off the final suture when the prince released a deep, shaky breath and turned his head to regard him. With a start Llew realized that he must have wakened sometime during the ministrations, yet had refrained from moving while the arm was being stitched. What control that must have required!

Upon turning his head to gaze on Llew, the prince had not moved again. Finally he spoke in a calm voice, "You cannot be who you appear to be."

That seemed like a good start to Llew, the prince at least was not trying to kill him . . . yet.

"And who do I appear to be?" Llew asked. He thought himself prepared for any response, but he was quite wrong.

"Well", the prince said slowly, "you appear to be my brother, returned from the dead."

Llew gaped at the prince; he had not known the prince had ever had a brother. It seemed a rather grievous omission in Moriganna's curriculum on the heir of Gwent.

"Well," he said slowly, "I think Moriganna would rather I have appeared to be you."

The prince hissed and drew back as much as he could without moving from the ground by the fire. A wicked hunting knife had appeared in his hand at Llew's words. "So this is nothing more than a plot of the mother of lies? What do you plan then? To kill me and take my place? To rule Gwent as Moriganna's puppet?"

"Look," said Llew, "I know you are having a bad day, and you might not be thinking clearly, but please consider what you just said. Moriganna would love that plan, in fact, it very much is her plan."

The prince blinked. "Ah, I see what you are saying. If it was your plan as well then there is a certain question as to why I am not outside and under the turf already."

"Precisely," Llew agreed.

"So you are not her pawn in all things then?" the prince asked suspiciously. "How do you explain your appearance? Surely she has you under a spell, a guise of some sort?"

"Nay," replied Llew. "Were that the case would she not have made us identical in appearance? I am here now because she was quite upset that we are becoming less alike as we grow. I think her original plan was, in fact, to wait until you were grown before killing your father and usurping you."

"Hmm," the prince mused, "it is true you are somewhat heavier set than I. They must have been working you hard."

"Afaggdu has been a demanding sort of arms trainer these past three years."

"Ah, I wondered where he had disappeared to. Yes, that could certainly account for it. Come closer that I may examine your face."

Llew's eyes flicked to the knife in the prince's hands.

The prince made a wry face, and then winced, probably because of his head wound. With a quick hand motion, the knife vanished. Llew carefully eased closer, well aware the weapon could reappear as quickly as it had been secreted away. Afaggdu had taught him that trick as well.

When their faces were within a foot of each other, the prince slowly, ever so slowly, raised his hand and touched the side of Llew's face. Llew held perfectly still while the fingers brushed against his cheek. It was bare, with just the faintest whiskers beginning to show themselves. Though hardly more than a boy's fuzz, Moriganna had insisted his facial hair be shaved daily, no doubt to better his resemblance to the prince.

A look of wonder came over the prince's face. "Surely not," he murmured, "it simply cannot be. Even the bones beneath your face match my own. Where did Moriganna get you from, and what is your name?"

"As for where she got me from I cannot say, but, so far as I know, I have lived all my life at her keep, somewhere past the eastern marshes. As for my name—only today I learned my real name is Llew. Yet I am now uncertain of the truth of this, and I know I cannot be called that near you, so perhaps I could go by Gwri? It is what I am used to, even though I was told never to use it again, as it is not my real name, just what they called me, on account of my hair, ever since I was but a spratling, underfoot and in the stables."

"No," the prince said, "your name is your own and you are certainly welcome to it. My full name is Llewellyn, so call me that instead. You were kept as a stable boy?"

"Well, only the first few seasons that I can recall, after my father, the old stable master, passed on. I was very young and have few memories of him. My mother died even before that, and of her I have no memory at all. Then I came to the queen's notice and she wanted me trained as she thought a king should be—at least so far as manners and history and fighting and horseback riding and such."

"Indeed," was all the prince said. After a bit, he added: "Truly Moriganna has much to pay for; an accurate accounting may well be more than she can afford, yet she has done better by you than she might have."

"Your full name is really Llewellyn? Moriganna never told me that."

"Indeed, I do not use it a great deal." The prince looked thoughtful. "So, Llew, will you accompany me home? You will find our generosity without bounds for this day's work alone."

"Gladly will I do so," answered Llew, "I was not really otherwise engaged, as it were."

"Excellent. Two will travel far more safely than one." The prince shifted his position, wincing as his arm moved slightly in the process.

"True enough," replied Llew. "And we will travel faster as well for speed is of the utmost if we are to have the least chance to save your father."

"My father?"

"Aye, Moriganna will not have envisioned failure here so her plans to kill the king must already be underway. Certainly she will want him dead before you—that is I—return, so that no taint of regicide would stain the heir."

"Llew! the prince exclaimed. "We waste time here! We must ride both by day and by night as we can to prevent this." He tried to rise, but failed and remained on the cloak by the fire, a frantic look in his eyes.

"Steady, your highness. We must make allowance for your injuries."

"We do not have time to make any allowances. We must move, now!"

Llew eyed the prince speculatively. "And when you weaken and are unable to travel at all? What then?"

"That shall not happen! You may leave me behind if it does."

"It will happen, your highness. At the very least the trip will take longer, if it can be finished at all. Consider the same situation as if you were a horse. Would disregarding your injuries speed up a long trek? Further, it is at least two weeks travel to Gwent by the most direct route. It is possible we will arrive too late, in any case. What will it serve for the heir to come riding forth in the wake of the king's death, yet in a condition unfit to immediately take up the throne? Leaving you behind when you may already be the new king is not a sound option either."

The prince groaned. "I thought I was the very soul of sound reasoning, but your logic is unassailable. We will leave at first light and travel as far and as fast as we may, though."

"Agreed," Llew assented. "Here let me bandage that arm, highness. We will want it kept clean that it may heal faster."

"Certainly, and thank you, Llew." The prince shifted to allow Llew to apply a dressing to the fresh wound.

"I hope you will not think me rude if I try to rest a bit now. Although my mind is racing with what you have told me, I know I must. I would try to eat also, but I fear with my woozy head nothing would stay down."

"Rest easy, your highness. Rest easy. In the morning we must move fast, in any case, for there are likely to be those of either Arawen or Moriganna, or possibly both, who will seek us. It is too much to hope for that they all have destroyed each other."

The prince's eyes were already closed, so Llew was not sure if that last had been heard or not.

"Nicely done," remarked Cymri, when Llew again thought to take hold of the amulet. "I was greatly concerned with what Prince Llewellyn's reaction would be to you. Trust is not a thing to be given lightly, yet the prince tends to be an excellent judge of character."

"Aye, I do not think that, were I in his place, I would so easily trust such a one as me, freely admitting to be from Moriganna. His reaction to me seemed rather odd, though, to say the least." The prince's intense wonder at their resemblance had surprised Llew with its depth and intensity.

Cymri cocked her head and fixed an avian eye on him. "Do not discount yourself too easily. Even in his current state the prince is likely to be highly perceptive, and he has probably noted things about you that you yourself are not aware of. There is certainly a rapport between the two of you that even a black bird can see."

"Heh, now who is discounting themselves? At any rate, sleep seems an excellent idea at the moment."

"Aye," agreed Cymri, "it would be—but the prince needs healing even more than you need rest. There is a healing chant I will teach you. I cannot perform it in my present state but it will greatly speed his recovery. I will teach it to you now and you must recite it over his wounds for at least an hour tonight."

Chapter III

Setting Out

The following morning Cymri applied her beak to the side of Llew's head before the sun had even crested the horizon. The sky had cleared but the weather had turned cooler.

"Ow, I wake, I wake! Leave off Cymri!" Llew sat up abruptly. As he rose to get some rations together for a quick breakfast, the prince roused and regarded him.

"Cymri? You named your bird Cymri?" he inquired.

"Nay," replied Llew, "she is not my bird, she is her own bird, and I only call her that because it is indeed her name; I had no part in it."

"I knew one by that name once."

"Hmm," mused Llew as he passed a few strips of dried meat to the prince, "a red haired young woman, about a head shorter than us, fancied herself a bard?" Cymri cawed loudly at this, though whether in amusement or outrage was not readily apparent.

"Aye, that would be her, the very same, do you know her?"

"Certainly," replied Llew, "and you know this bird as well then."

The prince's eyes went wide. "No, it cannot be," he protested.

Cymri cawed, "Yes, yes!" If anything, the prince's eyes grew wider.

"Cymri?" the prince asked tentatively. The bird pumped her head up and down.

"Oh this is terrible, Cymri, who did this thing to you?"

"Moriganna!" Cymri squawked.

"Of course she did!" the prince's eyes flashed dangerously. "She has much to answer for indeed, and so she shall."

"More than you know, even yet," Llew said cryptically. "But we had best discuss that later. Gower, up!" he commanded.

The horse had been sleeping in a corner, lying on his stomach, his head lying forward on his front legs. At Llew's command he jumped up in a most unhorse-like fashion, propelling himself up and forward using his back legs.

The prince took this additional oddity in stride and said nothing.

They each then took turns traveling out and behind the hut to take care of essentials. When they were both back, Llew shared out some of his meager trail rations.

"Highness, can you ride?" Llew asked after Gower was saddled.

The prince was still moving a bit gingerly but replied, "Yes, I feel much better than last night. Your skills as a healer do you great credit. But while we are together on this we are just comrades in arms. Dispense with formalities. Also, I would say to please call me Llew except that it will be better, I think, if you do as I suggested last night and call me by my full name, Llewellyn. Unless you prefer to sound like you are talking to yourself?"

"Nay, have no fear on that account your hi—er, Llewellyn,"

Llew said. "Of more concern is which route should we take? The barrow warrior was taking you eastwards so I should avoid that; southeast is all too close to Arawen's lands of Annwyn. Southwest leads us closer to Moriganna. Westward we might meet either followers of Arawen or Moriganna depending on how yesterday's events played out. Northward takes us into wilderness and ruin and deeper into Pictish lands. Beyond that is the sea and Dylan, I know little of him but he is certainly a personage we do not wish to meet."

"Indeed he is not," exclaimed Llewellyn. "What do you know of him? He explained little when we met."

"Ah, you have at least met him," replied Llew, holding Gower so that the prince could mount. "I dare say you may be more of an authority on him than I am, now."

Gower, curious at who was to be mounting him, pulled loose of Llew and commenced sniffing the prince thoroughly in a most unhorse-like manner. Somewhat taken aback, Llewellyn attempted to pet the animal on the neck to sooth him. It was a movement meant to gain the trust of a normal horse; Gower apparently found it pleasing as well, rewarding the prince with a couple of quick face licks. The prince cried out in an undignified manner and leapt back. Gower took a startled step backwards as well.

"It is alright," cried Llew. "That is just Gower's way. He really does like you." And to Gower: "Good boy, easy there, good boy, good Gower," as he reached out and stroked the startled animal's mane. "Gower is a little different from most horses is all."

"I can see that," Prince Llewellyn remarked dryly, looking just a bit flushed with embarrassment.

"Give him one of your meat strips. You will have a friend for life."

"Meat?" Llewellyn looked aghast. "You feed the creature meat?"

"He loves it, just a little though, he can also eat grass to live on and we cannot."

Llewellyn numbly offered a strip of meat to Gower. At least, Llew noticed, the prince did not seem to visibly react to the sight of the great beast happily wolfing it down and then panting. He got the prince on Gower's back with no further mishap.

Breaking camp, Llew led them southward by unspoken agreement. Although that path might take them directly between the domains of Arawen and Moriganna, it was the correct direction to travel towards Gwent, and it was away from other bad choices, such as remaining in an area where survivors of the skirmish the day before might be looking for them. The day was mostly overcast, although not so much as the day before; at least now there was some air moving. The grass here was predominately a moor grass; it was tufted in blue and moving in weak waves under the gentle easterly breeze.

It was not good farming land at all, Llew realized. The earth's limestone bones were far too close to the surface beneath the grasses. Indeed, in many places they showed through, areas of naked rock where nothing grew save for small purple flowers in the cracks, and orange and green lichens and mosses on the stone itself. The underlying stone also prevented trees from planting deep roots. The same stone kept rain water from draining properly so that the ground was mostly soft and wet, though not quite marshy. Nonetheless, it was suitable land for the grazing of herds of sheep and possibly cattle. That there were signs of just such use in the past, such as the herder's hut, and no signs of any now, bespoke how far into wilderness and ruin the land had fallen. From what Llew recalled of the geography of the region, this had probably been part of the hinterlands of the kingdom of Clwyd.

Though the prince's wounds obviously still pained him, he made no complaint. He was also full of questions. "Tell me, Llew, aside from the occasional word or two she manages in Tetheran, how is it that you are able to understand Cymri?"

"Ah, the short answer is that I wear a magical medallion, crafted by Moriganna, and it is somehow infused with the blood of both Cymri and myself."

"I have heard that Moriganna is not one who is inclined to do favors for others."

"You have not heard incorrectly. The medallion is also a curse in that it is a kind of prison. It is too heavy for Cymri to carry and, should either of us ever get more than a few miles away from it, she will die."

At Llewellyn's insistence, he allowed the prince to try it on, but it seemed the magic that allowed an understanding of Cymri's speech worked for Llew alone. "Ah well," said Llewellyn, passing it back to Llew, "at least one of us can understand her, and you can answer my questions easily enough. Why was she turned into a bird and, for that matter, why does Moriganna allow her to roam freely?"

"Heh, she does not allow either of us to roam freely, for all that we are doing so. To explain more than that is a rather long story, I fear. If you wish, I can relate some of it to you as we travel."

"I do not want some of it. I want all of it. You must tell me your story, clear up until I awoke to find you practicing knitting with my flesh."

"Wherever would I start? I can certainly not recall my own birth."

"That is for you to decide, but it must be the first pivotal moment in your life, the one that eventually led to you coming to my rescue."

"Well. I grew up in the stables—"

"Not that way. You will skip over too much if you try to tell it like that. That is hardly a good thing if this is to be our sole diversion during our travels. You must tell it as a story that you happen to know of, not one that you are actually involved in. Hearing you say: 'I did this' and 'I did that' the whole time would surely do it a disservice. You must also cover it with enough detail. This is your entire life we are speaking of. Done right, there should scarcely be enough time for the telling before we ride through the gates of Caerleon."

"I am not certain I can do as you ask, Llewellyn."

"Then we shall take it in small portions, and I will ask many questions so that I may retell it for the both of us. You said you thought your name was Gwri until yesterday? Very well, then we shall call it Gwri's Tale."

Chapter IV

Gwri's Tale: The Sprat

"Gwri! Drop that shovel and get a pair of bridles; these horses will not go up to the castle on their own. The master of horse wants them yesterday and you are all I can spare to go with me right now. Mind you do not embarrass me." The 'or else' at the end of that warning was unspoken.

Taken by surprise, Gwri just stared at the stable master for a moment. It was fairly rare for Braen to ask him to do anything other than muck out a stall, or fetch something, and he had certainly never been permitted anywhere near the castle.

Braen eyed him with disfavor. "Did you miss the part where I said I was in a rush?"

Gwri dropped the ashwood shovel as though it were on fire and darted away, returning a moment later with a bridle for each animal. It was actually a measure of Braen's confidence in Gwri that he took the first bridle the boy offered and began putting it on the nearer of the two horses. Each bridle was specifically fitted to a single horse and even the simple act of fetching them had required Gwri to note which two horses the stable master had so that he could ensure he brought back the right bridles for each.

Braen finished putting on the first bridle and turned for the second, then saw Gwri had already put it on the other animal and was sitting on its bare back, reins in hand.

"No one likes a show off," Braen grumbled. "I will let it slide because I did say we were in a hurry."

The queen's castle stood atop a low hill overlooking the village below. The village had no name of its own. It was simply the village at Caer Mallcoedwig. The locals needed no name for it and no one else knew of its existence.

Although Gwri had never before been allowed within a bowshot of the castle, the stable master was a frequent visitor and they were admitted without incident. After dismounting in the courtyard, Braen made no move to tether the horses or to leave. Instead they just waited.

Gwri took the opportunity to have a good look at his surroundings. For him, they were something new and it might be a long time before he had another chance to come here. To his unpracticed eye, there was activity everywhere as the folk of the keep went about all the chores of daily life. This included everything from livestock being butchered, wagons being unloaded, laundry being washed and hung to dry, and even children of some of the castle dwellers racing around while they played. Eventually, looking up, he was surprised to find he was being watched. His surprise turned to shock when he realized the watcher was the queen herself.

Gwri saw her so seldom, this mysterious enchantress who held all of their lives in her hands, that he did not think to avert his eyes. No one had told him that her subjects normally avoided eye contact with her . . . or that there was a good reason for doing this. In an instant, her unblinking eyes flashed to him like a hawk to a vole. Under that pitiless gaze, Gwri stood rooted, unable to move or even think. She stared for a long moment and then vanished out of sight back into the room behind her.

For his own part, Gwri did not understand what had caused such a reaction. She had never even noticed him before, yet catching her eye once had resulted in what he was sure was far too much attention for comfort. He knew nothing of what this portended but he knew he wanted no part of it.

A guardsman came over to them and, wordlessly, Braen gestured towards the horses. The guardsman glanced over the animals and nodded once before he took the reins and led them away.

Gwri felt an enormous sense of relief flood through him as they began to make their way to the exit from the dark fortress that was Caer Mallcoedwig. That relief was short-lived. His heart went racing when another guardsman interposed himself between them and the gate.

"You can go," he said to Braen. "Queen Moriganna wants a better look at this little one. If he survives, we will send him back later."

* * *

It was late afternoon when the stable master looked up from his inspection of a recently repaired gate and saw Gwri had returned.

For his own part, the boy was not sure what sort of reception he was going to get, but he tried to reassure himself that he had seen at least a flicker of relief in Braen's eyes.

"Well, look at this," announced Braen. "The prodigal son

has returned. It certainly looks like it could have gone worse."

That was an understatement. In addition to having survived, Gwri was wearing new clothing and even a fine set of boots, made and cut to just his size. These were the first boots either had ever seen that were made for a child.

"Well?" Braen finally asked, trying to mask his curiosity. "What was it all about?"

Gwri shrugged. "She never said. She just sort of looked me over, like the way that guardsman did with the animals we brought him, and then she told me I had a lot to learn."

Beginning to show some ire, he continued, "After that she turned me over to her servants and they washed me in a big tub of water like a muddy shirt!" If anything, his outrage went up a notch. "Then they made me dress up like this! They also took away my old shirt and breeches and would not give them back."

Braen idly tugged at one corner of his moustache and looked thoughtful. "That was it? Then they just sent you back?"

"They did," Gwri affirmed. "But," he added, "the steward said to tell you I have to go back every day so I am in time to clean up and eat midday meal with the queen. Then I am to have lessons of some sort, manners and history and something else—I do not recall what. It will not be until after the evening meal that I can come back here to do my chores, if there is time."

"She wants to eat with you every day?" Braen shook his head in disbelief and a suspicious look came into his eyes. "And what else was said, eh?"

Gwri hesitated. "She did say that there would be consequences if I was not there on time each day," he admitted.

Braen reached out, as if to grab the boy by his tunic, and stopped just short of actually seizing the finely made garment. "Consequences for whom?" he thundered.

Despite his long familiarity with the man, Gwri was just a bit intimidated. "You and me, is what they told me," he said in a small voice, "mostly for you."

Braen's anger changed instantly to seeming despair. He put his head in his hands and sighed heavily before looking back up at Gwri. "From now on, boy, you are living in my shadow when you are not there. Now, was there anything else—anything at all?"

The boy thought about it. "No, that was it."

Chapter V

The Sea Lord

"So Moriganna began preparing you to usurp my place at least seven years back, it seems. All because she saw what a close resemblance you bear to me," remarked Prince Llewellyn. "That seems rather a long wait."

Llew shook his head. "Seven years to her might be as seven days to you or me. No one knows how old she is, just that she is ancient. Planning ahead probably takes on a whole new meaning when you see time on that scale."

"When did you realize what she was up to?"

"Me?" Llew laughed. "I had no idea what she was up to, but I never trusted her. Not even when she adopted me and named me her heir."

"Heir to Queen Moriganna? So," mused Prince Llewellyn, "you really are royalty as well, and can honestly call yourself Prince Llew."

"All just a ploy of Moriganna's," Llew responded hastily. "I have never even told anyone but you that she had adopted me and named me her heir. It means nothing if she lives forever."

"Cymri knows of course?"

"I have never told her, but if she did not overhear it then she has probably worked it out through innuendos, or else through the little barbs that Moriganna and I tossed at each other from time to time, your highness," said Llew, momentarily forgetting he was not to address the prince other than by name.

"Regardless, Prince Llew, it is an honor to greet you, your highness. I hight Prince Llewellyn. Now, given that we are peers, you really must call me Llewellyn in informal settings. And this," Prince Llewellyn spread his hands out to indicate the entire wilderness around them, "is most definitely an informal environment."

Llew smiled and replied, "I will do my best to keep that in mind . . . Llewellyn, but please do not think poorly of me should I occasionally backslide."

"Oh no, certainly not. I will just tease you unmercifully whenever it happens. That is what friends do for each other, you know, or so I hear."

Llew could not think of how to reply to that. He was too caught up in the realization that no one had ever before referred to him as a friend.

By this time they had traveled out of the grasslands and had entered a forest of ash and spruce. Cymri occasionally flew ahead for short distances at a time, then returned.

"Two weeks to Gwent you say?" asked Llewellyn as he watched Cymri depart on one of her excursions.

"Well," answered Llew, "I am only going by the maps I recall seeing, and by my estimate of how old they are. It may take longer given the hills, forests, and rivers in the way; I am not even considering if we should come to trouble with our enemies."

"So what you are saying is that it is two weeks as the crow flies?"

"That is true, and I know what you are thinking."

Llewellyn chuckled, the first time Llew had heard him do that. "Do you?"

"Aye," said Llew, "you want to send Cymri ahead with a message, but it will not work."

"And why not?"

"First, you have forgotten that, long before she gets that far from me and her amulet, she will die. That is something of an obstacle, but it is not even the only one."

Llewellyn clapped his hand to his forehead, then winced with the unexpected pain. "I think that knock on my head must have jarred my brains loose, Llew."

"Not to worry, you have had a lot to take in during a very short period of time. I am surprised you can even remember my own name, even if it is borrowed from you."

Llewellyn actually gave a brief laugh and said, "Well, that is better than attributing it to early senility. How old are you, Llew? I would guess our ages must be very close."

"Moriganna told me my precise birth date. She even had some minor presents and delicacies for me each year on that date, but I think it was just so I would remember it. That is the way she thinks. Cymri told me later that she probably lied because the date she told me was the same date as your own. That is also Moriganna's way. If the wrong thing is the only one you know, then that is one less way for you to slip up and use the right one by mistake."

"Ah," commiserated Llewellyn. "No one should grow up under such a guardian. "So tell me," he continued, in a rather obvious attempt to change the subject, "you said Cymri's link to you was the first reason that my otherwise brilliant plan would not work. I have shrewdly deduced that this implies there is a second reason. What is it?"

"Well," Llew said slowly, "assuming we could make something we could use for ink, and that we could use it on something we could make for parchment, I still cannot read or write. Can you?"

"Nay," Llewellyn replied. "How very frustrating this is! When this is over, the first thing I shall do it learn to read and then to write."

"I believe," said Llew, "that I will as well. I never fully realized the usefulness of these skills ere now. In case I run short of time, though, I think I will first learn to write, and then to read, since writing seems the more useful to me."

"Hmm," mused Llewellyn, "I do not think it works like that. How would you read what you had written if you did not learn to read first?"

"If I have written it then why would I need to be able to read it?" asked Llew. "I would know what it said."

"Possibly," Llewellyn allowed. "We shall have to investigate the matter further. Taliesin can both read and write in many languages. He could advise us."

"He could if he were not still a tree," replied Llew, while reflecting that it had never occurred to him that there might be different flavors of reading and writing for different languages. Why would that be, when neither skill relied on making the actual sounds peculiar to a given language?

"What? A tree?"

"Yes, I am afraid so," Llew replied. "He showed up one day, declared he was Cymri's father, and wanted to rescue her. For his trouble, Moriganna turned him into a great oak that, so far as I know, stands within her keep to this day."

"Taliesin will not remain a tree long once my father hears

of it! We will find and storm this keep of Moriganna's and break the enchantment."

"Only if she does not turn us all into summer daisies for attempting it," said Llew.

"Had she that much power she would have no need of ruses to capture kingdoms, or alliances with sea lords to capture princes."

"Possibly," conceded Llew. "Taliesin hinted at as much."

"Troubling as Taliesin's transformation is, it does ease my mind in one way."

"Truly? What way is that?"

"It had not escaped my notice that you were wearing his sword. I was almost sure there was a good reason for it."

"Ah, one that did not involve me taking it from him, you mean. No, it is a very fine sword; no longer being used by anyone, and Moriganna is never loath to do the frugal thing. She intended that, when you were captured, I should take your sword and give this one as a reward to Afaggdu."

"Since the barrow warrior did not trouble itself to remove it from me, I believe you must keep Taliesin's blade, much as I would wish to swap with you."

Surprised, Llew asked, "A prince's blade for a bard's? Why would you?"

"Taliesin is not any bard, nor is he just a bard. His sword is said to bear a name and is also rumored to be enchanted such that it will never shatter, or even nick and grow dull."

"Well, then," replied Llew, "perhaps you should—"

"Nay, and thank you. I believe it serves better where it is at the moment."

Upon that finality, Llew decided a change in topic was in order. "Tell me about your encounter with the sea lord, the one you and Moriganna call Dylan," he suggested. "All I really know is he is some lord of the sea who can command the weather and the sea creatures. Moriganna set him to blow your vessel off course and to a place of her choosing, one where her creatures could exchange me for you."

The prince sounded pensive when he answered. "That the storm was his doing surprises me not at all. It had been storming for two days and we knew not where we were, only that we had far overshot our goal in a desperate attempt to save ourselves from a lee shore. It was late in the day, with night falling, when our fortune failed and our ship foundered on the rocks off the coast. We attempted to rescue the horses. We got them into the water to swim the short distance to the shore, but no sooner were they in the water than did vicious sea creatures attack and devour them all. It was quite horrible. That no men were likewise attacked was strange indeed, but we wasted no time in getting ashore, as you may well imagine.

"As we gathered on the beach, he came striding up out of the surf. He was very tall and powerfully built, with handsome features, beardless, but with long dark hair , yet you could tell, just by his eyes, that he was utterly without humor, conscience, or mercy. They were so very cold! He carried an enormous three-pointed spear and wore strange armor made of the hard parts of various sea creatures, but of what species I could not say. He had a dozen creatures with him. They were bizarre, misshapen, man-like things that carried coral spears but wore no armor, and they dripped white sea-foam where they stood. I believe they were his guards, but he did not need them. One of my men drew sword against him and was swatted aside like an annoying insect.

"He looked me full in the eye and, I confess, I was frightened, but I could see no point in showing him that. He spoke to me then in a deep voice, laden with much malice: 'Know little princeling that you survive only by my design. I have no love for your line and great is my desire to strike you down where you stand.' It seemed to me that I could feel his hate as a tangible thing.

"I hid my fear and said, 'Come then,' while drawing my own blade with as much bravado as I could muster. 'It may not be so easy as you seem to think.' Yet he never even glanced at my sword.

"He sneered then and said, 'A deal has been struck; your life is yours for a bit longer, and those of your men as well. Keep your weapons, you may need them to survive until a certain someone comes for you, and these are Pictish lands. The Picts are unfeeling brutes who will care little for you or any other. Do tell Moriganna, if you should see her, that I, Dylan, have kept my bargain. I leave you alive and unharmed, despite how it pains me to do so.' Then he strode back into the waves with his followers and was gone."

Llew gave a low whistle when the tale was complete. "I do not understand why he even showed himself to you. He said little and accomplished less."

"I have thought somewhat on that myself," the prince said bitterly. "He was boasting. There is some reason, real or imagined, why he truly hates those of the house of Gwent, and he merely wanted me to know it was he that had undone me and given me to Moriganna."

"That, at least, makes some sense," agreed Llew.

"We weathered the night on the beach and the next day we gathered what little we had saved and made all haste southwestward on foot. We had traveled barely half a day before we were set upon by Picts, first, then by Moriganna's mercenaries, who captured those few of us that remained, and then we were both attacked by Lord Arawen's barrow warriors. The rest you well know."

"I am sure I would have been frightened, too, but it sounds like you handled it as bravely as anyone possibly could have."

Llewellyn shrugged uncomfortably. "One has a role to play, and nowhere less so than in front of our own people. At that point, I still had people. It is now your turn. Where did Gower come from, and is he even a horse? I would like very much to know how you acquired him."

Chapter VI

Gwri's Tale: The Bag

The stable master was still fast asleep when Gwri arose at the crack of dawn, as he always did, and went to fetch water for those horses that were confined to their stalls. A year of eating at the queen's own table had seen him shoot up in size to the point where carrying two full buckets of water was no longer an especially difficult task for him. Certainly he was now far larger than any of the village boys near his own age.

He preferred to take the water from the nearby stream. He did not mind the walk and, even carrying the buckets, this method was still far easier and faster than trying to bring it up from the well, one bucket at a time. It also allowed him to be done by the time Braen woke up. This was important as the stable master would have insisted that Gwri use the well so as to keep him closer at hand. Braen, the boy had noticed, was more than a little paranoid about letting him out of his sight.

When Gwri arrived at the water's edge that morning, something was different. It took a moment before he figured out what it was. A crude jute bag had become snagged on a fallen log across the stream. It was right at the edge of one of the deeper pools and just above a series of rapids.

That would have been an end to it had he not kept a close watch on this interesting new addition to his environment. It was while he dipped his buckets to fill them that he thought he saw the bag make a small movement.

It looked almost as if something might be inside. Perhaps a fish had nudged it from underneath? He set the buckets down and fixed his gaze on the bag. Had it really happened? Could it happen again? He involuntarily jumped when it did just that.

Something is in that bag, and I am not leaving, he vowed to himself, *until I know what that something is.*

Getting to it was problematical. First, he had to find a way across. The bridge was much too far away.

"So," he announced to the bag, "you intend to make me do this the hard way." Gwri knew a nearby spot where the stones allowed him to cross. It required a series of leaps and short climbs to avoid getting wet, and that was only if he did everything exactly right. With all the overconfidence of a nine year old acrobat, he still made it look relatively easy.

As he moved down the other bank to the fallen tree, a new problem manifested. The many branches jutting from the tree's trunk would make it more than a little difficult to get out as far as the bag. He tried anyway but, just as he thought he could make it, they became too thick to allow him past.

Looking about, he spotted a rock protruding from the water off to one side. This started him thinking and it took only a moment to see how it could be done.

He deftly leapt to the rock while ducking under a branch. Then, because the rock was too small to stand on, he used it to spring back to the tree trunk, right next to where the bag waited.

Where he failed was in not realizing how much the sudden arrival of his weight would push the tree down into the water. This had the immediate effect of freeing the bag and letting it continue its interrupted journey downstream. It simultaneously caused him to lose his balance and land in the water. His attempt at grasping a branch failed and, sick with fright, he found himself following the bag down through the rapids.

He tried to extend a leg down to see if he could reach bottom but only succeeded in smacking his knee into an underwater boulder. The pain made him gasp and suck in a mouthful of water. He coughed it up while flailing to keep his head out of the water and simultaneously trying to avoid hitting the rocks. This was not entirely successful. His entire body smashed into a boulder. Then the current pulled him away and whirled him about just in time for his left side to be dragged at high speed down a long rough boulder, ripping clothes and skin alike. He did not scream, but it was only because he realized that getting more water into his throat to choke on would likely be the end of him.

The current dumped him into a large deep pool where the water was almost placid compared to the rapids. There! He kicked with protesting limbs, thrust himself forward, and seized the bag. It wriggled in his arms and something from inside made a loud whine. Before going over the far side of the pool he got his feet beneath him and touched the bottom, then he slogged out onto the embankment where he collapsed.

Something in the bag began vigorously thrashing about. Curiosity overcame his pain and exhaustion. The wet knot on the rawhide cord securing the bag was more resistant to being untied than even the fabled Gordian Knot. With some effort, he rubbed the cord on a jagged rock until it wore through. As he unwound it from the bag's mouth he was caught completely off guard by the wet and furry animal that burst out and began licking his face. It was a puppy, but what a monster!

As much to stop the tongue as anything else, he wrapped his arms around the beast and hugged it, rejoicing in its survival. He, Gwri, had saved its life and the thrill that brought him was intoxicating.

A better look made it evident the pup had to be related to the hounds in the queen's kennel, but why it had been thrown into the stream to drown was beyond Gwri's comprehension. He had always imagined that was only ever done with excess kittens, and then only by terrible fiends, of course.

"It does not matter," he told the puppy. "You are mine now and your name is Gower!"

Gower's response involved a furious amount of tail wagging as he squirmed and attempted to land another lick on Gwri's face.

Chapter VII

Mercenaries and Picts

"That," Llewellyn announced, after Llew had told him of rescuing the puppy he had named Gower, "was cheating. If you are implying that this Gower has anything to do with the Gower that I am mounted upon, then you still have more to tell."

"Patience," Llew said, and flashed a quick grin, "I will give you the rest as we travel, whenever I may, but it is a longer story and part of a longer one yet. In the meantime, since we are acting as though we are peers, I think it is my turn to ask a question."

Llewellyn attempted to glower at him but, after a moment, his lips quirked and he could not maintain the expression. "Fine then; ask away."

"So despite Dylan's warning about Picts you have seen none but those that attacked you and your crew?" Llew inquired.

"I have not, and I do not wish to ever see any more," the prince replied.

He said this just as Cymri flew back from one of her excursions cawing loudly in warning.

"Picts?" Llew asked of her, amazed at the timing.

Then he remembered to touch the medallion.

"No, Llew, not Picts. It is that scurrilous Captain Cai and his lieutenant. I just saw them on the way back. I am sorry I could not give you more warning."

"Wait," Llew objected, "they are forward of us?"

"Yes, Llew, they must have wandered past in the night looking for us, then decided they had gone too far. Oh, there they are now."

The two men in question had topped a small rise not a hundred feet away. They were on foot and looked a bit bedraggled but grim.

"Quickly," Llew said to Llewellyn, "he is a most skilled opponent but on Gower he may find me too much to handle."

"What about the lieutenant?" the prince asked.

"I have not taken his measure yet but he cannot be more dangerous than Cai. One way or another, this should be over very quickly. You trained under Afaggdu and other masters as well. If they do not both set their sights on me do you think you might hold him off for a few moments?"

"Oh, trust me, Llew, it would be a privilege. I am less than happy with these fellows."

"That is far enough," Llew called out, when the pair was perhaps thirty paces away.

Captain Cai had a mean looking grin on his face when he called back. "Hello boy, it is so good to see you—alive that is. And you managed to get the prince despite everything. Perhaps I begin to understand what Queen Moriganna sees in you."

"Where are the rest of your men?" demanded Llew. "And Afaggdu and the shape-shifters?"

"Dead, all dead, it was just far too many barrow warriors. We are not far from Annwyn here and Lord Arawen apparently knew more of your queen's plans than she knew of his. When the

Lord of the Dead decides to join the game all bets are off."

Llew was still having a difficult time believing Afaggdu dead. It would certainly take more than Cai's unsubstantiated word to make him believe it. Using a trick Cymri had taught him, in the recesses of his mind he put that issue into a wooden box and sealed the lid, then set it aside until he could either give it more time, or additional facts came to light.

"So what is the new game?"

"It is unchanged, mostly." Cai pointed his sword toward the prince. "We have no time for your prisoner so he dies now and we equip you in his gear, then it is out of this hellish Pict bedeviled, barrow warrior infested land and on to Gwent where we install you as king. Vast rewards all the way around."

"Not for you," Llew called, "you must know the shape-shifters were going to get rid of all your men. Not to sound too dramatic but they simply would have seen too much for her to let them live."

"Oh, aye, all of them save for Meirion here—he and I have been together a long time. Yes, I knew that my men were forfeit. Moriganna paid in advance for that, and I can always recruit more later, should I need them."

"You still would not have survived my coronation."

Cai's eyes narrowed. "Is that a fact? Well then it is fortunate plans must change. She needs me too much now for those kinds of games.

"Once we—" Cai was taking his first good look at the prince. "Why is he still armed? Which part of taking him prisoner did you fail to understand?"

Llew drew his sword. "Walk away, Cai. Approach any closer and your backstabbing days will be at an end."

Cai looked as though he had tasted something

unexpectedly unpleasant. "A little boy playing at grown-up games, and he does not even understand the rewards or the risks. If that is how it is, then so be it; I just need you alive. The fact you will be maimed will be easy to explain."

He appeared about to step forward when Cymri once again began cawing in warning. Llew touched the medallion.

"What is it this time, Cymri? I was not really expecting so many visitors here in the wilderness."

"Picts, Llew, Picts are coming!"

"Where are they, Cymri?" Llew cried as he looked about wildly and mentally castigated himself for letting Cai cause him to be so distracted by conversation as to neglect his vigilance. A couple of rogue mercenaries were not the only dangers out here.

Although they still traveled in a wide and open grassy area, it had gradually become bordered on East and West by distant trees. Humanoid figures had already appeared against the tree line to the east and were running swiftly towards them. The distance was too great to make out details but something in their proportions and the way they ran told him they were not human forms.

Llewellyn hissed and said, "There are fully a dozen of them but we cannot let ourselves be taken alive. If here our stand must be then so be it."

"Nay," responded Llew. "Fighting with Cai against anything else? We may as well plunge knives into our backs before we start, for he surely would before we finished!

"To our west are thick woods, we may be able to shake them from our pursuit there. Though they may know this land far better than we, it is an attempt we must make. Later, there will be time to sell ourselves dearly, if that must be."

Llewellyn nodded his head. "Agreed then."

"What are the two of you yammering on about," demanded Cai. "Think, boy, it is not too late for you, the entire plan is not beyond salvage. Your rewards are to be greater than any others', do not throw that away in a fit of misplaced gallantry."

Llew sheathed his sword while reaching down and taking Llewellyn's hand. The prince gave a well-timed leap that let Llew pull him up onto Gower's back to sit behind him. For a short time Gower would have to carry two. Even at a gallop, Gower was quite strong enough for this, at least for a while, but Llew knew such an arrangement could be only temporary at best. The need now was to reach the far wood and be out of sight before their assailants caught up with them. Gower clearly did not care for running before their foes, but neither did he resist when Llew urged him westward.

"Running?" Cai's voice was dripping with derision. "You cannot escape me that easily. The horse will only slow you down in the forests, and I will have you within a day or two, unless the Picts get you first."

Glancing towards Cai, it was obvious that he had not noticed the rapidly approaching Picts to his right. His palpable anger was blinding him.

"You will not get us Cai. The Picts might, but they will get you first." Llew gave a quick nod of his head towards the onrushing Picts to show what he meant. Cai did not look but his lieutenant did. Meirion slapped Cai on the arm and pointed. The mercenary captain did look then and Llew saw his mouth sag open in surprise.

"Gower, run!" Llew urged and they were off like a bolt toward the western tree line.

He could hear Captain Cai crying out at them from behind as he and Meirion were rapidly left behind. A quick glimpse showed the Picts had nearly reached the mercenaries. Then Llew turned his attention to the forest ahead, looking for a potentially good point of entry.

"Good bye, Captain," Llew said under his breath. He found he actually felt a bit badly about leaving Cai to his fate, even though he had likely been about to try to kill him.

Just before they reached the trees, the prince, still clutching to Llew's middle to hang on, jerked suddenly and shouted in surprise.

Chapter VIII

Gwri's Tale: Making it So

Of course, saying a puppy was his and making it so were two different things, and Gwri knew the difference. He might be able to keep its existence secret for a bit, but what about when he was up at the castle? Keeping Gower far from the stables was not an option, yet if the puppy began making loud noises he would surely be discovered. A confederate would be necessary and the only stable-hand that Gwri felt might be sufficiently discreet was Slow Tomos.

Even though he was an adult, Tomos was, frankly, slow and rather child-like. More and more often, as Gwri grew older, Tomos tended to ask him for help when he was confused and, when given instructions by Gwri, never questioned them. It seemed to Gwri that Slow Tomos might keep Gower for him when he was up at the castle.

Slow Tomos, enjoyed considerably more freedom than most. There was not much reward in pushing him any harder than he was inclined to work so folk left him alone. It helped that he was a very hard worker when he was inclined. Of course, he was also inclined to occasionally forget what he was doing and just wander off. When that happened, there was seldom any huge urgency in getting him back. Sometimes he disappeared for days at a time but, as he seemed none the worse for it upon his return, no one ever seemed to think much of it. Being slow, people just seemed to expect such things of him.

There were also not many with the patience to engage Slow Tomos in idle conversation so it was likely no one would ever even think to ask him where he had come by a dog.

Unfortunately, Gower was not an ordinary dog. He was almost certainly the get of some sire from the queen's own kennel, even though they did not normally have a large white patch on their chest. A cover story would be required.

That still left the problem of how Gwri would keep Gower fed. The puppy's eyes were open and seemed to be working fairly well. This meant he might already be in his second month and possibly partially weaned. Still, milk would work to augment the puppy's diet for a bit longer and Gwri knew a source that would not even involve stealing.

Carrying Gower, heedless of his own injuries, he made his way back to the stables. Sneaking in without any of the men seeing him was a bit tricky but, the only child in a world of men, Gwri had grown adept at such sneakiness. Obtaining another bucket, he made his way to the stall of a mare that had recently foaled.

The people of Caer Mallcoedwig tended to get their milk from cows and goats. Most were probably unaware that mares might be milked as well. Oddly, they probably would have found the idea of butter or cheese made from horse milk to be repulsive, if they even knew it was possible. Gower did not seem to share that viewpoint. He lapped it up eagerly until he could seemingly hold no more.

Solid food would not be a serious problem. Gwri was confident he could think of something, given time. The men were already well used to him relaying instructions from the stable master, even though only about half of those orders actually had come from Braen. To his credit, after some experiments to see how badly he could abuse this power, most of the orders that originated with Gwri were now aimed at maintaining the stables to a higher standard than Braen's own.

Fortuitously, he was able to find Slow Tomos in a nearby field where he was gathering hay.

"Tomos," he began, "I have a charge for you."

The big man looked up, affability written large on his simple face. "Hello Gwri, I will soon be done with this field. Did you have another for me to do?"

"Ah, no Tomos, not at the moment. You see this dog?"

"Oh, I most certainly do see the dog, Gwri. I think it is a puppy though. Whose is it?"

"Well that is what I am here about. Once he is grown, this puppy is meant to help us with the rat problems—particularly some that seem too big for the stable cats to deal with properly," Gwri lied.

Tomos furrowed his brow. "I do not know that any rats I have seen are quite that big, Gwri."

Gwri licked his lips nervously and answered, "Yes, well, it is the rats we do not see that are the concern. If nothing else, a dog will help us ensure there are none, once he gets bigger."

"Oh," said Tomos. "What is his name?"

"His name is Gower. Now," continued Gwri, "each afternoon I must travel to the castle. It is during this time you must be responsible for him, keeping him out of trouble and so on. You may keep him leashed and near you unless you cannot do your work with him there. Otherwise, you may keep him at your hut, but I do not wish to hear of him howling or creating a disturbance. Is this too much for you?"

"No, Gwri, I am happy you have selected me to do this."

"Me? I believe this is precisely what Braen would have you do."

Tomos smiled, "Even as you say, Gwri. I am glad to do it even if it were just for you. You do so many things for us."

Gwri was not sure whether he was more uncomfortable with someone assisting him just because they liked him, or because Slow Tomos, the most likely person he knew to be confused by anything, was not the least bit confused over who, using his proximity to Braen, was secretly running the stables in all but name these days.

Then Slow Tomos took notice of Gwri's injuries, and his eyes widened in concern, "Gwri, you are hurt!"

"Ah, it is not so bad as it may look. I am on my way to get some poultices and bandages from Braen right now," Gwri improvised. "Please take good care of Gower and I will be back after evening meal."

Leaving was not quite as easy as that. Gower, it seemed, was not the least bit happy with being left behind. Gwri soothed him as best he was able and then hurried back to the stables. Noon was approaching and he needed to get his injuries dressed quickly and get to the castle.

As he rounded the corner of the main building he ran smack into a completely frantic stable master named Braen.

"Ack! Boy, where have you been! I would whip you for the worry you have caused me save that I cannot take you to the queen that way." Then he saw Gwri's injuries and made a high-pitched noise Gwri had never heard before.

"What have you done to yourself? It is almost time to go and look at you! Even your clothes are ruined. What will the queen think? What will she do?"

"Calm yourself," Gwri advised. "I fell into the stream while fetching the morning water. It will never happen again. I was, ah, distracted by a white stag that came to drink," he lied. As Gwri well knew, Braen had a bit of a fixation on a white stag that he claimed to have seen in his youth. The stable master was certain it had been the Stag of Rhedynfre.

"They will make me bathe at the castle as they always do. And, as always, any clothing that is damaged or worn or even dirty will be replaced before sending me to the queen. It is a daily ritual of theirs. If we can but poultice and bind some of the worst of this we can still make it on time."

"You saw the stag?" Braen whispered in awe and Gwri felt almost bad at leading him on like this.

"Only for a moment, I was so startled I fell in and was swept downstream. Will you please help me bind these so we can get to the castle?"

The stable master shook it off. "At once, boy, aye, and if anyone does ask what has happened to you, be sure you explain it with no fingers pointing at me!"

Chapter IX

Forest Trails

Gower carried them swiftly into the cover of the far woods. Luck was with them and, within only a few minutes, they crashed through the heavy brush onto a game trail. Llew dismounted to lead Gower, but first there was another concern.

"Are you hit?" he asked the prince urgently.

"What?" asked Llewellyn in some confusion.

"I felt you jerk and cry out back there, I thought an arrow had caught you."

"No, nothing like that. We must hurry though. There were fully eleven of them and only seven of them went for Cai and company, the other four continued after us."

Choosing the direction that seemed to run downhill, Llew led the small party hurriedly down the trail. Fortune was still favoring them for they came to a small rill less than fifteen minutes later. The water was shallow with few rocks, and its bed was heavily carpeted with old leaves. A quick look back showed that no Picts were within view as he led Gower into the shallow waters upstream.

Llew very much doubted the Picts could use scent to track

them but, in any case, they would not find many tracks under the water. Half a mile up the stream he found a broad flat rock extending from the water up to the trees. He led them back out of the water there, betting the rock would dry before the Picts reached it. Even so, the woodcraft of the Picts was legendary. Llew had little doubt that, given some time, their trail would eventually be found.

Leading Gower, and with Llewellyn still riding, Llew carefully picked their way through the forest. It was old growth here and the trees were great hulking things, festooned with moss, that shaded the earth almost completely. This was fortunate in that it left the ground fairly free of underbrush, easing their passage somewhat.

"Llew, the cause of my surprise back there—I should tell you. It was Captain Cai and Lieutenant Meirion."

"Ah," Llew said, "yes, I felt odd, almost bad, about leaving them to that. Did they die well?"

Llewellyn shook his head slowly. "As I said, seven of the Picts went for them, it was hard to make out, but I think I saw Cai kill two of them."

"That is not too surprising. He was wearing armor and had a steel weapon and, for all his other faults, was supposed to be expert in their use."

"No, it was that," Llewellyn said flatly, "I saw the one you call Lieutenant Meirion kill the other five. It was so fast and, at that range, it was impossible to be sure, but I do not think either of them was even wounded. They were already looking in our direction before we reached the tree line. They may still be after us."

That took Llew by surprise. He stopped in his tracks and thought for a moment. As he did, he tasted an emotion and realized it was disquiet, perhaps even a little fear. Then he ruthlessly shoved it to one side, saying, "Moriganna is never one to stint when it comes to hiring the best she can find. Even so, they may have a time of it following our trail through all of this, and not being apprehended by a force even they cannot prevail against. Still, if we should meet them again, we probably do not want to discount the lieutenant overmuch."

"That does seem like a good idea, Llew," replied Llewellyn, in a perfectly delivered monotone.

Llew wondered where the prince had learned that style of droll understatement. He hoped it was not a common thing in Gwent. It then occurred to him that it might also be the prince's own way of dealing with apprehension.

It took only a short time to come to another game trail. Llew debated only briefly before taking it. Doing so would probably make it easier for the Picts to find their trail but, as their principal hope of escape lay in speed, the trail was the proper choice. Or so he thought, until they came to the pile of skulls at a point where the trail branched.

It was clearly a warning. They stopped abruptly and regarded it. The skulls surrounded a post on top of which was another skull, lashed down with leather strips that had strange symbols burned in to them.

"I have no idea what it is a warning of," remarked Llewellyn, "but it tells me we are on Pictish lands."

Llew sensed something then, in the comparative quiet, and raised his right fist, requesting silence. Faintly, it came to him. People sounds were in the woods. Camp sounds were emanating from somewhere ahead. Somewhere ahead and—

Llew continued to listen for a time, cocking his head repeatedly. When he turned back to Llewellyn his face was very grave. "I know not what we have blundered into. There are at least two camps ahead and one or more to either side. These are large camps; they make much noise and are unconcerned that they do so."

The prince's eyes widened. "We must get off the trail immediately. If there are so many it is only luck we have not already run afoul of them."

"I must concur," replied Llew.

Once again he led them off the trail and in amongst the ferns and trees. The problem, he noted at once, was that a horse could be seen from a fair distance as there was little cover between the tops of the ferns and the lowest limbs of the trees. Any lookouts, or even firewood gatherers, might spot them at any time.

Fortunately, the terrain was somewhat uneven. Low ridges, mounds, and shallow depressions helped break up any line of sight. Unfortunately, this also had the effect of slowing them further and channeling them in a way Llew was not happy with, as it seemed they must eventually pass far too close to the leftmost camp.

"What in the mind of Math are they doing?" Llewellyn asked in a hushed voice. "I thought they traveled in small groups only?"

"From what I have heard of them from Cymri and Afaggdu, normally that is the case. On occasion, however, a strong leader may bring them together for some special purpose. Perhaps there is a major raid or even a war in the offing?" ventured Llew.

"If there is then it is probably some new devilment of Moriganna or Arawen," muttered Llewellyn.

Grasping his amulet, Llew asked, "Cymri, can you find us a way around?"

"I will try," she called, as she took wing, disappearing rapidly amidst the trees.

She returned in what could only have been a few minutes. "This way passes far too close to the southernmost camp, yet I think it is the best we will find," she reported to him. "But Llew, they have a prisoner and I believe they mean to sacrifice him."

Llew paused only a moment. "There is naught we can do for him. He is already lost."

"Llew," said Cymri softly, "do you know what they do with prisoners when they sacrifice them?"

"Not really, does it matter?"

"It might, Llew. They put them in a wicker cage shaped in the form of a man. Then they start a great fire—"

"Enough, Cymri, enough! But what would you have me do? Get the prince killed in a vain attempt at rescue? How many Picts are at the fire? Twenty? Thirty? More? More would hardly be needed."

"Counting a few women and large children, at least sixty, but I think it might not be necessary to fight them."

"How then? They will be so impressed by me charging in on them upon Gower that they will immediately flee or disperse?"

"There is a way, Llew. Their willingness to burn others must have put it into my mind."

Llew bit back an angry retort. "Very well, I owe you much and your advice has been solid on too many occasions for me to discount it now. If you believe we can do this then we shall try."

Chapter X

Gwri's Tale: The Turnip and the Club

The servants at the castle clucked over the condition of Gwri's torn and bedraggled finery but they had new clothing and boots at the ready. They cleaned him up as best they could, given the many bandages and bruises he bore. Then he was sent into Queen Moriganna's dining hall. The table was set, but no one else was in there until, at the appointed hour, she swept in, an ornately carved wooden rod in her hand. She was very tall. She was also quite graceful but not, Gwri thought, as a woman could sometimes be, but more as a dangerous predator might be.

He remembered to hold her chair for her but she did not sit down. Instead she stopped and regarded him thoughtfully. Then she spoke. "I am told you arrived rather beaten and battered today. How did that come to happen?"

Gwri repeated his story about falling into the stream while fetching water, but he omitted any mention of a white stag. That would be too much detail and she might trip him up with it.

"So," she inquired, "you are certain it was not the work of those urchins in the village or one of those wretched men at the stables?"

"Oh no, your, uh, highness. The village boys mostly do not dare any more. They have had most of the fight drubbed out of them. The men at the stable would not dare hit me, either. The stable master would pin their ears to the wall."

"Very well, then you maintain it was just an accident?"

"Yes, your highness. It will not happen again." Gwri was beginning to sweat a little.

"Do you know what I thought at first, Gwri?"

"No, your highness, I do not," Gwri replied honestly.

"I thought—" She slammed the rod down on the tabletop with great force. This caused Gwri to actually flinch and he knew he would hate himself for that later. "I thought you might be trying to run away from Caer Mallcoedwig and, right now, I know you are hiding something."

Gwri shook his head in astonished denial before he could speak. "Your highness, I would never run away. Where would I go?" Meanwhile, he was thinking furiously about what a good idea that was. Good? When he got a bit bigger it would not even be a good idea . . . it would be an excellent idea. Surely he would have eventually thought of it himself? Free to go where he wanted, to see what he wanted, all with no one else deciding what he should do his time? Perhaps he could even start a rumor that he was a king or a prince in disguise and become some sort of a wandering hero. There were so many like that in the old tales that he was suddenly sure it must actually happen occasionally. Life would be perfect.

As though a curtain had been drawn past her, Moriganna's rage departed as quickly as it had appeared. She regarded him coldly for the best part of a minute before speaking. "I can see you are unhappy here, and your performance in your lessons has been disappointing. Yet I can also perceive that you are more than capable of mastering them. I will not fault my own skills in instruction so I am left to believe you are not properly motivated."

Uh oh, Gwri thought. This sounded like she had decided to start beating him, or worse.

"We will," she continued, "try a two-pronged approach that I call the turnip and the club. If you can begin doing well you will eventually be rewarded with a nice crunchy turnip. Run away again and you will feel the club."

Was she mad? Gwri shook his head to clear it. Of course she was mad, that was a given—but why a turnip? He already had far better provender than that. The threat of punishment, on the other hand, he understood very well. "Um, a turnip, your highness?"

"First," she said, drawing out the word as she did so, "let me show you a club, one of many I can employ."

Four of her grim guardsmen, the kind that almost never spoke and that were shunned by the others, came into the great hall and surrounded him on all four sides. Gwri wracked his brain desperately for ideas. This looked like he was about to get the beating of his life. Rather than their normal clothes or armor, all were wearing loose fitting dark robes. On some signal they unbelted their robes and, there was no other way to describe it, their faces began to melt and change. The robes slid off as they somehow grew taller. Standing around him were four . . . things. In form they looked like what might happen if gigantic slavering wolves had been made to walk upright and partially remolded to the approximate shape of men.

Gwri's heart quailed in his chest. He had heard many old tales concerning a multitude of strange and horrific beings, but he had never imagined meeting any of those terrors in the flesh, not really, not like this, especially while still a child, surrounded and unarmed. Their fangs were huge and they were close enough he could feel their hot breath on him. The claws on their forelimbs were equally terrible but, worst of all, were their eyes. They were soulless and cruel and he felt they saw in him only a bit of meat that they might snap up in a few bites.

"These," said Moriganna calmly, "are some of my shape-shifters. I have many more. They serve me and me alone. They can track you anywhere and are even more dangerous than they appear to be. They can also take many forms, becoming either beast or man, and you will likely never see them coming. Do not attempt to run away from me again." She then raised her voice in a shriek, "Ever!"

On that final word, the shape-shifters dropped to all fours and raced from the room at incredible speed and in total silence.

"Now," Moriganna continued imperturbably, "we shall speak of the turnip."

There is that turnip again, Gwri thought wonderingly.

"Have you ever wondered why you are the recipient of so much effort and time—my time and my effort? I would guess you have not. You simply see it all as a huge inconvenience. You disdain manners, you despise history, and you show only the mildest of interest in heraldry. Tell me Gwri, do you intend to work all your life in the stables? Or do you aspire to something better?"

It was something he had never considered quite like that. "Better would be good," he ventured cautiously.

"Better is an option, Gwri. There is a kingdom to the south that has no proper leader. It needs one and I have far too many other things to do which prevent me from dropping everything to go take charge of it. Instead I intend to give it something it has not had in a long time. It needs a proper king more than anything.

A king must be many things, however, and if he does not start his training early he will never be much more than a barbarian warlord. The world has those in plenty already.

"What that kingdom needs is a king of kings. Such a king must be one who is gracious and wise, yet he must also be well able to take charge and set things right when it is needed. Such a king must also be a puissant warrior with a firm knowledge of history so he does not revisit the mistakes of the past on his people for, just as they are required to honor him and comply with his commands, he is required to value them, and protect them, and make them as prosperous and as safe as is reasonable.

"Responsibility must extend in both directions or the very fabric of civilization is lost. As things stand now, should that happen, the forces of Fae and Annwyn will battle for the rights to gnaw the bones of the last men as they are dragged from the ruins of what could have been.

"I cannot wave my wand and create such a king. To create such a being I can only start with the proper metal and ensure that it is, step by step, forged into something much more than it otherwise could be. You are a quick lad but even a slow one could understand this. Do you?"

"You want me to become that king?" Gwri asked. It did not seem credible, but if anyone could turn an orphan stable boy into a king it would almost have to be Queen Moriganna. "Me? Why me?"

"Because you have what it takes, Gwri. I saw that in you when I first laid eyes on you. You also look like them so they will be quick to accept you once I have blazed a path to the crown for you."

"I might not make a good king," Gwri said.

"You will be a great king, but you will require my help to

get the opportunity. I confess I am not the warmest of people. Sentiment does not sway me in any way and if I saw a way to save the kingdoms of mankind by sacrificing you, even if it were with a ceremonial knife on a stone altar, then I would do so in an instant. Fortunately for you, I need allies, not sacrifices.

"The high kingdom fell a century ago. I saw it all happen. The great kingdoms were left leaderless for too long and, left to their own devices, refused to unify under a new high king. Now the great kingdoms themselves are collapsing. They will soon all fail and grass will grow in the roads. The lands will become a single howling wilderness, an unmarked grave for the dreams of man, with all the great castles fallen.

"Right now that fate is like a great flood wave rushing down a river towards us. Then there is you. You can become a great rock and I will place you in its path to deflect that wave. Together, we can save all that it might otherwise destroy. Will you aid me, and yourself, by becoming that rock? Will you let me make you a mighty king? Can you become a ruler who will live on in legend as long as men walk under the sun?"

Gwri considered it. He did not trust her further than he could throw a horse. Such a reward would be magnificent but he simply had no faith in her to deliver on it and, if she did, she would use him and throw him away; he was certain of that. Still, he could not say no. If he did that she would simply try harder to get him to say yes, and there would be no peace until he did . . . or until she came to believe that he never would. To say that she had a reputation for being vengeful when she did not get what she wanted would be to say that water had a reputation for being wet.

He had to say yes, for now. Yet even an apparent capitulation was risky; the Queen of Deceit was seldom easy to deceive. Even to appear to acquiesce he would have to make it believable. He had seen Braen negotiate many agreements. How to make this agreement seem as real as those?

He thought for a moment and it came to him. He had something she wanted now, yet she was only offering nebulous promises for things many years away and, in the past year, he had learned a great deal in the constant company of the stable master.

One thing learned was that Braen, and the people he traded with, would never have accepted such a deal solely on this basis. For something they had to deliver in the present they would insist on something received in the present, at least as an initial installment. He should do the same and try to get something in return, right then, that she would believe he valued. What would she believe might seal this deal for him?

It would have to be something she would believe he really wanted, something tangible, something easy for her to give. This was not hard to come up with. He knew precisely what he wanted more than anything.

"So I am to be a great king?"

"The greatest," Moriganna affirmed, "if you cooperate and learn your lessons."

"If I agree then could I have a symbol of our trust in each other right now?"

"Are you bargaining with me?" she asked in her very dangerous voice.

"Oh no, no your Highness, not at all," Gwri lied again. *How many lies am I going to tell today?* he wondered to himself.

"But a king should be an excellent rider. In all the stories I have heard they always are . . . yet, while I take care of them daily, my chances to ride horses are few and far between." Another lie! "To be really good at it I should start now."

"Yes," she agreed, "that does make a certain sense. I will

give instructions to begin your lessons in horsemanship. I will also have some of my guardsmen begin instructing you in the use of weapons as well, for the same logic surely applies."

"That would be wonderful, my Queen," exclaimed Gwri, meaning it, "but—"

"But what?" she demanded.

Something tangible, he thought to himself again. *It must be something I can actually touch right now.*

"Well, I think it would help me focus better on what I must do if I had something to look forward to when lessons were over. You have many horses; surely it would also make sense to give me one of my own?" He clenched his teeth and waited for her response.

The queen did something he did not believe any mortal man among the living had ever heard her do. She laughed. "Very well, my little one and future king, tis time you learned of responsibility and, should you fail in your lessons, of consequences.

"I can see today is already a lost cause. One of the servants will give you a jar of unguent of my own preparation. You are to rub it thoroughly into your wounds and bruises. It will be painful but you must show some resolve. It will be well worth it as you will find that in three days' time your little injuries will be all but completely healed. I will come to the stables then and we will pick out your horse. As that is also your birthday, you may consider this a birthday present. Your lessons will resume the day after."

"What?" he interrupted. "You know my birthday?"

Moriganna affected a yawn. "I know many things, dear boy. In case you are wondering, however, you will be eight. Until then, enjoy your time off. You will have little of it in the future.

"Oh, and one more thing. With the addition of riding and

arms training, you will need to be here directly at terce instead of midday."

The boy now named Gwri hesitated, torn in two by his desire to flee yet held in place by a problem.

"Yes, what is it?" she demanded sharply.

"My Queen, I must ask, what is terce?"

She sighed. "We do have much to learn or, rather, you do. It is the midpoint between sunrise and noon. When a king holds court it is the traditional time at which he begins. Now go. I have had quite enough of you today and for quite some time thereafter, yet three days of respite is all we can afford. Do not shorten it!"

Despite his injuries, Gwri was gone like an arrow from a bow.

Chapter XI

Into the Fire

When Llew explained to Llewellyn what Cymri had said, he found a point of view similar to his own. Worried as the prince was by the danger, or even delay, that a rescue attempt might entail, it was still something they had to attempt if Cymri thought they could do it.

It occurred to him that Llewellyn must have known Cymri from a very early age indeed, to put such stock in the bard's plan.

Llew and Cymri approached the camp carefully. Peering from cover of the heavy foliage on an escarpment overlooking the fire, Llew found himself looking down into madness.

The cleared area about the fire teemed with Picts. They were dancing maniacally, even the best dressed wearing little more than a breech cloth and daubs of paint, while drummers beat a savage rhythm and an eerie, penetrating pipe music came from flute-like tubes that some of the musicians were blowing into. Surprisingly, despite most being smaller and slightly darker in coloration than Tetherans such as himself, the Picts appeared to be completely human. Llew could see it was the ones wearing what he could now recognize as enormous wicker masks, and carrying wicker shields, that had made him, and likely many others in the past, question their humanity.

Three bonfires were before him. The center one was as yet unlit, while the others blazed merrily, curling the leaves of nearby trees. In addition, the center one was surmounted by the figure of a giant man, woven of wicker. If the two outer ones had contained such figures, there was little left by way of evidence.

"The prisoner is already inside the center one, Llew," Cymri informed him."

"Is he even still alive?"

"Oh yes, Llew, the Picts will not sacrifice a dead man. Besides, he was showing plenty of energy when they put him into it."

"Cymri, can we really do this?"

"Oh I think so. The hard part will be getting away afterward."

"It always is," he grumbled.

"Llew, he is a very young man, not much older than you or Prince Llewellyn. He deserves better than this and it lies within our power to give him that. The two men that they already sacrificed were probably his kinsmen. Like us, he is alone and bereft of any aid save our own."

Llew said nothing, There seemed nothing he could say.

"Now, look beyond and to the left, further back where the trees open up again. See those mounds of sticks and leaves?"

Llew glanced away and saw what she was referring to.

"Those are their huts, Llew. They are entirely made of branches, twigs, bark, and dried leaves. Do not they look very flammable?"

"I will allow as that they do," he agreed.

"I cannot carry much, but I can easily carry a burning bit

to drop upon the roof of one of them. Once it is burning, the fire will spread like—well, quickly, to the other huts. Most of their worldly goods are there. They will almost certainly rush to save what they can and that should be our chance here."

"A chance is all it is but, in the absence of any other, I find myself very enthusiastic about this plan, Cymri."

Cymri cocked her head and regarded him, checking for sarcasm it seemed. Then she took wing. She circled the camp above the maddened dancers, saw what she wanted at one of the outer fires, and swooped. Snatching a bit of wood that was burning only at one end, she carried it away toward the huts. The Picts, in the frenzy of their ceremony, gave no notice at all.

Two of them, wearing the fearsome wicker masks that extended half way to their waists, and above their heads by nearly a foot, advanced to the wicker man. One held a torch and the other brandished an intricately carved club. The one with the club struck the wicker man several times and yelled something in his own language, punctuated by wild laughter.

There was no way the club would have hurt anyone inside the cage but it must have gotten their attention. Llew could now hear someone inside yelling back at the Pict. Llew strained to hear but could not make out what the prisoner was saying. Conversely, the tone of voice was clearly one of defiance and anger, not fear or pleading. Llew wondered if, in the face of certain and horrible death, he could be so bold himself.

The Pict yelled back something in a mocking falsetto voice, and then laughed abominably. Llew put his hand to his sword and waited, resolved now that the prisoner would be freed if it lay within him to do so.

Cymri came flitting back and perched beside him. "It lit easily, although I had a bad moment where it nearly went out before it could catch. They will notice soon."

"Very well, thank you, Cymri. Could you get Gower and the prince and have them meet me at the end of this bluff, on the eastern side? Do what you can to let them know they should follow you. Once I have the prisoner hacked out of there we will need to move very fast."

"Done!" replied Cymri, and she was off again.

Moments passed and then there was a loud yell from below as all the music fell silent.

A tumult of shouts followed immediately, fading with distance as the Picts ran to their huts. Venturing a look, Llew saw Cymri had done her job well. In the direction of their dwellings, all that could be seen was smoke and flickering flames. Through this, the Picts ran in all directions, yelling and calling out to each other as they sought to salvage what they could.

There would never be a better time. Unsheathing his sword, Llew moved out of cover in a straight line for the wicker man. Although he had drawn his sword to help penetrate the wicker cage, it was fortunate he had chosen a tool which also had other uses.

As he approached within thirty feet of his target, death came for him. His only warning was a faint rhythmic noise from behind, the sound of what had to be a Pict's bare feet slapping the bare earth as he rushed towards Llew. Llew spun instantly, slashing to the side with his sword. He barely succeeded in turning aside the spear the Pict had been clutching as he ran for Llew's unprotected back.

The Pict ran on a few feet and whipped about to come at Llew again. Afaggdu, however, had been very specific on how a lone swordsman could deal effectively with a lone spearman and Llew felt a surge of confidence that seemed out of place with the situation. Before the Pict could charge again, Llew stepped quickly forward and was upon him, well inside the range at which the spear could be used effectively against him.

Unless this one had exchanged masks with another, he was, Llew noted, the same Pict that had beaten on the sides of the wicker man and mocked the prisoner inside. Anger caught at him and, seizing his foe's spear with his left hand, Llew slashed at the man's head with his blade, connecting on the first swing. This, Llew, had been led to believe, would end any fight in short order.

The wicker mask had not figured in the equation. Although it took some damage, the thickly interwoven willow switches were too dense to cut through in one swing. The blow was further weakened by the springiness that was the nature of the mask's woven construction.

The man bellowed as he attempted to pull his weapon free of Llew's grasp. With both hands on the spear, the Pict had a better grip. Llew managed to hold on, but it was a near thing and he had to let his footing shift lest he be drawn completely off balance.

Up close it was evident that this Pict was substantially larger than most of his fellows, larger than Llew, in fact, and was fully grown, with great corded muscles that were themselves covered in strange tattoos and wicked scars. It dawned on Llew, in a flash of awareness, that the man almost certainly had far more experience in combat that he did. Neither was time on his side. More Picts might return at any moment.

Over and over again, Afaggdu had cautioned him on the dangers of using a sword. This was because, tempting as it was, the sword was not a stabbing weapon. Stabbing would eventually only get your blade stuck. Indeed, none of the swords Llew had ever seen even had a proper point for stabbing. The sword was a slashing weapon, meant to beat aside defenses, deliver terrible damage, and then escape again so that its owner was never helpless . . . was never effectively unarmed.

When the Pict leader, for a leader he surely was, tugged on the spear a second time, Llew again held on but was drawn stumbling forward to come face to face with his foe. He found himself looking directly into the wide, furious eyes within the mask. He was too close even to swing his sword. Instead, he thrust it full into that terrible face with its wide maddened eyes.

His opponent screamed in torment and fell back, releasing his spear and ripping off the wicker mask. Llew had no time to regard the Pict's face except to see that it was strong and cruel. Even noting that much was remarkable, considering that the face was twisted in agony and covered in blood flowing from the left eye or, rather, perhaps where the left eye had been.

Llew hesitated for a full heartbeat, shocked by the blood and pain resulting from what he had done. The Pict was beaten and unarmed. It would be proper to take him prisoner now but that was not practical, not with members of his tribe likely to return at any second. Practical behavior would be to strike him down so that he would not be able to summon pursuit immediately or even describe the nature of his assailant. Llew was quite certain that this was what Moriganna would counsel. That automatically made it an undesirable choice of action in his own mind.

Llew drew back his sword and brought it whistling around against the wounded man's head, directly above his left ear. The warrior fell to the ground on his hands and knees, groaning. Llew had used the flat of his sword, thinking to spare the man by knocking him out. Afaggdu had told him that, despite what he had heard in so many stories, hitting a man on the head

72

was not really very likely to knock him unconscious without severely injuring him in the process, but it had seemed worth a try. Llew steeled himself and struck twice more in the same manner before the Pict fell motionless upon the ground. Llew did not bother to see if he was still alive; either he was or he was not and, if he was alive, it did not mean he would survive or that he would not be permanently injured.

Trying to further justify his actions to himself, Llew told himself that, although it was not quite the opposite of what Moriganna would have done, it was better than simply slashing him to death. Then too, an injured man might slow down pursuit or divert some of the pursuers to care for him. Afaggdu had taught Llew that as well.

Sparing what was meant to be a last cursory glance at his fallen foe, Llew noticed the Pict, like the others of his kind, had not been wearing any clothing save for the hideous wicker mask and a torc that looked like it might be real gold. *Doubtless*, Llew told himself, *this was stolen from some murdered innocent.* Angered, it was the work of a moment for him to retrieve it and put it around his own neck for safekeeping. Perhaps he might someday find who it should belong to and be able to return it. He scowled at the prone warrior and considered ensuring he was dead. It might not atone for the Pict's past misdeeds but it would prevent those that he would almost certainly commit if he recovered.

Llew recoiled from his thoughts and shook his head to clear it. As a warrior in a violent world, he had long since accepted that he might eventually kill an opponent in combat. He might or might not have just done that. He had not accepted that he would ever kill an unconscious and severely wounded foeman.

His emotions in check, Llew recalled why he was there. He turned and swiftly ran to the wicker man.

"Draw back if you can," Llew called to the prisoner inside, "I have to open this thing up fast and do not want you getting chopped up in the process." *And leaving a trail of blood for every Pict in the world to follow as we flee*, he thought to himself.

Llew hacked away at the wicker but it was frustratingly slow. The stuff was devilishly hard to cut. The sword blade almost bounced when it struck, resulting in very little damage. Llew stopped for a moment as he had a thought. Ah, the Picts would hardly have woven the whole thing around the prisoner. How would they have done it?

Llew forced himself to take the time to examine the wicker work. He was rewarded almost at once. Along one side of the torso were thinner twists of willow. Their placement reminded him very much of thread holding a shirt together. He learned it was certainly easier to cut as he forced his sword up through it. The front of the wicker man shifted. Llew finished the cut, sheathed his sword, and seized the wicker section that had moved. Yanking it hard, the cut strands of willow separated and stretched, pieces falling to the stacked wood below. He started to give it another yank when the man inside slammed into it from the other side, snapping the vines that still held as though they were so much rotten thread.

Together they ripped the panel down and, as the man inside struggled to climb out, Llew half dragged him out.

Another giant, thought Llew. The youth that emerged was at least a head taller than he was, and considerably broader and heavier as well. He had blond hair and beard, blue eyes, and was wearing furred boots, blue trousers, and a leather coat covered in small grey metal plates to the point where it resembled the scales of a fish. Definitely not a Pict, they had little use for armor, yet the clothing was unlike any Llew had seen. Perhaps it was like something he had heard of? Combined with the height and coloration it seemed to trigger some warning in his mind.

Suddenly he had it. This was not a Tetheran, this was a Northman!

Northmen had been raiding Tethera from as far back as any tale could tell. They were enemies, even to the point of being used by parents to frighten children into behaving. 'Be good,' children were told, 'or the Northmen will come and carry you away, never to be seen again.' Since the fall of the great kingdom their behavior had changed. They no longer raided and retreated. They now came in their long ships from out of the north and created colonies along the coastlines. They could never have succeeded in this were it not for the lack of a strong high king to rally the kingdoms against them. Even now, should the kingdoms unite, it might not be too late to throw them all back into the sea. Llew had many times heard that such a thing would, as the saying said, only happen when Pwyl's heir sat upon his throne . . . meaning it never would.

For an instant, Llew thought to draw his sword and treat the former prisoner more roughly than he had treated even the Pict chieftain. Then he recalled the reality of the situation. The Picts would make no distinction between the two of them.

"Can you run?" he asked.

"Ya," came the answer, "I will not be a burden. You will see! Although I am powerfully thirsty and water would be welcome when we can get some." The accent was strange, thought Llew, apparently Northmen were unaccustomed to making certain sounds, like that beginning the word "water," such that it sounded like "votter" when he spoke it.

Despite his assertion, the Northman ran clumsily the first

few moments, evidently still shaking off the aftereffects of his confinement, but he rapidly picked up speed and confidence. They passed by the fallen Pict and the Northman said, "Ah, that was Goll, so much to kill him myself I wanted. Instead another debt it is I must owe you."

He stooped and picked up the Pict's spear from where it had fallen. Llew hesitated for a second, not sure if he wanted an enemy warrior to have a weapon, and not sure what do about it if he decided he should stop him.

The Northman caught the look Llew gave him and misinterpreted it. "It will not slow me down, my drott. I, Helgar Olufson, so swear to you, but leave it here I cannot. My father, he always say to me, 'Do not you leave your weapons lying about behind your back in a field. You never know when you may need all of a sudden your spear!'"

Nonplussed, Llew gave him an uncertain smile and decided not to push matters. Indeed, he saw now that the weapon was not a Pictish one at all, nor was it of a style used in Tethera. It appeared the Northman might have been quite literal in referring to the spear as his own. The spear, with its treated haft and fine metal point, was something the Picts could not make but would have been more than happy to take for themselves. This was in direct contrast to the Northman's scaled armor that the tribesmen had apparently been quite content to consign to the flames with the owner.

Two minutes of hard running saw them at the end of the bluff where Llew had told Cymri to meet them. He was greatly relieved to see Gower and Llewellyn there as well and slowed to a walk to regain his breath. Apparently, Cymri had been able to make his instructions sufficiently clear. He had worried about that.

Then he found something new to worry about. A group of four Picts, perhaps the very ones that had chased them from the road into the forest, were cautiously approaching the pair. They were already within two hundred paces. Llewellyn had clearly seen them and was astride Gower, ready to bolt. Just as obviously, he was loath to leave before Llew had rejoined them. Then he spotted Llew and Helgar approaching and rode towards them calling out, "The enemy is upon us, Llew."

The Picts, apparently determined not to lose their prey after their long pursuit, dashed after them. Focused on Gower and the prince, they did not yet appear to have taken notice of the newcomers.

Helgar took one look at Llewellyn and looked again at Llew, then grinned fiercely before saying, "Your brother, saved us some he has!" With a brutal yell, he lowered his spear and charged straight at the oncoming warriors.

Llew groaned inwardly. The Northman's courage was incredible yet there was no strategy in this. They could have at least taken a better position and made the Picts come to them. Somewhere inside himself he gave a mental shrug. It was what it was. Llew drew sword and ran with Helgar, giving his own rendition of a bloodthirsty cry as he did so.

The Picts were thoroughly startled by the appearance of the newcomers and their seemingly crazed attack. None ran, but two slowed momentarily, leaving the lead two to outdistance them and meet Helgar alone.

It was like a wolf in a sheep fold. Helgar spun his spear end over end and knocked aside the spear of one of his opponents. Then, in a continuous fluid motion, as the butt end of his spear came in line with the Pict's body, Helgar thrust forward, driving the blunt shaft into the Pict's lower gut. The Pict dropped like a sack of onions, gurgling horribly. Helgar continued his spear's whirling rotation the instant the haft came off the Pict. It was almost as though it had not stopped spinning. The remaining Pict was momentarily unprotected on the side where his fellow had fallen and, again, as an end of Helgar's spear came in line with the second Pict's body, there was a quick thrust and Helgar withdrew his weapon. It was a killing blow, for this attack had been with the point. Droplets of blood flew from Helgar's spear and the second Pict joined the first upon the ground.

Now Llew caught up to Helgar and together, with whooping yells, they charged upon the two Picts that had hesitated only a moment earlier. Turning in perfect unison, the pair of Picts tried to run from them, but Llew and Helgar were already moving at full speed and were far too close. It was over in a moment.

Both now gasping for breath, they stopped. Helgar leaned heavily on his spear but found breath for a laugh. "Hoo boy, I have never seen a Pict run before he has even tried to fight! Scary fellows we be, eh?"

The violence he had just done would register on him only later, Llew realized, and it would be unpleasant. Worse, Llew knew from what more experienced men had told him that, as he killed more men, it would eventually become considerably less disturbing. Not for the first time he wondered about an issue that he knew Mercher and Afaggdu would think ridiculous: Could he still really be Llew if he changed that much?

But this could all be considered later. Rather than think about it now, Llew forced himself to grin back and clapped Helgar on the shoulder. "It was you that made them do that and yes, you are more than a little scary, my friend."

Behind them they heard a loud whinny, followed

immediately by the sound of heavy thudding blows punctuated with cracking noises and one short scream. Turning they saw that the Pict which had caught the blunt end of Helgar's spear must have regained some of his breath. He had then made an extremely bad choice in attempting to stand just as Gower, now riderless, had reached where he had fallen. Perhaps he had thought to leap on Gower's back and make his escape.

Helgar's eyes went wide with appreciation at the sight. "I never have much use for horses before but for that beast an exception I make. Even with only four legs, a son of Sleipner himself he must be."

Gower, satisfied that the Pict was not getting up again, trotted up to Llew and licked him on the ear.

Helgar gaped at that, then did something completely out of character with all Llew had ever heard of wild Northman warriors; he giggled.

Llewellyn was now coming up the path at a measured walk, then took alarm when he saw Helgar, apparently recognizing him at once for what he was. "Llew! Behind you!" he called.

Llew glanced behind him and saw only Helgar. As Llewellyn came within normal speaking distance, Llew raised his hand, palm out. "No, no, this is who was in the wicker man. Helgar Olufson, Prince Llewellyn. Prince Llewellyn, this is Helgar Olufson."

Helgar stepped up, now only slightly panting. "I greet you Prince Llewellyn, any brother of my drott will always be to me a shield brother."

As Llew had earlier, it was the prince's turn to look nonplussed. "Oh, ah, very well then."

Llew started to tell Helgar that Prince Llewellyn was not

actually his brother but then decided it was not the time or the place to try to explain why apparent twin brothers were not actually brothers at all.

Cymri chose that moment to land upon Llew's shoulder, startling Helgar considerably as he muttered a word in the northern tongue and stumbled backwards from her.

Llew obediently clenched the amulet. "Llew, you cannot linger here." she told him peremptorily.

"Tell me something I do not know, Cymri," he retorted.

"They found their chief, the one the two of you banged up so badly. He is alive and they are tending to him. He cannot even stand yet, and I think he is having great trouble seeing out of his remaining eye—you would think double-vision for a newly one-eyed man would seem almost normal—but he is also furious. Very soon they will likely do as he says and dispatch nearly every warrior they have after you. There is only one good way through the hills and forest and out of here. If they cut it off before you pass through it, you are lost."

"Okay, that much I did not know," agreed Llew. "Which way is it we should go?"

By way of answer she took wing and settled on the branch of a tree a few hundred feet away.

"Let us go quickly," Llew told the others. "The man I fought at the fires did not die and it seems he is their chief and his feelings are hurt. He is going to send every warrior he has after us and there is only one viable path for us out of here."

Helgar was looking at Llew as though he had seen a ghost. "You have black birds that come and whisper to you what they have seen? I know of only one that does that."

"Just the one bird, Helgar, and she has never really been one for whispering."

Helgar nodded uncertainly and followed when they started moving. They put Llewellyn back on Gower. They were not running now but instead were moving as speedily as they might, short of actually running or trotting. An hour passed and they came to a well-traveled path. They took it and continued on, heading downward and southward.

After scouting ahead to ensure they were not moving into an ambush, Cymri came back and landed on Llew's shoulder. Helgar gaped at this anew, but said nothing.

"Cymri," said Llew, in a low voice. "Helgar there keeps calling me a drott or something. I do not think it is meant insultingly so what exactly is he doing?"

Cymri gave a low whistle, an easy thing for a bird. "He called you a drott or did he say 'my drott?'"

Llew thought on that for a moment. "Come to think of it, I am pretty sure it was 'my drott,' Cymri. Why does he do that?"

"Well," said Cymri, "You had better get used to that accent."

"I am already beginning not to notice it," replied Llew, "but why do you say that?"

"Llew, if you were worrying about whether or not you could trust him then you can stop. And by the way, congratulations. You have your first fanatically loyal follower. A man of his race would gleefully leap upon a hundred foemen rather than betray his drott. You must have really impressed him, even saving his life probably would not be quite enough by itself."

"That is all I did," protested Llew.

"There must be more. Did you somehow distinguish yourself when the two of you took down that chieftain?"

"I do not think so, beside which, Helgar was still in the wicker man at the time and probably could not see it."

Cymri, cocked her head. "You took on a full grown Pict chieftain in face to face combat? He was built like an ox, too, and a head taller than you. Were you crazy?"

"No, of course not! Llew said defensively. "I did not have any choice; he sneaked up behind me and was already too close when I heard him."

Llew had never seen Cymri speechless before. It was a moment before she was able to say anything. "Picts are master hunters and almost undetectable when they wish to be. You heard a barefoot Pict coming up behind you across bare earth? Llew, even most wild animals would likely never have suspected he was there until his spear ran them through."

"Besides, it was not so hard," Llew continued. "I did exactly what Afaggdu taught me and, then too, the Pict had no idea that my sword was a serious danger when the only parts of him it could reach were covered in that huge wicker mask."

"Llew, you are scaring me. You won because he misjudged you, badly . . . very badly. And because of that inhuman sense of hearing you have. Ask Helgar if he knows anything about the chieftain. Like how many warriors he can send after us—that sort of thing."

"Helgar," called Llew,

"Yes, my drott?" came the immediate response.

"As I said, that Pict I fought is alive. Do you have any idea how many men a chief like that will be able to send after us?"

Helgar looked perplexed. "Why, all of them, my drott."

"Enough with the drott for now. Call me Llew. What do you mean by 'all of them.' How many are in his tribe?"

"It is not just his tribe, my—Llew. Goll is their war leader. He has already summoned all the tribes to rally for a great war against your people and mine. Now he has lost status by your defeating and maiming him. Only with your death can he quickly undo this. He will send runners to every tribe's camp and summon every Pict warrior there is."

Chapter XII

Gwri's Tale: A Boy and His Horse

As soon as he was out of the castle, Gwri made a beeline for Slow Tomos and retrieved Gower straight away. He sensed no one would question his right to have a puppy now, even if it had mysteriously appeared from nowhere.

The truth was as he suspected. If he was a boy so important to the queen that she was going to give him a horse, this made him a person that ordinary folk did not want to get on the wrong side of.

Rumors immediately spread that Gwri was being groomed as their dark queen's apprentice, and would soon become capable of similar feats of dark enchantment. Not even Braen give him a hard time about loafing about when it was by the queen's command.

The unguent worked as well as she had claimed, although applying it had been sheer agony. The results were apparent within mere hours when his wounds began healing faster than any human could reasonably expect. For those that knew of this, it just served as additional fodder for their ideas about his relationship with the queen. It was not normally her way to dispense her miraculous cures herself, there were servants at the castle that did that. Nor was it typically done for skinned knees and bruises, only for those in far more serious need.

On the morning of his first full day with Gower, Gwri had begun trying to teach him tricks. Despite his new status, the stable-hands laughed at that.

"What is so funny about training a dog?" he demanded. "Some of you train horses and they are not so clever by half."

"He is just a wee bit young for that, Gwri," said Yorath, one of the more senior of the stable men. "Give him a bit. He will probably learn a lot from you in time, but he is going to teach you a lot in the process—primarily about patience." The other men present laughed again at that, although there was no meanness in it.

Gower, ever ready to please, proved them all wrong as he quickly picked up commands such as sit, lie down, roll over, fetch, and half a dozen others, then proceeded to master them. The stable-hands quit their laughing at that point. It was not natural for a puppy that young to be that quick and clever—perhaps not for any animal.

Three days passed quickly. Having his own dog was an endless delight for a boy who had never had anything. Gower's unabashed adoration and love for him was also intoxicating. There had never been anything in Gwri's life to compare it to.

On the third day he and Gower were playing fetch-the-stick in the small paddock, where it was so constantly trampled and churned by hooves that there was no grass at all, when Braen hailed him from the main stable. Whistling to a completely mud-covered Gower, Gwri trotted to the main stable and around to the front, then drew up short. Queen Moriganna was there.

She regarded him with an emotionless eye, then

summoned him with one crooked finger. Without even checking to see if he was coming, she turned to her stable master. "Very well, Breen, show us your very finest. A fine mount makes a statement and I want it to be a very strong statement indeed."

Braen, tugged his forelock respectfully and replied in his most ingratiating voice, "Oh certainly, your highness. I would never dream of giving you less than the very best, but there will surely be a much better selection after the next spring foaling. If I could make it sooner I would, but a mare takes eleven months to make a foal, and even the gods themselves seem unable to do better. Oh, and it is Braen, your highness."

She had apparently been distracted by something that was on her mind, but now she turned her head to the stable master and asked, "What is Braen?"

"Braen is my name, your highness, not Breen."

Her eyes narrowed and Braen cowered from them. "Are you correcting me?" she asked.

Braen looked like someone who had only just discovered that he had a fatal illness. "Oh no, no, your highness, Breen is a fine name. You can call me that, certainly," he croaked.

"Actually," she said, "I may change a name now and then, but I only do so when I need to. Breen was your great grandfather's name, and you look more than a little like he did at your age. But you are Braen and we will not change that. Let us go in . . . Braen."

Braen let Gwri get the door for her and they entered. Within were no less than ten horses, five to each side in their own stalls, which the stable master had selected for her review. Gwri would have been thrilled to be given any of them. The queen walked past each, scarcely glancing at them.

When she stood at the end of the stalls that held her

candidates she said, "Braen, it was Braen, correct?"

"Yes, your highness," answered Braen anxiously.

"Overall, your service has been adequate, so I want you to know that I am not currently planning to turn you into a small cat and toss you into my kennels."

"Thank you, your highness." Although he said this quite calmly, Braen brought out a small cloth and began blotting enormous amounts of sweat from his face.

"But none of these horses will do. Three are too old, one is too small, two have too little spirit, two more have unfortunate markings, one is a mare, and the fifth one on the right is going to go lame and will eventually have to be destroyed.

Braen stood speechless; Gwri did as well, but for different reasons. This was not magic, he realized, this was just centuries of being around horses. Queen Moriganna might well be the best judge of horses in the world. Long life, Gwri realized, was not just the result of mighty power but was, itself, a mighty power in its own right. What else might she have learned?

Then Moriganna slowly turned and looked in Gwri's direction. Enunciating each syllable slowly and separately, she asked, "What . . . is . . . that?"

Gwri followed her gaze and looked down in panic as he realized the still mud-coated Gower had drawn her attention. "That is just my dog, your highness," he squeaked, all subterfuges discarded.

A cruel smile came across her face. "I told you that you could have a horse. I did not tell you that you could have a dog. This thing is enormous and it is still just a puppy, how could you ever hope to afford to feed it?" With that she inclined her rod at Gower and spoke a word. A nimbus of darkness appeared around Gower and the puppy began yapping piteously.

A red haze came down across Gwri's field of vision and he charged straight at Queen Moriganna. He gradually became aware he was making no progress in that direction. Braen and, although there was no telling where he had come from, Slow Tomos, had both seized him and were not letting him go.

Gower stopped his yapping and Gwri's rage fell away from him in an instant, all of his emotion re-channeled into concern for Gower. But Gower was gone. In his stead stood a young colt. It was a fine colt, indeed, it was a superb colt.

Moriganna gave voice to a short and wicked laugh. "You see Braen? Your mares and gods may not be able to produce a horse in less than eleven months, but I assure you that I am not so limited. Come tomorrow at terce, Gwri. Bring your horse." So saying, she swept out of the stable.

Disbelievingly, Gwri looked at the colt. It inclined its head to regard him. "Gower?" he asked uncertainly. The colt leaned its shoulders back; there was no other way he could describe it, for it would have been ludicrous to say that a horse was crouching, then it sprang towards him and began licking his face unmercifully.

"Ack, Gower, leave off you galoot! You are too big for this!"

Chapter XIII

A Hasty March

"Well, not all of the Picts will come," amended Helgar. "Maybe one man in every four will stay with their families and animals so that they are not left unguarded, even though Pict women are nearly as dangerous as the men. Also, they probably will not chase us for more than a few days. That would take them too far from their families and too far into the lands of their enemies before they are ready to go that far.

"If we stay ahead of them for three days, perhaps four, then turn back they will. We can hunt down Goll later."

"Why would we do that?" Llew asked.

"He will scheme against you forever, Llew. Begin to call him 'One-eye' behind his back his own people will. Heh. For the Picts, Goll and 'one-eyed' the same word may soon be. Stopping that he cannot do. Laughter will follow and he would stop that if he can—but he cannot easily do that while you live."

"How wonderful," remarked Llew. "Moriganna, Arawen, Goll One-eye, can I make any more powerful enemies?"

Llewellyn had overheard this last comment. "You are doing remarkably well in making enemies, particularly for a man of but fourteen summers. Bear in mind, however, that nearly every Tetheran alive, simply by being alive, is an enemy of those three."

"But not on a personal basis," Llew complained.

"Welcome to my world," replied the prince, "and you can probably add Dylan to that list when he learns you rescued me from whatever fate Moriganna had in mind."

"Oh, of course," groaned Llew, "Dylan. The reason I will not be taking any sea voyages anytime soon."

Helgar smiled dangerously. "Many great battles to fight we will have. Truly it is fortunate I am that it was you that found me in the wicker man."

Llew snorted, "Helgar, I think you can count yourself lucky that anyone found you there."

Helgar had sufficient grace to look sheepish at this. "Yes, but a bonus it is that it was one with many great enemies to fight. Sing of us until the world is destroyed and remade will your bards and our skalds.

"Or they will," he frowned, "if our names can be straight kept. Llew, how is it that you and your own twin brother have almost the same name? Some kind of shared, family name is it?"

"I will explain as we travel, Helgar, but suffice it to say that, although our names are quite similar, the situation is quite complicated. What we are not, despite appearances, is brothers."

Helgar furrowed his brow but only said, "I will look forward to hearing it, Llew, who is my drott."

"Helgar, you pronounce our words fairly well, but why do you speak as you do?"

"Do I still have an accent?" Helgar asked in heavily accented Tetheran. "I was assured I do not."

Llew almost managed to keep from laughing at that. "No, I am not referring to your accent."

"I am sorry, my drott, then take your meaning I do not."

"Sometimes your words are put together almost backward from what it would seem they should be. Other times you speak just as any Tetheran might," said Llew.

"Ah," exclaimed Helgar, "in the language of my people all my words would be in a different order from how your people speak. When I learned your tongue, I was taught to change the order I spoke your words in. Sadly, I am not a fast learner and I also get a bit excited at times. So I forget and slip between the two. Confusing to you it might be so try I will to do better—I mean to say it might be confusing to you so I will try to do better."

"Um, very well," said Llew, "but Helgar, do you not have friends and family of your own that you need to return to? Your fine metal armor tells me you are of no low station among your own people."

Helgar scowled. "My father was Jarl of Lindenjal, but he is dead and my worthless uncle rules now. I cannot return yet. It was to escape him that my older brothers and I fled through the wilderness, only to be captured by Picts." He managed to spit as he said the word Picts.

Llew thought instantly of the other two fires, burned down to no more than hot embers, each with the remnants of what might have been wicker men. He said nothing, not trusting himself to speak.

"So you have lost both your home and your family then?" Llewellyn asked quietly.

If anything, Helgar's scowl deepened. "Lost my home I have not. It is where it is and it will not move. When the time is right, when I have grown to where I can swing a great axe with but one hand like my father, when my name alone brings fear and panic with the word I am coming, then I shall take up a great axe in each hand. Then Helgar will return to Lindenjal and heads will roll. Many heads will roll," he amended darkly.

No one thought for an instant that Helgar was speaking figuratively when he spoke of heads rolling.

Despite fearing he was being foolish, Llew impulsively leaned forward to Helgar and seized him by one shoulder. "We have matters to the south that must be attended to now, Helgar. But when that time comes, I will support you in this as best I can."

Apparently it was the right thing to say. It certainly broke the ominous mood. Helgar snorted, "Such is your nature. I knew it when I first saw you. Such a thing is what makes a drott."

* * *

They made good progress, considering that they had no trail, although overall it seemed to Llew they spent more time going west or east than they did south, slipping sideways across boulder strewn open areas, and in and out of dark, thick forest in between.

They finally came to an opening in the trees where the ground was not covered in stone. To be sure, there were plenty of stones, yet the lea was primarily filled with grass. A few rangy sheep grazed upon it and directly across on the opposite side was a crofter's cottage. Solidly constructed of tightly packed stone, its roof was of thatch and a thin plume of grey smoke, little more than a wisp, protruded from the stone chimney.

"Ah," exclaimed Helgar, "good this is. We have little food and little time to forage. Now we can get some and continue without slowing." He noticed Llew's frown. "Ah, pay for it we would," he added quickly, "or leave our promise of payment, of course, my drott, Llew."

"It is not that good, Helgar. True enough we need supplies but we have little time to escort a crofter and his family down the mountains. Yet we cannot leave them here. The Picts will use their heads for their filthy fetishes or some such."

Now Llewellyn frowned. "You have the right of it, of course, Llew. It pains me to spare the time or effort but I concur. I see little choice in the matter."

The little party picked its way across the open pasture to the bare earth yard until they stood before the croft's only entrance, a rude wooden door bound by heavy, coarse rope.

Stentorian snoring could be heard within. Llew also noted there was more than one source, perhaps even several, and the hair on the back of his neck seemed to stand up.

"All may not be as it seems here," he whispered to the others. "Take station around the corners so that, initially, they may see only me. If it is only a crofter and his family it would be best not to frighten them. If it something else—"

Llewellyn and Helgar both nodded knowingly. His meaning was understood perfectly. They then led Gower around to the side of the hut, out of sight of anyone opening the door from inside.

"Hail the house," Llew called in a loud voice.

The result was disappointing in that the snoring continued unabated.

Llew tried again, with greater volume. This time, his reward was immediate.

At least one set of snoring came to a sputtering stop. "Huh, whazzat?"

Another voice said, "Wut?"

"Someone is at the door—get up you lot!" hissed an ugly

voice.

Llew dropped his hand to the hilt of his sword and backed up a few more feet from the door.

The door slammed open and a rough looking man hulked there with an axe. Seeing Llew he immediately smiled. It was not an especially friendly smile.

"Why it is just a boy in his father's armor," he exclaimed. "A little lost is ye?" He stepped out and more men crowded out behind him to either side.

Llew's heart sank. These were no crofters and a fight with a pack of bandits had no part in what he and his needed to do. Still, they were Tetherans so, while he held little hope for it, mayhap they could be diverted.

"Hullo there!" Llew chirped brightly. "I was just passing through the neighborhood and thought perhaps I should warn whoever lived here about the Pictish horde coming in this direction."

The leader guffawed and Llew's remaining hopes, such as they had been, fell away.

"And what horde would that be, little man?"

That, thought Llew, seemed a bit unfair. He was at least a head taller than the bandit and nearly as heavily built.

"Why the horde that their new war leader, Goll One-eye, has summoned, and the one with which he intends to cut a wide swath into the lands of all civilized people. The vanguard should be arriving by this time tomorrow."

Without moving, Llew leaned slightly forward and put the back of his hand along the side of his mouth as he spoke in a lowered voice, "They like to put people in wicker cages and burn them alive. I really cannot recommend staying here any longer than it takes to grab your belongings and some supplies." Then, while straightening at the waist, he casually took a step backwards to keep some distance between him and the semi-circle of what he was now certain were bandits.

It also helped to put him at a slightly greater remove from the incredible unwashed stench they gave off. Llew had to wonder how it was that, if nothing else, the rain itself did not occasionally wash some of their smell away.

The men around the leader shifted uneasily.

The leader seemed unconcerned. "Well that is a fine and friendly thing you are doing young fellow. Of course, we do not have much in the way of belongings and supplies so we will need yours, of course. But that is just the neighborly thing to do, eh? Sharing? That sword will be a nice start. Hand it over, boy."

Llew had the sword out in one smooth draw before any of the bandits could so much as blink. "Ah, this sword you mean? I really cannot. It was a gift from my dear father on his death bed and has been in the family ever so long. Besides, you look much more like an axeman and you have an axe already. Hmm, so do many of your, let us see, one, two, three, four, five, six—six friends," Llew announced loudly.

The leader snarled. "That is right, boy, seven to one it is and at those odds it does not matter how clever you are with that pig-sticker. Drop it, and whatever else you have of value, and run along and play."

Llew's stomach did a flip-flop. This was ugly and he did not like it a bit. Even so, he forced a short chuckle. "I said there were seven of you. I did not say there was one of me. I may not even be the one who is outnumbered here."

There was a loud thud and the bandit nearest the right corner of the cottage began to collapse to the ground, the butt of a spear now occupying the space where his head had been. Llew winced. Helgar's rules of engagement were more than a little rough around the edges. Llewellyn, at least, waited a decent interval while the next closest bandits to Helgar turned around. Then his sword flicked out in a blur, going left, then right, and two more bandits were removed from the equation before the astonished fellows could even finish lifting their axes. Llew made a note to himself that, between the two of them, the prince was probably the better swordsman. Afaggdu had predicted that might be the case, given that they had been forced to cut Llew's training short.

The bandit leader cursed and, along with his men, spun halfway to face both Llew and the sudden attack from the rear. "You want to play, you poxy little lord, then we right well will!" he bellowed.

"Ah," said Llew in a mocking tone, "that is just your temper talking. The numbers may now be only equal, counting Gower, and we perhaps seem a bit young when compared with your wealth of, um, age. But we," he continued in a deeper and more menacing voice, "are all trained and blooded warriors, accoutered with the finest in arms and armor—and we are certainly not playing."

And it was true, thought Llew amazedly. For all their rough fearsomeness and bluster, these remaining bandits had no more chance against them than a flock of chickens against an aerie of hawks.

One of the more imposing looking bandits, the only one not wielding a woodman's axe, dropped his knotted club and showed his hands were now open and clear.

The leader cursed again, "Damn you and your little crofter soul, Addfwyn! I took you in but I told you when you joined what would happen if you failed me!"

"I do not owe you anything, Meilyr," the man said quietly. "You took everything I had at the point of a knife, including my oath. If I am forsworn I cannot understand why when all you ever had was a stolen oath. Besides, I was just biding my time. Your days were already numbered—now they are over."

Addfwyn's voice was calm and low but, if looks could have killed, Meilyr would have already passed on.

Meilyr scowled and then turned it into an unpleasant grin. "Maybe, but do not count your coins before you have them." He moved back several steps, poised and ready for combat, evidently preparing to take them all on singled-handedly if he had to.

Then he spun and ran at top speed across the lea towards the tree line. It was so abrupt that even Helgar was taken aback. The two surviving bandits goggled at the sight, then glanced at the grim ensemble around them, even Gower was facing them, somewhat crouched, with his teeth bared and—could that threatening noise he was making be called growling?

As one, the last two sprinted after their departing leader, leaving their axes behind them. No one made any attempt to strike down the fleeing, unarmed wretches.

Llewellyn watched them run and said, while emulating a Northman's accent, "Scary fellows we be, eh?" Helgar laughed at this.

Chapter XIV

Gwri's Tale: Training Begins

The next morning, after leading Gower to the castle, their training began in earnest. Gwri quickly discovered that he was not nearly as physically capable as he had thought. Had he not worked all of his life, from dawn to dusk, in a job that demanded continuous use of his muscles? Was he not a strapping large boy, given his years, and one whose martial skills had eventually cowed all potential adversaries that were anywhere near his own age?

After spending a short time with an older guardsman named Mercher, Gwri began to realize that none of this seemed to matter. Mercher had apparently drawn the short straw when it came time to designate someone to train the queen's bastard brat, or possibly her grandson, depending on which of the latest rumors was most in favor.

They had both taken up wooden practice swords at the start. After Mercher had inflicted a few fresh bruises over top of the boy's older ones, Gwri got angry, but he found that the anger did not help him in the least. He finally ran completely out of energy, many bruises later, and was forced to ground his weapon.

Mercher directed a penetrating look at Gwri that revealed

nothing of what he might be thinking of his new student. "And what have you learned so far this fine morning?" Mercher inquired.

Somewhat red-faced from more than the exertion, Gwri considered various acrimonious responses before finally deciding on the simple truth. "I have not learned anything except that I am equally ineffective regardless of whether I am angry or not," he admitted.

"Excellent, that is a good start then," Mercher replied. "It means that you may have learned something of how much you need to learn. It is not until you realize your head is empty of what needs to be learned that you are ready to begin filling it."

This said, the old guardsman handed Gwri his own sword and nodded to the weapons rack. After he put away the practice weapons, Gwri spent the following two hours engaged in vigorous exercises that worked his muscles in ways that were wholly new to him. He was certain the next day would find him with sore spots in places he had never known he had.

Gwri also met briefly with his riding master, a younger man named Cadwallon ap Dew, another of the more experienced guardsman. Gower was still too young to ride, but there was plenty to do, despite that. Although the guardsman tried to hide it, he was clearly impressed by Gwri's familiarity with horses and even with his riding ability. Yet there was, and Cadwallon had been careful and thorough in emphasizing this, far more to becoming a master of mounted combat than knowing how to ride. Likewise, turning Gower into the warhorse he potentially could become would be a long and difficult road. This was despite, or perhaps even because of, the fact that Gower's potential was beyond anything the trooper had ever seen.

"Ensorcelled by the queen, you say? I can well believe it.

Just look how fine he is! I have never seen the like of him from any mortal stud, nor have I ever even seen any others of his breed. Yet I can scarcely credit it. You say he was a dog?" The veteran had looked rather askance upon learning this. "I expect we will have a great many bad habits to break him from," he remarked, as he watched Gower. That worthy was now sitting on his hindquarters and performing what appeared to be a futile attempt to scratch a flea with one of his hind legs.

By midday meal, Gwri was exhausted and sore. He was also both discouraged and unhappy with how long the road ahead seemed to be. He was certainly in no mood for all the frippery the afternoon would hold.

Today was different, however. When Moriganna caught him slacking she did not grow angry, or shout, as usual. Instead she just reduced her eyes to slits. This, by itself, was daunting enough to intimidate most, but Gwri was getting used to it.

"So, how you are enjoying having your own horse?" she asked. "If it is proving too tiring for you then I am certain there are other opportunities for such an animal in my service."

Gwri found he had much less trouble applying himself the rest of the afternoon.

Later, when he had time to think about it, his fear began to fade as anger suffused him. *How dare she threaten to take Gower!* As he further considered the matter, he realized two things, that she would not actually carry through, except in extremis, for it would remove the threat from her arsenal.

It was then he began to realize what a valuable lesson this was in and of itself. He thought he had been so clever in tricking a horse out of her. Now he was beginning to realize it was not so straightforward as that. Not only had getting a horse cost him his dog, it had also given Moriganna a hostage for his good behavior.

As he had discovered, Queen Moriganna was a cold and hateful creature with nothing but disdain for others, and no concern for them whatsoever except in how they could be a help or a hindrance to her. Despite this, even though people understood that about her, they still rushed to do her bidding and please her. This was not just because of her magical powers. In truth, almost no one ever saw her using them. Aside from this implied threat, her greatest power seemed to reside in her ability to manipulate people.

It occurred to Gwri that, if this was the true basis of her strength, he could study her and learn how she did this. That might even make him better able to protect himself against it. Likewise, he might be able to discern ways to get the same results for himself someday, although hopefully through other means.

It came to him in an insight that all rulers—all strong rulers, he amended—were probably master manipulators of men. Yet it seemed to Gwri that there had to be, as in most things, a right way and a wrong way to go about this. Moriganna's way, while possibly very effective, was clearly a wrong way. Also, while effective, it might not be the most effective. The heroes in the old tales always seemed to surround themselves with boon companions, heroes not unlike themselves but who would gladly help the hero, even placing their own lives at risk to do so, more because they believed in the hero than in the end goal.

Gwri had never had any friends or boon companions, and he had never seriously considered the possibility of finding any. That was simply something that only happened in tales, not in the real world. Yet, without even admitting it to himself, he had come to feel that just to be able to gather such people around him, true brothers-in-arms, almost seemed a better reason to seek a lofty goal, or essay a dangerous quest, than any actual reward its attainment might bring.

It also seemed to Gwri that to have others so thoroughly bonded to you that you did not need to rely on vicious schemes to gain their aid was a far better way to get things done. This planted a seed that, looking back later, he recognized as being the first time he wondered why someone like Queen Moriganna would really even care about saving mankind.

* * *

Winter passed and summer came anew and, all the while, Gwri and Gower both grew at a furious rate. In Gower's case, Cadwallon was perplexed. "He is growing fully twice or even three times as fast as any horse ever had a right to do," the amazed guardsman said, as Gwri rubbed the horse down after an especially vigorous training session. "I would proclaim it to be completely unnatural except that, given what you have told me of his origins, it would be just plain silly to ever pretend he was not unnatural."

"Perhaps it is because dogs grow so much faster than horses," Gwri suggested

"Perhaps," agreed Cadwallon, "or perhaps the Queen has slipped some of her potions into his water."

At some point, Gwri received a lesson on the Julian calendar, itself a legacy of the Roaming Empire's brief reign over the lands of Tethera. Greatly surprising him, Moriganna had claimed to know his real birthday, which she said was at midsummer on the fifth day of July. If true, this would be the year he would pass his tenth birthday. A month shy of that and already he was of a size and weight that approached that of some grown men. In practice bouts against a full grown guardsman of moderate skill his speed and vigor, coupled with his natural aptitude for anything having to do with weapons, would occasionally even allow him to win. The embarrassment of this for the beaten adversary was enough to limit the supply of those who would willingly spar with him, yet there were still plenty of guardsmen who could and did trounce him each and every time.

In the saddle it was a different story. He and Gower together were an unsettlingly effective combination. Even the best of the queen's riders had to be on their toes when it came time to practice mounted combat against them. Gower had risen to nearly seventeen hands and weighed in at around one hundred and fifty stones to Gwri's twelve. Despite his size, which was much larger than the cobs that most of the guardsmen rode, Gower was also extremely swift and, for a beast his size, he was extraordinarily agile. In addition to all of this, he was very smart for a horse and completely fearless, even eager, when it came to a fight. Unbeknownst to most, Gwri spent a good deal of his efforts in every match making sure Gower did not become too excited and hurt someone.

As for the other lessons, Gwri had surprised himself. Once he quit fighting it he had discovered the manners part of his training was not terribly difficult. Likewise, when you really let yourself listen to it, even history was not too bad, especially if you pretended it was stories instead. Gwri loved stories and would listen to them whenever he could. Listening to Moriganna recite history to him, which he always had to be ready to repeat back to her when she asked, he realized that she not only knew an enormous amount of history, she had actually been there when a lot of it had happened.

This gave the history a lot of detail and insight that no one else would have knowledge of, but it also had the disadvantage of

Queen Moriganna being was who she was. Most people she had interacted with came off badly in her telling, and Gwri came to understand that, while he was getting a great deal of history, he was also getting an extremely one-sided view of it. Other than outright hate and dislike, her typical attitude for most people could best be described as disdain.

"Enough," she finally declared one day.

"I know enough?" Gwri asked, scarcely able to contain the rising joy he felt at the prospect.

She dashed that with her next words, "Hardly, I simply have had enough of this. Things like dancing and such will have to be taught by another and I have other things to do, in any case. I already have a prospect in mind to be your instructor. With any luck, she should be arriving in the next few days. Continue with your arms and riding instruction until she arrives but, until she does, you will take your midday meals in the kitchen and go back to the stables in the afternoon until she arrives and is ready."

"Yes, your highness," he replied. He was still pretty pleased with getting a break from studies, plus, it sounded like he might no longer be subjected to Moriganna's withering disdain and mercurial temper on a daily basis. Perhaps he should bring up something that concerned him now? He had delayed thus far as he was not sure how she would take it, but she seemed in as good a mood as he was ever likely to find her.

"Your highness, there is an issue I have been hesitant to discuss with you."

She raised one eyebrow but, with a casual gesture, bade him to continue.

"It is my arms trainers. They are solid guardsmen and know their trade but they are what they are. I feel I have learned, if not all, the bulk of what they have to teach. I am not the greatest warrior in the land, but then I am also still quite young. As I grow and gain expertise in what they have taught me, my capabilities increase and even now some of the men are afraid to fight me in practice, but—"

"You think they have reached a point of diminishing returns, Gwri?"

"A point of what?" he asked, perplexed at this term that used familiar words in such an odd way. "I think they have reached a point where there is less and less of use that they can teach me. Their aid in my practice is useful, of course, but I feel there is much more that I need to learn."

Moriganna frowned and he found himself waiting for a potential lambasting.

What came was not that. "Gwri, I am not displeased by your progress in your weapons training, but recognize that my guardsmen, while not at all incompetent, are not precisely at the pinnacle of combat skill, even within the realm of men. For the role you must play, you do have far to go. It is well that you recognize this also. In truth, I am attempting to attract an instructor of the first rank to travel here and undertake to complete your training. "

Gwri tried, with only moderate success, to hide the thrill that coursed through him when she said that.

"It is a ticklish matter but one I have already recognized as a necessary one. There are certainly many issues, not the least of which is that Caer Mallcoedwig is not precisely the crossroads of the five kingdoms and I want that instructor to come here willingly.

"I am not nearly so picky in the case of your finishing instructor. In contrast, she will likely be most unhappy at being here but I do not care. She will do what I bring her here to do."

"I have noticed, your highness," Gwri interjected cautiously, "that we get no visitors at all. Only those whom you have previously sent forth on some task ever seem to come here."

"That is because there are many warlords—and others—in the world who would seek to force their attentions on us—could they find us. It would be to their detriment, of course, but I do not wish to be bothered until you are ready to deal with them. In the meantime it is simple enough to maintain a spell of misdirection upon this place. None may approach without losing their way and wandering off—unless they have been here in the past or are brought hither by someone who has already been here."

Gwri nodded slowly. She had just confirmed what only rumors had told him previously. It explained much.

"Go. We will speak again in a few days. In the meantime, apply yourself as best you can. You have a brilliant future ahead of you, but only if you help make it happen."

Chapter XV

A Dubious Refuge

Still watching the retreating bandits, Llew remarked, "I do not think we will see them again."

"He is a vicious one, that Meilyr," said the man who had stayed behind. "He will not rest until he settles accounts as he figures them."

"He might not have much choice in the matter," said Llewellyn. "Yon path to the south is the only way away from the coming Picts—and that is not the way they went."

Helgar chuckled. "Goll One-eye will have little use for them that they would like."

The man the bandit leader had called Addfwyn looked startled. "That was truth? The Picts are coming in a war group?"

Llew eyed him. "They are indeed, and what do we do with you?"

"Lord, take me with you! Even without the Picts coming, there is nothing I wish more than to be away from here."

"How could we trust you amongst us?"

"Your lordship," he began, and Llew did not correct him, "This was my croft before Meilyr came and took it from me. He forced me to choose between joining his band and 'sharing,' as he called it, or dying a very bad death. My wife and children are buried here; a sickness took them this past winter. It was cruel but I have come to realize it would have been crueler still had they been here when Meilyr and his band appeared.

"I need to be away from here, even were the Picts not on their way. Please, lord, I do not need much, a little food, indeed what remains of my herd and stores are yours, certainly, and I can give good service. I am not afraid of work."

He eyed Helgar apprehensively. "I am not certain of the Northman but a lord, er, lords," he added, glancing towards Prince Llewellyn, "especially those that travel without retinue, retainers, or even a shield-bearer, could make good use of me. I can take care of the horse, also your arms and armor. And I am a better cook than you might expect. Indeed, that is a large part of why Meilyr let me live."

Llew scowled. Without some reason to disbelieve what the man had said, he would now feel guilty if he sent him away. Plus, he mused, it would be the crofter's own rations they would likely be consuming for some time to come. But what if he was lying? Did he have the right to risk Prince Llewellyn's safety to protect his own conscience?

Apparently sensing something of his internal conflict, Llewellyn settled the matter.

"Addfwyn Croftholder," he began, "the high and the low justice are mine to administer. You are hereby freed and pardoned for any crimes committed while a prisoner of the bandit Meilyr. You are free to go or stay, or come with us and take oath—a real oath," the prince added. "There is no harm to fear from us should you refuse. Is that understood? But take the oath and then break faith with us and there will be consequences."

Addfwyn gulped. "Yes, my lord!"

"What is your full name?"

"I am called Addfwyn ap Sior, my lord."

"Very well," continued the prince, "do you, Addfwyn ap Sior, take this oath freely and of your own volition?"

Llew doubted the man knew the meaning of the word 'volition' but, in context, the gist of it should have been evident.

"I do, my lord."

"Do you swear true faith and loyalty to Lord Llew of Gwent?" Cymri, who had landed on Llew's shoulder at some point, started at this point, flapping her wings a few times before settling down.

"I do, my lord."

"To take him as your liege lord? To serve him in all things, never to falter, and in peace or in war, to meet your full obligations to him?"

"I do, my lord."

"And do you, Lord Llew of Gwent, accept the services of Addfwyn ap Sior as your loyal vassal?"

Apparently, Llew realized, that must be addressed at him. He replied in the only way that seemed possible: "I do."

"Very well," smiled Llewellyn, "my apologies for the incredibly short version but we really need to grab up what we can in the way of provisions and get away from here as fast as our feet may carry us."

"At once, my lords," acknowledged Addfwyn. "I will bring everything that might be of use out here and you can choose what you will. I have a pony to help carry it. The rest," he added as he started toward the cottage, "we can burn to keep the Picts from getting the use of it."

Llew nodded approvingly. "One question, Addfwyn. You

said your skill in cooking was a large part of the reason Meilyr made you join his band. What was the rest of the reason?"

"Oh," Addfwyn stopped and turned back, he twisted his hands together awkwardly while keeping his eyes downcast. In a quiet voice he said, "He needed more men, my lord. He had lost some."

"Did he say how?"

"No my lord, he did not need to. When they first came here they were nine. We had words and I killed two and crippled another before they overcame me." Addfwyn was silent for a moment and then, almost apologetically, added, "I did not want them near my family so they are buried to the west near the wood."

There was another silence before he asked, "By your leave, my lord?"

Finding his voice, Llew commanded: "Carry on . . . and do not forget to retrieve your weapon."

As soon as the former crofter had gone inside, Helgar announced, "I will get us as much of a sheep as we can easily carry and eat before it spoils. The rest into the woods they can go. Better the wolves eat them than the Picts." He then picked up a couple of the fallen axes and left to take care of that messy chore.

"Get twice what you would think that would be, Helgar. My horse can eat mutton as well as we and it will save time he must otherwise spend grazing."

Helgar bellowed with laughter as he headed for the nearest grouping of sheep.

Llewellyn snickered, "I believe he thinks you are making a jest with him, Llew."

"Mayhap," he replied, "but I would wager he still brings the meat I asked for."

The prince nudged the one whose head had met the haft of Helgar's spear. "What about this one? I would give long odds against him ever waking up but, for the moment, he still lives. Shall we finish him off? It would probably be a mercy either way, for if he does awaken then the Picts may have him soon after."

"Nay," said Llew slowly, "We cannot take him with us but I do not want his blood on my hands. We will leave him here and let the gods decide his fate. If he wakes, and it is in time, he may yet save his life."

"As you say," replied Llewellyn. "By the way, that was quite brave the way you faced down all seven of them. You handled it like you were born to do so and had done just that, many times before. There was never a trace of hesitation or even concern. I was very impressed. Not," the prince added hastily, "that I ever doubted you could do that."

"Heh," replied Llew, "It was easy when I knew I had the most stalwart companions any man ever asked for at my back—at their backs, for that matter. And thank you for stepping in with that oath. I was really in a fix trying to figure out what to do with our reluctant outlaw."

"I was happy we were able to save him from a life of banditry," Llewellyn said gravely. "He has had a hard life but I think it will be better now and I also suspect he will be of substantial value to you until the end of his days. I will go see what else is available, besides just food, which we might wish to supply ourselves with while the opportunity exists."

Llewellyn went inside and left Llew standing in the grass-free area before the cottage. His mind on other things, Llew reached down, seized the ankles of a dead bandit, and dragged him far enough away so that he would not present an obstacle to their getting supplies together.

Afterward, he was not far from the only trail that led to this lonely outpost. He walked over and looked down it. It snaked downslope between the trees until it was lost from sight. It was a far cry from a proper road but their progress along it would be substantially easier than it had been through the wilderness.

Llew took hold of his medallion. "Cymri, you are certain this is the only path of escape?"

"Before we speak on that, Llew, do you realize what happened back there?"

Llew snorted, "I made a serious enemy out of a little bandit?"

"No, silly," Cymri chided. "When you took that man as your vassal?"

"Besides ruffling your feathers quite a bit? I gained another mouth to feed and with no means to feed him, or pay him. In time it is entirely possible he will want to whop me with that big club I told him to continue carrying."

"You have to listen to everything that is said, Llew, not just to the parts that worry or intrigue you. Prince Llewellyn named you Lord Llew of Gwent."

"Yes, that seems more than a bit of a stretch but, under the circumstances, I decided it was a good time to let it pass."

Cymri sighed. "If anyone else said it then yes, it would be a stretch. The prince is the heir of Gwent. If he says you are a lord of Gwent then it is not a stretch. It becomes the truth. His father will certainly confirm it and find a title and some land for you; the alternative would be to shame his heir. Congratulations on becoming a real noble, no longer just Moriganna's pretend prince—and here you never thought all those lessons on table manners would ever be of any use."

Llew's mind reeled and it was hard to give meaning to the

black bird's next words.

"Do not let it go to your head. A title means nothing if you do not live to enjoy it." Cymri shifted her position on Llew's shoulder. "There is no good way to avoid this path. As I said, there is but one way in or out in this direction. The good news is that your feet have carried you quickly and there is no one blocking your path forward so far as I can see. Likewise, none yet press closely upon your heels."

"Yet?" queried Llew, waiting for the bad news.

"When they come they will progress much faster than you have so far. I do not think you can stay ahead of them for three days."

Llew rubbed his temples with his fingertips before replying, "Heroic as it might otherwise be, I would rather escape than make a desperate last stand against uncountable savage Picts. Is there some place we could hide and have them pass us by?"

"There are going to be a lot of them and so many of them are expert trackers I am very tempted to say no."

Llew blinked hard and turned his head to full regard her. "Tempted? Only tempted? Is it a hiding place you are thinking of or not?"

"Well," hedged Cymri, "it is a hiding place in that no Picts will dare to follow us, but they will know we have gone in."

"Still," said Llew, "that sounds like a refuge. They cannot wait for us to come out, regardless of how hungry we may get. An army, even an army of Picts, cannot stay in one place more than a few days. They will run out of food and game, and they will have neither stores of provisions, nor wagons to bring them more. Worse for them, their presence will eventually be noticed, boding ill for their undeclared war to be a surprise.

"Cymri," said Llew, "without surprise on their side, the

Picts have little chance for gain against the Tetherans. So far as I know they have no siegecraft and a properly forted up enemy would be beyond them. Meanwhile, Tetherans from hundreds of miles away would gather their forces and march. Even sworn enemies amongst them would put that aside until the Picts were driven back into the dark places of the wilds."

"That is true enough, Llew, and an excellent assessment. You seem to recall more of Afaggdu's training than just the sword it seems."

Llew recalled many hours discussing the finer points of strategy in the evenings while moving stone and wooden markers across the battle maps. It dawned on him now that Afaggdu had hidden all kinds of lessons in the banter while playing the war games. It was a pretty sneaky way to ensure his attention . . . and it had worked well.

He shook his head to refocus. "The Picts cannot enter and they cannot afford to remain waiting outside. So, in essence, this place you are alluding to is not so much a hiding place as a safe place for us?"

Cymri bobbed her head and regarded him. "It is," she said, "not a hiding place and it is not a safe place. It is just a place where the Picts will not follow us. It is called Cas-Eiddew."

Something that might have been dread tugged at Llew's heart upon hearing that name, though it was not one he could recall having ever heard before. "It is a proper fortress then? Who rules in this place that the Picts fear them so?"

"None know this, Llew. By day it is merely the sort of hilltop ruins you might find in a thousand other places. Tethera is ancient and no one has knowledge of all its past ages unless it is the Fae themselves, or something akin to them. These ruins may even be older than most. Only crumbling stones remain, deeply covered in ivy and thistle, but by night, some nights at least, the ruins are said to become something more; indeed, they appear to be not ruins at all but a great fortification that might shrug off the greatest armies ever assembled. There are even said to be flags and banners upon its walls and lights moving within."

Llew licked his lips nervously. There was no shame in admitting that this was frightening. It was the very stuff of which nightmares were fashioned. There were undoubtedly worse fates than death, worse even than a death that involved burning within a wicker man. It might well be better to face their Pict pursuers and try to die in combat than attempt such a place.

"What do those who approach it at night say? Are there at least men upon the walls or at the gate, Cymri?"

"Again, no one knows," she said. "I am certain that people have tried to approach it; indeed, there are tales of entire armies marching upon it. It is telling, however, that we have no accounts from any of them of what they encountered. This would indicate no one ever saw any part of those armies again."

"I am confounded," began Llew, "that I have not heard of this place before. Surely something so singular must be known in every corner of the land?"

Cymri ruffled her feathers in a motion Llew had learned was probably her equivalent of a sigh or, perhaps, a shrug. "Llew, the world is filled with a plethora of mysteries, too many of them dangerous and too many of those that are dangerous being both ill content to wait for victims and quite capable of seeking them out instead. The great kingdom is shattered and the five kingdoms are all, each in their own way, withering away from what they once were.

"Travel between them is dangerous for most and difficult at best. Creatures such as Arawen and Moriganna and, perhaps to a lesser degree, Dylan, are but a few of those who would encourage this state of affairs. By these measures, Cas-Eiddew is a lesser threat that most will never come close enough to learn of—and one that is easily avoided by any who do.

"In short, while in your travels you may gain knowledge of things that surprise you, you should never be surprised at not already possessing knowledge of them."

"Very well," replied Llew, "this sounds like near certain death and the Picts are wise to be afraid of this place. The question is, as deaths go, why should we prefer it over them?"

"Because Moriganna moves against my house," Llewellyn declared. Unnoticed by them both, he had approached and heard at least of some part of Llew's words, even if the royal could not understand Cymri's. "You yourself have said Moriganna is sending assassins against my father. If we choose death then we accept that. Moreover, if we cringe away from the unknown and accept defeat rather than face it, what does this say of us?"

Llew had already come to much the same conclusion. The decision was not a decision at all or, if it was, it was one that could be made without worry of later regret because there was only one proper way to make it. Llew found it reassuring that someone else felt the same way.

Llew gave the prince a sardonic grin. "Sometimes I like to take a stand against what others are telling me, simply to measure the strength of their arguments. Doing so vexed Moriganna to no end. Even so, I cannot imagine my decision would have been any different for it in this case. There are some fates to be feared more than death itself, yet even they are outweighed by our own fears of failure."

"Indeed," Llewellyn nodded, "we understand each other well, you and I. Now what of this place? You spoke of a strong point where there might or might not be men upon the wall? And yet the Picts fear it so much that they will approach it not? Why would it sound like certain death in either case?"

Llew explained and the prince furrowed his brow as he considered.

"Still and all," he mused, after Llew had finished, "we might camp amidst these ruins by day and see no threat, while the Picts are kept at bay by their own beliefs. We should likely be there at least a night but, again, it seems there is no certainty that this castle apparition would choose that night to appear."

"And if it does?" inquired Llew.

"If it does," Llewellyn responded, "then it may not be lethal or, if it is, we can go down fighting. If eldritch horrors seek to take form in our world so as to cause harm to us, then they can receive it from us as well, and we are all armed."

"You presume our weapons would not pass through them without harm?" Llew asked.

"Well, if they did then it stands to reason their weapons would pass through us in much the same way, and we should all have but a futile bit of exercise."

Llew shook his head and chose not to assail this logic. Cymri had mentioned the possibility of entire armies disappearing. "Did you find anything of use?"

"I found a few minor things, mainly blankets, those that were not overly soiled by those filthy bandits, and some water skins."

"On a cold night, a blanket is not a minor thing," said Llew.

Llewellyn gave him a level look. "True enough. You can take a look to see if there is anything else. I will remain here for a bit. Helgar is slaughtering a pair of sheep. It is a messy business."

"And that bothers you?" Llew asked, surprised.

"He has also taken off all his armor so as not to get blood on it. I suppose he feels it is easier to rinse blood off his hide than his gear."

"Ah," said Llew, glancing towards the cottage. "That would explain why he is naked. Given all that hair, I would have worried he was one of Moriganna's shape-shifters in the act of becoming a beast."

Llewellyn snorted. "That might explain it. Nevertheless, between an overabundance of sheep intestines and naked blood-spattered Northmen, I think I will just remain here a bit. I grew up in a great castle, not a butchery."

Llew grinned. "It falls on me then. I will go see if I can get things moving toward a quicker departure."

It was already late afternoon before they were ready to move, but they now made good time with Llewellyn again astride Gower and all of them free to move down the path at a brisk rate. Llew kept his bow ready at hand in case they came across game—mutton would get tiresome quickly—but failed to espy any creature larger than a sparrow.

As darkness fell they pushed on until the last possible moment. They then stopped just a few feet off the side of the trail. They had cooked a good deal of mutton before departing, and speed was of the essence, so they made no fire. Llew assigned himself the first watch, then it would be Helgar's turn, followed by Addfwyn's and, last, Llewellyn's. Llew deliberated a bit but, even while feeling a bit guilty about his lack of trust, asked Cymri to keep an eye on Addfwyn during his shift.

When his shift was over, Llew slept fitfully. A single dream kept returning to him in which he ran heedless through a dark forest, slashing down endless Picts as they leaped out of hiding and into his path. Something he knew to be much worse than any Pict was chasing him, though he had no idea what it was. To his dreaming self it seemed a terrible thing to slash down so many men in such a hasty and uncaring manner. Yet failing to move fast enough to stay away from whatever was chasing him seemed immeasurably worse.

Eventually he awoke, somewhat rested in body but not, perhaps, in mind. Llewellyn was shaking his right shoulder.

"Llew, I think I can see my hand at the end of my arm now. The darkness fades and we must be away."

Once he had shaken off enough of his grogginess Llew saw that Helgar and Addfwyn were already up and ready and had saddled and loaded Gower and the pony for good measure. There was no camp to break and, in unspoken agreement, they all decided to forgo breakfast. In only moments they were able to begin shuffling south along the path again, picking up speed as the light improved. Llew felt himself come awake by degrees.

They came to a wide expanse of weathered grey and white rock across the trail. While it was flat enough to lead Gower and the pack pony across, it was heavily furrowed and irregular. Pieces both small and large were prone to crack off beneath their feet and hooves.

Combined with large patches of moss and lichen, the morning dew made it very treacherous to travel on. No one fell but, at one point, the pack pony started to slide and had to make an awkward jump to avoid a bad spill. The animal landed badly on loose stone slabs and, again, nearly fell before righting itself. Llew spent a lot of time holding his breath until they had negotiated their way to the far side.

At some point that morning, Cymri landed on his right shoulder. Llew was so used to this that he scarcely noticed it.

What took his attention off everything else was when a similar weight landed on his left shoulder. Taking care not to move any more than was necessary, he turned his head slightly to see what was there. Then he slowly reached his hand up and gripped the medallion.

"Cymri, who is your friend?" he asked, while not taking his eyes off the newcomer. It was another large black bird not at all unlike Cymri in appearance. It regarded him and Cymri, flicking its gaze from one to the other and back again.

Cymri sighed and responded, "He is not my friend, he just wants to be. He has been dogging our trail since well before we even left Caer Mallcoedwig.

"I have been trying to explain to him for some time that my father would just never approve but he is more persistent than clever. Until now I could always get away from him by coming to you; apparently he has decided you are not so scary as he had thought.

"He should leave again when it becomes clear I am *not* interested in him. Just please, whatever you do, do not give him any—what are you doing?"

"It is just a little trail biscuit, he must be really hungry, look how he gobbles it up."

"You gave him food? How could you!" Cymri squawked almost incoherently.

"Cymri? Is that a problem?"

"Yes! Of course he gobbles it up! These wild birds are always hungry and it is much better tasting than most things he would find in the wild. He has already decided you are safe to be around and now you have given him food! We will never be able to get rid of him!"

"Oh," said a baffled Llew, and then, "How is this bad? I

always thought it would be a tremendous thing to have a real pet bird although, in truth, I had kind of hoped for something more like a raptor, perhaps a falcon. This is good though; I am going to name him Cilgwri."

Cymri just sputtered. It was a rare occasion when she could not find something to say.

Helgar said nothing during this exchange but it was obvious he found two large black birds perched on Llew's shoulders to be even more unsettling than one had been.

"Helgar? Not you, too? You think Cilgwri is a problem?"

His friend seemed to take a moment to collect his thoughts. "It is not that, Llew. I worry only that you may soon rip out one eye, hang men from trees, and Gower will grow four more legs, perhaps."

Llew shook his head. He was getting quite accustomed to Helgar, but Northmen really were a strange breed.

It was fairly uneventful after that. By evening, Llew had trained Cilgwri to say his own name and Llew's as well. While he was not a trained bard, he was actually pretty clever for a bird. They then spent another fire-less night in the wild.

In the morning they did not load the pack pony. Apparently the jump on the rock surface the day before had injured the creature and it was now lame as a result. With speed being of the essence, Llew did not argue as some of the provisions and gear that it had been carrying were placed on Gower and in their own packs. Most of it simply had to be abandoned. After this, Addfwyn shooed the poor creature away from camp and into the wood.

"I cannot just kill her," he explained, "so this way there is at least a chance the Picts will not get her either."

On the trail that morning less than two hours had passed

before Cymri gave a caw and launched herself to the right of the path. Discerning what might or might not have once been a game trail in that direction, the little party made their way along it as quickly as the terrain allowed.

It was none too quick. Little more than an hour had passed before they heard a virtual cacophony of bird noises behind them, seemingly from where they had departed the open trail.

Helgar grimaced, "Clumsy savages they are; some of those birds live only in the swamps of the Pictish wilderness. Come here they would not."

"They must know that—and that there is a good chance we know that as well. I expect it amuses them to call their fellows thusly. If it frightens us in the process, so much the better," said Llew.

Helgar snorted. "It is not frightened I feel when I hear them do that. It is insulted I feel. Even if they are coming to kill us, and think they have the men to do it, it is most foolish of them to want me to feel that way."

"Cymri," Llew said, "the scouts could be within a bowshot of us within the hour. Shortly after that they will probably be close enough to attempt a direct attack on us. How far have we to go?"

"That all depends on how close they are willing to come to Cas-Eiddew before breaking off. At the rate you are moving it will take you at least that hour. Although," she added, "you need not worry about being within a bowshot of them."

"Really? Is their aim that bad?"

"Oh no, they have wonderful aim . . . with spears. They probably will not throw them, however, as they would then only have their knives and those are mostly stone."

Llew was incredulous. "They do not have bows?"

"Oh they do, but their ways are not your ways, Llew."

"You can say that again," he muttered, thinking of wicker men in fire pits.

"Seriously, Llew, despite your upbringing in, of all places, Moriganna's own stronghold, you think like a Tetheran and, because of that, you think everyone else must think as a Tetheran does as well. Persist in that belief and you will fail to understand things that may save your life, or else offer great opportunity.

"Picts have bows but they are not nearly as well made as those of Tetherans. Other than yew, they do not have access to all the finer materials that are necessary. They are confined to rawhide instead of hemp strings. They also do not have metal for arrowheads save what little they can loot. It is also not practical for a nomadic people to make their bows as big as our war bows. With shorter range, less power to penetrate, and stone headed arrows, they have come to see bows, like slings, as being little more than tools for hunting. They would no more think to use them in battle than you would think to use a shovel or a cattle switch.

"Since they mostly fight amongst themselves, this barely matters as they are all on a relatively equal footing and believe that honor is best won on foot, face to face, in melee. Against Tetherans with iron tipped arrows and hemp bowstrings, it matters a great deal."

"I should say so," replied Llew. "My instructors made me do special exercises every day for six years just so I could draw this bow. They also made me shoot a quiver full of arrows every day and my accuracy is still not the greatest—but against unarmored opponents? War arrows would be a ridiculous waste."

"This is but one of many reasons why, despite the Picts living here long before the Tetherans came, and originally in far greater numbers, the Picts are the ones now normally confined to the wilder places, while the Tetherans rule the five kingdoms.

"Well, Tetherans and Northmen these days, at any rate." she amended.

"Thanks for clarifying that," Llew remarked dryly. All the same, he took his quiver from Gower, checked to make sure it was ready, and slung it for ready use. Then he strung his bow, a six foot monster cut to his own height, and carried it in his hand thereafter.

It occurred to him that this might be an area in which he was far more capable than the prince. Afaggdu had been very surprised to find he was being trained so extensively in the use of the bow. That probably meant Llewellyn had not been.

He remarked to Llewellyn, "If they seem likely to catch us I will have to take Gower back while you and the rest proceed on foot as quickly as you can manage."

"I see," remarked Llewellyn, coldly. "Very well, he is your horse, certainly."

Before an hour was passed they heard shouts behind them. Glancing back, Llew could see three Picts at first, and then a fourth came into view about a quarter of a mile behind them. The question was whether or not they would attempt to close, with the numbers being so even, or if they would hang back and wait for reinforcements. They had to know his little band had teeth.

The question answered itself when, having seen their quarry, they broke into a fast trot.

Llew pursed his lips grimly. He already knew what he had to do.

"I need Gower," he said curtly.

Llewellyn regarded him wordlessly, then reined in, and dismounted. "Come Helgar, Addfwyn, it seems we must find our own way to Cas-Eiddew."

Helgar was confused. "My way is with my drott."

"No," corrected Llew, "right now it is not. Help the prince get there as quickly as possible. Gower cannot carry us all, in any case, and I will need him to move fast."

Helgar looked as if he would argue but then, noting that the prince and Addfwyn were already on their way, froze, clearly uncertain what to do.

Llew wracked his brain looking for the words that would have the desired result. When he found them he knew this would be blatant manipulation of the lowest sort, but he used them anyway. "I have already given you my trust, Helgar; can you not give me yours?"

Helgar's jaw dropped, aghast. He fumbled for words that would not come while Llew continued to speak. It was such an unfounded accusation that Llew felt sick at heart for making it. He was certain it would not have been necessary if he could have spared a few minutes to instead reason with Helgar.

"If you really mean to help me, you will get Llewellyn and Addfwyn to Cas-Eiddew safely because I cannot do two things at once and," added Llew, "the other thing that must be done requires a bow."

Helgar's mouth snapped shut for a second and he straightened. The warring principles within him had reached an accord and he simply replied, "Yes, my drott. It will be done as you say." Then sprinted after the prince, while calling back, "But if we are there and you are not, coming back out I am!"

Llew smiled tightly and drew a light hunting arrow from his quiver as he regarded the approaching Picts. There was certainly no reason to expend one of his precious war arrows on an unarmored target—especially when he had no intention of hitting. It was a pity, he suddenly realized, that he did not have a smaller bow. It would not have had the range but he could have used it from Gower's back, allowing him to shoot repeatedly, while falling back only a bit between shots.

The Picts came on but were still a little over two hundred and fifty paces away, not really within close enough range for him to hit them, yet they were close enough he might scare them and slow them down. Llew drew back his first arrow as far as he could stand it, took aim, and released. The arrow flew high and was lost to view.

The Picts saw him take the shot and froze. They had not expected this. Llew, in turn, had not expected them to freeze. In the silence, Llew could plainly hear the sickening sound of his arrow thudding home, a long moment after it suddenly appeared in the lead Pict's chest.

Llew had chopped off a head, stabbed a man in the eye, and slashed another down with his sword in less than two full days, but none of those had managed to have the impact on him that this had, it felt like his intestines had frozen and turned to stone. Certainly he had been aiming at the man, but he had never expected to hit him, not at that range. He mentally kicked himself when it occurred to him the light hunting arrow had flown much further than a heavier arrow would have.

It was not that he was particularly averse to killing his enemies, when he had to, but this death simply seemed so unnecessary. Scaring them would have been just as good. The only upside was that this would most likely scare them just as much as a near miss or, likely, even more so.

It was clear the Picts had not realized they had entered into range of his arrows, or even considered that one of their quarry would turn back to make them the hunted. Prudence demanded his next action be to nock another arrow. The Picts watched him do this and were clearly torn on whether to charge or retreat. As Llew began to aim, they seemed to suddenly realize that just standing there was a not a good thing to do. As one, they faded back over a rise.

Llew was not terribly worried about them attempting to flank him. Given the semi-open nature of the terrain, they would have to go several miles around to approach without crossing the interval between him and the spot where the dead Pict still lay.

As he stood guard, he discovered he was already less bothered by the death. The man had, after all, been coming to kill him. When he looked for emotion within himself about the man's death Llew found there simply was not much there. Yet, a few moments earlier, with the sound of the arrow hitting still fresh in his ears, he had been sick at heart. It bothered him that he could so quickly become a different person and it bothered him more that he had so little control over this process.

The three that had retreated had not gone far. He felt certain they still watched. Even so, every moment they were confined to inaction, his companions could shorten the gap between themselves and Cas-Eiddew.

When the Picts emerged from cover again, perhaps half an hour later, there were over a dozen of them. Without hesitation they began loping in his direction. For his own part, Llew fired one arrow at the point where they were most thickly grouped, then fairly leaped onto Gower, and the two of them raced after his companions before the arrow had even landed.

They caught up with the others after a short time. Llew dismounted and urged the surprised Llewellyn to take his place on Gower. When the prince at first demurred, Llew was adamant.

"You are not yet fully healed and we can no longer merely

walk. I had some luck delaying them but there are now too many for my bow. Now is the time for running and that means that on foot you will only slow us down."

Llewellyn looked him full in the eye and said, "Forgive me. We are truly brothers-in-arms yet I misunderstood and so misjudged. It was a thought you are unworthy of and I am less worthy for having thought it."

Llew grinned, for some reason it struck him as more amusing than insulting. "You thought I was abandoning the lot of you? Phew, and here I was worried that you were mad at me."

That was not at all the response the prince had expected and, caught without a ready rejoinder, it was relatively easy to get him to climb back into the saddle. The party broke into a trot as soon as he was up. Llew was not sure how far it was they had to go and reasoned that, while it was essential that they pick up the pace, they did not dare burn all their reserves too early. While the others could not yet detect it, Llew could hear the Picts behind them whooping it up and, presumably, exhorting their fellows to run faster. He wondered briefly if their pursuers would really stop short of entering the ruins.

And then they were there. Low walls and broken columns, abundantly covered with thistles and ivy, lay strewn across two large hillsides. The ruins stretched to cover the saddle between the hills. The companions plunged directly in between two low walls while, behind them, Llew could hear the welcome sound of silence. The Picts had ceased their pursuit.

Chapter XVI

Gwri's Tale: The Kennels

As Gwri exited the main keep, he glanced at Gower, waiting patiently to be ridden home to the stables. It occurred to him there was something he had wanted to do for a long time.

Being as casual as he knew how, Gwri sauntered the length of the courtyard, past the castle stables and all the way to the kennels. As he entered the long low stone structure, he wrinkled his nose. While he did not normally mind doggy smells, this was entirely too much at once, even for him.

Inside was precisely what he had expected. There were many pens for the great hounds and kennel keepers moved between them, changing out feed and water, and bringing in dogs from the practice yard, then leashing new ones and taking them out. His presence did not pass unnoticed and the keepers whispered between themselves before one scurried off out of sight. Gwri was hardly surprised when, a few minutes later, the kennel master himself bustled out to stand before him.

He was a florid little man, quite short, and it seemed he was almost as wide as he was tall, both from side to side and front to back. "Yes, your lordship, is there something I can help you with," he asked, his nervousness evident.

Gwri had initially thought that it was rather amusing how Moriganna's people treated him. She had never bestowed any sort of title upon him. He was still just Gwri, an orphan with no apparent prospects and no skilled trade, despite now having a horse, and wearing weapons and fine clothing she had given him. After a time, he had discovered that one got used to being treated as though one were aristocracy and, thereafter, scarcely noticed it. Sometimes, however, he did think about it and wondered if perhaps it was too easy to get used to. It was then that he worried whether or not he was still the same person he had always been.

He had to be careful here. He did not want to lie outright in case some news of this visit got back to Moriganna's ears.

"Greetings good kennel-master, sirrah! As you may be aware, the queen has decided I should be better versed in a great number of areas." That part was completely true.

"Certainly no one could claim to know too terribly much about the workings of Caer Mallcoedwig without being familiar with the kennels." It might be a stretch, but this could also be considered true.

"It has been decided that I should come and be given a basic familiarity with your kennels by the mastermind of the entire operation, namely yourself. I hope this is not a bad time."

Technically, this was true, although it was laying it on a bit thick, and it was on shaky ground as it also implied that the queen herself had sent him, despite the fact that only he had decided he should do this. There was also the problem that he did not remember the kennel-master's name, and was not even sure he had ever known it.

The kennel-master's apprehension melted away and he positively beamed. "Well, of course, that is absolutely correct! The kennels are an essential element of Caer Mallcoedwig and I am very glad to hear this is so well understood. Come, come, young sir, let Oswalt ap Hire, breeder and trainer of the finest hounds in all the lands of Tethera give you the tour as, for you, I am happy to make the time."

Gwri graciously accepted this invitation and was treated to fifteen minutes of visiting the pens, the birthing rooms, and the training yard.

Finally getting a word in edgewise, he asked, "The hounds are all very similar to each other, not at all like the dogs I see in the village."

"Ah," exclaimed Oswalt, "they are a very special breed. Queen Moriganna brought the first of them with her when she left Annwyn."

"When she—what?" exclaimed Gwri. "She was in Annwyn? Was she a prisoner of the Lord of Death?"

"Ah forgive me, your lordship; you are so close to her I assumed you knew."

Wonderful, thought Gwri, sarcastically and to himself, *people think Moriganna and I are close.*

"It is not something we discuss but, to answer your question, yes and no. Yes, she dwelt there for many years but, no, she was not a prisoner unless, perhaps, she was a prisoner of love. Reportedly, she and the Lord of Annwyn were, um—close. That is, of course, no longer the case. Indeed, I would suggest never speaking of it in her presence. Yet it is necessary to understand why her beasts are descended from the hounds of Annwyn."

"They are hell hounds?" Gwri asked, shocked to his core. "But they are not white; there is no white on them."

"Well, no, of course they are not what the frightened peasants call hell hounds. We simple humans would not be able to control them were that the case. They have been interbred with both wolves and wolfhounds, which in turn are bred from an ancient breed of dog taken from a faraway land. Those that show any white are partial reversions to the hounds of Annwyn and must not be allowed to breed. Those that show other colors are partial reversions to the ancient breed, or to wolves, and also cannot be allowed to breed."

"That sounds like a lot of dogs being killed," Gwri said unhappily.

"You misunderstand, your Lordship. Mallcoedwig hounds, although not generally known by that name, are extremely valuable, nearly as much so as the fine horses Braen breeds. They are a major source of income for her highness's coffers. We sell nearly all of the ones we cannot allow to breed. Even they are worth far too much coin to do otherwise with. Why, one or two of them alone is often sufficient to take even the best armored warrior right out of his saddle, whereupon the beast's handler can make an easy end of him."

"So they are mixing with the dogs of the five kingdoms? This would seem an eventual disaster waiting to happen."

"They are not allowed to breed; the queen enforces this herself by some dweomer she places on them before her merchants take them away. Some few we do destroy. We cannot sell hounds that are seriously deformed, unremittingly savage or, worst of all, darkly deceitful and far too cunning for anyone's good.

"Really, it is very few that are destroyed, your lordship, perhaps only one in a hundred or more, but it is absolutely necessary if we wish to maintain the integrity of the breed. We are not monsters. We care about Mallcoedwig hounds, we truly do. Yet to truly preserve a line it is necessary to eliminate all those that merely resemble it. We lose far more because—well, to other causes."

"What do you mean other causes?"

Oswalt licked his lips nervously. "It is not really all that many, on average, just a few more than because of the throwbacks, really. It is scarcely worth worrying about."

Gwri raised his hand, palm out, to interrupt. "The primary cause, please, Kennel Master Oswalt. I believe you were on the verge of saying it."

"Ah, so I was, it seems. Please, your lordship, it is meet that you should know but, I beg you, please recognize that this is a subject requiring considerable discretion."

"You have my word," declared Gwri.

"Well, frankly, your Lordship, it is the Pwacca."

It was Gwri's turn to hide his confusion again. "The Pwacca you say?"

"Yes, even so. We try to be careful but every so often a Pwacca finds its way in and sires a litter of pups. Obviously, when that happens they are lost to us."

"And then you are forced to destroy them, too." Gwri concluded sadly.

"Oh no, my lordship, the queen would feed us to—well it does not bear thinking about. No, we turn the offspring over to her highness."

"Very well then, pray tell me, what exactly is a Pwacca? I do not believe I know them by that name."

"Perhaps not by that name, your lordship, but you do know them. We all do. You know those guardsmen that do not mix with the others? The ones that barely speak to anyone outside their own ranks? The ones that seem so very fearsome without it being immediately obvious as to why?"

"Ah," said Gwri, "you mean the queen's shape-shifters."

"Yes, well, I suppose they might not be terribly frightening to you or her highness, but to the rest of us—" Oswalt shuddered.

"Wait," demanded Gwri incredulously, not bothering to correct him on how frightening they were to him as well, "shape-shifters come from these kennels?"

"I do not know where the breed originated; I suspect her highness's enchantments, but aye. They are not men that can take the shape of animals. They are animals that can take the shape of men. The new ones must come from our kennels because they cannot breed amongst themselves. Although some of the pups are female, all of the adults are male.

"Normally, it seems they can control their shape but sometimes they take a form that is four-legged and nearly mindless, with animal instincts prevailing. Then it is that they are likely to try to break into the kennels and find the bi—, pardon me, breeding females that are ready to sire a litter."

Gwri's mind reeled with this so he attempted to backtrack temporarily. "The ones you do destroy—is it common practice to place them in bags and toss them into deep water?"

The kennel-master sounded shocked, "Oh absolutely not, your highness! We would not treat any of our hounds like that! No, we try to wait until they begin to be weaned so we can administer an herb to their food. This herb takes them into a deep sleep from which they will never waken. We burn the bodies; we do not heave them out hither and yon. If necessary to take them earlier than they can be weaned, then we do it very quickly so there is no pain or fear.

"What you describe would be cruel and senseless. To do as you suggest would be monstrous, indeed it—ah," the kennel-master snapped his fingers. "It is something the Pwacca might do to cull one of the litters we pass on to the queen. As to why they would be culling their own numbers? We do not judge the pups in any way before we turn them over. Perhaps a pup is too vicious, or not vicious enough, or is not smart enough, or large enough, or it is deaf or mute, or cannot change shape, or does not smell quite right, or simply has markings on its coat they do not like. Who can say with such as them?"

Leaving the kennels, Gwri saw that Gower was still waiting patiently. He stood for a considerable time and regarded his noble steed from a short distance away. Eventually the great horse noticed him and trotted over. Gower quizzically regarded his motionless master for a moment before attempting to lick him on the face. Gwri narrowly averted this, then mounted and rode back toward the stables. Together they moved as naturally as though they were but a single creature.

The prisoner arrived three days later.

Chapter XVII

Met by Moonlight

Llew and his companions continued on into the ruins, threading their way to the top of the greater hill. It was evident to them all that if the Picts did decide to venture in, this vantage point would provide the little party with the most possible warning, and would take the Picts the longest to reach of any point within Cas-Eiddew.

From the way the Picts were wildly gesticulating to each other, he could see a spirited conversation was under way, but even his superb hearing could make out nothing of what was being said, even presuming it would have been in a language he could understand. He very much wanted to know if the Picts were arguing on whether or not to enter the ruins, or perhaps to simply leave rather than attempt a waiting game.

When no attack was immediately forthcoming, there seemed little point in not setting up a small fire and trying to get more comfortable. It was already late in the afternoon and there seemed no chance at all they would be able to leave the ruins before nightfall. Llew tried to suppress an involuntary shudder at the thought.

Just as they could see the Picts, the Picts could see them. Clearly it did nothing to make them happier.

"They look so angry their teeth might well never unclench," remarked Helgar.

Their fear of this place must be great indeed, thought Llew, *if it can overcome their antipathy towards us and prevent them from entering, even in broad daylight.* More Picts kept arriving in ones and twos, and often small bands, until, by twilight, there were well over a hundred milling about. Still, they remained several hundred paces outside and made no efforts to either advance or create a camp.

The stars began to come out and the sky continued to darken. It would be a full Moon that night but it had not yet risen. In the meantime it became so dark that the Picts could no longer be seen. Despite this, and the fearsome reputation of the place, Llew and his party were extremely tired. The prince insisted on taking the first watch as the others tried to sleep. Nonetheless, they slept fully clothed and armored, with weapons at hand.

Around what must have been midnight, there was a loud commotion from the direction where the Picts had been. From all the yelling and shrieking and clanging and thumping, Llew would have thought every last Pict had found a poisonous snake in their bedrolls all at once. The clamor continued for about thirty seconds and then it was quiet again.

This had wakened everyone. Gradually, the party settled back down again, with Llew keeping the watch. Thus it was that he heard the distinct sound of what could only have been a large stone being gently rolled aside somewhere very close. Trying to hide his movement, he silently reached out his foot and tapped Helgar and Llewellyn on the bottoms of their feet, twice each. They came awake quietly and, seeing and hearing no visible danger, had the good sense to slowly and quietly take hold of their weapons.

From near at hand, Llew heard Gower paw the ground with his hooves. Cymri fluttered her wings, probably from the top of the rock wall next to where they had camped.

Llew felt more than heard the slow measured footsteps as something approached. This was because each footfall caused the ground to vibrate beneath him. Finally, unable to stand it any longer, Llew sprang up, trying desperately to see his foe in the dim starlight. Helgar and the prince had also risen, weapons in hand, prepared as they could be for whatever might come.

Yet nothing came. Slowly he turned about, attempting to see what might have joined them. As he came around to his starting point he saw that nothing had joined them. Indeed, it was the other way around. His companions had all vanished.

Panic stricken in a way that even the barrow warrior had failed to achieve, Llew called their names desperately, but to no avail. There was no answer at all. Then, after a few moments he realized he could hear a chuckling in the darkness.

"Show yourself," he cried.

The chuckling stopped and an amused voice, that was gruff yet somehow not deep, replied, "I could ask you to do the same."

"What do you mean? Who are you? What have you done with my friends?" Llew demanded.

"My goodness," said the mysterious voice. "Three questions all at once, just boom, bang, slap! No hint of payment for answers either. You sound young. Is that the way of young people today? Just demand whatever they want and with never a thought of recompense?"

Llew's hearing told him the speaker was up high and fairly

near. He was probably atop one of the taller stone walls of the ruins. Which meant it was unlikely in the extreme that the speaker was the source of the brutish footsteps.

"So you wish a ransom then? A payment for people that you have kidnapped and who had no quarrel with you?"

The voice hardened slightly, "No one asked you or them to come here. No hospitality has been given or received. However," the voice continued, "we have no interest in any ransom a mortal could likely pay. No, we would have taken you as well and asked no ransom were it not that you are different."

"How so?" Llew said tersely, as he slowly turned, sword before him, trying to detect whatever he was faced with.

"Well, it is almost embarrassing to admit," the voice began, "but we cannot see you. None of us have ever encountered a mortal that could escape our eyes for we do not see with our eyes alone. Yet here you have done it, and we want to know how."

Llew almost fell to his knees in surprise. The monsters could not see him? Perhaps there was some hope here after all. He took a cautious step forward in the direction the voice seemed to be coming from.

"Hold a moment, mortal! Invisible or not, you will not gain by searching for me. I am not easy to find either, and invisible or not, you would find no benefit in such a confrontation."

"So," said Llew, "you claim not to be able to see me, yet I take but a simple step and you are instantly apprised of it?"

"Eh? I said we cannot see you, not that we could not hear you. You mortals have ears like wooden blocks and even so most of you scarcely use even that small capacity. Plus," the voice chuckled, "you are about as quiet as a rockslide when you move."

"So, you have not taken me, yet you claim you could

overcome me easily?"

"Perhaps easily, perhaps not so easily, but yes, we are quite daunting and our numbers are great. Even death is but an inconvenience to us for, indeed, it is common knowledge that we have all died before."

Llew felt gooseflesh rising all over his body at hearing this but spoke again, managing only with difficulty to keep the fear from his voice. "The question is evident and still without answer. What do you want?"

"We want nothing from mortals save to be left to ourselves here in what you call Cas-Eiddew."

"Fine," replied Llew, "release my friends to me and we shall go and never return. You will have what you wish so far as we may grant it."

"Nay mortal, if we are about to be inundated with invisible men like yourself we will need to know the why and the how of it."

"I can hardly tell you why when I have no idea myself!" protested Llew. "Clearly my own companions have no problems in discerning me."

"Be that as it may, still, we are sporting folk. I am prepared to make a wager."

Llew scowled, "I have little choice it would seem, but if I win you will release all my companions to me unharmed and let us go in peace?"

"We could do that," came the rejoinder.

"That was not an answer," Llew retorted. "And what is this wager? Must I defeat this great hulking giant that tried to sneak up on me through the ruins?"

"You heard that?" the voice expostulated. There was a brief pause before it continued, "Allow me to withdraw my accusation comparing your ears to wooden blocks. Indeed, there is a little bit of the hidden ones in you, I would wager."

"So that is your wager?" asked Llew.

"What? No! Wait, no, neither that nor anything to do with fighting giants, either one or many," the voice expostulated in a rush, obviously taken aback by Llew's question.

"The terms are these. Thirty paces before you a great boulder has been rolled aside—"

"By the giant," supplied Llew. "Yes, I heard him do it. It sounded just like a rock slide, and that was before he came stomping out sounding as though entire mountains were being tossed upon the earth, one after another—"

"Enough!" boomed an enormous voice that had not spoken before. There was silence for a moment and then, from the surrounding darkness all around Llew, a horrendous grinding noise began that sounded like many dozens of great boulders being rolled aside.

It did not take much effort for Llew to clamp his mouth shut and wait silently.

The small voice was back, chuckling, "Oh my, you made me lose my patience and that is hard to do with someone who has had as long to develop patience as I have.

"The wager is you will go to the boulder that was rolled aside, the first boulder," the voice amended, "and proceed down the tunnel you will find there. This leads to a series of caves and tunnels; some contain challenges and, altogether, they serve to form a gauntlet of various encounters. You may even see some that you know there, but they may not be as you know them," the voice added cryptically.

"Pass through the gauntlet, remain alive, and you will get what you have asked for."

A vague memory recalled itself to Llew, "You must release us within three days' time at the latest," demanded Llew. "I have heard far too many tales of folk emerging back onto the surface only after a century has passed there, with all they've known and loved long passed into dust and faded memory."

"We are not faery folk and have nothing to do with their tumuli," retorted the voice, sounding insulted. "Very well, if you cannot complete the gauntlet within three days we shall consider that you have lost, even if you remain alive."

"Now, wait a minute—" began Llew.

"No, those are the terms, you altered them yourself and we will not change them."

"Um," said Llew, "I am sorry if I seemed to be comparing you with the faery folk," he ventured.

"Noted." said the voice. "The conditions stand, however. After it is over—if you are still alive—I will tell you what we are so you do not make such mistakes in the future.

"Also," continued the voice, "if you are able to survive the gauntlet and we still cannot see you, we will grant you a boon. Again, in the future, if you have one, do not be comparing us to those wretched Fae. They would never make such a generous offer unless compelled.

"And, before you put your invisible foot in your invisible mouth again, yes, the challenge is a fair one. We have deliberately given you at least one chance in two of surviving because we are not conniving faery folk. It is also much more fun for us to bet on amongst ourselves with the odds not overly tilted in one direction or another," the voice added.

"Verily, I must thank you for that," Llew replied sarcastically.

"That can wait," chuckled the voice. "The moon rises in

just less than an hour. You do not want to be out here on the surface when it does. If you are . . . well then, as you mortals say, all bets are off."

All around him, Llew heard great stones being rolled back into place. He called out in a loud voice, "May I speak with one of my comrades before we begin?"

Silence was his only answer.

Chapter XVIII

Gwri's Tale: The Lessons of Cymri

The prisoner was brought in under guard in late afternoon.

That the queen's men should be escorting a captive to Caer Mallcoedwig was not precisely an unprecedented event, but it was noteworthy and all the more so as the captive was a very young woman, dressed more like a man than a woman. There was also a variety of musical instruments attached to the outside of her saddlebags. More than anything, this implied she might be a bard, but no one had ever heard of a woman being a bard before.

Her clothing was green while her hair was a fierce red, nearly the same shade as Moriganna's own. Riding a horse with her hands bound before her, she still looked utterly composed, and somehow regal and aloof. She regarded her surroundings with what seemed a complete lack of interest, but Gwri had the feeling that her eyes missed nothing. They even settled on him for a few seconds and, just for an instant, Gwri fancied he saw her eyebrows rise in surprise.

She was very pretty, Gwri thought. Moreover, she evinced a kind of look that seemed to say to him she would be very interesting to speak with and that here was someone he might wish to become better acquainted with.

A short time later, a runner from the keep arrived to tell him that Queen Moriganna wished to see him at once. He accompanied the messenger back and was led to the queen in one of her work areas. Many books lay open on the tables. Small flames burned beneath small containers of various sizes. Hung from the rafters were collections of all manner of dried things, and lining the many shelves were jars with a variety of contents, some weird and mysterious, others grotesque or even disgusting.

Seeing him she merely said, "Give me your hand, either one, and do not be concerned, I only need a few drops of your blood." Seeing his hesitance she added, "No. Fear of such a small hurt is unacceptable and you need not be afraid of anything else. I am only making something you need and that will serve to your benefit at least as much as my own."

Gwri was not the least bit interested in showing fear before her so he proffered his hand as asked. There was no real alternative, in any case. She took a small pin from her hair and pricked his thumb. A drop of blood appeared which she deftly caught it in a small glass tube. She squeezed out a few more drops for good measure. He was then summarily dismissed.

* * *

Gwri was unsurprised when the next morning saw him ushered into the keep after his morning arms training. The bathing and dressing had long since ceased to bother him. It had simply become a routine part of his life. Midday meal, however, was decidedly different. Gwri was not the only guest at the queen's table.

He thus found himself playing the gentleman and holding the seats of Queen Moriganna first, and then the red-headed young woman, in turn. Her manlike clothing was gone and she was wearing an elaborate gown in a pale shade of pastel green.

Once they were seated, Moriganna spoke, "Lady Cymri ferch Taliesin, I give you Gwri. Gwri, this is the Lady Cymri ferch Taliesin.

"Good day to you, Lady Cymri. Your presence graces this table and is most welcome," Gwri responded dutifully.

Lady Cymri glanced sharply at Queen Moriganna before looking back to Gwri and replying in kind, "Your words are most gracious and kind, Gwri. I am honored to be here and thank you both for having me."

Servants bustled in with the first course and Gwri could not resist asking, "So, and what brings you to our simple secluded cantref, Lady Cymri?"

"Did you mean other than Queen Moriganna's huntsmen?"

Moriganna said nothing, leaving Gwri feeling rather awkward. "Well yes," he admitted, "I did witness your arrival yesterday so I knew that much. I was hoping you could tell us more about your activities before you fell afoul of her highness's men. If this is uncomfortable to you then please forget I asked, I implore you."

Again, Lady Cymri looked at Queen Moriganna. "He is not bad at all. There is no dirt under his nails. The manners are good, if a bit on the obsequious side. Certainly his vocabulary is coming along nicely. Perhaps you missed your calling, your Highness."

"I rather doubt that," the queen replied calmly. "At any rate, you told me that after meeting with him you would give me an answer on whether you would willingly assist in completing his education."

"Even while I am to be a prisoner here?" asked Cymri.

"Even so," Moriganna replied evenly.

"Tell me again, in front of him, of his origin please."

"His father was my stable master in the village until about six years ago, when he died. His wife had already passed on a couple of years before that. The boy was nearly old enough to start making himself useful so the new stable master kept him on. At least that is the reason he gives. Frankly, I think the man might be a bit soft but he does his job well. In the last few years, particularly, he has really begun to show some aptitude so I allow him some minor failings. A few years ago I noticed the boy assisting him and—well, you must see why."

"I certainly do," Cymri said grimly, "it is completely uncanny and I am quite likely a better judge of that than even yourself."

"So and so," replied the queen. "I began his training at once. A late start, perhaps, but I feel it is possible to make up for lost time given that he has no other distractions."

Gwri took in all of this exchange but was able to make little of it. Asking questions was not an option at the moment so, instead, he strove to remember every word and nuance so that he might possibly decipher it later.

Abruptly, the red-headed young woman turned her attention to Gwri and, for the first time, addressed him directly. "Gwri, does any of that conflict with anything you know?"

"I do not quite understand all of what either of you are getting at, but what I think I do understand does not conflict with the truth." Gwri knew better than to call Queen Moriganna a liar at her own table, but neither was he willing to praise her honesty. Fortunately, she had not said anything at this meal that was not, so far as he knew, the truth.

"Gwri," said Cymri, "I need to know a bit more about you before I make my decision. It must be in your own words and much of what may seem to be unimportant to you may be very important to me. Will you answer my questions completely and without seeking to evade their intent in any way?"

He swallowed and nodded assent. To Gwri's untrained eye she was well past his age but had only very recently attained full womanhood. She was the first female less than twice his own age that had ever taken an interest in him for any reason. This made her both beautiful and fascinating. If she had asked him to go try to do handstands on Gower as he galloped in circles around her, Gwri would have been willing to give it a try, despite the fact he had never quite managed it, even with Gower simply going in a straight line.

With that, she began her interrogatory. Gwri had never imagined his life story would take longer than a few seconds but she was amazingly thorough. She wanted details, even on things that seemed of no importance whatsoever. Though they had eaten virtually nothing, the meal was long over before she seemed satisfied.

Queen Moriganna looked extremely bored. "Well, Lady Cymri? Are you content?"

Looking less than happy, their visitor responded. "As you say, he seems of good intent and not simply a tool you have somehow conjured up. I will teach him the finer points of life in the courts and such skills as he does not yet have. You realize that when my father comes for me this will all come to a crashing end?"

Moriganna smiled in such a way that, while no sneer was evident, one could almost feel there was one hiding behind it. "If Taliesin comes here he will discover nothing he has the power to change and yes, before you ask, I do know the limits of his powers."

Cymri changed course, "Obviously, you must travel to the court on a more or less regular basis, despite our never having met there. Have you seen the prince of late?"

Moriganna took a delicate sip from her wine cup. "Assume that I have. What would you draw reference to?"

"There is the small matter of the prince's martial skills. For a child his age, they are unparalleled; he has also had access to some of the finest instructors in all the kingdoms. Do you believe your Gwri here will be able to do nearly as well? If he does not have equivalent skill he will not be credible in the least."

"I think you may leave that to me. Gwri is not without some native skill. He regularly overcomes grown men that are trained to the sword, often more than twice, or even thrice, his own age. Further, I can, and will, obtain instructors of corresponding skill to those that have trained the prince."

"So, if I train him, then what?" asked Cymri.

"Then eventually he goes south and finds his destiny. After that you may remove the medallion I have given you and you will be free to travel wheresoever you wish. Nothing you might say to anyone at that point would be of any use, and most would not, in any case, believe it to be the truth. Remove the medallion before that time and your life, as you know it, will be over. Likewise, if the medallion and Gwri are more than a handful of miles apart, you will die."

Startled, Gwri glanced to Cymri's neck. Indeed, there was a silver medallion upon her breast, suspended by a delicate looking silver chain about her neck.

"It hardly matters," remarked Cymri. "You would likely kill me if I did not agree to train him, and I would not wish to escape and leave an innocent like him to be a pawn in your dark plans."

"So you say," said Moriganna. "Leave us now; I would speak with the boy a moment. I will send him to your chambers when we are done here."

Demonstrating impeccable manners, Lady Cymri excused herself to leave the table while Moriganna rather rudely dismissed her with a wave from the backside of one hand. The queen waited to speak until after she had left.

"I am going to make a bit of a speech here, Gwri, but have you ever known me to be enamored with the sound of my own voice?"

"Indeed, I have not, your highness, Gwri replied.

"Very well. I have told you something of the stakes we play for here. This girl looks very sweet to you, I am certain, but bear in mind that the same reason we want her here to train you is the very thing that potentially makes her very dangerous. Her roots are planted deeply in King Pendaran of Gwent's court at Caerleon and she knows the prince there rather well. She is also something of a bard."

"Surely not!" exclaimed Gwri, "I have always been told there are no female bards."

"It is not a normal calling for women, and there are many good and practical reasons why it is not, but her father is Taliesin, the Chief of all Bards, and adviser to King Pendaran and his forebearers before him. With centuries of tenure in both his craft and that position, there are none to gainsay him if he chooses to dote on his only living child and even accede to her wishes to play at being a bard herself. In any case, she is perfect for our needs as she has considerable knowledge of the bardic lore, experience with the inner workings of the court at Caerleon, and a good deal of personal knowledge of the false prince.

"This prince is the son of King Pendaran who, himself, is not a real king but an usurper. His family was only intended to be stewards for the kingdom, yet allying themselves with Lord Arawen of Annwyn gave them the nerve to claim that the kingdom should rightfully be theirs.

"I know you have heard many stories of the Lord of Death from me, and from others, for all of your life. Lest you think them exaggerated, make no mistake; the dead march in his armies. They are slain warriors he has looted from the barrows of the dead like so many clay jars and they are every bit as terrible as in any tale you have ever heard.

"They know no fear, will follow his orders without question, and cannot be properly slain as they are already dead. They can be destroyed, but doing this is not an easy thing. One to one, my own shape-shifters are easily a match for them but, while I have many shape-shifters, he possesses entire legions of barrow warriors. Fortunately, they are somewhat limited in that they cannot remain animated indefinitely when they are away from Lord Arawen's influence.

"Pendaran's secret alliance with Lord Arawen is foolish beyond measure as Arawen's ultimate aim is the death of all men, everywhere. Indeed, that accomplished, he would then proceed to continue killing everything else until he strode across an entire world bereft of life. The only sound remaining would be that of the wind howling through the ruins.

"We cannot simply march in and rescue the kingdom of Gwent. Pendaran also has substantial numbers of trained warriors, enough to preclude a simple military conquest even before considering how the Lord of Death might attempt to upset our plans. Their only major weakness in the short term is the prince himself, the sole heir to the kingdom. This can be made to work against them as you are the very image of the prince himself.

"It is what drew me to you in the first place. When the time is right, we will borrow a trick from the Fae and take the king's son, leaving you as a changeling in his stead. That is the whole point of all of this. We have been blessed in your extreme resemblance to this pretender prince but, unlike with an infant changeling, to make it work you must be every bit as a prince yourself, with all the skills and mannerisms the pretender has gained thus far.

"It should be impossible for even King Pendaran to detect the substitution himself, but it scarcely matters if he does for when you are grown and newly come into your manhood my agents will induce him into abdicating in your favor."

"But I am not a prince either," Gwri protested. "I have no more claim to the throne than this impostor."

"Give me your hand, Gwri."

Gwri had long since learned that resistance to these kinds of demands was less than useless. He stood and walked the length of the table to where she sat and extended his left hand to her.

"Kneel," she demanded.

Gwri complied. Nothing else was an option.

Quick as thought, she seized his extended hand with her right and he felt a tiny prick as she stabbed him in the ball of his thumb with something sharp. A single drop of blood appeared.

"Ouch, again?" he demanded.

"Behave as a man, not a child," she ordered, then closed and opened her left hand and a drop of blood was there on her thumb as well. With a flip of her wrist their thumbs came together and the two drops of blood were squeezed together. Gwri had heard of this practice among the warriors. Since he had no intention of sincerely promising to be a blood brother to Moriganna, he was not unduly disturbed by it. It was simply wasted effort on her part.

Then a kind of shocking fire burned within his thumb, swelling almost instantly to consume his entire body. Gwri gasped and shook and might have fallen save that Moriganna still held his hand in a grip like unto a blacksmith's vice. The feeling was gone as suddenly as it had come upon him and he gasped again, but with relief.

Moriganna looked shaken herself but said, "Whoever you may once have been is no longer of consequence. With this blood and, by the oldest laws of the land, our lines converge. You are now Gwri ap Morigan, my adopted son and my heir in perpetuity. Rise, Prince Gwri."

In a daze, he stood, feeling barely able to focus his thoughts. Moriganna was now his mother? He had not wanted this!

"I think," Moriganna said dryly, "that we will forgo the traditional maternal hugs and kisses, my son. I am well aware of your feelings about me and many of them are justified. I do seek power for power's sake and not just to save the existence of mankind. I know in your youthful idealism that you find this objectionable. I also know you do not care for my methods although, if you ever attain my wealth of experience, you may be somewhat more flexible in that regard.

"It does not matter. We both wish to save mankind's candle from being extinguished. You wish it because it is the right thing to do; while I do not wish to be left with nothing to rule. Now, however, you are very much a prince so that should dispense with your last objection."

"But not a prince of Gwent," Gwri replied.

Moriganna's smile was chilling. "Oh, but you are, my son. You simply do not know your family history well enough. At one time I ruled as high queen over all the lands you have ever heard of, all of Tethera, the Great Kingdom. It is a long story but, after several generations, I was eventually betrayed and barely escaped with my life when our lands were taken from us by an usurper.

"Now it is time to take back what is ours and save all that we both hold dear from the machinations of the Lord of Death. I tell you all of this because Cymri is dangerous, albeit necessary. Whatever she is, she is loyal. She would never have agreed to assist us in any way against her impostor king if she did not see a strategy to turn the situation to her advantage. In this case, she intends to work her wiles on you and persuade you to defect. Regardless of what she will attempt to make you believe, your interests coincide entirely with my own. I am showing you the turnip again."

Gwri wondered if perhaps turnips had been considered a delicacy when Moriganna was younger.

"Another thing. I will not countenance my son spending his nights bunking with the stable-hands in the village. Your room will be that on the fourth level of the eastern tower. Have the servants clear out whatever they have stored there and bring suitable appointments to furnish a room fit for a prince."

"Am I to be a prisoner of this castle then?" he asked stiffly.

Moriganna frowned at him before saying, "Of course not, you are a royal now. This is where you belong and the only lock on your door will be one you hold the key for. Cymri's rooms are off the west hall on the third floor. Go ahead and go to her now, yet remember what I said. She has much she can teach you, but her interests are not your interests and she can only escape if you go with her. Then recall my shape-shifters and know that your escape is not something that can be attained, no matter how persuasive she may be."

Chapter XIX

The Gauntlet

The night breeze had begun building in strength and was making a low wailing sound as it passed through the ruins before Llew found the boulder that had been rolled aside, revealing its passage downward. He certainly hoped it was the wind making those noises. While he had many questions he would have liked to have put to the mysterious voice—as well as his sword and dirk—he did not for an instant doubt what it had said about his not wishing to be on the surface when the moon came up.

The passage entrance itself was a somewhat square opening, framed in massive and cunningly fit carved stones, set into an earthen bank. Long grass and ivy covered the embankment where the boulder would not have blocked it. It was a very large boulder of dark stone, covered with a considerable quantity of lichens and mosses. It did not get rolled aside too often—not with that kind of growth on it, decided Llew. The way down looked to involve oddly over-sized stone steps, with the walls and ceiling of more cut stone, although the dim starlight made it impossible to see more than a few feet within.

Llew did not doubt he would enter, yet still he lingered.

All the tales he knew of concerning men encountering magical creatures suggested that, not only did such beings tend to eschew outright lies, many, if not most of them, could not lie if they wanted to. Yet this was not at all the same as saying that they could not be duplicitous and false. In fact, if the vast majority of the tales were consistent on anything, it was that supernatural creatures of all sorts loved to mislead mortals but took great pride in doing it through omission and redirection.

At the other extreme, there were also, Llew recalled, certain types of creature that would delight in telling deliberate falsehoods. It was also believed that there might exist some that were incapable of telling the truth under any circumstances. In such tales, a clever hero, after realizing this and recognizing it for the limitation it was, would turn this problem back upon them and trap them into giving up needed information. While it made for good stories, Llew tended to doubt such creatures existed. He had learned from Moriganna that lies were of most use if they could be hidden amongst truths.

He put his hand on the great worn boulder. On an impulse he tried to roll it himself, first one way, and then the other. He threw his full body into it and arched his back but gave up before he strained himself. He needed to conserve his strength, and the stone had not budged. It might, he thought, be magically held where it was but that was an unnecessary complication. The stone was just too big for him to move.

Llew grimaced, perhaps it was good he had not been able to get to wherever the voice had been and with his blades unsheathed. If the creature that could move this massive stone could also throw a lesser rock with any accuracy then it would take just one such missile to bring down even the mightiest of men in full armor. Still thinking grimly on this, he entered the darkness and began to descend.

At first he was feeling his way along, he had to extend each foot with care while his hands stayed fast against one wall. It was, he decided, inconsiderate of the voice not to have provided him with a torch.

Then he noticed that from below there was a faint glow emanating upwards. The light increased as he descended and, rather than speed his passage, it served more to slow his progress even further while he endeavored to see what was causing it. The answer was astonishing. As he reached the bottom of the stairs they ended in a great sand-floored chamber within which danced hundreds of small lights.

Llew gazed at them in wonder. They seemed almost like fireflies, but no firefly ever burned that long or that steadily.

Llew tried to capture one in his hands but it took only a few endeavors to teach him that this was quite impossible. They evaded him easily, but he could now observe that they were not insects. In fact, they had no bodies at all; they were just as they had first appeared—glowing points of light and apparently nothing more.

The cavern was roughly ovoid with a ceiling that ran to over twenty feet high in the center. The walls were a mixture of living rock, chiseled where necessary, with some man-made sections of cut stone. A chill passed over Llew. In this case it occurred to him that "man-made" might or might not be entirely correct. There was a tunnel opening on the far end of the chamber. Llew was disinclined to regard an empty chamber as part of his challenges and was heading for the far side to continue his when he noticed the metal bars covering another opening not far from the exit. At that moment, all at once, and without any fanfare, the lights went out and he was plunged into total darkness.

Llew placed his hand on his sword, considered for a moment, then slowly drew it and waited. The silence was near absolute. He could actually hear a kind of ringing that he knew was only in his head or his ears. Then came the unmistakable squeal of metal being dragged against stone. Llew never for an instant doubted that it was the lattice of metal bars being swung aside. As best he could, he took a fighting stance facing the noise and tried to listen with every bit of his ability.

Thudding sounds came to him now. They were footsteps, probably, but not the careful plodding gait of the unseen giant, earlier. These were closer together, of a kind that might be made by a creature with more than two legs and not as heavy as the giant, perhaps, but much less cautious. He could tell when the creature entered the cavern proper. Then it stopped.

Llew still could not see a thing. His eyes were not adjusting which just meant that there was no light at all to adjust to. On the other hand, he could hear the creature fine. It was breathing heavily enough for a dragon, he thought, although he had never heard one.

The footsteps resumed, coming directly towards him. Fear, at least fear of anything other than failure, had not been heavy on his mind when he had fought the barrow warrior or even the Pict chief, Goll. Now, however, he could feel it in every fiber of his being. He knew he was gripping his sword too tightly, but it still felt as if his hand might go nerveless at any moment and simply drop it.

Now the creature grew very close indeed and Llew prepared to strike out blindly at it, a desperation move. "Stay back!" he cried out. "Come no closer! Stay right there!"

Miraculously, the footsteps stopped. Then a heavy yet

somewhat muffled impact occurred right in front of him and displaced air rushed past him, carrying with it just a bit of sand. Had the creature sat down in the sand right in front of him? Somehow he did not doubt it could perceive him very well. Could it have that much disregard for his sword?

As Llew's mind whirled, seeking some way to resolve what he should do, a warm gust of humid and unpleasantly fragrant wind blew into his face. It was either larger or closer than he had realized. A hot gaping maw must already be in position to seize him and devour him whole. Llew drew his sword back and was just starting to sweep it forward before him when he hesitated.

He knew he was terrified and completely out of control yet somewhere there was a small part of him that was reminding him of exactly what Afaggdu would have had to say about that. It would not have been approval. And there was something else. Llew strained his almost panic-stricken brain to try to realize what it was and then it came to him—there was something about the smell of that breath! It was not a good smell, but it was oddly familiar, even if he had not smelled it in a long time.

Now he nearly did drop his sword as his arms suddenly went weak and even his legs felt a bit wobbly. "Gower?" he whispered incredulously. The answer was immediate as something wet, strangely soft, and about the size of a small shield, made two quick passes up his face, knocking him backwards to sit on the floor in the process and sending his sword spinning away.

"Arghh!" he spluttered. "Gower, lay off! Stop it you big galoot!"

As quickly, suddenly, and completely as they had turned off, all the lights resumed their duties and Llew could see.

Big galoot was right, marveled Llew as he squinted again in the dazzling illumination that had seemed not nearly so bright earlier. Sitting before him was Gower, but it was a Gower he had not seen in years. It was Gower as a dog again. Yet Gower had never been this large. Gower had been destined to be a huge dog, to be sure, hence Moriganna's snide remark about feeding him, but he surely would not have become anything like this. He was as big as a—here Llew's mind shied from the thought for a moment—Gower was as big as a horse.

It occurred to Llew that this did not make much sense. If the strange people of Cas-Eiddew had broken Moriganna's transformation of Gower, allowing him to be a dog again, why had they not broken it in its entirety? Why had his size remained so large? Surely that was part of the spell as well?

It did not matter right now. He clambered to his feet and, leaving his sword where he had dropped it, seized the giant beast in a fierce embrace about the neck as Gower thumped his massive tail on the sand floor.

After a moment, Llew lifted his head from where it had been half buried in Gower's fur. "Whew," he said, "someone needs a big doggy bath if he is going to be sleeping with me again!"

Llew was immensely cheered. With Gower at his side there was little he need fear of a physical nature. Surely, even one of those strange creeping giants would hesitate before such a large and sharp-toothed animal as this. He glanced to the far opening and noted the barred door had closed again. "Okay boy," he began as he turned back to Gower then gaped. Gower, if he had ever been there, was gone. Llew was quite alone again.

He retrieved his sword and sheathed it. Not having Gower to protect him meant he had to stay ready. This felt rather unfair because it seemed to him he had passed a sort of test and getting his companion back would have been a perfect reward.

Cautiously he moved to the other opening. This proved to

be another tunnel, carved right through living rock and heading down at a steep angle. Trying to scan everything at once in case some trap loomed in wait, he followed it while taking slow deliberate steps. The ceiling varied wildly in height, rising to twenty feet in some places and dropping to as little as five in other. The latter slowed him even further as it was necessary to walk hunched over.

* * *

Llew soon lost track of time. After what he thought might be more than half an hour, but less than an hour, he heard the faint sounds of music. As they grew closer they resolved themselves into the sweet dulcet tones of an accomplished singer. They were accompanied by music from a harp that was played, so far as Llew could tell, with a skill beyond reproach. The tune was neither sad nor cheerful. The best description seemed to be haunting, although the words themselves were in a language he did not know.

He peered out into another large limestone cavern. Unlike the others, this one was of natural origin. There was no sand, and the ceiling was festooned with stalactites reaching down to corresponding stalagmites. They were quite dry and dead. Whatever waters formed this place were no longer coming here.

Llew's attention was riveted on the figure in the center of the cave. It was a woman in courtly attire, seated upon a stone rising from the floor and with her back to him. Her fine gown swept away behind her in a semi-circle. Long red hair flowed down her back, well-brushed and lovely; it was unconstrained by ties or ribbons of any sort. It was she that was singing and playing a small harp she held in her lap. By the voice alone, Llew knew her at once. It was Cymri, restored to her human form.

A great flat-sided crystal sat before her and served as an enormous mirror. Within it, he looked upon her front. He edged closer, using extreme caution and watching for potential traps.

It was odd. Despite the mirrored surface of the crystal, she evinced no recognition that he was there behind her. Puzzled, and with growing suspicion, he slowed and stopped. "Cymri," he called.

She ceased singing and held her head frozen in place. He watched her eyes in the mirror, as they darted everywhere, trying to seek him out. She continued to play but did not speak.

"I am right here." Llew gave a brief laugh. "Can you not see me either?"

Her eyes in the mirror flashed to look almost straight at him but, again, her head and body moved not at all. Then she did something even odder. She very slowly and deliberately rolled her eyes upwards and then down, in an arc, until they were looking at her reflection.

Llew tensed, this was very strange. Again, she looked in his direction and, just as she had before, rolled them up, over, and down to her own reflection.

Llew's mind reeled as he tried to process this. It almost had to be a warning, but against what? In the first challenge the situation presented him with something strange and terrifying. The nature of the challenge had been for the lack of knowledge and unfamiliarity to frighten him into attacking a creature dear to him. To defeat the challenge had required him to figure out what was going on while he resisted the temptation to simply lash out before assessing his potential foe's intentions.

Would they give him the same challenge twice? Llew did not think so. It did not fit any of the folk stories he had ever heard. Plus, he had not yet been tempted to draw sword—quite the opposite, in fact. He had been given soothing music and a trusted friend who was in no danger. Sudden fear blossomed in Llew and he snatched out his sword just as the thing on the rock spun about and leaped for him.

What it was could not be known. Llew had a simultaneous glimpse of wicked claws, several fanged maws, and what must have been dozens of eyes, large and small, all over it. Almost of its own volition, his sword swung against it, through it, reversed itself, and slashed again as he rapidly backpedaled to avoid bodily contact.

It screamed horribly from many mouths as he hacked off chunks of it that fell to the ground and burned with a cold blue fire when they struck. Llew felt himself losing control, panic becoming red rage. He began striking again and again at a pace he knew could not be sustained, even though it now seemed that he was tireless and possessed of endless strength. He was determined not to countenance this abomination's continued existence in his world for one moment more than it took to remove it.

And then it was gone. There was nothing left. The pieces had all burned away and left not even a residue behind. All that remained were a discarded harp laying near the stone the monster had been perched on and, nearby, the remnants of what had been a gown. It was but a thin disguise the monster had burst out of in midleap.

The fight, Llew realized, as his mind and senses came reeling back, had probably concluded in under a minute. He was unharmed but completely exhausted as his rage fell away. He was safe, the creature was gone, and the world was a better place. His sword was clean as, whatever ichor had befouled it during the fight, it had burned away to nothing—as the rest of the monster had. He barely had the strength to sheath the blade, his arms trembling uncontrollably as he did so. Then he leaned on the stone the creature had been sitting on and attempted to recover his breath and strength.

It was as Llewellyn had said to him on the road, he realized. When eldritch horrors took form and sought to deliver harm in the world of men they could not do aught but become vulnerable to receive it as well.

"Llew," Cymri's voice said.

Llew jerked his head up and staggered to his feet, half drawing his sword. Then he saw it was her reflection in the mirror that had spoken.

"Llew," she said. "Can you see me? I cannot see you but I heard your voice and I know that . . . thing did not fall away into pieces without help."

"Cymri?" he asked as he gaped at the mirrored surface.

"Yes, certainly it is me. I cannot see you and your voice sounds strained, are you injured?"

"Nay, Cymri, I am fine, I just got a bit carried away in the moment." His eyes narrowed. "Of course if you are Cymri that begs the question of why you were helping that thing lure me in so that I would be off my guard. That is not really the kind of behavior I would expect from her."

"Llew, how often have you met me trapped in a mirror with some hideous creature compelling me to sit and sing as it so chose? I was unable to move at all save by its will, with the exception of my eyes alone. Although it may not have seemed like much I tried to warn you as best I could."

In truth, Llew realized, without the small warning from her rolling her eyes, the monster would likely have had him. It most definitely was not something an enemy would have done.

"My apologies, Cymri," he responded. "Your warning, while oblique, was timely. How do we get you out of that mirror?"

She seemed confounded. "You ask me that? I should as well ask you why I am in this mirror, and where did that creature come from, and where are we, and why are you invisible?"

Llew sighed. "What is the last thing you recall?" he asked.

"It was night, we were in the ruins and you awakened us because you heard something. I was hopping about on the wall because it was too dark to fly. A flash of light—I do not know what happened but I was here, forced to perform in front of that thing that was wearing a gown identical to my own for hours and—" she gave a sudden cry, "—how did Moriganna's spell get broken?" Then she flushed, "And who was it that dressed me in this gown after they broke that spell?"

Llew suppressed what would have been a flippant answer on that last question. He had been about to say "Everybody," just to see if he could cause that blush to deepen, but he caught himself just in time; this was not the time or the place. Instead, he replied, "I do not have answers to any of those except that we are beneath the ruins of Cas-Eiddew and this is a series of tests the powers of this place are subjecting me to. They want to know why they cannot see me. For that reason they have promised our safe departure should I succeed in passing through all their challenges alive."

"It is always all about you, is it not?" she commented.

"I am sorry? What?"

"Never you mind, Llew. So you have no way to get me out of this mirror?"

"I could try to shatter it," he mused. "That might do it."

"Ack no! Even assuming you could do it there is no way of knowing whether I could survive that or that it would not bring enormous misfortune upon you!"

Llew furrowed his brow. "So how do you propose we do it?"

"That is an easy one to answer, Llew. You simply go complete your challenges. By their own admission they must then let us go. That means they will get me out of this mirror. As they are likely the ones that put me in it, they should be able to do so readily enough."

"So I leave you here?"

Cymri sighed. "How can you be so clever some times and still say things like that? Of course you do. Now go finish as soon as you are ready, I badly want out of this place."

Llew shook his head slowly from side to side. "Very well, but know that should they renege on the deal, or try to change the terms, they will not do so without cost."

"I would expect no less. And, Llew, could you see fit to take that harp with you? It plays like a dream, and it is unique in my experience."

Llew thought for a moment before asking, "What about the one you are holding?"

"You think I forgot about it?"

"I did not say that," Llew protested.

"I lack faith it will not melt into moonlight or some such when I am released. It might be nothing more than a reflection of that one. Go now, I will be fine, but Llew?"

"Yes?"

"Do not lose a challenge!"

In actuality, Llew took at least half an hour's rest before he felt ready to press on. After reiterating his determination to get her out at any cost, he moved through the cavern and down the next tunnel.

This one seemed to twist about itself while descending. Sometimes the angle was so precipitous that Llew had to turn and face backwards as he climbed, more than walked, his way down.

* * *

Eventually, although Llew could not say how long it had taken, the slope diminished and the tunnel led into a larger cavern, much as the others had.

Waiting for him in the center was a large Northman.

The man was a brute, dwarfing even the Pict chieftain, Goll. He wore armor formed of overlapping metal scales and an axe across his back. What an axe it was! It was double-bladed and looked capable of felling large trees in a single swipe. The Northman stood and stared at Llew. Then he drew back his lips in a huge toothy smile, the kind of smile a dragon might make when contemplating a small herd of sheep that had strayed into its cave.

Llew drew swiftly and dropped into a crouching stance. Against such a weapon as that axe he could not hope to block its swing. Survival would lie in staying nimble and aware, and in dodging each swing altogether.

As Llew drew his sword, the Northman reached over his shoulder, seized the great axe, and brought it into a two fisted grip before him.

Llew began to circle to the right, edging just a bit closer with each few steps. The proper tactic would be to get inside the swing of the Northman's weapon. That axe would be almost useless if he got inside its range. On the other hand, the Northman's enormous size was enough to make him wary. If Llew got too close, the Northman might not need a weapon.

The Northman hefted his axe for a strike and turned to

stay facing Llew. Llew edged a bit closer. The Northman took a pair of half steps towards him as well.

Llew found that troubling. Why would the Northman do that? He had to know Llew must come to him. It did nothing for him and it opened him up to the potential for a misstep or even of being caught off balance.

Llew stopped circling. The Northman remained facing him. On a hunch, Llew cautiously took a step backwards and watched as the Northman did the same. Praying he was correct in his assessment, Llew sheathed his sword and stood up straight.

He was rewarded by the warrior returning his axe to its sling across his back and standing up straight as well.

Llew knew that there was power in the number three and it was his lone idea at that moment. "Helgar, Helgar, Helgar," Llew intoned. "Can you speak?"

And the Northman spoke! "Llew, it is good to see you! Even better that my drott was far too clever to fall for these shadow-skulker's tricks! My voice was gone. Mine own limbs were not my own! Except for smiling to try to show I was not your enemy, I could do nothing but act as you did. I truly feared we were about to fight."

Llew smiled. "Afraid you might have to kill me?"

"A little bit, ya. But thinking more likely you might kill me. It would be a very poor outcome for Helgar, either way, would it not?"

"Indeed it would, and for me as well," Llew replied dryly.

The Northman, was shrinking a bit in size and starting to resemble Helgar as he furrowed his brows. "But my—Llew, how did you riddle it was me?"

"Well," said Llew, "moving towards me when you already had a good position was just the deciding factor. I have already

169

encountered Gower and Cymri. Neither was what they seemed to be. It is almost like our hosts are trying to teach me a lesson with each encounter that fails to kill me." Musing aloud, "I wonder if either outcome might constitute advancement towards whatever they are really after?"

His brow still furrowed, Helgar asked, "What lesson would this have taught?"

Llew looked into space and reflected while speaking slowly, "With you I would guess it was something about how I should not judge and treat everyone from a certain tribe or group in the same manner, just because they are members of that group. Further, treating them that way is only likely to bring about a reaction that wrongly confirms that I am right to do so. You were not threatening me with your smile, but, by taking it as I did, things might have escalated . . . badly. Admittedly, it is a very odd concept."

"They must be very strange creatures indeed," agreed Helgar.

"Still," added Llew, "there may be something to what they seem to be telling us. One may only look at the two of us to see that."

When Helgar did not reply at once, Llew glanced sharply in his direction. He was not surprised to see there was no sign of the muscular youth. Only the giant axe that lay upon the sandy floor gave any clue he had ever been there, for there were no footprints whatsoever.

Llew groaned in dismay. He knew what he must do. Llew retrieved the heavy axe and jury-rigged a way to carry it slung over his shoulder. He then checked and made sure he could shuck it instantly if he came to another fight.

He continued on.

The next tunnel barely descended at all. Compared to the earlier passages it was spacious and easy to stride down. Llew distrusted it at once. The earlier paths were more difficult but offered no obstacle beyond that. Perhaps this clear passage was made to hide a horrific trap. He slowed at once and began examining everything around him as he went, yet no pit opened at his feet. No terrible trolls sprang up out of the sand. Despite this, rather than allaying his suspicions, they only increased as he continued.

* * *

At length he came to an ornate wooden door that opened to the largest cave of all, a veritable cavern. Intricately carved pillars of stone rose to support a ceiling that appeared to also be of finely worked stone. The floor had been worked with large flat stones and the walls were hung with fine tapestries. A raised dais at the center had an elegant reclining bed of sorts upon it. Resting on it, apparently in repose, was what could only be a beautiful princess. Fine golden hair fell about her head and she was wearing the most ornate gown Llew had ever seen or heard of. As he approached he could see it was made of a heavy blue material and embroidered with a king's ransom in gold thread. Blue and silver gems were brilliantly manifest on much of it and, most especially, on the bracelets, rings, necklace, and coronet that she wore.

Llew approached, alternately stunned, bewitched, bemused, and suspicious.

Recalling what he had said to Helgar, he did not doubt that there was some trick of appearance at work here. Was he meant to awaken her with a kiss? That seemed rather contrived. It also might be exactly what was intended so she could change into

171

a gorgon and turn him into stone, or a harpy that would claw him apart. If that was so then they might expect that he would suspect that and instead make it the necessary course and—the layers of double thinking involved could, he realized, quickly escalate beyond any mortal's ability to even begin to understand them.

Not knowing what else to do, Llew approached more closely and just observed. Staring at her beauty was not difficult at all. Trying to think while doing so was somewhat more difficult. Mind reeling with possibilities, he searched for patterns.

Three challenges so far, thought Llew, *all of them involving what?* Was the common theme just that things were not always what they seemed to be? Certainly there was that but, beyond that, what? Clearly he needed to mull this one over a bit.

There was, he considered, the fact that, in each case, the one he encountered had not been free to directly communicate with until the challenge was beaten. Gower was a dog, Cymri had been trapped and ensorcelled, Helgar had likewise been under another's control. There was a pattern! The sleeping princess was likewise unable to speak with him. Was it important that they not be able to speak with him? Certainly it was! None of the challenges would have been nearly so dangerous had they been able to communicate with him at the outset.

So this challenge might not be dangerous could she but speak to him. *But why*, he had to wonder, *would it be dangerous in the first place?* Llew mentally kicked himself. That was not the question here and he was letting himself be sidetracked. The real question was what would she have told him if she could communicate with him. What would the others have communicated? Why, that they were his boon companions, of course! So would this encounter plead the same? With Cymri and Gower and Helgar accounted for he was running out of companions. The only ones he had not yet encountered were Addfwyn and the prince and this was clearly not either one of them. Indeed, he realized guiltily, the gown's neckline was cut sufficiently deep that he knew full well that could not be the case. Unless—

Llew scrutinized the princess more closely. The hair was the right color, although far too long, and as for the features? He felt a chill as he made himself realize they were not sufficiently different to rule the possibility out. The certainty of his sudden conviction fell across him like a cold wave.

His first reaction was outrage. They had used an illusion on Helgar, certainly, in making him appear to be a full grown warrior and a stranger. But this? This was unforgivably insulting! They had enchanted the prince to appear as a princess! The prince himself would be mortified and ashamed at being seen in such a way. Was this some carefully calculated insult by the creatures of Cas-Eiddew? What could they have against the prince that they would do this? Or was it aimed at Llew himself? Was it intended to force an insurmountable divide between him and the prince? Surely the prince would never want to even see him again after this, for that could only serve to remind him of this shaming. Truly, a lesser man in such a situation and astride a throne might have ordered that Llew be quietly done away with.

Whatever the answer was, he realized he had but one course. He could not bypass this encounter, nor could he retreat. But how, he wondered, should he wake the prince if, in fact, it was him? The folk tales provided no guidance. Given the circumstances, a kiss, after all, was quite out of the question!

"Prince Llew?" he called urgently. Nothing happened and Llew prepared to call twice more to see if perhaps three namings would suffice, as they had with Helgar. Before he could call the second time, however, the figure abruptly sat up.

She first glanced about wildly; then she noticed her gown. She placed her hands near her waist and ran them up it, ending at her bosom, as though assuring herself that the gown itself was real. Her hands then went to her long hair, lifting it up to inspect it without comment after which she drew it back with a seemingly practiced gesture.

Ignoring Llew completely, she cried out to the chamber, "And what is the intent of this? What possible purpose of yours could it serve to expose me thus? Are you enemies of Gwent, per chance? Why? And what is it to such as you?"

No response was forthcoming. "Speak to me!" she shouted with sudden heat.

Llew's own voice was exceedingly cautious for the voice, although perhaps a bit higher than it had been, was most certainly that of the young prince, and his doubts had long since passed away completely. She was indeed he. "Uh, your Highness?" ventured Llew.

Considering he was standing in clear light in front of her and not ten feet away, her reaction was unexpected. Her hands flew to her throat and she leaped up and away from him. Crouching quickly, her hands went to the small dagger she wore. She turned slowly in place, as if seeking him out, although he stood in plain sight.

"Llew?" she ventured. "Are you there?"

"Aye, and I am," he replied, "at your service, um, Llewellyn? Your Highness?" Llew braced himself for the attack she looked quite ready to make.

Her reaction, however, was considerably less abrupt. She stood up straight and removed her hand from the sheathed dagger's hilt. In a raised voice she called out, "Llew, I am trapped in this room. Are you at the door?"

Llew gulped nervously. She obviously could not see him, just as Cymri could not. She might not be pleased at what he had to say now.

"Nay, I am in the same chamber, only a few feet away. I think a glamour of some sort has hidden my aspect from you that you may not perceive me. Perhaps in some way similar to the glamour they have drawn upon you."

She visibly gasped, returned her grip to the dagger's hilt, then released it again and sagged a bit, casting her eyes downward in front of her.

Seemingly resigned, she looked up again in Llew's general direction. "So you can see me then? See what they have done?"

"Do not fret about it, my prince," exclaimed Llew. "What they have done they can very well undo and I may soon be in a position to demand a boon from them! I will get them to turn you back into a man and you and I can forget this ever happened. We would speak of it never again. It will not have happened!"

"I doubt that will be possible, Llew."

"Certainly it will," he protested, "have I done other than serve your interests since we met?"

"No Llew, you have been amazing, truly. The brother I never had, er, did not know. But," she continued, "for whatever reason it may be, our captors had a purpose in revealing me thus and it has not gone away. 'The kittens have escaped the sack,' as they say in Owent."

Llew felt his mind running hither and yon as it tried to take in the hidden meanings in that statement.

In an attempt to at least temporarily edge away from what felt like deeper waters, he asked, "What do you mean, the brother you did not know? Is that not the same as the brother you never had?"

"Nay, Llew, I was told that he, with our mother, died shortly after we were born. I now believe those that told me were lying or were deceived."

Llew did not know what to say. His brain felt like thick porridge, so long did it take him to puzzle some meaning out of the words.

"You believe that we might be brothers?"

"No Llew, I do not."

Llew felt a vast relief pour through him.

"My brother did not have a brother, only a single sister."

Such was his state of mind that it took him a moment to put that together. And just like that, as though it had never existed, the relief was gone again. Llew had no words at all. None would come.

"Llew, you are the only Llew there truly is. I am Llewellyn. You are my own twin brother and I am your sister. I am certain of it. I suspected it when I first laid eyes upon you. Now I know it. You are the rightful heir to Gwent, my lord."

Chapter XX

Gwri's Tale: A Ride in the Woods

"The reason that rulers learn history is because they make enough mistakes already, without repeating the ones of the past," Cymri explained.

"So they never mess things up the same way as someone else did?" Gwri found this a bit difficult to believe.

"Oh no, of course they do. They do it all the time. Many never even bother to learn much of anything about the past except, possibly, some heraldry or some such. No, humans are as humans are, and most find it easy to rationalize. Coming up with reasons for not doing things they should do, or else for doing things they should not do, is often eminently more tempting than actually buckling down and doing the right things."

"But do we not have bards whose responsibility is to learn these things for us?" demanded Gwri. "By your own admission, you cherish history, heritage, and lore and do your best to preserve them."

"You may not always have a bard at hand, Gwri. Besides which, how would you know the bard was giving you sound advice? And just who is the ruler supposed to be? Is it the one with the title or the bard telling him what to do? You might just as well become a tool of Moriganna if you are content to wear a crown and have someone else always telling you what to do."

Gwri grimaced. That shot had sunk home.

"No, bards are frequently confused for advisers or entertainers, and we can perform in those roles, but our real purpose is to teach. We do it through stories and through songs, because that is the best way to keep people's attention."

"Ah," said Gwri, "tell me again of High King Math and the Bone-fortress of Oeth?"

Cymri laughed and the trill of her voice sent shivers up Gwri's spine. After nearly a year of seeing her every day for lessons in all manner of things, he was smitten beyond recourse. She was much too old for him, certainly, and what a great pity that was but, even so, her company was a delight and she seemed to honestly like him. She had told him the Prince of Gwent was not, as Moriganna maintained, a scion of an usurping line, and that he was also a good person, and Llew found that, since it was her telling him this, why then, it must be so. He had long since decided that if the chance came to throw in his lot with Cymri and her friends, rather than with Moriganna, he would seize the opportunity with all his might.

In the meantime, she had carefully coached him on how to make it appear that this was not the case. For example, although there was no way he could hide the fact that he clearly liked her, he had to appear to be skeptical of her claims that Moriganna was the villain. Likewise, he could not appear to accept that King Pendaran was a well-meaning monarch whose line had taken up the throne a century before. Not through treachery but because High King Pwyl went mad when his own queen killed their only son and seemed intent on destroying everything and everyone in

Tethera. The situation had gone beyond unendurable and only a catref king by the name of Bran, Pendaran's great-grandfather, and, formerly, Pwyl's greatest friend, had been in a position to do what had to be done.

Gwri knew this was true because of an expression that even the common folk of Caer Mallcoedwig were prone to use. 'When Pwyl's heir is crowned high king,' was, after all, just another way of saying, "Never," as Pwyl's only heir had predeceased him.

"Math's story has not changed since I told it to you last month, nor has it changed since I told it to you last spring. What you really need to know most about High King Math is that he was the son of our first high king, Mathonwy. Can you tell me why Mathonwy matters?"

He groaned at this. He knew all about Mathonwy and, while he was important, Gwri much preferred studying Math. His adventures were, by far, the more absorbing.

He recited, "Our masters of old, the Roaming Empire, abandoned our shores to deal with issues closer to home after High Queen Boudicca fought them to a standstill. They would have left anarchy behind them, save that the three great peoples of the south, whom she had led to freedom and victory, proclaimed their allegiance to High Queen Boudicca. She then inaugurated the great Kingdom of Tethera. When she passed on, there were a great many that saw it as a chance to become a great king themselves. Eventually, this chaos coalesced into three kingdoms that looked as though they would exist in a perpetual state of war with each other. Mathonwy swept all that aside, reformed the Kingdom of Tethera, and proclaimed himself high king. That saved Tethera.

"But then," Gwri continued, with much more animation,

"Math ap Mathonwy took up the crown and the Fae decided it was time to end the rule of these upstart mortals. That was a mistake! Once they had learned that lesson, the Picts, believing us weakened, decided it was time to throw all the Tetherans back into the sea and turn back the clock to when they alone dwelt here. Again, Math taught them a hard lesson—can we at least discuss his battles?" Gwri pleaded, trying hard not to sound overly plaintive.

"I think," Cymri said, "that now is the time you take your daily ride, not learn more of Math. Gower, poor beast, looks forward to it all day, and you should not seek to cheat him of it."

"But I was not—" Gwri began to protest, then gave it up. "You are right, of course, Cymri. Tomorrow, then."

Cymri gave him a wry grin as she stood to escort him to the outer door of her rooms. "Tomorrow we shall see. There are still an awful lot of other things we need to find time to squeeze in between your ears."

* * *

Gwri and Gower had a long tradition of taking rides through the dark forest surrounding the tiny island of sunlight that were the fields and village of Caer Mallcoedwig. There was nothing especially dangerous to a mounted rider unless, of course, you counted Moriganna's shape-shifters. They were probably the reason there was nothing else dangerous there.

He was effectively leashed to those woods as he could not travel more than a few miles away from her amulet without risking harm or death to Cymri. He also was not under any illusions about the shape-shifters being unable to catch him and bring him back should he stray too far.

It was therefore a considerable surprise when he spotted a stranger on the forest path ahead. Gwri slowed Gower down to a walk and scrutinized the man as they approached each other.

The stranger wore a shabby robe with a cloak that came up over his head in a cowl. His hands were empty and he bore no visible weapons. He was also a fairly old man, judging by his posture.

"Hello great prince," he called, in a rusty voice, as Gwri drew within easy earshot. "Can you spare a moment for an old man seeking his daughter? She was lost in these woods and I am at my wit's end. Have you seen her?"

"Nay," replied Gwri. "How long has she been missing?"

The old man was peering at him strangely. "My lord, could I ask that you push back your cowl a moment?"

"Very well," Gwri replied and pushed it back, revealing his full face.

The old man staggered back a pace in apparent shock. "Prince Llew? This is madness; what are you doing here?"

Gwri was astonished. That the stranger did not know him was to be expected, but to think he was someone else was something else altogether. And what was the old man even doing here? No strangers ever came to Caer Mallcoedwig and few of Moriganna's minions ever went anywhere else. Those that did were reputed to be incredibly close-mouthed when dealing with outsiders. He had also called Gwri a prince. That Moriganna had supposedly adopted him, making him a prince in the process, was not known to anyone besides himself and Moriganna. Embarrassed by it, he had never even told Cymri.

In a flash his sword was out and pointed at the man. "Perhaps I am Prince Gwri instead, but I must ask how you know my station—just who are you?"

The old man threw back his own cowl and then straightened up. The man who now stood before him was neither especially old nor was he young. Nor was he especially short or tall but, instead, a very ordinary looking man indeed, except perhaps for a certain sense of presence that he radiated. His eyes were bright and keen and were fixed with a rigid intensity upon Gwri. He seemed to have no awareness of the sword whatsoever.

"Llew? You do not know me? Thousands of days together in your short life and you have forgotten me? Do you at least recall how you came here? We parted not a hundred days ago in Caerleon. Does even your father know where you are?"

Now it was Gwri's turn to be utterly confused. "I think you are mistaken. You cannot be this close to Caer Mallcoedwig without knowing where you are, and I have spent my entire life here. I am not your Prince Llew, I am Prince Gwri, the one and only, but you have not yet answered who you are—and what is this nonsense about my father?"

The man continued to regard Gwri with a curious intensity. "Very well, I am Taliesin, Chief of all Bards. Have you heard of me at least?"

Gwri's surprise was complete and he blurted, "Cymri's father?"

"Aye!" Taliesin said, his eyes now flashing fiercely. "You know of her then. Where is she! Is she alive? I have searched an entire year and it has brought me only this far."

Dropping most of his caution, Gwri lowered his blade, then he thought again and re-sheathed it. "Your search has brought you far indeed. Your daughter is my own tutor and is imprisoned within the central keep of Caer Mallcoedwig. It is a stronghold no man should be able to even approach, save by the will of Queen Moriganna."

Now it was again Taliesin's turn to be visibly startled. "That ancient witch? She is the one who has taken my daughter? Is she well? Has she been harmed?"

Gwri tried to keep track of all the questions. "Yes, she is an old witch. Yes, she took your daughter. You did not specify whom you were inquiring about, but I will tell you that Moriganna and Cymri both seem quite as well as ever, and neither has been harmed."

"Very well, thank you Prince—Gwri was it? You display an odd sense of humor in pretending that I might care about Moriganna, regardless of how I phrased my questions. Are you truly unaware that you have not spent your life here, and that you actually belong far to the south in the kingdom of Gwent?"

"What?" Gwri demanded, and then a thought occurred to him. "King Pendaran rules Gwent. Is his son named Llew? Is that who you think I am?"

"The thought had crossed my mind," replied Taliesin in a droll tone of voice.

"Well," said Gwri, "it seems we must resemble each other."

"And you sound alike. You even dress in similar fashion. Did Moriganna dress you that way and teach you to use the same polite ways of speech as well? Did she also teach you of riding, and even instruct you in the use of a sword?"

"Dressed me in fine clothing, yes. As for the sword, that was Guardsman Mercher. Riding was mostly on my own, although Guardsman Cadwallon helped in training me to fight on horseback, and in training Gower. As for polite ways of speech, some of that was Moriganna, yes, but a lot more of it was your daughter, Cymri."

"Astounding. So you are someone who just happens to look precisely like Prince Llew of Gwent and is sufficiently trained to act like him as well?"

"I believe you have stated the situation perfectly. As to why this should be so you need only ask yourself as to why Moriganna would want such a thing. The extent and simplicity of her plan is finally clear, even to me."

"I see," said Taliesin, narrowing his eyes. "So you believe she is planning to swap you for the prince and then rule through you? Is there some reason I should not irreparably damage these plans now?"

Gwri had no difficulty understanding that. "One reason would be that killing me might be more of a challenge than you expect, for reasons completely unrelated to my own modest skill with arms." Indeed, if Taliesin attacked him it would likely be impossible to prevent Gower from stamping him into a fine red goo. "For another, your daughter is very fond of me. She has even offered to help me escape, when the time is right. She would be most wroth with you should you manage to kill me."

Taliesin laughed at this. "I do not want to kill you, my false Llew but, were I to try, I doubt very much your brave words could stop me. As for my daughter? Well, Cymri is a red-head and as fiery as they come. She has been angry at me before, and likely will be again, yet I endure."

Uh oh, thought Gwri. Whether Taliesin could best him or not, there would be nothing good in either winning or losing. Gwri thought furiously, then blurted, "There is also this, if I die, the instant that I do, Cymri will perish as well."

"A bold claim," Taliesin said skeptically, "yet it sounds like a bluff to me. Pray, how would this be implemented?"

"Cymri wears a medallion that the queen obliged her to place around her neck. It is forged with the blood of us both and cannot be removed without doing something terrible to her and, should I ever not be within a few miles of her, it will kill her outright. Obviously, if I were dead there would be no more of me available anywhere. There would then be no way for her to stay within a few miles of me."

Taliesin swore quietly to himself but Gwri's hearing was well able to catch the words. Despite growing up in a stable, he did not know what most of them meant, but he made a mental note to find out.

Finally, Taliesin said, "This is very bad news, as you must know. If I could return her to Caerleon it is possible we could find a way to defang this curse." He looked up at Gwri. "You said she offered to help you escape; would you be willing to come with her if she escapes instead? I will guarantee I can find ready employment for you in King Pendaran's court."

"Very well," Gwri replied, "it seems all paths conspire to take me south. If I go, it may as well be with someone I like and that would be Cymri. No offense to you, of course."

"None taken, Gwri, and thank you. Please return to this Caer Mallcoedwig and tell no one of our meeting. When I come and collect my daughter just be sure you are ready to travel."

"You will not even be able to get in," objected Gwri.

"Ah, what does Moriganna have there, thirty or forty guardsmen?"

"In permanent garrison?" Gwri waved his hands, "They come and go as they are sent and summoned but yes, that many is likely at any given time. Also, there are the shape-shifters. Perhaps they are not as numerous as the guardsmen—although I suspect she has more elsewhere—but they are far, far more dangerous."

"Hullo," Taliesin said with a grin. "I am a bard. Nor I am just any bard; I am the Chief of Bards. If by shape-shifter you are referring to something derived from the so-called beast men of yore then they will be even easier to deal with than the humans. As for Moriganna? Most of her spells require enormous amounts of preparation and, as for the rest? I can defend against them quite adequately, thank you."

"You are a match for Moriganna and all her men and creatures?" Gwri asked, uncertain if he could possibly believe this.

"If I have time to compose a rather specific song and she has no warning I am coming, then yes; yes I am."

Amazed, Gwri had nothing to say to that.

"Gwri, I am a father and I have come to rescue my only child. I am quite good at judging people and their emotions. These are essential tools of my trade, and I have had centuries to refine them. If I read your face and voice correctly, you are quite fond of Cymri. Will you give me away and spoil her chance at freedom?"

"Nay," said Gwri, "you already know I will not."

Taliesin smiled. "In truth, I did know that, I just wanted to make sure you knew it. Very well, I need some time to put together the performance I must give. If you could gather whatever equipment you will need to travel quickly I will come sometime in the middle of the night."

Gwri sighed. He had never planned to help Moriganna but this would irretrievably commit him against her. Did he have a choice? Thinking it through, he decided he did not. This was a move a would-be hero could not avoid. He had heard enough of the old tales from Cymri, and from others, even before she came, to know that doing Moriganna's bidding would eventually make him nothing more than a villain. With wry amusement he realized that he would not even get to be the villain if he remained. He would simply be one of the villain's minions.

"I have to bring my horse. I have to."

"I think that is a very good idea, Gwri. Could you have a

few more in mind and be ready to bring them as well? We will need mounts for all three of us, and some spares would be good, too."

"Two spares it is then, Gower will never need a spare. He could carry forty stones weight all day and all night," Gwri boasted.

"He is a magnificent steed, Gwri. Was Gower a gift from Moriganna as well?"

"Hardly," Gwri answered. "Everything I have, even my name, has been given to me by others—except for Gower. Gower has always been mine and mine alone."

Chapter XXI

The Spriggan

Then, at the moment when Llew's disorientation was complete, the princess changed into a giant rock troll and leaped upon him.

At least, Llew waited for it, but it did not happen. Apparently this was not that kind of challenge. *Too bad*, he thought distractedly, he was sure it would have been simpler.

There was long pause that finally grew awkward.

"My lord?" asked the Princess Llewellyn.

Llew finally found his tongue. "You and I, brother and sister, I . . . do not see how that would be possible, even so, princess." Her title came haltingly from his lips; using it had taken conscious effort.

"Come sit," she suggested. "You look a bit wobbly."

There was nothing within the chamber upon which to sit aside from the divan the princess rested upon.

"That is not necessary," Llew said bravely. Then he sank to his knees where he had stood. His legs just did not feel at all sturdy enough to continue to bear his weight.

Llewellyn gave him a warm smile before saying, "This

seems a familiar discussion. I am your younger sister, Llew. You must call me by my name now, when we are in private. You may even use it in public on some occasions. My name is Llewellyn. It may help if you say it once."

Llew shook his head from side to side for a moment in a futile attempt to clear his thoughts. "Llewellyn," he began. "What you propose is . . . simply not possible. Your brother died. You said so. I assume he was buried with your mother. Even if there had been a substitution, a dead child left for a living one, it would have failed. Your mother, the Queen, must have had trusted servants who could not have been fooled."

"Bah, the witch left some piece of her magic to hide the fact you were taken. Perhaps it was another child magically made to resemble you. It is not impossible. At least some of her power is real. Cymri is proof of that."

Llew shook his head again, but this time only slightly. "In the old tales, magic applied to the living usually does not survive death. Likely, if Cymri died as a black bird, her body would again become that of her true self."

"That is said not to be true of changelings, Llew. In fact, they usually do die soon after the exchange but their magic is not undone. The magic of changelings is that of the Fae; therefore it is different from all other enchantments. The introduction of a changeling could explain it perfectly."

"Not so," objected Llew. "As told in all the tales, the changeling takes on the appearance of the babe but the babe takes on the appearance of the changeling. In such a case I would still bear the semblance of whatever the changeling's true form was, and that would not be human.

"Changelings are the Fae's half-breeds, and even the other half is never human. Therefore I could not have been exchanged for a changeling." Llew felt himself getting a slight headache from the logic involved.

The princess frowned and said, "There is that, but I have not heard that the original always takes the changeling's form, it seems it might go either way. Still, in all the old tales, if a changeling and the one it was changed for should ever again be brought into each other's presence then the spell is completely broken."

"Are you suggesting Moriganna somehow brought me and the babe's remains into close proximity to purposely break the spell?"

"Perhaps," replied the princess, "and perhaps not. "Be mindful that if her intention was to do so then that sly schemer could have found a way. She is not titled the Queen of Deceit for no reason."

Llew raised his hands, palm out in surrender. "Peace, I give up for the nonce. We can take this up again later. We still have many things to do, and that has not changed." So saying, Llew rose to his feet and extended a hand to the princess. "Shall we be on our way?"

Then he paused, feeling quite the fool. Like the others before her, the princess was gone.

It was easy to find the way out. Behind a tapestry, on the wall opposite the entrance, was another passage. The way here was wide and flat. It was also high enough that there was never any need to duck his head.

Like Cymri's cavern, the cave it opened up into was not the result of any chisel. It was hung with gleaming stalactites with multicolored stalagmites reaching to meet them. Water droplets slowly dripped and fell between, creating a shimmering sheen over it all. In the glow of the fairy lights it was beautiful.

Something sat on a raised stone in the center. Apparently it was waiting for him. This had to be Addfwyn, decided Llew. He was all that was left.

The figure appeared to be a small man, perhaps no more than three or four feet high, with a bushy beard surmounted by an enormous nose. His garb was strangely archaic with such oddities as his foot gear ending in points that curved up and around from the tips of his toes.

"Addfwyn?" Llew inquired.

Through his thick beard the little man smiled and his eyes crinkled with mirth. "Nay lad, I am not your farmer turned man servant. My name is Hafgan and you have beaten the challenge fairly."

Llew blinked in surprise. The voice was the one from outside.

Anger surged up in him, "Where are my companions? What have you done with them?" he demanded heatedly.

"Peace lad, they are unharmed and you will be brought to them. There simply is no room in here for all those Picts you left outside."

"Picts?" exclaimed Llew. "I have no Picts for companions!"

Hafgan's face wrinkled in perplexity. "Well they came with you, we just assumed—"

"No," Llew said emphatically, "they are no companions of mine! They are quite the opposite I should say."

"So you have no claim on them?" Hafgan asked in a thoughtful manner.

"Nay," stammered Llew, caught by surprise at the wording of the question. "What will you do with them?"

Hafgan danced a gleeful little jig before replying, "Do not worry yourself about that, lad. Oh, and do not look so concerned!

We will not harm them. It is not really our way when we have no need to. We will merely indenture them to the Firvulag for a bit and turn a tidy profit; then they will be released and with all their memories of us cleansed away. It is necessary, in any case. If they are not friends of yours then it would not do to have them following you when you leave," Hafgan added.

"What is the Firvulag?" Llew asked confusedly.

"To answer your first question, the Firvulag are not a who, nor are they a what. They are the deep ones. You may have heard them referred to as the black dwarfs. They will work your Picts hard but they will release them unharmed when our contract expires. We insist on that in the terms and even such fearsome ones as the Firvulag in all their numbers have little inclination to earn our wrath."

"And how long will they be held?" queried Llew.

"Contracts with the Firvulag are always for one hundred years, no more, no less."

"That seems a bit harsh, even for Picts," objected Llew. "What is it that gives you leave to barter away their lives?"

"Leave? There are two things that give us leave, lad," replied Hafgan. "The first being that you renounced any claim to them. You cannot deny it for you said it, and this is a bad place for denying the truth, whatever it may be. The second being that we are not taking their lives, only their time, and that in compensation for such time of ours as they have wasted."

"The Picts are humans," interjected Llew, "much as we might like them not to be. A hundred years may as well be their lives for I doubt any will last nearly so long as that."

"They can, they will. The Firvulag will not let them escape work by dying, or even by aging."

Llew thought this through. "So you will be unleashing a

small army of Picts on the world of a century hence?"

"Yes and no, lad. When they are released we will see that they blend in somewhat. If Tetherans still exist then the Picts will probably become convinced they are all Tetheran crofters. At that point they will want little more than to find brides, grow turnips, and raise hordes of crofter brats."

"They would probably consider that a fate worse than death," Llew commented, thinking of what he had seen of the Picts. Then he wondered why it was that everyone more than a few centuries old was so concerned with turnips.

"That will not be our problem," declared Hafgan. "Now, on to other matters. Although we now have an inkling as to why, we still cannot see you, so I believe you have a boon coming?"

Llew's thoughts came to a sudden halt, seemingly tripping over themselves as he tried to shift his mind to this new topic in mid-stride. "Wait! You think you might understand why you cannot see me? Could you share that with me? It might have an impact on the nature of the boon."

Hafgan pursed his lips in mock disapproval. "Oh, it is really quite simple now. During the challenges it was obvious you have no clear perception of who you are. If you cannot even perceive yourself, then how can you expect us to?"

Llew wrinkled his forehead in perplexity. "I can see myself fine. My companions see me as well."

"They see what is presented to them. They do not see you as you are because what you are is unknown, even to yourself. We cannot see you because we have learned to look past what is presented to us and focus only on seeing things as they see themselves."

"That seems a real problem," remarked Llew. "Anyone without a keen knowledge of who they are could pose a very serious threat."

"Nay," said Hafgan, "your kind is far too rare for that. For a fact, you are the first we've seen—or not seen—you know what I mean. Most people know enough of themselves that we can at least see an outline."

"Perhaps you were not watching the challenges as closely as you suggest. Princess Llewellyn says I am her elder twin and true heir to the kingdom of Gwent. How can you claim that I do not know myself?"

"Oh that," Hafgan waved his hand dismissively, "it fits the facts as she knows them but it is, of course, quite incorrect—either that or you do not believe it."

"What do you say?" exclaimed Llew.

"We can see her very well. Yet her telling you who you were did not make you visible. Therefore, she is wrong and you are not who she says you are, or you do not believe you are who she says you are."

"So then I am the changeling?"

"Hardly. A changeling most likely would have sickened and died. Neither human nor animal milk may sustain them alone without the presence of elder magic. Ergo, since a stable seems an unlikely place to find that, it is very unlikely you are a changeling."

Llew abruptly decided it was time to change the topic. "A guide," he declared, "For my boon I want a guide to take us to Gwent by the most expedient path."

Hafgan lowered his chin and fixed Llew with an unblinking, emotionless gaze. There was an air of unspoken menace in it. "Do you really want one of us traveling with you?"

Llew stopped to think about that. Worded that way, it did sound like a much poorer idea. Still . . . .

"You said you would tell me what you were if I lived? What are you?"

"I did indeed," said Hafgan, while giving Llew a speculative look. "You will not again be confusing us with the Fae. We are the watchers at the gate, the unyielding enforcers of old, the implacable doom of oath breakers, and the unstoppable force of retribution. We are what your kind calls . . . Spriggans." At this he crossed his arms in satisfaction and appeared to be waiting for an expected reaction.

"What?" asked Llew, confused by the unfamiliar term.

Hafgan scowled. "Spriggans. We are Spriggans."

Llew shook his head. "I confess it is not a name I know."

Hafgan's face, what could be seen of it over his beard, was rapidly growing deep red. Seeing that, Llew hurriedly added, "Ah, I am sure you are very fearsome and I shall surely not mistake you for any simple Fae. In fact, you mentioned I might have some hidden folk heritage of my own and, indeed, if that is true then I could only hope that—"

"Enough!" shouted Hafgan, raising his hands and bidding Llew to leave off. "Forget your flattery. If the mortal folk have forgotten what a Spriggan even is then it can only be because we have removed ourselves from their awareness for far too long. You desired a guide? I would guide you myself so that you and any others we encounter shall once more remember that Spriggans exist and cannot be long ignored."

"Um, thank you?" said Llew uncertainly.

"Well?"

"Well what?"

"Are you going to invite me to join your band or not?"

"Oh!" Llew exclaimed. "Hafgan, I believe that today there is going to be splendid weather to take a bit of a walk. It will be good to stretch our legs and see some of the countryside. Perhaps we might even find some wild berries, or pack a midday meal to consume beside a rushing brook. Would you care to accompany us?"

"Thought you would never ask. I accept." Hafgan then narrowed his eyes suspiciously. "You do not seem to be very frightened of me."

"Perhaps it is because your face is such an honest one," Llew suggested.

"See? There you go again. This could be a very long trip, or at least seem like one. Alright, follow me now and I shall guide you out of here. First, however, we will need supplies. You and your motley band had scarcely two sticks of dried meat to rub together."

So saying he gestured to two very large bundles that had apparently been up against the back wall the entire time. "You pick one and I will take the other."

Bemused by this, Llew asked, "You knew I was going to ask for a guide in advance?"

Hafgan snorted. "Not hardly. It was in my head you were going to ask for supplies."

Llew went to pick one up and nearly pulled himself down on top of it. With a heave and a grunt he managed to get it up to a height where he could barely manage to carry it. Hafgan picked up his own bundle with one hand and positioned it on his right shoulder. Llew said nothing but resolved not to get in any arm wrestling matches with Spriggans.

"Wait," said Llew, "you skirted around the subject of any hidden folk heritage I might have."

"Oh that," grumbled Hafgan. "Yes, now that we have seen a bit of you it is rather evident you have a tiny bit of Coraniaid somewhere in your family tree. Just a tiny bit, and so far back you need not worry about it. Their claim to fame was that their hearing was so good they could hear any sound that the wind carried. In that way they could thus avoid any danger moving upon them. Think how much poorer even your hearing is than that and you will have some idea how far back in your family tree they are."

"Coraniaid? What are they? How does my sense of hearing tell you they were far back in my line? I could just be the nearly deaf grandson of one."

Hafgan snorted. "There are none left, and have not been any for a very long time."

"What?" demanded Llew. "You just told me their hearing was so good they could avoid any danger!"

"I said any danger moving upon them. Poison does not move so you really cannot hear it coming."

"They were all poisoned? All of them?" Llew was aghast.

"It can be a rough and treacherous world, lad."

It was just a short trek up yet another tunnel before Llew spotted a welcome sight. It was sunlight! Then he found he had to cover his eyes from the painful brightness. Fortunately it was barely dawn and so soon became bearable. They emerged just a short distance from where the party had camped, and Llew was surprised everyone was there again, although all of them were fast asleep, even Gower, Cymri, and Cilgwri. Cymri was a bird again and Gower a horse. The princess, however, was still wearing her fine blue gown and considerable amounts of jewelry.

"Hallooo!" He called as they strode into camp. Instantly, companions were rolling, and flapping, and stamping and doing all the other things people and creatures do when waking from a deep slumber.

"What is it, my drott?" exclaimed Helgar. Then, spotting, Hafgan, "And what is this? You found a dvergr?"

Llew glanced over and saw Princess Llewellyn as she stood, still wearing her blue gown and other accoutrements, and words failed him. She glanced down and saw what she was wearing and words seemed to fail her as well.

"Oh," exclaimed Helgar, after a long pause, "and you found a valkrie as well? Hello, I am Helgar, if I am dead then glad am I to have one as beautiful as you to carry me to the sacred halls."

She gave him a disapproving eye and said, "I think you had better plan on carrying yourself, Helgar Olufson."

Hafgan interrupted at that point. "Nay, Northman, she is no valkrie and I am no dwarf and you are not dead—not yet at any rate. That could change if I ever hear of you confusing a Spriggan for a dwarf again. In the future, bear in mind that a Spriggan does not care to be mistaken for a dwarf, or anything else for that matter."

While he might have been teasing before, Helgar's eyes went large with alarm and he was clearly done with any attempt at humor. "A Spriggan? Here? Llew take care! Did you hear that? Tis a Spriggan!"

"Oh excellent," exclaimed Hafgan, approvingly, "finally someone who at least has some idea that there is such a thing as a Spriggan."

Llew set his bundle down with a relieved groan. Hafgan did likewise, although without the accompanying sound effects.

"Yes, he is a Spriggan," returned Llew, "and his name is Hafgan. He has brought us some much needed supplies and will be joining us on our little trek."

"But, my drott! If he is a Spriggan—"

"And," continued Llew, "he has this fine axe for you." Llew

unstrapped the weapon from his back and extended it to Helgar.

Helgar blinked in surprise as he took it and said, "Now I do not think that—ooh, she is a shiny one is she not?"

As Helgar admired his new axe, Llew turned to the princess. She was now looking at him intently. "I thought it was just a dream," she whispered. "I thought that when I awoke I would be safely back in my disguise and all would be as it was."

"Would that be a good thing?" Llew asked carefully.

"Nay," she replied, "I think this is far better, dear brother. What do you think?"

At this, Llew recalled what Hafgan had said about his identity. In the space of his next heartbeat he also realized that this was not the time to discuss the issue with her. "Llewellyn, I believe there is nothing," he answered cautiously, "that could make me any happier than to be your brother."

"So, Llew," Helgar said, "this then is your sister? And she has the same name as your brother? It must be very confusing in your home."

"The term is 'your highness,' Helgar," said Llewellyn. As we approach Gwent, this is how you must refer to Llew, and to me as well, when others are about."

Helgar frowned. "Getting all high and mighty as we approach your kingdom, are we?" There was a pause before he added, "your highness."

Llewellyn had the grace to immediately look contrite. "Oh my, no, friend Helgar—well, no more than is absolutely necessary. You are a boon companion of my brother and therefore of myself as well. It is just that things are more formalized, down here, and it will forestall many difficulties when we are in public. For myself, you may forever call me by just my name, Llewellyn, when we are in private."

"I daresay," she added. "Llew will petition our father for a title for you as well. You have certainly earned one for your role in returning the future king to his land and his people."

Helgar appeared about to say something that might not have been politic when Llew hastily broke in. "That would certainly be nice, Llewellyn, but Helgar already has a title we can use even without petitioning, uh, father." That word felt very strange on Llew's tongue.

"He does?"

"As the last of his house he is the rightful Jarl of Lindenjal. As I understand it, a jarl is not unlike a cantref king. Is that not correct, Helgar?"

Helgar looked perplexed at the question. "My drott, I know little about what a cantref king rules."

"Easy, Helgar. When we reach a cantref you can compare its size to Lindenjal. Would you say Lindenjal has more than one thousand subjects?"

"Well," considered Helgar, "we Northmen do not like to stack ourselves into tiny places as your people do."

"So in comparison?"

"I am thinking," announced Helgar grimly.

Hafgan started to say something, but Llew caught the movement as he opened his mouth and interrupted him. "Whatever clever comment you were about to make, Spriggan, let us pretend it was not going to be about Northmen and thinking. This is important to some of us."

Hafgan, closed his mouth without speaking but his expression conveyed disappointment.

"This is only a guess, Llew, but although Northmen spread themselves out more, Lindenjal is also very large so perhaps there are even more than that. Of course, one Northman is probably worth—"

"No," Llew interrupted, "let us not consider that at the moment, either. While I doubt not that it might be the basis for a spirited discussion, now is not the time or the place." Llew clapped Helgar on the back and looked towards Llewellyn. "You see? If Lindenjal is at all comparable to a cantref then Helgar is at least a cantref king in his own right."

Llewellyn frowned, although she appeared to be mulling it over. "A cantref king in exile is what he would be."

"Even so," affirmed Llew. Still, we are all three of us highnesses, so we may address each other on that basis.

"Ah," Hafgan broke in, "I may have neglected to tell you I am the King of the Spriggans."

"This is getting ridiculous," groused Llew, "seven in this band and four of us are royalty?"

"It is worse than that," said Llewellyn.

"What? Do you mean to say that Addfwyn is also a king in disguise?"

"Nay Llew, or at least I know of no reason to presume he is."

"That really limits the remaining possibilities. It must be either Cymri or Gower then."

"Very funny, brother. Know then that Taliesin, the Chief of all Bards, was adopted by Elffin, King of Ceredigion. When his time came he sat the throne until his son, his only heir, died young. After that, rather than sit and go mad with grief, he chose to wander as a bard is wont to do.

"People nowadays think Ceredigion is ruled by the kings of Dyfyd but, in truth, they only hold it in perpetual stewardship for Taliesin. He arranged that rather than abdicate. So Taliesin is a king and that makes our Cymri a princess as well."

"Princess Cymri," mused Llew, "I would try calling her that if I was not afraid of getting pecked. So five out of seven of us are royals then?"

"Unless more secrets come to light about Gower or Addfwyn—ooh, or maybe Cilgwri—it appears so," Llewellyn said.

"Ridiculous," complained Llew, "if we are all royals we must be going about it wrong because we certainly seem to have to do everything ourselves. Almost everything," he corrected himself, after glancing towards Addfwyn.

Steadfastly ignoring all the drama and strangeness, Addfwyn was already sorting through the bundles Hafgan had provided. His evident pleasure at finding cookware and provisions and even spare clothing and blankets was refreshing. Although he had not thought of it before, Llew realized he had not, until that moment, known what the man would look like when he was happy.

Addfwyn looked up from his inventory. "Excuse me, your highness," he said, addressing Princess Llewellyn. "Marvelous as it is, your current attire may not fare well as we travel. I believe this is a set of armor and other items that you may find more practical, particularly given your experience with such."

Llewellyn looked at him sharply. "You are not surprised to see me thus?"

"Me? Oh no, your highness, I knew you were traveling in disguise when you were taking my oath. A poor man like me, I would have been ushered from this world long since if I did not have the habit of paying attention to everything."

"And you said nothing?"

"It was not my place, highness. I knew you had your reasons and it was not for such as me to be meddling and asking questions about them."

The princess chuckled, "Oh you are a find, Addfwyn ap Sior. Never change."

She took the stack of items he proffered and went off behind a nearby wall for privacy.

Addfwyn continued to go through the new equipment and supplies. He also set aside a considerable bit of not-too-fresh mutton that he judged they no longer needed to carry with them. Llew was pleased to see that. Mutton was hardly his favorite food to begin with and, in recent days, it had fallen still further from the top of his list.

He did not really notice when he sat down and leaned back against a nicely slanted slab of stone. The morning sun was warm. His eyes started to close and he tried to resist, then realized he had not had any real rest for at least forty hours. This was despite an almost never ending series of grueling physical activities. A short nap before they started might be for the best, after all. The last thing he remembered seeing was Hafgan, apparently discussing the supply situation, while he squatted down beside Addfwyn.

Chapter XXII

Gwri's Tale: A Tree in the Courtyard

That night, as Gwri waited in his room, he could not sleep. He just lay there, fully dressed, with his armor and weapons close at hand, and listened. Few realized just how well he could hear. Gwri had been a long time realizing it himself, until he had again and again found himself in situations where he could hear what no one else with him could. Lying there he could hear the castle settling down for the night. Guards walked the walls, their faint footsteps perfectly audible to him. The gate remained open, but two guards were always stationed there. Gwri could even hear what they said to each other as often as not.

Eventually he heard music, it was not far away and it was coming from the direction of the gate. He flew to the window that faced the courtyard in time to see Taliesin stride in. He played a haunting tune upon a fantastic harp of finely worked wood ornamented with what could only be gold and precious gems. The two guardsmen never moved. Gwri glanced up at the guardsmen upon the walls. They, too, merely stood there, unmoving.

With a ferocious growl, a pack of seven shape-shifters poured out of their barracks, then slowed and stopped and gradually began to merely rock back and forth upon the pads of their paws.

For Llew, that clenched it. Taliesin could clearly do as he said. It was time to go. But then he heard a voice he knew all too well. "Enough, bard, desist. Your ridiculous plan has failed." Moriganna stood upon the hoarding outside her solar, overlooking the quadrangular courtyard.

"Foolish witch," Taliesin retorted, striding to the corner nearest where she stood, "all your schemes have come to naught. You have my daughter and I have come to take her. Did you think I would not?"

"I never discounted the possibility that you might try," she said smugly. "I even deemed it possible you would find a way through the veil I maintain about Caer Mallcoedwig. Observe!"

She gestured to two guardsmen who had emerged onto the hoarding with her. Between them, bound fast, they half walked, half carried, Cymri.

Seeing them, Taliesin redoubled his efforts and the tempo of his tune picked up speed in an intricate rhythm. Gwri groaned internally, he knew those two guardsmen. He knew all the guardsmen. Was it coincidence Moriganna had used these two in particular to bring out her hostage? He was sure it could not be. She really had made preparations in case Taliesin showed up.

She called down to Taliesin then, mocking him, "My, what a performance this is. A woman should count herself fortunate indeed to have a handsome man come play his harp so eloquently below her window. Was it your intention we should elope? Oh, how my father would have raged should he have caught you making this attempt." In a harder voice, "It is wasted effort, these men cannot hear your siren songs, for the deaf never shall."

Taliesin cocked his head and gave her an unpleasant smile,

then drew all the fingers of his right hand down across his harp. It made a horrendous, discordant noise that Gwri wanted, more than anything, never to hear again. Every guardsman and shape-shifter in sight collapsed in a heap, like puppets with their strings suddenly cut. Even the two men holding Cymri did likewise.

Taliesin ceased playing and gave her a pitying smile. "You never really understood how sound works did you, mighty queen? Deaf or no, if a tree falls in the forest, and there is no one that can hear it, it will still have an impact."

"Ah," she hissed, "your pretty instrument is Uaithne. I really should have recognized it, but it has been some time."

"Your time is over, Moriganna, you are alone and your lesser tricks will not work upon me. That leaves you only your blade and, although I know well your skill with blades, it is not superior to my own. Surrender. Hiding in a dark forest is no place for you. You were ever meant for grander places and I will ensure that King Pendaran's mercy is just that. Consider, Arawen is our enemy as well; with you joined with us he can be thwarted and mayhap even defeated. You could be a tremendous ally to us and the king is ever generous to those that serve."

Improbably, for a moment, Gwri thought she might have actually been the slightest bit swayed by Taliesin's words. Then he had spoken the word 'serve' and a hard and hateful look of pure malevolence swept over her face.

"I will never serve again!" she cried and reached out to seize the amulet Cymri wore—before ripping it from her neck.

The effect was instantaneous. Cymri collapsed out of sight. Taliesin shouted in anger and started forward while Moriganna spun and held the medallion out at arm's length, its face angled down directly towards him. He took perhaps three steps and then could not lift his foot for another.

Roots had sprung forth from his feet and legs and dug into the ground. He twisted and groaned and dropped his harp. He reached for his sword—perhaps he meant to cut himself free—but found he could not draw it. His fingers had become long stick-like things that did not bend properly. He twisted and writhed again and turned his face straight up to the heavens with a gargling cry of anguish and pain that cut off at its peak. Then he twisted and thrashed again. His body expanded incredibly and there was an enormous noise like the crack of a giant whip. Taliesin was gone. In his place stood a huge oak tree, appearing just as though it had been growing there for centuries, save that the branches and leaves still waved to and fro with the energy of their sudden growth.

Taliesin's harp still lay on the grass near the tree. Nearer still, a fine sword lay in its scabbard, still attached to an old leather belt. Other debris was scattered about, including a torn cloak and a worn out boot split right down the seams.

Moriganna leaned heavily upon the hoarding's railing. When she finally lifted her head, Gwri saw that there were white streaks running through her auburn hair, yet even as he watched, they diminished and lessened.

Gwri could not take his eyes off her. She had turned a man, a very powerful man, into a tree in an instant. How could he dare go against her will as he had planned? He narrowed his eyes as he regarded her. As he had planned? That was still his plan. His only advantage was that she did not know he had meant to flee from her this very night. It was, he decided, rather a good thing he had not yet played his hand.

Just then a large black bird attacked Moriganna. It fluttered and pecked at her and it was altogether strange in that not only was it attacking a person, but it was doing so in the middle of the night. Then Moriganna held up the medallion again and spoke a word. The black bird fluttered to the boards at her feet, whereupon she picked it up by its legs—not terribly carefully—and strode back into her solar.

Gwri stayed in his room and listened carefully. He heard her roust some servants awake and send them off on errands. It seemed the whole castle had fallen unconscious save for himself, Moriganna, Taliesin, and Cymri.

Thinking of Cymri tormented him. He could not hear her anywhere now and he knew there was nothing he could do for her at the moment. Moriganna may have killed her, but Gwri deemed it unlikely. He told himself she was probably just going to be placed back in her rooms to wake up. Moriganna was not nearly ready to call his training complete.

Would Cymri still be willing to carry on with the training while her father was a tree in the courtyard? Of course she would, he realized. Just as Moriganna had ensured his compliance by threatening Gower, she now had a hostage for Cymri's good behavior. That was her way and perhaps the greatest single reason why Gwri was determined to escape and overturn all her schemes for him.

She had said she would not serve again? Once free of her he would be able to say the same thing!

Chapter XXIII

Southward Bound

When Llew awoke he noted they were now loading the gear and supplies onto a small shaggy pony. It occurred to him to wonder where they had gotten the pony. He was on the verge of asking and then decided not to look at a gift horse askance.

Helgar and Llewellyn had been sitting and resting on a log nearby, although not sleeping. Llewellyn was wearing a very finely crafted suit of polished light mail that fit her perfectly. It did nothing to disguise her gender. Llew wondered if the Spriggans had just had it lying about, or if they had made it for her in a single night. Gower waited patiently with them, although Cymri was nowhere to be seen. Now, seeing his master waken, Gower suddenly lifted his head and regarded him. Thus alerted, Helgar and Llewellyn noted he was awake as well.

"Our needs drive us to hurry on, Llew," said Llewellyn quietly. "It is not fair to you, who labored so hard all through the night on our behalf, but there it is. We will try to help balance it, somewhat, by ensuring you need not stand a shift tonight."

Llew stood and stretched. "I dare say I will survive. Do not worry overmuch about a little missed sleep." It was a good act;

Llew's eyelids felt so heavy he was not certain how he was able to keep them open. Resisting the temptation to lie down in the grass at his feet and close them was almost more than he could stand. He sighed inwardly, wondering if, perhaps, it would get better at some point, like catching a second wind.

"Hold a moment, I would speak with Cymri before we start." The limits on how far she could travel from him ensured she would not be gone long. Sure enough, after a few moments she returned from wherever she had been and landed on his right shoulder. A moment later, Cilgwri alit on the left.

Llew took hold of the medallion and said, "And good morning, Cymri. You will be happy to know we have secured your nice new harp. Her response was a particularly loud caw, followed by a squawk.

"Uh oh, Cymri, do we have a problem?" he asked.

When no answer was immediately forthcoming, and worried that her mind might have reverted to that of a bird, Llew cautiously asked another question, "Cymri? Caw twice and hold up a claw if you can still understand me, please."

Cymri cocked her head and just looked at him. Llew felt a sinking feeling in the pit of his stomach. Then she cawed twice, lifted a claw, waved it at him, and put it back down.

"Thank goodness," he exclaimed, "she is still in there!"

The rest of the party was looking at him oddly.

"No, this is a good thing. Despite the medallion no longer letting me understand her, at least we know that her mind is still in there and she can still understand us. I was afraid that her transformation might be like High King Math's and her mind had spent too long trapped in a bird."

"Ah," said Helgar, "you thought perhaps your enchanted bird's brain had become just a normal bird brain."

Llewellyn casually extended her arm sideways and placed it on Helgar's shoulder. Then she pushed him off the log. It was no mean feat, given his size and bulk, but she was not a small woman herself and every bit as tall as Llew.

"What did I say this time?" asked Helgar plaintively, as he picked himself up off the grass.

Although Llew wondered what Helgar meant by 'this time' he pressed on. "Let me amend my words. This is not a good thing but it is better than I feared. At least we are on the way to Caerleon where this entire curse might be broken."

A thought occurred to him. Handing Cymri to Llewellyn, he tapped Hafgan on the shoulder and led him off away from the others for a short distance. "Hafgan, is this something to do with using her in the gauntlet, the part where she sat in the crystal and appeared to speak with me?"

"Should not be," answered the Spriggan, then rubbed his chin thoughtfully. "Well, it should not be if Moriganna crafted her spell properly and refrained from using any non-standard cantrips—by which I mean shortcuts. Of course, this is Moriganna we are talking about. She can be pretty lazy sometimes. For example, you know your friend there is not really even a black bird, right? Never has been."

"What do you mean she is not? How is that possible?"

"Just that she is not. She thinks she is, and the rest of you mortals do, too, but that is as far as it goes."

"No, that is not possible. How then would she fly?" Llew objected.

"It is a strong spell. It has her completely convinced."

"But—but, she eats like a bird; she sits on my shoulder."

"The power of belief is a strong thing, lad. All the same, when my sight works at all it does not mislead me."

"Wait a minute," Llew said feeling his way to firmer ground. "Regardless of whether her form is an illusion, you said you see people as they see themselves, yet you infer you see her as a human? Why would you not see her as a bird as well?"

"Because underneath all that enchantment stuff she still knows that she is really a young pale-skinned lass with lots of freckles and red hair—although I wager she would be really unhappy to know how wild and full of twigs it is now."

"So, then what? Does she still have that harp—twin to the one I took with me? Is she still wearing that fancy dress she was wearing when I saw her in the crystal? "

"Nay, lad, she was never actually in the crystal. It is a bit complicated but, although she controlled it, there was never anything in the crystal save an illusion of our own."

Llew's mind was spinning like a wheel on an overturned cart. "How has she not frozen to death during the winters? She had no winter clothing when she was transformed and she has been a bird for years. She is still wearing that traveling bard outfit?"

"Ha," exclaimed Hafgan, "still trying to trip me up with trick questions are you? That was also two questions but I can answer them both with one question of my own. Since when do birds wear clothes?"

He turned and sauntered back to the group then, but Llew's hearing was too good not to hear what he muttered to himself as he went. "Yes, indeedy, a lot of freckles."

Llew's eyes kept flicking from Hafgan to Cymri and back again as he gasped like a fish for a few moments. Then he narrowed his eyes, closed his mouth, and returned to Llewellyn.

"What was that about?" she asked him.

"Absolutely nothing," Llew replied in a steely voice. Then

he abruptly laughed. "Heh, 'How then would she fly' indeed," he said, mimicking himself. "Hafgan knows precisely how to get my attention and string me along.

"Beware, dear sister, our new guide has a wicked sense of humor and no shame at all in flicking our reins." He glanced over at Addfwyn and Hafgan and saw they were ready. "Very well then, let us press on."

It occurred to Llew to query Hafgan on how well he actually knew the terrain beyond Cas-Eiddew. It sounded like it might have been centuries since the Spriggan had traveled anywhere.

"Lad, tis in my immortal blood," Hafgan responded when Llew asked. "I was here when these hills and valleys were made. Until they are gone, no matter what comes, I shall know them." He turned and took a step to the south, then abruptly stopped and put his hands on his hips. "Hmm," he mused, "Perhaps my mind is going but I truly thought there used to be a knoll there, and a road leading past it."

He looked up at the unhappy faces of Llew and Llewellyn and laughed. "Young people today have no sense of humor. There never was a knoll and, as for the road, it is of no account. Do you think I need a road? I knew this land before there were any roads. It may have gotten a bit larger and a bit distorted but that is of no account to one such as me."

So saying he started down the hill away from Cas-Eiddew.

* * *

They traveled thus for three days. By early afternoon on the third day they were passing the remains of what had been cultivated fields, neatly lined with low stone walls and each one dotted with a small crofter's home. Llew judged, by the general state of disorder in the fields and random destruction and decay of the homes, that it had been a decade or more since men had dwelt here and made this land their own.

Helgar, with his long legs, had ranged out in front of them by several hundred paces. Addfwyn, still leading the pack pony, was trailing them by several dozen paces.

"What has happened here?" Llew wondered aloud.

It was Llewellyn that answered. "The same thing that happened in many other places. The kingdoms are in a bad way. Since the time of High King Pwyl and the fall of the great kingdom the situation grows steadily more dismal. They do not prosper; that which does not grow and renew itself can only decline. It is a decline that a prophecy says will only be ended when Pwyl's heir is crowned high king."

"King's Pwyl's only heir was murdered as an infant a century or more past, was he not?" objected Llew. "We knew that prophecy where I grew up, but no one believed it. We just used it as a fancy way to say 'never.' King Pwyl died without heirs over a century ago. Indeed, it was the murder of his only son that caused him to go mad."

"That is correct but it does not matter," replied Llewellyn. "Even if the child that was murdered had a twin brother, with an unbroken line of sons to this very day, no heir of his would ever be allowed to attend his own coronation, or likely even be suffered to live for that matter. Not after King Pwyl's atrocities. The phrase 'When Pwyl's heir is crowned high king' or 'When Pwyl's heir sits upon the Serpentine Throne' is just a quaint way of saying 'never' because the very idea of such is intolerable and will be throughout all time."

"We have wandered off the subject," Llew said. "I

understand the decline of the Tetheran kingdoms but I was looking for a more specific reason for what happened to the people here. It does not appear the land has had a drought, or that the soil has become barren. The Picts do not normally raid this far to the south. Was there a plague?"

"Aye, but it was not one involving disease. This was a human plague. As the reach of the kingdoms becomes less there are always petty men willing to try to use that to their advantage. Whether they be petty nobles, or simple bandit leaders trying to make themselves into warlords, the end result is the same. They war upon each other and it is what they seek to control that is destroyed in the process. It is a sad fact that most of what they seek to control wears a human face."

"Are we at risk from these bandits now?" asked Llew as be began scanning the terrain more closely.

"Not here," said Llewellyn. "The destruction is too complete. Those types do not care about farming or any other sort of honest work. With nothing left to steal, and so maintain themselves, they have moved on to greener pastures."

She looked sharply at Hafgan. "Unless others already move to reclaim this area?"

He regarded her archly, lifting one bushy eyebrow before replying, "I think not, your highness. The taint of mortals is still too strong here. Let their iron scraps rust away to nothingness for a century. Also let whatever unpleasant rituals they performed upon the fields and homes fade and flicker out. At that point, some of the Fae might consider taking up residence. It will not be the pretty fairies, or the elegant forest kings, nor any of the high ones such as the Tylwyth Teg, the blessed folk, or the Children of Don. They will not care for the taint. It will still be too strong, even faded as it will be.

"No, more likely it will be the Firbolg, or Kobolds. Perhaps even some of those nasty things that followed the Northmen down. Helgar's people used to call them Formorians."

"Do you mean the Fomorii?" Llewellyn inquired.

"Nay, lass, had I meant the Fomorii I would have said so. The Fomorii are some rather disagreeable folk that live in the sea. No wonder you folk lost all knowledge of Spriggans when you cannot even recall the differences between the people of the sea and those creatures from the icy north."

"None of them will settle here. It will not happen," said Llew. "This decline is only a reversal of fortune that has gone on far too long already." Although he himself had spoken them, the words surprised him. Where had he gained this conviction that it was time to do something?

"Heh," said Hafgan, "and who will end the decline? You?"

"I will do what I can," replied Llew evenly.

"That time has passed, young one. You cannot turn every stone back to rest as they once did."

"Nay, friend Hafgan. I do agree. The decline will not be ended by going back to what was. It will be lifted by taking us forward, by learning from our mistakes, and rising to new heights as yet unheard of."

It was self-evident; the only way to meet the future was by going forward, not trying to return things to precisely what they had once been. Somewhere inside himself, Llew knew that was an absolute truth, but he could not for the life of him figure out why he knew it. Somehow, that part of his mind that was always listening, while never speaking to him directly, must have been working constantly. He *knew* the answer could not involve simply turning back the clock. That would never happen.

He turned to Llewellyn and caught a glimpse of her

looking at him with an unrecognizable expression, possibly wonder? Her mouth was half open, apparently in shock or surprise. She noticed him looking at her, snapped her mouth shut, and recomposed her face.

"Llewellyn?" he asked in surprise. "What is it?"

"Well it is bravely said, dear brother. I both like and mislike the sound of it. Between ending the schemes of Moriganna and Arawen to seek power over all mankind, driving the Picts and Northmen back to where they came from, and dealing with whatever Dylan's black heart devises, you must still win the allegiance of four more kingdoms."

"Me?" asked Llew. "Why me?"

"Llew, have you never wondered why both Moriganna and Arawen have centered their plots on our own kingdom of Gwent? It is because it is the greatest and most powerful of the five. If the Great Kingdom is to be rebuilt, Gwent is the foundation on which it must stand. If Gwent falls then so, in time, must the others fall as well. And you are going to be king of Gwent."

That, reflected Llew, was something he was having a difficult time making himself accept. There just had not been any time to think about it since Llewellyn had told him about it sometime in the night before.

"Consider the Picts then," he said. "I do not care for them in the least, but driving them into Annwyn is a poor solution. We will find another. And, as for the Northmen? Having met Helgar I know I must find another way there as well, rather than simply driving them back into the sea.

"But what of our father?" he asked. "What is he doing to rebuild? I doubt it is coincidence that Arawen and Moriganna both are moving against him now."

Llewellyn took a moment to compose her answer. "Well,

part of that is probably driven by Arawen being forced to counter Moriganna. That is, by the way, almost certainly the only reason neither of them has enslaved all of the kingdoms in the past few centuries. I think each is far too busy countering the other to devote more than a fraction of their attention to the final goal.

"To more directly address your question, give some consideration as to why I was forced to spend my entire life disguised as my own brother."

Llew started to speak, then hesitated when he realized he was too tired to give this reasoning its due. "Something to do with keeping the nobility from getting restless because they are without a male heir?" he guessed.

"Nay, Llew, it is because the heir of Gwent was contracted at birth to marry Princess Bloddeuwedd, heir to the throne of Gwynedd. These two kingdoms united was, or is, my—our—father's next step in his plan to reforge the great kingdom."

"He was just going to marry you off to whomever? For reasons purely political?" Lew exclaimed.

"No, Llew, he was just going to marry you off. There are reasons why he would not marry me off to Princess Bloddeuwedd."

Llew granted her that point and managed not to blush.

She shrugged, "Why not an arranged marriage? We are born rich and powerful, but we pay a price for that in responsibilities. Responsibilities place constraints on our lives but to deny these constraints would be to deny our responsibilities. That is selfish and when selfishness causes great suffering, it is also evil.

"Our father paid this price himself, willingly, and would not expect less from us. Our mother was heir to Glywysing and in their marriage the two lands were healed to once again become greater Gwent. This was another reason why it could not be let known that the expected heir from that union was gone."

It came to Llew in an instant and he exclaimed, "This is why Moriganna started moving when we were born. Rebuild the great kingdom and her plans become much more difficult." After a moment's more consideration, he added, "I am certain it took a fair amount of effort for her, or Arawen, to tear it down in the first place, neither would be pleased for that work to be undone."

Llewellyn smiled with approval and said, "Very good, Llew. You will be a most perspicacious king indeed!"

Llew smiled back.

"And a fine husband for Princess Bloddeuwedd," she added mischievously.

Llew, in his fatigue, continued to smile for a moment longer before the impact of what she had said hit him. "Umm, what? Wait a moment—"

He did not get to finish as, from up ahead, Helgar had turned from where the road crested a slight rise and was running back to them. From what he knew of Helgar's shy and retiring nature or, rather, the lack thereof, Llew was inclined to interpret this behavior as somewhat ominous.

He put his hand to his medallion almost reflexively although there was no reason to do so. Cymri could hear him just fine. "Cymri, quickly, what has him so alarmed?"

She had been perched on his shoulder for several hours but now she launched herself quickly in the direction Helgar was coming from.

Llew and Llewellyn put on their helmets and checked their weapons. Hafgan had a fair-sized hammer for a creature his size that he had attached to his belt, the hammer's head snugged against the belt itself in a kind of sheath with the handle projecting down through it. He now loosened the bindings and checked to make sure it could be easily removed.

Cymri was up high now and over the road as Helgar reached them.

"Easy, Helgar, what is it that it is so urgent?" Llew asked.

"Many men, my drott, perhaps even too many for us. Some of them were guarding a bridge in the valley ahead but others were there on horses. Perhaps patrolling they were, but saw me they did, and now coming they are."

"They are on horseback? All of them?"

"All of the ones that are coming. They bear shields showing a black anvil on a gray field," Helgar hesitated a moment before adding, "Llew."

"We will not outrun them on one horse," Lew decided. "It is possible we might not want to."

He looked up again towards Cymri and was relieved to see her winging her way back to them. "Iolo, Iolo," she cawed loudly.

Not sure what that meant, he suggested, "Let us all gather here and be ready for whatever comes."

After a few moments he thought to glance behind them to Addfwyn and the pack pony and saw only the pony was there. Of Addfwyn there was no sign. Llew sighed inwardly. Well, the man had been a simple crofter, after all. It did not surprise him that the possibility of being on the receiving end of a cavalry charge on an open road was a bit too much for the fellow.

Cymri landed on his right shoulder. He re-clasped the medallion and, once again, was reminded she could no longer speak to him. Then she again cawed, "Iolo, Iolo."

Llewellyn regarded her intently. "Cymri? Do you mean to say there are men out there bearing King Iolo's heraldry?"

Cymri pumped her head up and down affirmatively and

once again cawed out, "Iolo!"

Llewellyn placed one hand on Llew's left shoulder and announced, "Not to worry, dear brother. Whoever is coming, they wear the colors of King Iolo's men. His fealty is pledged to King Pendaran. This is excellent news. With plenty of men and fresh horses we will be in Caerleon within a matter of days!"

Llew turned to Hafgan. "Your help was most welcome, friend Spriggan, if not so easily won. Will you be leaving us now?"

Hafgan stroked his beard with one hand and seemed to contemplate the question. "Nay, your highness," he replied, "I will stay on if you will so permit. For a time, at least. I wish to remain a bit and witness how this plays out, and perhaps I will see how you mortals handle this hospitality you seem to expect."

A dozen riders, armed and armored, crested the hill and closed the distance between them at a gallop.

Chapter XXIV

Gwri's Tale: A Queen's Gift

Morning came like any other. Gwri had dozed a bit before dawn, but it had been nothing like a full night's rest. It sounded very much as though the castle had returned to what passed for normal. The guardsmen were guarding once again. The servants were servanting again. He was exhausted from the lack of sleep the night before, and most others seemed a bit under the weather as well. Arms and riding training, usually a cathartic release for him, was just a hazy blur that morning. After that, he was sent to bathe and dress for lunch with the queen.

Entering the great hall it was immediately apparent to the discerning eye that all was not normal. Although much reduced from the middle of the night, Moriganna still had some small white streaks amongst her dark red tresses. Likewise she had some bruising on one side of her face that might have been caused by something like a bird's beak striking her but failing to break the skin.

Of Cymri there was no sign.

He halted, feigning confusion. "Will not Cymri be joining us at table, mother?" As soon as it left his lips, he kicked himself for adding mother to the end of his question. Sarcasm did not work if the one who heard it did not understand it to be sarcasm and, if she did, she would only pay him back in some manner he would not appreciate.

Wonder of wonders, this morning she overlooked it. "I had a somewhat vexing night, did you hear none of it?"

"Nay," Gwri replied, "I slept like a stone."

"Hmm," she smiled slightly, "you and many others. Harp music can have that effect on people it seems. It was, however, a very rewarding night. You may have noticed a large oak tree in the courtyard this morning?"

"In truth, I did, but I thought it might not be polite to speak of it. Certainly no one else was doing so."

"No, I would rather imagine they would not. I value discretion in speech and they know it. Still," she continued, "as to Cymri, she apparently tried to fly the coop in the night with the oak tree's assistance. Which is what makes her fate so amusing."

She rang a small chime and two servants brought in a large birdcage and sat it at Cymri's place at the table. Within the cage was a sad looking black bird. Gwri had never realized a bird could look sad.

The bird croaked something and Moriganna said, "No, my dear, you do have to do it. It will be a cold winter and you do want my woodsmen to seek their firewood a bit further from the castle than might otherwise be their first inclination."

The bird croaked again.

Moriganna glanced at her, then up at Gwri. "Oh my, how rude we have been. Here we are having a conversation and you can hear only one side of it. Let us fix that at once. There is a medallion by your wine goblet. Put it on."

Gwri looked askance at the device, but he did not move to

touch it.

"Oh, do not be silly. You are my son; I would not seek to control you with such a thing. Unlike Cymri, you will find it quite as easy to remove as it was to put it on. You do need to wear it, however, to continue your lessons. Further, Cymri needs you to wear it to keep her alive. You would not do that for her? That would seem rather rude and even thoughtless."

Was she telling the truth? It scarcely mattered; he would have to put it on, regardless of what the truth was. He picked it up as if it were dripping with venom, then carefully settled it over his neck.

"See there? Was that so difficult? Now touch it with one hand and hold your hand there."

As Gwri slowly complied, Moriganna again turned her head and spoke to the bird. "Now you can tell him yourself why it is so important he do this."

"It is the only way you can understand me now," said the bird, in Cymri's voice.

Gwri jumped to his feet in surprise, knocking over his wine in the process.

"No, no, Gwri. We have discussed this before. A ruler is never surprised, even in the face of the unexpected," chided Moriganna. "Your thoughts, dear Cymri?"

"It is not that you never want to show emotion," said the bird. "It is that you do not want to show emotion until you are ready to show emotion. When the unexpected happens you must be able to maintain a calm exterior and inspire confidence. Sometimes, however, you may elect to show outrage or anger but you should not be furious when you do. It is far too easy to make mistakes, or say ill-considered things, that can be inconvenient.

"Unfeigned surprise, however, is something you just

generally do not want to show at all, ever. When you do show it then do it on your own terms; make it appear as though it is feigned, as you might, for example, if a small child gave you a gift."

"Why Cymri," Moriganna exclaimed, "I think that is excellent advice. Not that I always follow it, of course. I am definitely the type who will tell her followers to do as I say, not as I do."

"I think that may be an understatement, Queen Moriganna."

Moriganna laughed dryly, "Ah, the art of the delicate insult. Yes, every ruler should learn that. I can see Gwri's education for the throne is still in good hands, ah, I mean wings. You two probably have much to talk about, and I find that after the night's exertions I am not terribly hungry. I will excuse myself to take some rest and leave the two of you to talk.

"First, however, I will tell you both that since I need no longer worry about Cymri taking any unexpected journeys, she may now have complete freedom to fly outside whenever she wishes. It is necessary for her health, and I am never needlessly cruel.

"Second, Cymri no longer needs much in the way of accommodations. Just a perch will do. Consequently, I want you to move into her rooms, Gwri. She can remain there, of course, but"—Gwri thought he detected a muted smirk—"I want you both to understand I want no improprieties while you are sharing rooms."

So saying, Moriganna swept from the room.

"Cymri," Gwri began, "I am so sorry—"

"Never mind that, Gwri; it is not your fault. My father appeared during the night and attempted to rescue me. He nearly succeeded but now he is an oak tree in the courtyard. He would have succeeded had it not been for that wretched amulet being close at hand. With my blood in it she was able to use it as the focus for a spell my father would normally not have been vulnerable to."

"An oak tree?" Gwri exclaimed. "Can he be changed back? For that matter, can you?"

"Moriganna says she can revert us both, but that she will not do so unless I continue your education and, even then, will not do so until it is too late for us to betray her plans."

"That could be years!" Gwri interjected.

"Yes, Gwri, I am fairly sure it will be. But some day," she added, furiously flapping her wings as she spoke, "we will set things straight and there will be a reckoning."

Chapter XXV

The Anvil

At Llewellyn's insistence, Llew was astride Gower and in front of the party. "They will expect to see our leader mounted and at the forefront, and who else would this be but the Prince of Gwent?" she had asked rhetorically. "Just do not allow them to put you in a subservient position. Neither age, nor experience, nor even who has the most men, has anything to do with that.

"Keep in mind that you are not representing yourself but something much greater, and everything you do will reflect not merely on you, but on your kingdom and your father, the king. These warriors that are coming serve their lesser king, but you—as the heir—*you* are the Kingdom of Gwent. If you assert your role as if it is nothing more than the way the world is meant to be, why then, they will fall into their proper roles without questioning it."

It was only that this advice followed so closely what Afaggdu had tried to teach him that allowed it to penetrate Llew's nervousness in such a way that he could understand it."

The warriors came to a halt, spread out in a not quite semi-circular one-deep line that spanned the road and was several times wider. Perhaps he looked more daunting than he felt? The leader advanced a horse length ahead of the others and, apparently not feeling himself in immediate danger, removed his helmet.

He had a harsh face and it was clear he did not like what he was seeing. Llew sighed inwardly; he did not like what he was seeing, either. He was pretty sure he recognized the type. Cai had once had several such men in his service. They were petty bullies who were overly impressed with their own authority. Llew theorized that, while men like them sought such positions, they had neither the charm nor the kind of skills needed to win further promotion.

"It is difficult," the leader began, "to credit what I am seeing: a dwarf, a Northman, a girl in armor, and whatever it is you are supposed to be. Could you be a lost troupe of entertainers, perhaps? Although I do not believe I could credit any of you as being a bard."

Cymri flapped her wings and cawed loudly at that. This, in turn, caused Cilgwri to do the same.

"Oh, and you are starting a menagerie as well, I see. Still, you really should have included a bard. I suppose it is not surprising that you did not. They have reputations to maintain, after all."

"There is a harp on their pack animal," observed one of the warriors closest to it.

The lead horseman grimaced, "Unless you intend to play it yourself, Rhodri, you had best keep that mouth shut. I would not care if you were the king's own mother rather than a motherless second cousin. When I desire your observations I will tell you."

The warrior made a mock cringing motion but said nothing.

"That goes for all of you," growled the leader, speaking to

his men. "If I want your opinions I will ask for them."

Then, addressed to Llew, "I am Lunid ap Rhein. Just who are you to dare travel across Einionault without the express permission of King Iolo?"

"We had planned on asking when we got there, actually," replied Llew. "Although, we do appreciate you and your men coming out to escort us in."

The patrol commander's face colored as he waved furiously at the abandoned farmlands around them. "You have been in Einionault for hours!"

Llew looked around at the feral lands surrounding them. "Really?" he asked, somewhat dubiously. "I am not certain it really counts if all the people leave and even the king's men have pulled back to a new border."

Lunid ap Rhein appeared to be a very quick tempered man. Llew imagined he could see the man's face go almost directly from being slightly florid to puce purple while barely flickering through a bright red on the way.

At this point, Llew realized he had better cut this off before the man had a seizure and went into convulsions or, worse, ordered an attack. "Tell me captain, is King Iolo still sworn to King Pendaran of Gwent?"

The troop commander paused in his budding tirade as if turned to stone, and then cautiously replied, "Aye, he is—"

"Very good," said Llew, cutting off the captain and removing his helmet as he did so. "I am Prince Llew of Gwent. It is a matter of some urgency that I meet with King Iolo immediately."

Lunid ap Rhein was clearly at a loss for words. His mouth hung open in a strange way and Llew realized he was seeing what people were referring to when they said someone's jaw had dropped.

"What do you think?" hissed one of the mounted warriors to the man next to him. "Is he really who he says?"

"Well," remarked the one he had spoken to, "he is wearing some pretty nice armor and just look at that warhorse! I have never seen its match. It is probably worth more than all of Einionault just by itself."

"Stolen?" suggested the first.

"Not a chance," came the reply. "A trained warhorse—and you can tell it is trained—would stomp almost any thief to pudding if he so much as tried to touch it without its master's permission, and there is no question he is its master. They are so perfectly bonded they might as well be a centaur."

The one the leader had called Rhodri shushed them both, whispering, "Be quiet, the both of you. I was on the guard detail when King Iolo traveled to Caerleon a couple of years back. The captain went, too, and both of us saw the prince. He may have grown quite a few inches, but put some meat on the boy we saw and this young fellow sure looks like him. Further, look at the way he handles himself; he was born to command. No common thief or bandit can fake that! You want some advice? If there is even a chance he is who he says then you do not want to be the one to do him ill, despite whatever orders you are given."

Even after being ordered to be silent, these men certainly like to talk a lot, thought Llew. *It is fortunate for them that their captain does not share my own gift for hearing.*

Lunid still had not spoken and Llew was beginning to worry that the man's mental balance might have taken too strong a hit. Resolving to take charge, Llew started to ask that he and his friends be taken to this King Iolo but realized at once that was not the way to do it. The captain was off balance now but would recover and might then start trying to think of petty ways to delay them. Give a man like him an inch and he would claim a furlong, especially if he was given a chance to think on the strangeness of a prince riding in, unannounced, with scarcely any escort whatsoever. Being purposely difficult would bolster a small minded man's image of himself and make him feel important. Llew really did not care how the man thought about himself; he also did not want it to slow them down.

He decided to try to emulate Moriganna when she was in one of her less malevolent moments. It was an attitude where she was not so much distant as she was seemingly unaware of those she commanded, other than as extensions of her will. She behaved as if no resistance was expected, or even imaginable, and somehow that tended to make those receiving her orders feel the same way.

Except for himself, Llew corrected, and smiled inwardly. He must have been a constant irritant of the first order to such as her. It was a miracle he had survived long enough for her to put some distance between the two of them with tutors.

In a quieter, emotionless version of the command voice Afaggdu had taught him, Llew said, "You and your men will escort me to King Iolo at once. Oh, yes, and we will need more horses for my companions."

Lunid ap Rhein made a strangled noise that might have indicated compliance. It was hard to be sure.

* * *

It was after dark when they rode up to Caer Enion. As the name implied, it was a dark, almost black, pile of joyless stone set in vertical defiance of the low hill on which it sat. A single torch was lit beside the gate, and another was atop the ramparts. From inside came the light of a few more, through various arrow slits.

"So very dark it is here, darker than the inside of the Trickster's heart. These should be rich lands. Why are they so miserly with simple torches?" Helgar asked, almost plaintively.

"We should call it frugal, Helgar. They are merely being frugal. It is a clear night. When the moon comes up they will have plenty of light, and it will be quite nice out here," Llew answered.

Hafgan chuckled. "Moreso than at Cas-Eiddew, at any rate, Northman. Count your blessings."

"Yar," said Helgar. "I hope they are not frugal at their table as well. I do not dislike the way your people cook food, my Llew."

"I would wager King Iolo has never hosted a jarl at his table before," Llew commented.

"Then glad am I to offer him this opportunity," Helgar said.

Llewellyn held up a hand. "Bide a moment. I have had a thought. If a jarl is the equivalent of a cantref king, is he sworn to a gwlad or possibly a high king?"

Llew felt as though his stomach was trying to do something unsettling. That Helgar's people might already be sworn to another's service had never occurred to him! "Is there a Northman high king?" he gingerly asked Helgar. The answer could be most unwelcome.

"Well of course there is a Northman high king!" exclaimed Helgar and Llew felt like his stomach was redoubling its efforts at something. Perhaps it was attempting a cartwheel. If it turned out his stomach was an acrobat it might be quite at home in this troupe of entertainers that Lunid ap Rhein had accused them of being.

"Indeed, there are several," Helgar continued. "Although we do not say high king; we say kuningaz. That is part of the reason we Northmen have come and stayed here to live, Llew. There are several of them and agree on which of them is the true high kuningaz is something they have not done. Until they do, it is quite dangerous to be a jarl in the old lands. You are very likely to pledge yourself to one who might later turn out not to be the true kuningaz."

Helgar grabbed his cloak where it encircled his neck and yanked upwards on it while letting his head loll to the other side. It was fairly clear he was pantomiming a hanging.

Llew struggled to take it all in but Llewellyn got it first. "So you would be perfectly in your right to swear Lindenjal's allegiance to a Tetheran high king?"

"Yar, that could be done, once I settle that small dispute with my uncle. No one would dare question my right to do so then." A strange look crossed Helgar's face and Llew somehow knew the Northman had just had an idea. Llew had to mentally slap himself to keep from commenting on how strange 'having an idea' looked on Helgar's face.

Llew knew Helgar was not stupid. It was just that Tetherans tended to think of Northmen that way. It was probably, at least in part, because their use of a language so different from their own often left them sounding rather cloddish.

"What is it, Helgar?" he asked instead.

Helgar's eyes gleamed. "This is a very good idea, Llew. I will settle my difficulties with my uncle. Then I will swear to you, although, as you are my drott, I have already done so. Once Lindenjal has, other jarls in the south will want to as well I think. It will solve many worries we all have about all those pretenders in the old lands. Then, with the power of the Northmen at your back, added to your own forces, we will make you high king!

"Moriganna and Arawen and those rotted Picts and sea

devils and all the rest—they may fight—but we will triumph and it will be glorious!"

"If you can set aside the prophecy it could work, or be the core of something that could work," said Llewellyn thoughtfully.

"Prophecy?" asked Hafgan. "What are you mortals going on about now?"

"The Great Kingdom cannot be restored until High King Pwyl's heir takes up his crown," Llew and Llewellyn recited simultaneously.

"Hmm," said Hafgan, "had not heard that one but I do not get out as much as I probably should. All the same, I think the big lad has solved another problem for you. It is a good thing you said what you did about moving forward and not trying to return things to what they once were."

"What are you referring to?" asked Llew.

Hafgan smiled and said, "Why, what to do about all those Northmen. If there are that many of them already settled in Tethera then you might never be able to get rid of them all at this point. Might as well put them to work and collect some taxes."

He laughed at their surprised faces. "Now what say we get on with it and check on this fellow's hospitality? Personally, I could eat a dragon, were there any left." With that, they rode up the hill and through the open gates into King Iolo's fortress.

Chapter XXVI

Gwri's Tale: The Coming of Afaggdu

Several seasons passed and spring came again. A morning arrived when Mercher did not appear for arms training.

This was outside Gwri's experience. While he considered whether he should go check on the man, a harsh voice called from the shadowed doorway of the training armory, an especially thick-walled stone building, low and massive, set between the wall and the training yard. "Mercher has some things to take care of, I will be his substitute for a bit. Care to start with a bit of a practice bout? I would like to see where you are in terms of your training."

"That would be fine," said Gwri evenly. "Do you know which practice sword I prefer or shall I come in and get it?"

"Sword?" the voice said. "Who said anything about swords?" And then a figure rushed at him from the doorway. The man was huge, a bit taller than Gwri but built like a barrel. Instinctively, Gwri ducked and rolled to the right in the nick of time to avoid the initial rush. The new trainer had too much inertia to stop immediately but went several paces past and then turned to Gwri with what might have been a grin.

At that point Gwri saw the other's face and realized he was

not fighting a man but, instead, some sort of ogre. He cried out in surprise and fled into the armory where he slammed the door and threw the bar.

Outside he could hear the hoarse voice bellowing in laughter.

Gwri thought furiously. He had only had a glimpse of the other's face. Had it truly been a monster? Perhaps not, but it was not just the face, the entire head had been monstrous.

"Oh, do not be ashamed, lad," called the voice. "I am Afaggdu and my face has had that effect on many, even some of the greatest and fiercest of blooded warriors."

"What are you doing here?" Gwri called back.

"Why laddie, I told you. I am here to train you. For a ridiculously large amount of coin, your queen has engaged my services to take your arms training to the next level, as it were. I will not harm you—well, I will not maim or kill you, at least not on purpose. What more can you ask of a man training you to survive and triumph in a cruel hard world? Now come on out and take a good look at my ugly helmet of a head. You will get quite used to its sight before we are done. If it gives you nightmares in the meantime, you have my apology, but no sympathy. I have had to live with it all of my life."

Steeling himself, yet feeling a bit foolish, Gwri unbarred the door and came out to the small practice yard. The one who had named himself Afaggdu was leaning against a target post. He waited patiently while Gwri took a good look at him.

Afaggdu had a wide forehead and a single immense eyebrow stretching across both black-grey eyes. The eyes themselves were not quite level with each other. His nose was not especially long but was enormously thick. His lips, below his huge mustache, were both wide and long. He also had a remarkably broad chin, and this largeness continued throughout the jawbone. His face was not at all proportioned like a normal man's. It vaguely resembled that of a large cat, perhaps a lion if they appeared in real life as they did in heraldry. Thick-necked and broad-shouldered, Afaggdu also looked hard and fierce.

Long, thick, wolf-gray hair fringed his pate but, other than that, he was mostly bald. This only made the travesty that was his head more visible. That head itself was enormous, far larger than any normal man's. It was also lumpy and misshapen, even appearing to be corrugated, as though it had permanent waves embedded in the bone of the skull beneath the skin. Likewise, there were some terrible scars upon that head, apparently from a variety of injuries. Many of them were indicative of wounds that Gwri could scarcely credit had been survivable.

Afaggdu waited throughout his long stare, then raised the right side of his eyebrow improbably high. "It is the head is it not? Yet it has been a blessing. When old Scurlock caught me upside of my skull with his mace, my brains, such as they are, did not go flying hither and yon. I did not even fall. He was so surprised that it gave me time for a two-handed swing that cleaved him in twain. My eyes were crossed for two days and the headaches lasted two weeks, but I am here and he is not. I had a similar encounter with a Northman once, although he was using an axe."

"Wait," interjected Gwri, "Moriganna hired you to train me, you said? Where did she even find you?"

Afaggdu frowned in concentration. "Hmm, it was four or five years back we began speaking. She saw me with another student and knew she wanted me, but I was not available. Still, she sent an agent every few months after that, sometimes even coming herself, and kept upping her offer until I could no longer say nay."

"She came to you?" Gwri asked. "May I ask where?"

"Why at Caerleon, of course, I have been arms instructor there these past five years to a fellow who, it just happens, bears a face identical to your own."

"You were in the Kingdom of Gwent? You were Prince Llew's trainer?"

"Indeed, lad, I was one of them. A very talented study he was, too. It falls on me to bring you up to the same level. I expect that means we have some work to do."

"A moment more, please?" Gwri asked. "I understand Gwent is more than half a moon's travel to the south?"

Afaggdu lowered the right side of his eyebrow while lifting the left outrageously. "Oh, it is at least two weeks, possibly more."

Gwri shook his head. "I see her daily and, in all the years since that began, she has never been away from Caer Mallcoedwig for more than a few hours."

Afaggdu shrugged, "I cannot explain it and I do not have to. She is an enchantress. That is all the explanation we are likely to get, and it is more than sufficient to explain any number of strange things. Surely, this is not the first odd thing you have seen?"

"Oh yes," Gwri remarked sourly, "we have strange things happen all the time. See that huge oak tree over there by the great hall? That was a bard named Taliesin that came to visit one night; a few minutes later he was a tree, His daughter was a red-headed bard and is now a bird that teaches me in courtly ways, heraldry, and the old tales, every afternoon. For that matter, my horse used to be my dog."

"My," said Afaggdu, after a long pause, "that . . . does sound strange. It seems all the more reason for not getting too inquisitive about what the queen does in her spare time. If it is a concern of yours, my advice is to wait and watch. For the moment, however, you need more training and I need to get paid . . . so let us focus on that instead."

The days, weeks, and months that followed were not easy ones but they were instructive ones.

Afaggdu was deadly with a sword and any other weapon imaginable. He insisted that Gwri be at least competent with all of them. "You never know what you will be forced to use when you are not fighting in a nice tidy practice ring," he often said. Likewise, he would seize upon things that were not weapons at all. They could be ropes, farm implements, tools, even a saddle, and drill in on how they could be used in a pinch.

And then there was barehanded fighting.

This was entirely new territory for Gwri, as the only thing he had experienced previously that compared with it was back in the days when the village boys used to pick fights with him. Nowadays, when he passed, they just lowered their eyes and tugged their forelocks, as they would have for Moriganna herself. Gwri was not entirely comfortable with that, but it was better than being the target of their pranks and attacks.

Afaggdu put an enormous amount of their training time into fighting with no weapons at all. This involved a lot of punching and kicking, rolling and feinting, and even wrestling. These were not areas where Gwri seemed able to even begin to approach Afaggdu's level of capability, but Afaggdu seemed satisfied with his progress, once he began to accept there was no alternative but to fully apply himself.

"You are quite strong for your age, lad, and you will get better over time. Moreover, many otherwise mighty warriors will just stand there waiting for a death stroke if disarmed, or their weapon breaks. Their training tends to support the belief that they are helpless against an armed man unless they are also holding a weapon."

Gwri shuddered. Perhaps because of his training with Afaggdu, he doubted he could ever, under any circumstances, accept his own death without whatever resistance he could still manage.

"Remember this above all else, young prince. I have told you this before and I will tell you again. Your job is to stay alive regardless of what happens and, either keep on fighting or escape. You are never dead until your light goes out for good. Do not have any silly ideas about how retreating from an uneven battle is unmanly or some such tripe. If you find yourself in that situation, just get out and come back when the odds are more to your favor. Now the time may come when you feel the need to fight a holding action, perhaps to buy time for someone else, but even then you are fighting to win. If that is not possible you should have at least some idea for an attempt at escape once you have accomplished your purpose."

"And if that is impossible as well?" asked Gwri.

"Lad, accepting that something is impossible makes it so, whether it already was or not. So the trick is never to accept that something truly is impossible when it is your last chance. Go down fighting and you will dislike yourself less in the next world. Likewise, when a man is fighting to kill you, do not let the fact he has lost his weapon stay your hand, even if he wishes to surrender."

Gwri blanched at that. "Is that not a bit harsh?"

"Nay lad, if he was serious about surrendering then the time to do it was before he got close enough to smack you with his sword. Moreover, if his mates are still trying to kill you or yours, or you think it is likely a ruse, then you have no time to secure him and no obligation to try. When someone tries to surrender once in close combat they can only hope, not expect, that it will save their life."

In line with this way of thinking, Afaggdu had a myriad number of what Gwri would have thought of as dirty tricks. Now Gwri was forced to learn them as well. Whenever he made even the slightest protest about unfair tactics, Afaggdu would give him a pitying look that made him feel quite young and stupid. This was usually followed by some variant on how unlikely it was that he would ever be fighting a foe with anything like his own level of personal integrity.

"Do you think a barrow warrior of Annwyn will fight fairly and honorably? Or do you think that fighting fairly and honorably against a horror risen from its burial mound—and utterly obedient to the will of an overlord whose only goal is the extinction of all life, everywhere—is more important than winning? How about one of Moriganna's shape-shifters I have been hearing about? Or a Pict who would as soon cook you up and eat you as look at you? Lad, if the one you are fighting is ever as fair and honorable as you yourself would seek to be, why, chances are you would not be fighting at all outside of the practice yard, or perhaps a duel."

In all the many ways they fought and practiced, there was one way in which Gwri came to hold his own against the mighty Afaggdu. On horseback, specifically with Gwri mounted on Gower, was when he himself became a mighty force that could give even Afaggdu pause and, occasionally, a defeat.

Gwri had protested initially when Afaggdu decided to continue their training in the evenings, after dinner was over. As it turned out, this was not like his physical training during the mornings. Afaggdu had maps of many battles, some of which had never even actually occurred. Using bags of carved stones and pieces of wood and ivory to represent units and heroes, he would show how various battles had occurred, or might have occurred had things gone differently. Eventually, he and Gwri would take turns moving the units of opposing forces, dicing for the outcome when their pieces attempted to occupy the same ground, or otherwise came in range of each other's weapons.

Gwri loved this best of all and, once he had gained a sufficient understanding of the basics, would sometimes find himself directing the winning forces, although he could never quite be sure if Afaggdu was not letting him win occasionally to bolster his confidence. If he did, Gwri decided, it was very subtle. Afaggdu certainly would never admit to such a thing; it contradicted his stated values.

Gwri grew at a furious rate as another year went by, and then another, and still another. His voice changed and grew deeper and his strength developed until it was second only to Afaggdu's. His growth and his training made him formidable enough that none of the guardsman, not even the best of them, would willingly skirmish with him any longer—certainly not without a direct order.

With his mentor's aid, he and the bowyer created a bow equal to his own height that no one but he and Afaggdu could even draw. If his accuracy left something to be desired, nothing he ever hit would fail to notice his arrow. Gwri was assured that, even at two hundred paces, his war arrows would easily pass through an armored rider and the mount as well.

Gradually, Gwri found himself in a predicament. Despite the fact Afaggdu was clearly a mercenary, willing to sell his services even to the like of such as Moriganna, he was a man that Gwri had come to admire. Their relationship was more than instructor and student and he slowly began to realize that one of the greatest joys in his life was winning the ugly man's approval when he did something well, or mastered a new skill.

Worse, Cymri seemed to have taken a great liking to Afaggdu as well. When Gwri pressed her on it she would only claim that, despite all appearances, he seemed to be a good man who could be trusted to do the right thing.

Gwri found himself hoping desperately that this was true, despite the facts indicating otherwise. After all, he reminded himself, Afaggdu had trained with Prince Llew for years. Those two could very well have shared a similar bond, yet here he was, training Gwri to defeat and depose his former student.

Everything came to a head when Afaggdu and Gwri were summoned to Moriganna one evening.

She was in her solar, a dark room with many tapestries and draped with hangings the color of dried blood. Woven rugs from some far off place covered the floors and various braziers slowly burned, emitting oddly sweet odors as they did. There was no fireplace at all, a strange omission given the fiercely cold winters at Caer Mallcoedwig.

Gwri's first thought upon seeing her was that she looked quite angry. Fortunately, it did not seem to be directed at Afaggdu or himself. Recalling Afaggdu's first advice concerning dealing with her, Gwri did not inquire but waited to see if clues would be forthcoming.

Scowling, she strode up to him and seized his chin in her left hand, holding his head so he stared directly at her. She raised her right hand and seemed about to hit him but, instead, a bright light appeared, apparently resting on her palm. She continued to gaze directly at him a bit, then roughly turned his head to the left, and then to the right, taking a moment to study each side.

Abruptly she released him and stalked away as the light in her hand faded out. "Arggh," she cried, "we have a problem."

Gwri wondered at the way she used the word 'we.' Apparently the Queen of Deceit was not above deceiving herself that in Gwri she had a co-conspirator.

To Gwri: "The so-called Prince of Gwent is growing up. Unfortunately, as he grows he begins to look less like you and that resemblance is all important for our plans. Right now the difference is minor. Had I not been watching so closely, even I might not have noticed. Still, now that a divergence has begun, it will only get more pronounced over time. Our opportunity is in less than three weeks. That is when we must move out."

"I was to have another three years with the lad," Afaggdu protested, "a total of six you said. So far as my own training is concerned he is but half ready. It might be a bit more—he is a good learner—but he may not have closed the gap with Prince Llew yet. That one is not standing still just because I am no longer there. I need at least another two years before I can assure you that Gwri is ready."

Whirling about, Moriganna fixed her gaze on him. "We have no time for assurances. It is now or never and I will not accept never. Too many other forces are in play for this opportunity to be wasted. Time now weighs heavily and I do not have the luxury of another twenty or thirty years in which to devise another approach."

"I am fairly sure your plan involved waiting until the false prince was on the verge of his majority, three years from now, before making the exchange," said Afaggdu. "What about the training from the bird? Is that also unfinished?"

"I believe it is," she responded. "The best I can do is send you both with him to continue to advise him and train him as opportunity allows. The bird girl cannot be trusted, but only Gwri can hear her, so she cannot betray us. What about yourself?"

"I stay on the job I was hired for," Afaggdu said hotly. "A man has to have standards."

"Very well then, I have contracted with a certain someone to deliver the prince to us on the northern coast in a month's time. That rendezvous is in a particularly rough wilderness and much too far to the east for my comfort. My guardsmen are loyal but they are not prepared for this kind of an expedition. I am bringing in a mercenary company of thirty mounted men who, unlike the normal sell-swords available in this land, will have good reason to die fighting before betraying my trust. Accompanying them will be no less than fourteen or fifteen of my most ferocious shape-shifters.

"You will have minimal supplies, as speed will be your best ally. The mercenaries will have their own captain but, if he and his lieutenant both fall, you will take charge. The shape-shifters will have their own leader and will neither give nor accept orders from any man, but they will know my will in any matter that is likely to arise and, so long as that will is served, they shall not give you any difficulty."

"The commander," interjected Afaggdu, "do you have a name?"

"His name is Cai. Do you know him?"

"I know of him," Afaggdu grumbled. "He is scum. It is a good bet that his mercenaries are as well, for who else would serve under him?"

"Be that as it may," snapped Moriganna, "while he takes our coin, he is our scum. Once you have the prince, give Gwri a day or two to take in his mannerisms and his speech patterns. Then take all of his belongings and equip Gwri with them. You know what to do with the heir himself. Now go, prepare and equip yourselves as you see best. Do what you can with his training in the little time remaining. Gwri, you will take your meals in the barracks hall, at the servants' tables, or in your own rooms, as you please, but I will be much too busy for our daily formalities."

They went. Once they were well away from Moriganna, Afaggdu leaned over and whispered to Gwri, "Well here we go, lad. It is much too early but, since it is upon us, it is time my niece and I had a few words with each other—and with you as well. Let us go and speak together in your quarters."

"Your niece?" Gwri almost blurted it but remembered to keep his voice down just before the words escaped his lips. "Your niece is in Caer Mallcoedwig?"

"Aye, lad, my niece is here. You have even met. Her name is Cymri."

Chapter XXVII

An Unexpected Host

It had, Llew thought, been a rather good evening. Despite his still being so terribly behind on sleep, he had managed to enjoy himself thoroughly. King Iolo's effusive greetings and an impromptu feast had given him a kind of second wind. While Hafgan had declined to sup with them, and stolen off to eat in the kitchen, the rest of them had partied and laughed, told some heavily abridged and edited tales of their journey, and each had been praised for their part in things.

Curiously, Llew had decided at some point not to mention that the dwarf servant traveling with them was the king of the Spriggans. Let Hafgan make his own introductions if he chose not to eat and drink with the rest of them. Meanwhile, the wine and ale had flowed freely and Llew had taken advantage of the opportunity to get a bit more of both than he had ever previously been allowed.

None of which explained why he was waking up in what appeared to be a dungeon, nor why he was chained to the wall.

He quickly looked to his right and regretted it intensely. Whatever he had been drugged with had left him with a terrible headache! Fortunately, it was fairly dim in the cell as even that little bit of light seemed a bit too bright. Easing his eyes open gently, he could see Helgar chained to the wall a short distance away. He appeared to be alive but unconscious.

Carefully looking to the left, he saw Hafgan, similarly in chains. Unlike Helgar, he was wide awake with a bemused look on his face. This seemed so inappropriate that Llew just gaped at him for a moment.

"Heh, so you are awake, lad. Been meaning to ask you about the hospitality of men considered against the hospitality of Spriggans."

"Urg," replied Llew. "I feel almost as though you let this happen just to be able to say that."

"Not I. Not my fault if you mortals cannot hold your wine and ale. It is also not my fault that your King Iolo is an oath breaker. I do not know why he and your so-called father are no longer seeing eye to eye, but, if I were to guess, I would say he got a better offer."

"What about Llewellyn?"

"Calmly, lad, I think she is unharmed. Being of the fairer species she gets a better grade of dungeon, which is why we do not see her here. I do not think Iolo knows quite what to make of her but he is still hoping she is valuable to someone. Your mount is in the stable still. I heard the guards discussing it a bit earlier. Apparently the local master of horse tried to saddle him this morning at dawn."

"He will not like that," Llew worried. "I hope they do not hurt him."

"I would count that the least of your worries. From what I heard, the master of horse here is now the man who was mastered by a horse. In fact, he may never ride one again, even if he lives."

"Ouch," said Llew, with feeling.

"Yes, I would guess it does not really matter how much experience you have with horses if what you are dealing with is not entirely a horse."

Llew shuddered. "That hardly bears thinking about. Imagine climbing into a saddle only to find yourself riding a great wolf or a lion. Whether injured or not you might never be willing to ride again."

He put that thought away. "Hafgan, we cannot stay here, our speed is paramount."

Hafgan held up his hands, showing the chains around his wrists. "We are not going to find much speed like this, lad."

Llew tried his own chains and found they were quite adequate to the task of keeping him there. "Perhaps some ancient Spriggan magic might be in order," suggested Llew hopefully.

"Heh, Spriggan magic is probably not quite like you think it is, lad. All the same, they have taken our arms and other items but amongst mine there is a horn. If we can retrieve it and get outside tonight, while the moon is up, good King Iolo will be most unhappy should I also be able to sound it."

Llew's spirits sank, "Small likelihood of that."

"Patience, lad, we have some time yet in which to work out the details."

"Why is Iolo doing this?" asked Llew. King Pendaran is no simple cantref king; he will crush this traitor like a beetle on an anvil when word gets out. Word will get out, regardless of what happens to us. Too many people saw us ride in and I can tell you with complete certainty that even the soldiers have little discipline in holding their tongues."

"Well, I am not doing anything else at present, lad, so let us consider that question. Obviously, Iolo must be allied to, or at the mercy of, a much larger power."

"Aye," Llew scowled. "That is only logic and I will not contest it."

"Well, if we are going to play this game you have to do your part, too, lad. You must think. Does King Pendaran have any enemies? Do you?"

Llew laughed bitterly. "Perhaps a few. Do you think Iolo has thrown in his lot with the Picts and that the long arm of Goll One-eye has caught up to us?"

"Almost any enemy, before that one," agreed Hafgan. "What would be the worst case?"

"Moriganna," Llew said emphatically.

"Nay, think about it. She is the devil you know, but at least you are somewhat familiar with her, and she is not, for all her wicked ways, truly the worst possibility."

Llew's heart froze. "This is true, but what would Arawen, Lord of the Dead, seek to offer one such as King Iolo, aside from an early grave?"

Hafgan tsked, "You know of him as a dreadful force but, more than that, he is a schemer and conniver without match. Centuries of experience have shown him how to look into almost any being and then to choose a path that will lead to that one's destruction. As you and the princess pointed out earlier, he might long since have finished with the destruction of all Tethera were he and Moriganna not constantly upsetting each other's carefully laid plans.

"Your answer is that he would find out whatever it was your King Iolo wanted most in life—then he would offer it to the fellow at a reasonable price. The deeper price would be hidden, for it is the hook within the bait. Once the first deal is sealed, Lord Arawen has his prize, for now more deals will follow, each on worse terms until, in the end, the deal-maker is nothing more than an instrument of Arawen's will, to be used while he is useful and tossed aside when he is not."

Llew sucked in his breath before speaking. "So you believe it is possible that King Iolo is the tool of Lord Arawen in all this?"

"Aye, it seems likely for it is certainly the method by which he obtains his dark goals. Also, there is the matter of how King Iolo would fare if it became known he had betrayed his oath and imprisoned his liege lord's heir."

"A cantref king would not long survive such a thing once it became known," Llew agreed. "Not without a powerful ally indeed. Certainly Arawen has attempted to kidnap the heir before now, for whatever reason he may have. The only thing that might have changed is who the heir actually is."

"Or perhaps not," muttered Hafgan, enigmatically. Then he beamed at Llew, "Care to wager on how long it will take him to send some barrow warriors to collect you? He may even come with them to make sure of their prize, so long as there is no chance of his enemies finding out and setting a trap or an ambush for him."

Llew paled a bit at the thought, or perhaps it was the persistent lingering effects of whatever had been done to him the night before.

"Hafgan, we cannot be in this cell when he comes for us!"

"Oh, I am with you on that, lad. This is not the way I would want him to find us. We will wait until it is dark and then break out."

"Just like that?" Llew rattled his chains for emphasis. "And that door does not look like a solid kick will spring it open, either."

"Just like that, trust me, lad, I have a plan."

Then Helgar woke up and they had to explain it all to him while he held his head and groaned pitifully.

The guards brought them a bucket of water and some stale bread about midday. There were no other visitors and that was probably as well, thought Llew. Anyone else might have been an interrogator and they had nothing to tell one. They certainly had very little knowledge of value to their captor, and Llew had no desire whatsoever to see King Iolo, until he was free and, preferably, armed.

Except for that, the day was uneventful. He even managed to take a few short naps. Helgar went far beyond that in that he apparently had no difficulty whatsoever in grabbing more rest when there was nothing else to do.

It was after one of these naps that Llew awoke and found the little bit of light that had been streaming through a narrow slit in one wall had vanished. It was night at last.

"Psst, Hafgan," he whispered, "is your plan ready?"

"Indeed, lad, are the two of you ready?"

"Aye, speaking for myself I am more than ready," said Helgar.

"I assuredly am," replied Llew, "but I might as well not have eyes at all for how blind I am in the darkness."

"My eyes are sufficient, lad, so do not worry on that accord, but tell me, what do you hear of any guards and such with those amazing ears of yours?"

Llew squinted his eyes shut, a pointless exercise in the darkness, and strained to hear all that he could. Eventually he could hear the sounds of a castle after dark. These included sentries walking the walls, cooking sounds, the occasional whinny or stamp of a horse, even occasional snatches of conversation, although not even Llew's fantastic hearing could begin to make out what was being said. It was just too far and too transient.

He slowly pulled in his focus, concentrating on the cell door and what lay beyond it. It was very quiet but at length he could detect what sounded like an occasional belch and the sound of ceramic mugs being set down hard on heavy wood.

Again he whispered to Hafgan, "Beyond the door and quite a bit further in I can hear what might be someone having dinner or drinking."

Hafgan humphed quietly. "I guess that will have to do, we cannot wait all night. Lord Arawen can travel quickly and could arrive at any time, depending on how fast they sent word to him."

The cell suddenly felt different. It took Llew a moment to realize that the difference was caused by something very large being in the cell. Softer than stone walls, it was something that absorbed a lot of the normally unnoticed background sounds that would have hit the far side of the cell and bounced back. Apparently, it was noticeable enough that Helgar caught it, too. Both men froze in place.

There was a clinking noise of a chain, followed by a loud snap, and the sound of a chain falling to the cell floor. Then something was lifting the chain that held Llew to the wall. The snapping noise recurred, this time much closer. The same sounds repeated once more, this time from Helgar's direction.

Llew could sense the massive presence in the cell move slightly away from them, towards the direction of the cell door. Llew strained to hear what was happening and felt nearly deafened when there was suddenly a loud metallic screech. Then it was quiet again for another moment before something heavy was set on the floor near the exit. A long silence ensued and then, as suddenly as it had appeared, the massive presence was gone.

Llew was holding his breath, trying to hear anything at all

that might give him an insight into what had just happened, when Hafgan spoke again. "Alright your highness, you and your—friend—need to very gently pull your chains out of the ring on the wall. You are each going to have a length of the stuff dangling from each wrist but we will have to deal with that later."

Llew traced his chains and found it was as the Spriggan had said. Something monstrous had apparently seized them and pulled them apart.

Before he could ask questions, Hafgan spoke again. "We have a problem, lads. The door is open but there is a second door down a very narrow corridor with a very low ceiling. That corridor is keeping me from opening it as I did the first."

Llew found the corridor and, ducking very low, made his way down it with Helgar and Hafgan following in single file until he could feel the door. It was at least as stout as the one on the cell itself had been.

"So now what?" Llew whispered.

"You are asking me?" complained Hafgan. "I kind of thought I had already given pretty good service with the chains and the first door."

"Fine," said Llew, after thinking on the matter a moment. "In many stories one of the prisoners will pretend to be deathly ill to draw the jailers into coming. It's an old trick that should really only work in stories, because any guard worth his salt would be prepared against just such a ruse. In this case, however, it may actually serve us because they will believe the inner cell door to still be secure. They will certainly not be expecting us to be standing just behind the first door they open."

Helgar grunted, and then said in a low voice, "It is good enough for me, Llew. I want nothing more than to get my bare hands on them. That is all it will take."

"Very well then. Hafgan? Would you go back to the cell and yell for the guards? Something about how the prince has been poisoned or some such?"

"It is worth a shot, lad. My advice to you is let the barbarian rush them as soon as they unbolt the door. This is precisely the kind of thing his kind love best and they get lots of practice doing it when breaking into other people's homes."

"Hey now!" objected Helgar, none too quietly.

Just then there was a knock at the door.

"Who is there?" asked Helgar, before a frantic Llew could shush him.

"My lord Helgar?" came a voice. "Is Prince Llew with you?"

Llew shook his head in disbelief; he knew that voice! "Addfwyn?" he called.

"Yes, my lord, please bide a moment while I find the key."

Chapter XXVIII

Gwri's Tale: Lessons are Ended

As soon as they closed the door, Gwri checked to see that Cymri was on her perch and then put his hand on his medallion. "Cymri, Afaggdu is claiming to be a relative of yours. Would that be true?"

"Well of course it is," replied Cymri. "What? You cannot see the family resemblance?"

"Ack!" said Gwri, turning to Afaggdu, "Let me try to understand this. You are actually a brother of Cymri's mother?"

"Nay, lad, Taliesin is my bonny baby brother."

"Brothers? How by Math's golden torc can the two of you be brothers?"

Afaggdu grimaced and gestured towards his hideous features, "What? You cannot see the family resemblance, lad?"

Cymri cawed in what had to be laughter as Gwri put his head in his hands and gave it a good shake.

"Ha," laughed Afaggdu. "We never get tired of that one. Alright then, it is a bit of a story but the short of it is that our mother was a very powerful enchantress. It is even possible her father was a godling of some sort. When we were born, great things were expected of us. The reality being I was the ugliest babe anyone had ever imagined, and a sickly child as well. Tal came along about a year or so later and, if you can credit it, was actually a bit on the simple side."

"The Chief of all Bards?" Gwri asked, his skepticism easy to see.

"Aye, amazing, eh? Moreover, Tal did not precisely resemble my father in the way he should have. Worse still, he was more and more starting to look like someone my father knew and did not especially care for, especially not in the vicinity of his wife, if you take my meaning.

"Our mother, being who she was, decided not to take the easy route by putting us in a weighted bag and dropping us into a deep place. Instead she obtained—and the particulars of how is another story in its own right—two cauldrons of special waters. Anyone dipped into the first would become the fairest and wisest in all the land; anyone dipped into the second would become the best and sturdiest warrior the world had ever seen and, as she reasoned it, a warrior like that could not be sickly.

"Since both of us needed the first cauldron's water, the one for fair and wise, she decided to go for the whole ball of wax and dip both of us in each. It did not work, of course. Once she had dipped Tal in the one that makes you the fairest and wisest in all the land, well, it only stands to reason that there cannot be two people who are the fairest and wisest in all the land and the same goes for being the best and sturdiest warrior. But the prophecies on the waters were not false. There is no contesting of wits possible with Tal, and I am certainly a pretty sturdy warrior and fairly skilled as well. Why, blooded warriors often will drop their weapons and flee just at the very sight of me. Taliesin and I, we do not even pass into old age because if I were old and infirm, or Tal old and senile, then that would make the prophecies false—"

"Just how old are you?" Gwri interrupted.

Afaggdu shrugged. "Who could know? Why would I keep track? But it took me centuries of searching to learn just that little bit of our history. I am still not sure what happened between our parents but, not long after being dipped in the cauldrons, as we were still infants when it happened, we washed up on the beach in Ceredigion. Tal was on that huge enchanted harp of his, and I was on a wooden shield. Like the harp, that shield had powers, too, but it has long since been lost. We were found and taken to the king and he made us his sons, but he always liked Taliesin better. Who would not? So Tal became the heir."

"Taliesin is a king? I thought Ceredigion was a part of Dyfyd?"

"He is and it is. After a century or so on the throne, he got antsy and wanted to hit the road. His own son had tragically died young so, rather than abdicate, he got the king of Dyfyd to agree to keep an eye on things. Tal is still king, but I doubt he finds time to spend ten days a decade on his throne."

"Hold a moment," Gwri said, not sure if Afaggdu was not having him on. "Everyone knows about Taliesin. Story after story mentions him. Why is it no one knows anything about you?"

"Well, lad, although he is wonderfully clever at disguise, Tal draws attention everywhere and at all times when he is not disguised. He cannot help it on account of him being the Chief of all Bards, and clever and good-looking to boot. Me, on the other hand, I get a certain notoriety every now and again, but then I switch from being called Morfran, the name our royal dad gave me, to being called Afaggdu for a bit, while I keep a low profile. People seem only too glad to forget about me. You saw what happened when Tal went looking for Cymri; right away Moriganna knew precisely who he was. Compare that with how she had no knowledge of me when she saw me in Gwent or, if she ever had, she had since forgotten me. Most folk do not study my face so closely that they can recall its details later."

"I would wager they don't," agreed Llew.

"The name Morfran might have stirred some memory in her of a connection to Tal, but Afaggdu did not. Afaggdu was just another sinister looking mercenary. She was only too ready to believe I was some sort of monster like unto some of hers, just because of how I looked. When I began to suspect she had taken Tal I finally took her next offer to become instructor to her fosterling, as she called you.

"Then I got here and saw you and I began to have an inkling as to what was up. Make no mistake, I am as fond of Prince Llew as I am of you—at least now I am—at the time I considered just lopping off your head, along with Moriganna's. When I was younger I was a bit of a hothead and would likely have done just that, but there is something about living a long time that makes you tend to think more before you act. Lucky for you some unfortunate experiences made me older and sadder and a bit more willing to take a better look before I waded in swinging."

"Thank goodness for that," Gwri breathed.

"Alright then, lad. I had hoped for a few more years to work on your both your martial skills and your sense of values and such, but it is already upon us. We have come to the fork and there is no retreat."

Gwri steeled himself for whatever was coming.

"Now," Afaggdu continued, "I know you do not much care for Moriganna. I understand that, but can you take the next step?

Will you actively support us against her?"

Gwri remained motionless while the words passed in through his ears and seemed to bounce around his brain for a while. Then he chuckled; he could not help it. He chuckled again. This time it turned into a full blown laugh and would not stop.

Afaggdu and Cymri, the ogre and the black bird, turned their heads in unison and looked at each other in puzzlement. It was so comical that Gwri, on the verge of recovering, started laughing again. Eventually he ran down and dried his eyes on his sleeve, then put his hand back on the medallion.

"I am a bit confused," ventured Afaggdu, finally. "Was that a yes or a no, then?"

"Yes, Gwri," chimed in Cymri, "say 'yes' or you may otherwise never find a place for yourself in this world."

Gwri glanced from one to the other. "I already told Taliesin I was in. I had the horses for our escape all picked out. The gear we needed was assembled and ready, waiting for our escape."

Cymri flapped her wings excitedly. "You spoke with my father?"

Nothing would do then but for Gwri to recount the entire episode.

"My goodness," said Cymri, when he concluded, "you lie very well indeed. I was quite convinced that, when I told you of my father having come, it was the first time you had heard of it."

"So and so," said Afaggdu. "This will be a bit easier for you now than it would have been then. Moriganna will be giving us the horses and an honor guard as well. The trick will be getting away from that honor guard once we have picked up the prince and before they kill him for us."

"A couple of dozen mercenaries and a dozen or more

shape-shifters will be difficult to outrun." Gwri opined.

"Nonsense, lad, a little deadly nightshade in their evening rations and they will be in no shape to chase anyone."

"You would poison them all?" Gwri asked, horrified.

"Oh no, lad, tempting, but no. I would use the right amount. They would just be sick as dogs for a day or two, but the hallucinations alone would tend to give them other things to worry about besides chasing us. Now the shape-shifters are another matter, it is actually a considerable weakness of theirs. After they partake they will likely be out of it until we are halfway to Gwent."

"Then this should all be as easy as falling down a well?"

"Well, lad, that is what I always used to think on things like this until I noticed something that changed my mind."

"Ask my uncle what changed his mind," Cymri demanded.

"Cymri wants to know what changed your mind," Gwri relayed to Afaggdu.

"Oh that? Just that these sorts of affairs have never, ever, gone as smoothly as I thought they would."

Chapter XXIX

The Escape

A long minute passed before the lock made a scraping noise and the door swung open. Addfwyn stood there, backlit by burning rush torches in the room behind him. Also in that room were two guards, one slumped across a table while the other lay on the floor.

"Ha ha," chortled Helgar as he strode forward and picked up Addfwyn in a mighty bear hug. "You are a very crafty crofter! Had me fooled completely when you disappeared."

Addfwyn was slightly unsteady when Helgar set him down.

"I think," said Llew, "you had us all fooled. We certainly underestimated you in many respects. What happened?"

The manservant licked his lips nervously. "Well, my lord, when I heard Jarl Helgar describe the heraldry the guardsmen bore, I recognized it as that of King Iolo. He has a pretty poor reputation and I felt, quite strongly, that there might be a problem . . . so I sort of slipped off and followed on foot, sneaking around the patrols where I had to. Then, when I got here, I just started pitching in and working alongside the castle staff. No one questioned it. I was just another servant. A simple story here and there and that was enough. Who would believe I was willing to work here if I was not being paid? So I learned all about what had happened and I shifted myself to the kitchens—I really am a good cook—and, when it came time for someone to bring a tray to the jailers in the dungeon, I made sure it was me."

"So then you drugged their food or drink?" Llew asked admiringly.

"What? Oh no, my lord, that sort of thing is much too uncertain for something as delicate as this, and I did not have any drugs or anything like that. I just coshed them each behind the ear while they were eating. Then I heard a loud voice behind the door to the cells and . . . here we are."

"That is amazing Addfwyn. How much am I paying you?"

"Not a thing yet, so far as I know, my lord."

"Excellent, I am doubling it as of now."

"My lord is most generous."

As they armed themselves with the guards' weapons, Llew asked the others to bide a moment. He took a lit torch from a wall sconce and quickly retraced his way to the cell, ducking low again for the narrow corridor connecting it to the guard room could not have been more than four feet high. One glance in the cell showed him what he had more than halfway expected to find. The formidable cell door had been literally torn from its hinges. It must have happened in that one quick metallic screech he had heard earlier—then something had set it down gently to lean against the wall.

Llew tried to get his mind around this for nearly a minute before he remembered the large boulders being rolled aside in the dark at Cas-Eiddew. Had Hafgan brought an invisible giant with him? How had it gotten into the cell and then escaped again? The hairs stood up on the back of his neck. Hafgan had hinted something at Cas-Eiddew, something about those who had already died once? Could it be the shade of a dead giant? Perhaps that was the real reason why Hafgan had bid them wait until after dark for their escape. But why had the giant then not opened the second door afterwards as effortlessly as it had the first?

Mysterious as this was, Llew knew he had to shelve it for now. Time was at a premium and someone might check on those guards at any time. As he turned back to the tiny corridor leading to the guard room, he was again struck by how cramped it was. Could this be why the giant had not opened the second door? A creature of that size would not have been able to enter the tiny confines of the corridor to get to second door. Yet, as he further considered it, that made no sense either.

A giant might not have been able to get down that tight corridor to reach the second door but, surely, if it could pass through walls to appear in the cell with them, it stood to reason it could just as easily have appeared in the guard room and ripped the door off from that direction. Something that powerful would have had no difficulties with two guards. Was it because the guardroom, rather than being dark like the cell, had been well lit by comparison?

He pushed the conundrum from his mind. There were other things of greater priority to attend to. Somehow they had to find Llewellyn, rescue her, find Cymri, get to the stables, get Gower and additional mounts, get the gates open, and outride anything King Iolo could send after them.

As he reentered the guardroom, Helgar passed him one of the guards' swords. Llew hefted it experimentally. Then he added trying to find what they had done with his own sword and other gear to the tasks ahead of them, and sighed heavily. Why not add jumping over the moon to the list as long as he was at it?

First things first, they had to find Llewellyn.

"The princess is in the wide tower adjoining the king's rooms." said Addfwyn, "I know this because I arranged to take her meal to her guard earlier."

Very well, Llew amended to himself, first they had to rescue Llewellyn.

"I believe we can ascend from here to where the servant's halls begin and reach her that way. At best we may encounter no more than another servant or two."

Llew nodded as he absorbed that. First, they would have to rescue Llewellyn. "I see, thank you very much Addfwyn. It appears you truly are at least as amazing as Llewellyn suggested you might be. Your pay is hereby trebled."

Helgar laughed, and even Hafgan acknowledged this with a chuckle.

"You do not, by chance," continued Llew, "already have a plan for secretly getting my horse out, as well as enough horses for the rest of us, supplies to continue our journey, and a way of getting the gates open do you?"

"No, my lord, I do apologize."

"Humph," said Llew, "well I suppose you will get better at this with time." Despite the urgency of their situation he was having a difficult time keeping a straight face as he said this.

"Yes, my lord, certainly," answered Addfwyn. "But the stables are off the main courtyard, and I was able to hide some few essentials for our journey under a pile of hay in the loft there. We will need to take more than just horses for ourselves, however. We must take all the other horses as well, in order to slow pursuit, and then drive off the ones we do not need later."

Llew sagged a little and even Hafgan looked a little agog at this.

Helgar took it all in stride. "What about the gate? Did you find a way we may more easily open it?"

"Oh, it is already open, my lord Helgar. They seem to be expecting allies to arrive tonight and do not want to insult them by presenting a closed and barred gate when they arrive."

"Never mind quadrupling his pay; you already tripled it, now you need to redouble that," Hafgan said dryly.

The small group quickly climbed a stone staircase to what might have been the main level of the keep and waited at the top while Addfwyn surveyed the hallway they had to pass through. When he gave the signal they hurried down it several paces and into another narrow passage, this one ending in spiral stairs, both steep and tight, going up. Another short passage followed by another twisting stair and they were before a short narrow door.

"This is the servant's entrance into the king's rooms," explained Addfwyn. "His last wife died in childbirth, along with the child, and his only son was killed a few years ago leading a patrol that was trying to run down some cattle raiders from Powys. There may be servants preparing things for the night, but he will still be down in his hall, more than likely."

Llew swung the door open quickly and barely avoiding a young woman carrying a tray who had been approaching from the other side. She dropped the tray and gaped as Llew gaped back. Then she opened her mouth preparatory to a scream. A blur moved past Llew and promptly seized her, covering the lower half of her face with an enormous hairy hand.

Helgar winced and looked at the others. "Hurry to bind and gag her if you would, please. I was going too fast to get a proper grip and she is biting me."

Addfwyn ran into the largest room, which must have been

the royal bedchamber, and emerged with an armload of what must have been the king's own extra garments. Working together and using the king's clothing, and strips torn from it, to both bind and silence her, Hafgan and Addfwyn had her immobilized and gagged in moments.

Helgar shook his injured hand ruefully. "What a bite she has! Yet she is young indeed to have teeth so sharp and so many of them," he marveled.

Llew had taken the time while they did this to poke his nose about. Luck was with him when he found the king's sitting room, a smallish area just off of the bedchamber. On a table were a dozen or more weapons and one harp. Most of their other belongings that had not followed them to the dungeon were there as well.

"Better and better," exclaimed Llew, and they quickly gathered up everything they could carry.

"Now then, which way to the tower, good Addfwyn?"

Addfwyn shook his head. "I am not quite sure where the door is, my lord. The tower stands against the south wall of this room and I know that you have to be in here to get into it. There is no entry at ground level."

"Truly?" said Llew. "Then let us tear down these tapestries and seek a secret door."

This was another of those tasks Helgar was especially good at, Llew noted. The third tapestry he ripped down had an oak door bound in iron behind it.

Helgar regarded it skeptically. "It is not very secret, Llew, are you sure this is the right one?"

Forgoing a response, Llew strode past and attempted to open the door. He was unsuccessful. This door actually had a lock built into it, something he had never seen before. He threw his shoulder into it and found it no more yielding than a stone cliff. While he backed off for a moment, Helgar took the opportunity to throw his entire body against it with no more success than Llew had enjoyed.

Llew was on the verge of asking Hafgan if perhaps he had a friend that would care to take a shot at it when he heard a familiar caw. Turning and looking up, he saw Cymri and Cilgwri sitting on a beam between the rafters. Reflex sent his hand to his medallion which he had only just recovered from King Iolo.

Llew smiled, "Why, hello Cymri, how good to have you rejoin us, and hello to you, Cilgwri."

They both cawed at him and flapped their wings, earning Cilgwri a disapproving glance from Cymri.

Llew gestured to the indestructible door, "Care to take a turn at knocking this down?"

Rather than answer, she picked up something shiny in her beak and flicked it down in his direction.

Llew, surprised, still managed to stumble forward and snatch it out of the air. He found himself holding a bronze key. He gaped only a moment then turned and stuck it in the lock.

"I am not certain why, Cymri, but this feels like cheating," he commented.

"Rather do things the hard way?" Hafgan asked. "Using your head is good, but using it as a battering ram is not so good, lad. I like this better. Turn the key."

It turned with a satisfying click.

Cymri ruffled her feathers and cawed.

Hafgan said, "She says she supposes you could lock the door again and she could take the key back to its owner."

Llew had to restrain himself from picking up the Spriggan and using him as a battering ram, not on the door, but on the thickest stone wall he could find. "You can understand what she is saying without the medallion?" he hissed in his loudest whisper.

Hafgan looked hurt then leaned closer to Llew and covered one side of his mouth with the back of his hand while he whispered in reply, "Ah now lad, I told you. She is not really a bird. It just follows naturally that she is not really speaking in bird language either. To me she is every bit a human mortal like yourself, albeit with many more visible freckles, and she speaks the same language you do."

"It was funnier the first time, Hafgan."

"Ah, she says be careful with that key and do not lose it like King Iolo did. He has been looking for it much of the day, ever since it disappeared from his night stand next to an open window that Cilgwri was flying near this morning."

"It sounds like Princess Llewellyn missed lunch," Llew said thoughtfully, trying to put Hafgan's attempt at humor out of his mind.

"And dinner too, but she probably valued her privacy more," retorted Hafgan.

"Good point," responded Llew, and he opened the door.

He just had time for one quick glimpse of a fairly well-appointed bedchamber with a spiral staircase leading upwards on the far side before he was almost run over by Llewellyn charging out. "Cymri already signaled to me you were close," she exclaimed. "Oh, how I wish you had been faster. They keep marching in through the open gate, too many to count. All of the castle's servants and most of its guards have gone into hiding but I do not know how we may escape now."

"Umm, slow down, I beg you, princess. Who is marching in?" asked Llew.

"Who is not correct or, rather, there is no who. The

correct word is what. Barrow warriors are what. They just keep filing in with no end."

"Well now," exclaimed Hafgan, "it sounds like Lord Arawen may have decided you were a prize worth collecting in person, your highness." To Llewellyn, "Did you see a dark gaunt fellow among them? It would have been someone who was not a barrow warrior but not looking more than marginally like a mortal man. Possibly he would have been riding some sort of wretched steed?"

"I am not certain, but there was a living man, or something that looked like one, leading them and he was riding a mount not unlike what you describe."

"Aha, and those stairs you just came down, they lead to the top of this tower? It is a high place where I can see?"

Llewellyn nodded, clearly puzzled about where this was going.

"Excellent. If your highnesses and such others would care to come up to take in the sights, well, I would say you have earned it."

"What about Gower? What about mounts for us all and getting out of here?" inquired Llew.

"Oh, lad, it is not that big a place. If the courtyard is full of barrow warriors you would all have your brains plucked out and eaten before you could take three steps towards the stable or the gate." Hafgan glanced at Helgar, "Well, except you of course, even a barrow warrior cannot get blood from a turnip."

"Hey now," warned Helgar.

The Spriggan grinned, "Nay, do not trouble yourself, I was only making a bit of a jest."

"Very well," said Helgar, sounding only partially mollified.

"The jest is that barrow warriors never eat. What would

their rotten bellies do with food? Let us get up to the top; I think you will like this."

Chapter XXX

Gwri's Tale: Departure

At forty-seven mounted men, it was very nearly a small army that assembled in front of Caer Mallcoedwig three weeks later, early on a foggy, late summer morning. To Gwri's surprise, Moriganna came out to him as he sat waiting on Gower.

"Ah, there you are my little king-to-be."

Gwri bit his tongue. She was tall for a woman, very tall, but he was already a head taller than she.

"How is your new armor fitting?" she asked.

"It fits well, and it looks splendid, but—"

"Yes? Is there a problem?"

"It is the helmet," Gwri admitted. "The antlers are not large but they make me feel silly. They are also not the best in a fight; a helmet should be smooth. That way an opponent's blow, should it land, might slide off and exert less force upon both the helmet and the head inside. The antlers could prevent that by letting an opponent's weapon gain purchase."

"My," said Moriganna, "you have been learning. I have great hopes for you. But," and her voice turned colder, "you are not meant to be fighting. Your training is superlative, what you have of it, but the only reason you have it is because I want you to be able to play the role. Some practice bouts in the yard are one thing, but you have never been in a real fight. You will have ample people around you to take care of any real fighting that might need to be done. Play your part and leave the combat to them. Any serious injury to you and all of this might be for naught."

"Yes, your highness, but why antlers? Were I going to be alone in the woods I would live in fear of poachers."

"You will not be alone. Also, the antlers may be helpful. Certain old tales mention another rider with horns upon his crown. Your appearance now may win you a moment's doubt should any familiar with those stories encounter you. It might even send some fleeing away without ever drawing close. Of a more practical nature, the royals of Gwent also have the stag predominant in their heraldry. It may help if you are unable to obtain the prince's helmet.

"That looks to be a stock sword from my armory. Give it to me and take this one instead." She snapped her fingers and a servant ran forward to hold up an opened wooden box to Gwri. Inside was a wondrous fair sword. The blade looked as though it had been made entirely of silver while the hilt appeared as finely worked pure gold. Gwri drew his sword and placed it in the box with his left hand while taking the new one with his right.

Although he had only caught a glimpse of it a few years earlier, he was certain that this was Taliesin's sword. Like his harp, it had been found near the tree that he had become. Gwri shifted the sword in his hand, felt the heft and balance and marveled at it.

"Gwri, have a care out there," Moriganna said in a tone he had never heard before. With a shock, he realized it sounded almost like concern. "Whether you believe it or not, you have lived a rather sheltered existence. Now you are going out into

Tethera, where very little is ever precisely as it seems.

"Do not shrug off my warning. Consider that I am named the Queen of Deceit, the Mistress of Deception, one of the greatest powers in the land, and it is me that is telling you this. There are old dangers out there, and new ones as well, none of which would hesitate to swallow you whole. Beware of everything and trust no one."

On that note, Gwri wondered, why would she arm him with something that would scream to the court in Gwent that he might have had something to do with Taliesin's disappearance? Someone there, probably several someones, would surely remember and recognize such a unique sword. He started to ask her about this, then realized he did not dare. There was no way he could reveal that he knew its provenance without revealing he had seen the whole affair. Moriganna was clever enough to start unraveling more from that knowledge alone.

Instead he asked, "Why such a sword? I thought I was not to fight."

"Nothing is beyond the realm of possibility, but once you have the prince's sword you will wear it instead, and give this one to Afaggdu. He will be expecting it."

With that she was gone off to speak with Cai, the captain of the mercenaries she had summoned for this expedition. It gave Gwri time to reflect on how she had showed nothing but complete confidence that he would do exactly as she had told him.

Moriganna and Captain Cai were far enough away from everyone else, especially with all the noise the assemblage was making, that they were quite satisfied no one could hear them. Gwri, of course, could hear them quite well.

"The situation is this," she told Cai, "The prince is sailing around the coast to Gwynedd to present his respects to his future bride. A sometimes ally of mine, a lord of the sea named Dylan, is following the prince's ship. When it is in position, a few days from now, he will raise a storm and blow it far off course to where we have agreed upon, then he will sink it. The crew and passengers will be permitted to get to shore but without mounts or supplies.

"The area is home to a great many Picts, hence a need for protection. Dylan is supposed to hold and safeguard the prince and his people until your arrival. All the same, the sea lord refused to so swear, regardless of all threats or cajolements. I even had a difficult time extracting his oath to leave the prince alive and unharmed. Consequently, you must be prepared to enforce our will upon him and his subjects. You have the forces to do so, as long as the both of you are on dry land.

"For the bulk of the prisoners, I will send others to collect them from you. You will know these others when they contact you.

"Speed is of the essence. I do not overly trust Dylan and, worse luck, the place is not terribly far from the borders of Annwyn. I want the prince alive and kept that way at all costs until Afaggdu is done with him. All of his gear is to be given to Afaggdu's student. That includes everything, armor, sword, even his coin pouch and everything in it. Will that be a problem?"

"Nay, your highness, you are paying well enough that even a fat coin pouch should pose no undue temptation. Will the Picts pose any danger to our own men and . . . other things?"

"A mounted force like yours they will have little liking for. The shape-shifters I am sending with you will ensure that. If the natives do overcome their reservations about attacking you, it will be easy to make them regret it."

At that point, Cymri landed on his right shoulder. Gwri had become quite used to this. Since being changed into a bird there had been no need to confine her to the castle. As Moriganna had promised, she was leashed to Gwri and, at five miles distant, became deathly ill; a bit further would certainly kill her.

Gwri put his hand on the medallion. "Are we ready?"

"Ha," said Cymri, "just let me finish packing. Actually, I am not sure if I am more eager to get away from this wretched fortress or to get away from that stupid bird that likes to harass me when I am out flying."

Shortly after that, with no apparent signal, the shape-shifters began trotting their mounts away. Cai called an order and the mercenaries followed in close order. Afaggdu looked at Gwri, shrugged, and they took up the rear with Cymri riding in her usual perch on Gwri's right shoulder.

Chapter XXXI

An Ancient Enmity

From the top of the tower Llew saw nothing whatsoever to like about their situation. It was precisely as Llewellyn had described it. Ranks of barrow warriors, standing silent and implacable, filled the castle's center. Except for a small area near the keep's entrance, there was no ground visible.

Llewellyn wrinkled her nose. "Oh the stench!" she exclaimed. "Were they not already dead, that alone would kill them."

Llew eyed Hafgan, "We could really use a little good news here, friend Spriggan."

Hafgan scowled at the assemblage below them. "Aye, well, it is a bit disappointing, I must admit, lad."

"Oh? And what could possibly be disappointing about this, your shortness?" inquired Helgar. Some part of Llew marveled that the Northman was actually employing sarcasm. He realized he had started to think Helgar was not quite capable of it.

Hafgan seemed to take no notice of it, although Llew had the sudden conviction that, had he not been preoccupied with what he was looking at, the Spriggan might have actually enjoyed receiving a little sass back in his direction.

"It is Lord Arawen," said Hafgan mournfully.

Llewellyn let out an incredulous noise at that. "Yes, I suppose having Lord Arawen here is a bit disappointing, not to mention all those decaying wights he brought with him, and yet disappointing would not have been my first choice of words."

"Nay," replied Hafgan, "you misunderstand, lass. The disappointing part is that yon miscreant on the horse is not him. I had rather hoped it would be, but he was either too wily or too cowardly this time."

Llew rubbed his ears, convinced they were not working correctly. "Let me get the straight of this. You were hoping Lord Arawen would come for us?" he asked, disbelievingly. "You are unhappy he did not?"

Hafgan sighed. "Truth is I have been waiting to catch him where I could get to him for a long time. It seemed a good bit likely he would be coming to collect you personally and, in the process, give me a good opportunity to collect him instead. Instead he sent Garl. Not nearly as satisfying, but he will have to do. Ah well, it is a start."

"And how would you care to go about collecting him? He looks like he may have brought a few friends."

Hafgan raised one eyebrow, then lifted up the horn he had recovered from King Iolo's bedchamber.

Llew raised one eyebrow himself, and said, "You mentioned that horn earlier. Is it some magical artifact that can lay our enemies low from a distance? What is its power?"

Hafgan looked amused, "Nay, lad, where would you get such an idea? Tis a horn. Its power is that it makes noise when it is blown." So saying, he put the horn to his lips and blew mightily. The horn had a wide deep voice that echoed across Caer Enion.

It sounded, it occurred to Llew suddenly, like the sound of doom.

As hundreds of barrow warriors and their leader turned their heads to regard the top of the tower, Llew could not help but think that the doom he had heard was their own.

Hafgan replaced the horn on his belt. Still standing on the parapet, he waved at the mounted figure before the door to the keep, and to the men that stood near it. One of them, Llew noted, was King Iolo himself.

"Yoohoo!" called Hafgan. "Hey there, Garl, long time no see."

The being Hafgan had dubbed Garl turned to King Iolo and Llew could hear him ask, in a voice both cold and brittle, "Why is your dwarf jester up there making noises at me?"

Iolo did not seem to have a ready answer but Hafgan's hearing was good enough that he caught the question as well.

"Garl, oh little Garl, have you forgotten me so soon? It has only been, what, two or three centuries? The one who holds your leash has, most assuredly, not forgotten. It is why you are here and he is not for, despite all his ambitions, he is a great coward, while you are of so little regard he has sent you to your death on the off chance this little scheme of his might yet be accomplished."

Garl sneered. "And just who are you, dwarf, that you think you can threaten me with a legion of barrow warriors at my feet?"

"Why, Garl, you do not recognize me? It is I, Hafgan. We have met before. Mayhap you did not get a good enough look last time, for you may have been too busy trying to outrun your master after he lifted his robes and made like a rabbit back to Annwyn. That you are here, and he is not, says he, at least, has not forgotten."

"Hafgan?" Garl said uncertainly. Then, with more force,

"The years have not been kind to you little one. If Hafgan you are then you are a much diminished Hafgan, and now you will prove that even an immortal dwarf may die. Against the might of the barrow warriors my master has given me there is no means by which you might prevail."

Hafgan laughed, "Dwarf is it? Is that the best you can do? Or," he said, eying Garl speculatively, "perhaps little Lord Arawen never made clear to you what I really am? There is a reason why he does not yet possess the forces to sweep all before him. The barrows of the west are closed to him and he may no longer seek his rotting recruits here. You may have some idea why that is, or perhaps not. Arawen knows if you do not.

"It is my doing! My brethren and I now guard the barrows of the dead and Arawen will never violate them again while we yet survive. Instead he must watch as his forces are gradually spent in numbers greater than he can replace. It has made him desperate. Desperate enough to risk losing you in an attempt to get what he wants by guile since, after all, brute force was not serving him well."

Garl looked back up at Hafgan and said sardonically, "It appears I am in position to accomplish a great deal with brute force."

Hafgan did not reply, he merely hefted his hammer and stepped off the parapet.

Horrified, Llew leaned over the side and saw him falling. There was no way to save him; all Llew could do was watch as their would-be guide plummeted to the paving stones below. Then it seemed to Llew that the falling form simultaneously became both blurred and larger, just before it hit, cracking the stones upon which it landed with a colossal impact that shook the entire tower.

The whole party gaped. Where Hafgan should have landed was a dark giant, fully ten or twelve feet in height and holding a hammer whose head was larger than any anvil Llew had ever seen.

For a wonder, the barrow warriors did not attack it but even seemed to cringe back a bit. Certainly Garl was cringing a bit. Of King Iolo and his men there was no sign, they must have fled into the keep.

"So," the giant exclaimed in a voice like thunder, "it is time to remind people what a Spriggan is. Spriggans hold all the barrows in the land. We prevent the dead from being disturbed and we do it with brute force. When brute force is insufficient we just use more of it."

Garl recovered some of his aplomb sufficiently to spit out, "You are mad. Even you are no match for this. Even you will fall. My warriors will swarm you and tear you apart, a bit at a time, and that will be an end to you."

The giant laughed but it was not a pleasant laugh. Seemingly from nowhere, there were suddenly a dozen more giants around the outskirts of the courtyard and two stood in the open gate. "Now," he asked Garl, "did you want to give the order to attack or shall I?"

"Take them," shrieked Garl. "No prisoners, kill them all!"

Like waves at sea, the barrow warriors surged and they surged in every direction that a giant stood. It did them little good. The giants swung their hammers and clubs in great arcs that cleared every opponent they could reach. They stomped on the few that miraculously survived the great sweeps of their weapons and all the while they just kept swinging.

Llew and the party watched with awe for nearly a minute. The bulk of the barrow warriors were still up, but it was amply clear this was not a battle they could win, or even survive. The outcome was foreordained. The two giants in the gateway were quite sufficient to ensure none of the barrow warriors would be leaving early—if they even had the wit to do so. Garl apparently saw the doom that was coming. He fled into the keep.

Llew felt completely ineffectual. There was simply nothing he and his friends at the top of the tower could do to help. Then it occurred to him that there was something they could do.

"Iolo!" he yelled to them, straining to be heard over the astounding cacophony in the courtyard. "We need to capture Iolo before he rallies his men, or escapes the castle, or whatever his new plan is."

Llewellyn, Helgar, and Addfwyn all had their weapons out. They had understood him well enough. With Cymri fluttering everywhere, and barely landing for scant moments anywhere, they quickly descended to the tower room where they had found Llewellyn being held.

They arrived in time to meet King Iolo and six of his warriors just entering through the door from his quarters.

"Surrender!" Llew and King Iolo both yelled simultaneously. Seeing as how neither one of them had the least intention of surrendering to the other, both sides came together with yells and roars and weapons flailing.

"I need the prince alive," warned Iolo. "Kill these others."

Helgar guffawed, "That easy it is not!" He had acquired a large shield from somewhere and, disregarding the mace he was holding, slammed two of the men facing him into a wall with so much force that they bounced off before falling to the floor. Only one was able to even begin to make a shaky attempt at regaining his feet. It was then that Helgar used his mace. The remaining two men neither ran nor surrendered, but they did seem a bit uncertain about pressing the attack overmuch.

Llewellyn had but two men facing her and they clearly did not take her seriously. One grinned and made a quick feint at her even before his partner was in position to aid him. Llewellyn made an odd twisting and slashing motion with her weapon that was evidently not a feint because the guardsman suddenly looked shocked and fell over backwards. It was impossible to know how skilled he had been but the remaining man was now taking her quite seriously and, worse, as skilled as she was, he was clearly the more experienced. It was all she could do to mount a full defense and hold him off though it was clearly just buying time.

Llew was unable to help anyone as, although he had only one opponent, it was King Iolo himself, and he seemed to be a veritable demon with a sword, perhaps even more formidable than Afaggdu, were that possible. Llew was only surviving by giving ground constantly and attempting to interpose various pieces of furniture between them. This went on and on and Llew despaired of how it must end.

An odd realization came to him. He was terrified of losing this fight, but not because it would likely end in his death, that just elicited an unhappy emotion, something like losing a complicated game in the opening moves. What he feared was failure; it would mean the deaths of all his new friends and help turn the world into a playground for such as Moriganna, Arawen, Dylan, Goll One-eye, and perhaps even King Iolo.

There was a loud splintering noise and a groan to one side. Both he and King Iolo sneaked a glance to see what it was. Addfwyn had apparently been keeping a low profile, as only a lowly born servant could, but when Llewellyn and her opponent's melee had swept past him, he had used the opportunity to break a chair over the guardsman's head. Amazingly, the man was still in the fight but only barely; the tide had clearly turned in the princess's favor. It was obvious he could not last. In the same glimpse, Llew could see that one of Helgar's two remaining opponents had fallen and the remaining fellow, with an unexpected display of good sense, had dropped his weapon and was trying to surrender. Fortunately for him, Helgar was in good spirits and had not entered one of the murderous battle rages that Northmen were well known for.

King Iolo must have taken it all in as quickly as Llew did for he sprang backwards and was out the door towards his quarters in an instant.

"Stop," yelled Llew, giving chase. "You have no place to go."

They ran down the short hall and into a small storage room. At the back of it was a tight spiral staircase. King Iolo went down it and warning bells went off in Llew's head. The staircase was far too constricted to fight in and, if the King chose to stop at the bottom, anyone still in it would be hard pressed to even defend themselves.

Yet he could not give up the chase. It had occurred to Llew earlier that things could become very bad indeed if Iolo was able to rally many of the troops that had gone into hiding. By his estimations from the night before, there had to be at least forty or fifty more of them somewhere.

A half formed thought sprang into Llew's head and he glanced about hurriedly. There were several barrels in the storeroom but, they were too large. There were also crates of many different sizes but those would not roll. If only there was something he could use to—aha. There were a number of smaller casks. Llew dropped his sword and, snatched one up with both hands, discovering as he did so that he could only barely manage the weight. The thing was filled with liquid and was not at all light. Still, fear and panic lent him strength and he managed to heft it up before flinging it down the stairs; he then heaved a second for good measure. They rolled and bounced down and around and out of sight, caroming off the walls as they went.

Llew listened and it took no special sense of hearing to catch the yell that changed into a scream. Accompanying it were more thuds, the sound of wood shattering, and splashing noises. Retrieving his sword and holding it before him as best he could, Llew made his way down the staircase.

Iolo was fetched up against the far wall of the corridor at the bottom. He was laying in what had to be a very uncomfortable position. Llew was shocked to see that Iolo, and all of the corridor around him, was completely covered in what appeared to be blood. Then he saw the remains of the broken casks and he realized that, because of the odd color and consistency and the very volume of it, it must be a mix of lamp oil and red wine. The smell of spirits in the air was so strong that Llew suspected it was winter wine, made by putting wine outside in the winter, then repeatedly removing the ice as it partially froze. What was left was the essence of the wine, the spirits. Even a large man could quickly be in his cups from drinking just a small amount of it.

Seeing Llew with his sword, King Iolo tried desperately to rise, but discovered his left leg was broken and neither was his left arm working especially well. That he had other, less visible, injuries was a given.

He settled for turning a hateful glare on Llew. "So is this the way the heir of Gwent fights? By rolling barrels at a man's back?"

Llew had been full of emotion for some time but this was the first time that day that he felt genuine outrage wash through him. "Perhaps not," he returned icily, "if that man had not been running away like a coward . . . and that after violating every code of hospitality known."

King Iolo sneered, "You think the Lord of the Dead cares about such things? In the end we will kill all so that we may rule all. This is only the most minor of setbacks; the end is inevitable for death comes to all things. For some," he said, eying Llew balefully, "much sooner than for others."

Llew snorted, "Have a care, Iolo. Lord of Death? Your master, Lord Arawen, has already claimed that title. He would probably look askance on you usurping it."

"Spare us from the wisdom of fools, little boy. Do you think King Iolo could have done what we have done? He is a guest in Annwyn at present, but be of good cheer. It is a bargain he entered into willingly, although he will not like the true price when we bring him hither in a moment. No doubt you and he will have much to discuss."

"Wait," stammered Llew, "you are not King Iolo?"

"We are, and we are not," replied the fallen man, "and we will be gone in a moment despite anything you may do—so listen carefully.

"Although we shall not have you quite yet, it would not do for either you or us were you to fall into Moriganna's claws. Yet she has invested far too much in you already; she must make another attempt to salvage that investment ere you return to your father."

"How do you know this?" demanded Llew.

"Fool princeling, do you not yet understand? We know her well and have fully taken her measure. We have contended with that pretentious witch for many centuries now. She has interfered with so many of our plans even we have lost count. She is the bane of our existence. Yet she will fall with the others in the end. All that is needed is to prevent her progress in the interim. That means she must not recapture you. That is something you should not desire, either."

"Arawen?" Llew ventured incredulously. "You are saying you are Arawen?"

"That is Lord Arawen to you, little prince. Now listen carefully for no one knows more of Moriganna than we do. She will come at you when you least expect it. It will not be at a busy moment but at a quiet one. Her essence is hiding strange shapes under the guise of more familiar ones. We may be the Lord of Death, but she is the very Queen of Deceit.

"No, you do not get to ask questions," the injured man snapped as Llew opened his mouth to do just that. "You are welcome to do yourself in, or surrender to Garl if he is still around, but, since both those things seem unlikely, you must recall what we are telling you if you wish to survive. Moriganna is a deceiver. She will catch you off guard while she is disguised as someone you know, as someone you trust. You must not trust her!"

Sheathing his blade, Llew said, "You are trying to sow distrust between me and my friends. This is no less than I would expect of you, if you are indeed who you insinuate you are."

Ignoring his injuries completely, the fallen man fixed Llew with a gaze of glacier calm and menace. "There is no insinuate about it. Let us be clear, we are who we are and your only hope is to die before we do come for you. That is acceptable to us for we care not about human pain and suffering; it is merely a minor consequence of our works. It is not our goal. I tell you what I tell you now only to give you a chance, however slight, of avoiding Moriganna's machinations. Should she be successful, it would be an inconvenience for us, but that is all. Whereas for you—she will not kill you, but what she will do is something you will like even less.

"If you should run across Garl, do give him our hopes for an efficacious escape. We would like to see him back in Annwyn so we may have a protracted, and somewhat disagreeable, discussion on his past service to us, and on whatever future there is in store for him, or the lack thereof. If he can redeem himself in even the tiniest margin by helping prevent Moriganna from getting her claws back into you, why then, the nature of that conversation might change. You may tell him we said so.

"In any eventuality, you are warned, do with it as you may. We are leaving now."

"You are not going anywhere," Llew grimly declared.

"In a moment you will be able to say hello to King Iolo. As we said, we are certain you can find much to talk about."

The injured man's eye suddenly rolled up into his head and he began shaking convulsively. The shakes stopped after just a few seconds and then his eyes refocused, glancing hurriedly in all directions before finally coming to rest on Llew, who was still standing in the entrance to the staircase.

"Churl! What have you done?"

Llew took a step into the corridor, being very careful not to slip on all the oil that was puddled about. Was this really King Iolo? Had Lord Arawen somehow possessed him and then released him? If so, had he really released him, or was this some ruse of the Lord of Death?

The injured man attempted to move and began discovering the full extent of his injurie. "Stay back, I warn you," he called, and punctuated it with a loud groan.

Llew discounted the threat and continued to regard the man. Was this an opportunity or a trap? In either event, what should he do?

"Did Rhodri send you to assassinate me?" the injured man demanded. "He must know he stands to inherit should I fall." With considerable effort, he abruptly leaned to one side and got his good leg under him. Crying out with the pain, he pushed himself up and snatched a torch from the wall before waving it at Llew. "Stand back, I will not tell you again!"

"Easy," urged Llew. "We can discuss this now and wait to kill each other until later. If it even if it comes to that. Either way, it is certainly not something we can do out of order."

King Iolo swung the torch at Llew again and Llew was obliged to take a half step backwards. The king made a one-legged hop to swing the torch again and then it happened. With one leg broken he had no way to regain his balance if he slipped on the oil and lost it—and lost it he did.

Time seemed to freeze for Llew. He saw the king toppling forward and down, the lit torch in his good hand. He saw the oil and spirits that had drenched the walls and puddled on the floor. And, finally, he saw that he was standing in at least half an inch of oil and spirits himself.

Time returned to something like normal, and Llew was charging back up the spiral staircase at a pace he could not have imagined even a moment earlier. He felt more than heard an enormous in-drawing of air below him. Then came a tremendous fwoosh and Llew had a good guess as to exactly what that sound portended. He reached the supply room and threw himself flat onto the hard floor as flames shot up and out, over the staircase. For all their fury, they only lasted a scant second before receding. He heaved a sigh of relief before he noticed the soles of his boots were on fire.

Llew leapt up and turned all his efforts to stamping out the flames. With all the oil on them, this was not an easy thing.

That done, he looked up and saw Helgar and Llewellyn regarding him from the doorway into the supply room. They had odd looks on their faces, and he suddenly felt very awkward.

"Yes?" he asked.

"Well," Llewellyn said slowly, "I am not surprised Moriganna saw to it that you learned to dance, but is this really the time or the place? It did not even seem especially skilled."

"What?" exclaimed Llew. "My feet were on fire, thank you!"

"That may be overstating it, but it was not bad," said Helgar, "some teaching I can give you and you will be ready to revel with Ægir himself."

Llew started to respond, stopped, tried to start again, and stopped again. "Come," he said at last, "we should try to find our way out to the courtyard. I dare say Hafgan and his friends have stomped the place flat by now, and Iolo's men will not stay scattered and hidden forever."

He cautiously led them back down the spiral stairs. The oil and spirits had burnt off, for the most part, and there was surprisingly little smoke. Most of it had gone down the corridor rather than up the staircase. The remaining traces of haze, coupled with the occasional small bits of fire still burning here and there, gave the place a surreal feel. Helgar made a gesture in front of himself that might have been the outline of a hammer or something similar in shape.

The mortal remains of King Iolo lay near where they had fallen. Only his ornate torque gave clear evidence of who he had been. The blast of fire had hurled him against the wall like a rag doll, and his broken leg and arm were quite obvious by the angles at which they lay.

"My drott, what have you done?" Helgar said in an awed voice.

Llew was still annoyed by the dancing comments and trying not to look at what had happened to King Iolo. "What does it look like I did? He was the better swordsman so I picked him up and bounced him off the floor a few times, then he made a rude comment about Gower so I summoned a ball of fire and threw it at him."

Helgar gulped before speaking. "My drott, that is a most handy thing to be able to do— scary—but very handy. Did Moriganna teach you that, too?"

Llewellyn rolled her eyes. "He is just teasing us, Helgar. There are remains of casks here and it looks to be something in them was set to burning."

"That is correct," said Llew, "There was quite a bit of it but, even so, I never imagined winter wine would be so flammable, even mixed with oil. I wonder if it was really winter wine? Or perhaps the lamp oil was not precisely what it seemed to be?"

Llew did not want to take the time but gave them an abbreviated version of what had happened after he began chasing King Iolo and deliberately stopping before he got to the issue of his boots being aflame.

"So Garl is still about," observed Llewellyn. "Centuries old enchanters, especially ones that are dedicated to evil, should probably merit a bit of caution."

They made their way down the corridor in the direction the smoke had traveled and rounded a corner before coming across a group of four of Iolo's guardsmen. They were prepared for trouble and had their weapons out. One of them spotted Llew's party and issued a warning. As one, they all turned to face the apparent threat.

"All right, Llew," Llewellyn said softly, "I think you know

how to play this."

Llew put on what he thought of as his command disguise. It really did, he thought, seem as if it transformed himself into someone else when he did this, giving control of his body and his mind to an arrogant stranger. Not, he suddenly thought with a shiver, entirely unlike what King Iolo had done with Lord Arawen.

"You men," he called, "I require an escort. Know you who I am?"

At least one did. "You are Prince Llew of Gwent, your highness."

"Very good, sheath your weapons, and accompany my person then. If we should spot a little gnarled man in a gray robe who is a stranger to this place I want him apprehended or killed at all costs. Is that clear?"

"Your highness," one of the men said doubtfully, "forgive us, but King Iolo has made some accusations against you and ordered you held until you could be taken to your father."

"Is that what he said? Treason will ever attempt to justify itself, of course. In fact, King Iolo was a traitor and had broken oath to align himself with Lord Arawen of Annwyn."

The guardsmen gasped at this and several made gestures to ward off evil. That Llew had spoken of their king in the past tense went unnoticed.

"But you need no longer worry on that account. His plots exposed, Lord Arawen has fled and his forces lie crushed in your courtyard, all save that weasel of an emissary he sent and whom I very much wish to speak with."

"Begging, your pardon, your highness, we are sworn to King Iolo and you place us in a predicament. Perhaps if you were to sheath your weapons we could all go to him and sort this out?"

"Very well, I am a reasonable man. We will all sheath our weapons and you will send one man to see King Iolo. Even as we speak he is just down the corridor and around the corner near the back stairs to his quarters."

The guardsmen glanced at each other. In a voice he plainly thought Llew could not hear, the apparent leader said to the rest, "Make no mistake, we are caught in a hard place, but this is a good chance to get ourselves out of the worst of it. Do as he says. Grwyl, you go get the king."

Grwyl sheathed his weapon and approached the party, then slid past them at the greatest distance the corridor would allow.

He was gone only a minute before sliding back past them and returning to his fellows.

"He is dead!" he exclaimed as he reached them. "King Iolo is dead!"

"Are you certain?" asked the one that had sent him.

The man shuddered, "Beyond a shadow of a doubt."

"Yes," called Llew, "I wanted you to see for yourselves. He is quite dead. He died badly, as one would expect of one who allies himself with barrow warriors and their ilk.

"Until some succession is established, his lands are now forfeit to his liege-lord, my father. As prince and heir I am obliged to put them right and bring back some semblance of order. The sooner we are about that, the better. Accept my authority and do my bidding and we will get started. Otherwise, I suppose you could go try to find this emissary of the Lord of Death and place yourself under his orders, but know that, without his barrow warriors, he may not be around much longer.

The lead guardsman saluted. "Your highness, we are at your command."

Chapter XXXII

Gwri's Tale: The Wild Growth

By midmorning they had skirted along beyond the north end of the lake and its several spurs, then moved out of the wood into what appeared to be an endless marsh. Gwri knew from maps that it was not actually endless; a couple of days and they would be out of it.

It took three. Worse, dealing with Cai, the mercenary captain, made it seem twice that long. He was always very careful to speak to Gwri as though he was a vassal speaking to his king, but Gwri thought he could hear the sneer behind his voice even as he spoke. Knowing nothing of the keenness of Gwri's ears, Cai also said a great many unflattering things about Gwri to his own troops when he thought they would go unheard.

Gwri came to despise him so much that he briefly considered calling him out, then clamped down on the temptation. It could not help their plan and might actually imperil it. Even if he won—and in his more honest moments with himself he had to admit that was not a foregone conclusion—Cai's lieutenant would just take over, and there was no plausible reason to duel him. He was a quiet man who did his job and did not irritate anyone. Gwri tried to console himself by thinking a lot on how what they were about to do would probably wreck Captain Cai's world.

Putting his hand to his medallion, Gwri asked Cymri about the unexpectedly long time it had taken to get out of the marshes. Afaggdu made a noise but, when Gwri gave him a quizzical look, he simply said, "No. It is a good observation on your part. Let her answer it. I am but your arms master, this is her bailiwick."

"This gets a little complicated, Gwri, but it has to do with Annwyn," she told him.

"Annwyn? Gwri asked, perplexed. "But Annwyn is far off and to the east."

"Yes, it is, the east and the north, but it was not always there, bordering what remains of the Great Kingdom where other lands once were. It appeared slowly, over time, beginning a few hundred years ago. Dead things and horrendous beasts came prowling and the area became more and more dangerous. Eventually there was only Annwyn, with its dreadful master and his terrible minions.

"It was thought that Annwyn had come into our world and somehow displaced the lands that had been there. The truth is worse. Tethera somehow has come into Annwyn's world and left behind whatever world we were in. We know little about what lies beyond our borders for, ultimately, there is only Annwyn and the sea. No ship which passes over the horizon and out of sight of our lands ever returns."

"What about the Northmen?" he asked. They come from someplace else."

"That is true enough, but they come from the North, hugging the coast of Annwyn to get here. Even so they lose at least one ship in every three."

"This is all strange and terrible!" exclaimed Gwri. How is it that this is not common knowledge?"

"With no solution or explanation, it would only serve to frighten people, Gwri. Also, many do know of it, but most of those choose not to dwell on it. Few would care to run around panicking the countryside over something that has no explanation or cure. Of those that do, they tend to be considered madmen and are not taken seriously. In any case, most Tetherans are more concerned about bringing up their children and bringing in their crops."

"Yet how does this relate to why our travel is slower than expected?" Gwri asked again.

"I am getting to that. It is because Tethera has been growing larger since being brought to this world. We most often call it the Wild Growth."

Gwri swallowed, then asked, "Growing larger?"

"Yes, Gwri, Tethera is constantly growing larger. We do not quite know why. It never does this where anyone can see it, but it does it all the same. Consequently, the larger towns and villages stay the same size, but the space between them grows larger. The wilderness areas grow the fastest.

"This land is now much larger than it used to be, with ever greater distances between the abodes of men. Strange things lurk in the wilds that never did before, and ruins are sometimes found that no one remembers being there in times past.

"This growth would seem a good thing, for we value land, but it actually works against us. It makes trade and communication between the kingdoms more difficult. It provides more wilderness for Northmen, who continue to come down past Annwyn, hugging the coast in their clinker built ships, to build colonies upon our shores where we cannot easily dislodge them. And, all the while, the numbers of the Picts mushroom as, being nomads, they thrive with the advent of more wilderness in which to dwell."

It was all so odd and frightening that Gwri had nothing more to say on the matter. He did wonder if she was somehow having fun at his expense.

After the marshes came an area of hills so large that Gwri was unsure if they were not really mountains. He asked Cymri about it.

"Nay, Gwri, no mountains these. To see real mountains we would have had to travel west and north from Caer Mallcoedwig, not east. Ah, but I have never dared travel more than a bit over the forest and lake around your home. You have no idea what it is to soar above these hills. Almost, I think, I could choose to give up my former life and remain as I am, rather than give it up. If only I had a means to do both."

Gwri snorted, "Perhaps Moriganna can do it herself, but I cannot imagine any other who might. Somehow I doubt you are ready to become an evil enchantress."

"That would be a stretch, yet it cannot be the only way. High King Math could do it, Gwri. The gods loved him so very much that they bestowed upon him the power to take the form of any creature he could imagine."

"Yes, you have told me. Now that is a gift worth having! Yet I thought you told me such gifts always came at a price"

"Well, it did come with a price, although not one he ever had to pay."

Gwri's raised eyebrow indicated he was ready to hear more.

"You have really made raising your eyebrows part of your

repertoire, Gwri. Uncle Afaggdu has at least trained you to do that."

It was true, he realized. He raised and lowered his eyebrows a lot, but it had only really started when he met Afaggdu. He idly wondered what other habits of the world's ugliest warrior might had rubbed off on him.

"The price," Cymri resumed, "was that if he remained too long in any one form, his mind would slowly become like unto that of the form he was in. Allowed to go too far, his mind might never have returned, and he would have remained in whatever form he was in, forever."

Gwri started to say that if she had the same problem she would already have become a bird brain for good. Then he realized that might be a cruel thing to say to her and managed to bury the impulse to blurt it out.

Chapter XXXIII

A Plot Unfolded

They picked up six more guards on the way towards the courtyard. Llew dispatched two of the original four, along with four of the new ones, to go seek out others in the castle. They were also instructed to get all the rest of the servants out of hiding, as well. When they reached the entrance hall they had another surprise.

Hafgan was waiting for them. He was leaning casually against one wall, a sardonic grin on his face. He was dwarf-sized again but Llew made a mental note to never again even think about dwarves and Hafgan in so much as the same thought.

"I would wager you will not mistake a Spriggan for anything else ever again," Hafgan chuckled, still in an exceptionally good mood."

"Aye, Hafgan, that was amazing, truly. You and your sneaky friends came all this way just hoping Lord Arawen would show his ugly face?"

"Well," said Hafgan, "in addition to being really good at employing brute force, and a bit of stealth, turns out that Spriggans are also very good at holding a grudge. Especially when it involves Arawen."

"You and your friends were doing good, needful work up here," praised Llew. "All the same, I wish you had been with me when I met him a short time ago."

Hafgan bounced up off the wall, eyes agog. "What? You have seen him? Where is he?"

"Easy, friend Hafgan, he is gone, and no hound or hawk could catch him, but yes, he was here. We even spoke for a short time."

Hafgan looked like he was searching for his next words when Llew forestalled them. "You met him also; in fact, you even saw us speak with him."

If the subject had not been so dire, Llew might have laughed at the look on Hafgan's face. As it was, he took pity on him and told him, "King Iolo, it was King Iolo. Somehow the lord of the underworld possessed him and walked among us in his body." Llew shook his head, "We spent the night drinking and feasting with him and never even suspected." Llew thought about it a moment, "I suppose we should count our blessings that you snuck off into the kitchens early on, so he did not recognize you, either."

Hafgan found his voice, "So how did he escape?"

"He just went away and Iolo was back," Llew raised his hand to forestall Hafgan's questions, "but Iolo is dead so we can know no more than that."

It was clear that Hafgan was thinking furiously. Then he said, "Nay, your highness, it might be that we can. Come see what I have outside."

Llew and the others followed Hafgan out into the courtyard. Llew had been inwardly cringing at what it must look like out there, but he was shocked to his core by the reality. Of the smashed remains of the barrow warriors, there was nothing left. What looked like a dozen or so dwarves stood in a group around something in the center, yet the courtyard itself was completely free of any sort of remains.

Llew blinked twice and took a second look. "How is this possible?" he asked of Hafgan.

"You did not think we Spriggans were a messy lot did you? But come, see what we have."

The Spriggans parted respectfully to let Hafgan and Llew approach whatever it was they were standing about. For an instant Llew took it to be a severed head, then realized it was a living man buried up to his neck in the center of the courtyard.

Addressing the head, Llew said, "My goodness. Garl is it? I did not recognize you at first, without your body that is."

Garl did not speak but the glare he returned said a great deal.

Hafgan cleared his throat. "Garl here knows the way it is. He has been trying for so long to get into barrows that, obliging Spriggans that we are, why, we are likely to put him in one. On the other hand, he has spent centuries trying to avoid death. He has done every reprehensible act imaginable in his pursuit of ways to cheat it. It is somewhat ironic that this even includes pledging himself to the service of the Lord of Death."

"Will he answer our questions?" Llew asked.

"I think he has already indicated he would rather not, but there is one question he will have to answer." Hafgan patted Garl on the top of his bald head and said, "And that is whether or not his life, for the sake of which he has already broken many oaths, and all bounds of decency by the standards of any race, is more important than his single oath to Lord Arawen."

Garl grimaced, but said nothing.

Llew thought for a moment. "But why should that be a decision?" he asked. "He must know that King Iolo was actually Lord Arawen. We had a considerable discussion together although, admittedly, it was cut somewhat short when he suddenly recalled a pressing engagement and had to return to Annwyn."

Garl still did not say anything, but it was evident that Llew had drawn his undivided attention.

Llew rubbed his chin and seemed to stare off into empty space, ruminating. "I do recall that he did say to tell you, if I saw you, that he was looking forward to seeing you safely back in Annwyn. It was something about your future that he wanted to discuss. Honestly, it did not sound like a very encouraging future unless you were willing to help me with Moriganna."

Perhaps, thought Llew, Garl's jaw would have dropped but, being buried up to the top of his neck, there really was not any place it could drop to. Then he made a garbled sound and spat dirt. "What," he choked out in a voice so hoarse it was difficult to understand, "what were his exact words regarding what helping you would gain me?"

Llew continued to pretend it was a struggle to recall, then said, "Aha. It was something about how if you were you to aid in keeping me out of her grasp then 'the nature of that conversation might change.' He said I could tell you he said so."

Garl snarled, "What a poor attempt to deceive me. Deceit is the one thing Moriganna might have had a hope of training you in and clearly she failed miserably. Lord Arawen would never speak thusly."

"No, no," Llew disagreed, "that is fairly much exactly what he said, except that he kept referring to himself as a plurality. Are there a whole bunch of him inside of whatever passes for his mind? People would think very oddly of me if I went around calling myself 'we' and 'us' all the time when it was just me."

A remarkable change came over Garl's face, the anger and fury vanished and was replaced by a calm, almost friendly aspect. Indeed, it seemed as if another man completely was buried in the courtyard. In a voice only slightly less harsh, but with no hint of any hate or disrespect, he answered, "Your highness, it is merely the way he speaks. I think it may be an outmoded manner of speaking from some past age that he still indulges in. Please forgive my earlier doubts; I will aid you as I may." Garl attempted to smile but it looked more like his face was cracking.

"Very well," replied Llew, "let us test this new spirit of cooperation and then see if Hafgan and his folk are willing to dig you up. You came here with hundreds of barrow warriors for the express purpose of capturing me? Do you know who I am?"

"Why, your highness, as you have discovered, you are the rightful born heir to the throne of Gwent. This young woman with you is your sister, Llewellyn who, hiding under a man's name, has had to masquerade as you almost since birth in order to maintain Gwent's alliances and avoid the general anarchy involved should it become known that there was no male heir.

"Moriganna is a liar and a deceiver as you well know but in this she was merely wrong, not lying, as she is also an idiot. She has told you, incorrectly, that you are a just an orphan lad that happens to bear the precise semblance of what she thinks is the Prince of Gwent, your sister clothed as a man."

Hafgan cleared his throat, "your highness, could I speak with you in complete privacy for a moment?"

Llew spared him a puzzled look. "Very well, friend Hafgan."

The two of them retreated across the courtyard to the side

of the stable and Llew asked, "What is it that you must speak to me of now? Whether he is telling us the truth or not, I want to hear what he says, now that we have him talking."

"Remember this while Garl is in such an affable mood," Hafgan said. "You must get your answers quickly. This whole happy ally thing will not last. Sooner or later it will occur to him that, while his Lord Arawen has suggested that he will let him survive if he does this, you have made no such promise yourself."

"Why would it matter? I cannot execute him outright if he is cooperating!" Llew exclaimed.

"Shush, lad, perhaps you cannot. It is a mark of how much I like you that I will now tell you a secret that you must hold dear. Spriggans will not normally kill mortals, or at least, not deliberately. Do not ask why. It is a very deep part of what we are. However—"

"Bide a moment!" exclaimed Llew. "That gauntlet you put me through could easily have gotten me killed!"

"No, lad, it could not have," Hafgan retorted, followed by a quick chuckle. "You were never in any danger. That ordeal was necessary, but it was never dangerous; it was only meant to seem so in order to get your attention."

Llew was gathering his breath for a rush of invective when Hafnar cut him off. "Keep your mind on the current target. That's Garl. Now, Garl here would be much improved by a century long stint amongst the dark dwarves. The work would do him good and so would making him a farmer at the end of it."

"I do not know that I can send a man to a century long servitude in the depths of the earth when he has cooperated with me," objected Llew.

"He is not cooperating with you, he is only telling you what he wants you to hear, nothing more. It does not absolve him of centuries of crimes. Nothing he does for you at Arawen's bidding will change his nature. If you let him, he will go forth from here and continue to commit horrors against your kind, even your own subjects. Worse, every new death he causes will be one you will share some responsibility for. Why? It will be because your deliberate actions and, here is the key part, *while knowing the cost in advance,* will have allowed them to happen.

"Whether you are to be a true king, or merely pretend to be one, you will have hard decisions to make at times. Hard decisions with serious consequences are things a king cannot shy from. A fair and just king would order Garl's death in a heartbeat. The only concession given might be to allow him a swift and private execution in exchange for services rendered. You are still too soft for that, so be glad you have a viable option."

Sensing Llew's uncertainty, he continued, "I will make it even easier for you. Your only real decision is whether to execute him or leave him to me and mine. If you try to free him, my lads will be enraged and likely kill him themselves."

Llew wondered why so many decisions he found himself faced with were either not really decisions at all or else were ultimatums. "You just said Spriggans cannot kill mortals."

"You have to learn to pay closer attention, lad. I said Spriggans will not normally kill mortals, I did not say they could not. If they kill him they are quite likely to cease being Spriggans. I would be a poor king if I permitted that to happen so I would have to do it myself to spare them. Then I would no longer be a Spriggan. That would be a poor outcome for the help I have given you."

"Nay, Hafgan, I will do nothing to jeopardize your crown or your . . . sprigganhood? In any case, one less king would do us little good and might well be disastrous. This group apparently needs five royals just to muddle along."

"Heh, your fellow highness, try six. My lads have been hiding all about this place since they followed us here and have heard many things. The residents are claiming that your steed is the 'King of All Horses.'"

"What? Gower? Why?"

"Well," said Hafgan, somewhat diffidently, "as horses go he may behave strangely but in all other matters he appears to be the very epitome of all a horse should be. Further, I am led to understand he is cutting quite a swath through the local mares and the new master of horse is more than happy to let him do so."

"What are you saying? Does that mean what I think it does?" Llew asked, dreading the answer.

"Oh aye, in the not too distant future they should be getting some outstanding additions to their stable." Hafgan paused and looked thoughtful, "Or possibly their kennel."

"Let us hope Oswalt ap Hire never hears of this," Llew muttered.

"Who, lad?"

Deciding that the conversation had already digressed sufficiently, Llew turned on his heel and returned to where Garl was mostly interred.

"Very well, Garl, no dissembling, why does Arawen know that I am the true heir to the King of Gwent, while wily old Moriganna does not?"

"Your highness, when you were born, she sent her men with a changeling to intercept your mother while she traveled. They were to substitute the changeling and bring you back to Moriganna with none the wiser. The changeling would probably soon sicken and die, as they are wont to do when cared for by humans in the absence of magic. At some later date of her own choosing, Moriganna would simply have had to produce you—her perfect puppet king through which she could rule."

"What actually happened?"

"Her huntsman returned to her and told her their targets had never come to the ambush point. Instead, after some of the queen's party had taken ill, they went to an inn where the queen and the boy prince died. The changeling she had obtained at great cost, and that they now carried, was useless."

"What actually happened?" Llew repeated.

"They actually told her that. That did happen."

"Very well, so what was the truth behind their lie?"

"The truth is that, unfortunately for them, we were able to ambush them. They told us they had already made the swap and offered you to us you in exchange for their lives. After a time they agreed that Lord Arawen would be the better master to serve and they returned to Moriganna keeping you, for the time being, to serve as the changeling babe. You no longer appeared to be a threat and it gave their story more credence."

"No doubt it would have amused you to have her unknowingly order the destruction of the very prize she sought," Hafgan added in an ominous tone.

Garl glanced worriedly at the Spriggan, then continued, "She returned to her stronghold. No doubt she had ordered her master of horse to dispose of you, but here something happened we did not expect. He must have actually been a bit soft and, given that he knew that you were actually human, and therefore not a changeling, he balked. You wound up with the stable master and his wife to raise as their own.

"Meanwhile, word came out that the girl babe had died while the boy had survived. We took this to mean that the master of horse had lied to us and not made the swap at all. Instead, he had taken the changeling back to Moriganna to be done away with. So we thought the girl and the changeling were dead, when actually it was only the changeling.

"Lord Arawen was most displeased the real boy was still alive and still in position to inherit, but he took some consolation in how much this would have discomfited Moriganna. Changelings are obtained only from the Fae folk, and only at a dreadful price. Her purchase price was wasted unnecessarily if the boy prince was the one that had survived. Indeed, we believe that, in her fury, she executed her master of horse in short order, the only one who knew who you truly were. This would have eliminated the only person who could have linked you to the changeling that should have died.

"Some years later she realized her stable boy bore enough resemblance to the Prince of Gwent that she might still carry off her scheme, even if at a later point in life. Eventually, we became aware of what she was planning and decided do something about it. Dylan sold out Moriganna to Lord Arawen and told us where we could snatch you and the real prince as well." Garl tried to shrug but this was apparently difficult to do when buried up to the chin. "Things have not gone so well since then," he added.

Llew pondered what Garl had said, not entirely sure what to ask next. Fortunately, Llewellyn had a few questions of her own.

"How did you know what Moriganna believed was false?"

Garl raised his eyebrows and said, "You told what you knew to what you thought was King Iolo at the feast last night. Although he did not choose to reveal himself to me as my master, he told me that much."

"Hmm," mused Llew, "so I did, yet that was rather late in the game. This army of barrow warriors you brought was already on the move. In truth, it was almost here. Why bring so many? Why bring any at all? Surely they expose Arawen's control of Caer Enion?"

"Collecting the heir seemed just a last minute bonus. They were to counter the forces we believe she has sent to kill your father."

"So you were to save my father? You expect me to believe that?"

"No, because that is not the reason we were sent. As far as we are concerned, it was never about your father. We were sent to overturn Moriganna's scheme. Saving your father was only a way in which to accomplish that purpose. Lord Arawen does not care about your father one way or another. Again, the aim was simply to crush Moriganna's plans decisively. She is the only real obstacle to Lord Arawen taking control of all of your little kingdoms."

"We shall see about that," Llew said darkly. "Very well then, if Moriganna's agents are after my father, how could you hope to stop them with barrow warriors? No one would allow your cadaverous minions into Caerleon."

"They would not have to enter. We would not even have gone to Caerleon because Moriganna's agents would not have gone there."

"How so? demanded Llewellyn.

"Because someone, probably Moriganna, must have told the king that Princess Llewellyn was fleeing toward home from this direction, and he is coming for her. No doubt Moriganna's shape-shifters are waiting in ambush for him along the road somewhere, even as we speak."

Chapter XXXIV

Gwri's Tale: The Chase Quickens

On the sixth day they reached the River Dee. It was not a terribly wide river. Gwri was certain he could have thrown a stone clear across it, but it was too deep to safely ford. They lost most of a day cobbling together rafts and running ropes to shuttle all the horses across. Everyone got soaking wet and it was fairly miserable as things got cooler. The evening weather could be somewhat chilly at any time of the year, and the warmth of summer was slowly fading as the season drew to an end.

At this point, Captain Cai and one of the shape-shifters had a heated conversation. Cai was insolent and dismissive, while the shape-shifter was outright hostile and taciturn to the extreme. Although he had known they were capable of it, Gwri had never heard a shape-shifter speak before.

The upshot was they had reached a point where the prince should have been, and yet there was nothing. The words of the shape-shifter were too low and guttural for even Gwri to make them out, but he heard Cai clearly, as he ended the exchange, saying, "You have the noses for it. Find them!"

The shape-shifter called several more of his kind to him

and they began moving around the area, frequently stopping to sniff the air. One of them cried out in what must have been triumph and the others came running to him. They all sniffed, took a long moment, then raced for their horses.

"Move out," snapped the captain. "Those we pursue do not have horses, but they do have a head start, and these are not friendly lands."

They rode for perhaps an hour before coming across a small battlefield. The battle was over, although only quite recently. Gwri stared. Corpses of men lay everywhere. The dead were Tetherans, they wore the armor and clothes one would expect of a prince's retinue, but there were no weapons. There were also no other bodies.

"What happened here?" Gwri asked of Afaggdu.

"I would say it was Picts, lad. They are ruthless savages, every one of them."

"They killed what? Forty men? And took no losses of their own?"

"No lad, they are not immortal. They do not even wear armor. There is a good chance they took even more losses than these boys did. They just do not leave their dead behind when they can avoid it."

One of the shape-shifters had dismounted to check the corpses. Gwri watched with disgust while it touched a finger to the blood on one of the bodies, then appeared to taste it. He held up two fingers. Two others circled the area and pointed in different directions than that from which they had come.

"He is saying this happened about two hours ago," Captain Cai relayed to all present. Then he glanced at Gwri, "Your highness, I must ask that you stay out of this skirmish to come. Regardless of how safe and one-sided it may seem, we simply cannot afford you getting killed at this point."

"Or even scarred, eh?" queried Gwri.

"That is of a less concern," Cai said in a dismissive voice. "King Pendaran is the only one of consequence who might still detect the exchange, but it will not matter. He will probably die tragically just hours before his son, who was presumed lost at sea, returns to his side."

Afaggdu waited until the mercenary had ridden off a short distance, then spoke in a low voice to Gwri, "I did not think Moriganna would let that go undone. We will do what we can to prevent that as well. I do wonder, though, what Cai thinks will happen to his men when all this is finished. They would be entirely too many witnesses for this sort of thing, and he is too clever, in a nasty sort of way, not to know it. Surely it has dawned on him that this is what the shape-shifters must be for?"

"He is a cold fish but, as you say, he is clever. Perhaps he has a private deal with Moriganna," Gwri suggested.

"Well he certainly might think he does, but she does not trust him enough for that."

"Are you sure she does not?"

"Pretty sure, lad. She has promised me a substantial bonus to put him down the instant you are king. I held out for that lovely sword you are wearing. Little does she know it is my brother's blade."

Gwri was taken a bit back by that. His arms instructor had a ruthless side, but he was certain Moriganna had misjudged Afaggdu badly if she thought he would serve as a hired assassin, no matter what the price. Still, if he saw Cai as a menace he might do it anyway. *No,* Llew corrected himself, Cai was a poisonous snake and Afaggdu saw nothing commendable about dealing with such as though they were anything else. It was likely, then, that the mercenary captain's days were already numbered.

"Now, not to change the subject, lad, but you notice our good Captain Cai does not seem upset?"

Llew glanced at the captain, then back at Afaggdu, "He is calm as can be. Why is that?"

"It is because the prince is not here among the bodies. That means he still has a chance to succeed and get paid, plus whatever bonuses he was offered for a live capture. Also, there will not be much of a fight now, when we overtake them. Mercenaries like nothing better than to collect pay for very little risk.

"Be ready. They will not be moving far or fast and we will run them down in short order. There cannot be more than a handful left, and unmounted men against our force would have to outnumber us hugely to be a threat.

"Hopefully, if there are any men left guarding the prince, they will have the good sense to run. This may be hard to watch and harder to accept, but keep in mind that we may not be able to save them. Yet we do have to get the prince out of here, else many more than a few royal guardsmen and sailors will die."

"What about the remaining Picts?"

"They went off in a different direction. The Picts, for all their ferocity, are tribal sorts. They cannot suffer endless casualties without ending their own line. We should have nothing to deal with save what little of the prince's men yet remain."

Chapter XXXV

The Hand of Moriganna

Llew and Llewellyn had both heard enough. Under their direction Caer Einion was mobilized and very little sleep was had that night. The armory was opened and more horses were brought in from the village. At dawn, they would ride out, accompanied by a guard of forty of the late king Iolo's men.

Garl would ride with them as well, a watchful Hafgan at his side. The other Spriggans had all melted away and disappeared at some point. When Llew asked the diminutive king about it, his reply was simply that Spriggans were not terribly concerned with Moriganna, or King Pendaran, and were quite confident of Hafgan's ability to keep Garl on a short leash.

Cymri would wing far overhead, keeping a watchful eye on everything. Llew hoped she could spot Moriganna's ambush before they encountered it.

The plan itself was a simple one. By traveling quickly, and spying ahead, they hoped to reach the enemy before the king of Gwent could reach their ambush and, with any luck, Llew's force would take them at least partially unawares, and from an unexpected direction.

Llew sincerely hoped Moriganna was running low on shape-shifters. It was never far from his thoughts that his own small party, even if one was a Spriggan, and even when accompanied by forty men, and a very questionable ally in the person of Garl, was still nothing like the three hundred barrow warriors that Lord Arawen had summoned to deal with the same problem.

Another problem was much easier to dispense with. Using Hafgan as their interpreter, Llew and Llewellyn spent a short space of time talking with Cymri about the late King Iolo. It seemed his wives had both died, along with his only child, and he had no living siblings, or uncles. *Finally*, Llew thought thankfully, *I face a problem that circumstances have made easier to resolve, rather than more difficult.*

After speaking with his guards, he and Llewellyn went straightaway to the armory where a large group of guardsmen were outfitting for the coming expedition.

"Rhodri ap Nynniaw," he said abruptly, as he strode up to one of the guardsmen, "kneel."

The guardsman's face betrayed puzzlement and not a little trepidation but he did as commanded. Several of the other guardsmen looked concerned but none intervened.

"Do you, Rhodri ap Nynniaw, swear to serve my father, King Pendaran of Gwent, in all things and with all of your loyalty and courage, so long as either of you should live, and after that, his heirs, whomsoever they may be?"

Still looking confused, Rhodri said, "I will your highness, and gladly, too."

With a practiced move almost too fast to follow, Llew drew his sword and stopped the blade so that it just barely touched the top of Rhodri's head. "Then, pursuant only to my father's approval, I hereby crown you King Rhodri of Einionault, long may you reign."

It was too sudden for Rhodri to take in all at once. "S-sire?" he stammered.

Llew sheathed his sword. He and Llewellyn both came forward and, each taking one of Rhodri's hands, pulled him back to a standing position. "Welcome to the brotherhood of royalty," said Llew, giving him what he hoped was a companionable embrace.

"Aye," added Llewellyn, "I understand the duties may be onerous at times, but it has its compensations." She proffered her hand and King Rhodri recovered his wits sufficiently to receive it and bend to kiss it.

"But sire," King Rhodri protested. "Iolo and I were related, it is true, yet I cannot say that there is not some better claim to the throne."

"It matters not," Llew replied airily, "just before he died, Iolo suggested to me that the throne would be yours upon his death." Which was actually true, sort of. "That he did not have time to publicly declare you his heir matters not. I heard it. Who questions it?"

The armory was extremely quiet for a moment until a nervous guardsman dropped a shield he had been polishing.

Once the noise had stopped, Llew said, "Your people have already prepared your predecessor's chambers for me and mine. With your permission, I will retain them until we leave."

"I think that might be best, Prince Llew," said Rhodri, already recovering some aplomb.

"Of course," warned Llew, "celebration must wait. We still need to ride at dawn with forty of your finest. Now we will leave you to prepare yourself and your men as best you see fit."

King Rhodri stood straight and saluted smartly, right fist over his heart. "Yes, my liege, we shall not disappoint you."

An odd look came over King Rhodri's face, "Although I believe I will take a moment to further exhort one of my captains to even greater efforts."

Llew smiled, "Would that be a certain Lunid ap Rhein by name?"

"Why that would be the very one, your highness."

"Not a bad idea," said Llewellyn, "both a duty and a compensation at once. Just please try to be sure you balance the two."

Llew turned to all the open-mouthed guardsmen who had been watching the exchange. "Well?" he growled. "I hereby give you King Rhodri. I trust you all remember how to greet your new king?"

For their part, the guardsmen all fell to one knee and each pledged fealty to King Rhodri.

Upon leaving the armory, Llew withdrew into an alcove and motioned for Llewellyn to join him.

"Llew, what is it?" she asked with concern at the strain she saw on his face.

"Llewellyn, how do you do it?"

She looked puzzled as she asked, "Do what?"

"I am trying to put the best face on everything, but I am so far out of my depth I am drowning," Llew began. "Everything, from evading Picts and facing down bandits, dealing with enchanted creatures in their own lair, ordering grown men many times my age about as if it were the most natural thing in the world, putting a bold face on when dealing with the Lord of Death and his ancient minion, even crowning King Rhodri just now—it is all just an act.

"I am pretending to be a hero and a prince, a warrior and, most of all, a grown man, yet all of it feels unnatural. It is not me doing it. It is a role I am both playing at and hiding behind. No one is more surprised than me when people continue to take it at face value, yet there is so much at stake if I fail in a single performance!"

"You need some rest," Llewellyn said gravely. "You have had so little since this all began."

"It is not just that," he insisted.

"Shh, I know, Llew. Come, I will tell you a secret. It is not just you. I have felt that way my entire life. The only thing that helps is experience and, more than that, knowing that you are not alone. Many people are in the same shoes."

"I do not think Helgar ever has such doubts."

Llewellyn giggled, "No, I rather suspect not, but we might be surprised. There are also many other people who do not ever feel this way, but I do not think it is because they are more capable. I believe it is because they just are not in the habit of thinking about such things. It is not their nature. I used to envy them because they seem happier. It may indeed be that they are happier. But I would not exchange places with any of them. I think, by taking so much for granted, that they miss a great deal in life.

"Keep doing what you are doing, Llew, no one could do it better."

* * *

It was an exhausted Llew who returned alone to the king's chambers nearly an hour later. Llewellyn had stopped off along the way to confer with some of the chief servitors, while his personal guards had remained just outside the king's inner sanctum, guarding the entrance. With luck, he hoped he could still get in three or four hours of much needed sleep.

He met Addfwyn coming out of the royal bedchamber. The former crofter held the doors for Llew and offered, "I hope the room will meet with your approval, your highness."

"I am sure it will beat sleeping on the road by a considerable margin, Addfwyn, thank you."

Llew paused at the entrance to the bedchamber, closed the doors, and wryly considered the unaccustomed luxury. Someone, probably Addfwyn just now, had even prepared a basin of still-steaming hot water, with scented soap and embroidered cloths, and placed it on a piece of furniture that had a small yet incredibly valuable looking reflecting glass fixed on the wall behind it. He could not pass this up!

Tossing aside his tunic and baldric, Llew washed his face and neck with the great abandon of a man who has needed just that for several weeks. He dried his eyes and nose, then lifted his head and peered into the looking glass to see the results—which was when he noticed that someone was standing directly behind him.

He spun about, reaching instinctively for his sword, but he had already taken it off and leaned it against one wall.

Addfwyn was there, but only for a moment. His form rippled and Moriganna stood there in his place.

Llew gaped for a moment before he demanded, "How did you get here so quickly? And how did you get in here?"

The Queen of Deception laughed lightly, "Did you really think to escape me that easily, my stable boy son? I made you all that you are and, even though you are not yet fully forged, you are proving to be as well-made as any accomplishment of mine should be. You even sent that vile nuisance, the one that calls itself the Lord of Death, packing for his dreary little land. Now but one step remains, we remove Pendaran so you immediately ascend to the throne, and our success is then complete."

Llew straightened, "I am not yours to command any more, Moriganna."

"Silly boy, you were never not mine to command. Recognize that. Also recognize that this is not the way it need be, going forward. Then we can get about the business of restoring the great kingdom. I know that is what you want as well. As a bonus, we will make you high king in the process. Oh, will not that infuriate Lord Arawen beyond measure?"

"I will not be your puppet, Moriganna."

"It will not be like that, Llew. You will be king and, after that, high king, with all that implies. To all and sundry I will simply be your adviser. All kings have them, all kings employ them. When you grow old and pass on I will ensure a smooth transition of power to your heirs. Your line will prevail throughout all the ages of this world. I will personally see to it, for it is my line as well."

"That will not do, Moriganna, I know you far too well. Such a world would be little more than your village at Caer Mallcoedwig writ large."

"Bah, my subjects do not starve, nor do they freeze in the winter—any winter. When they are severely injured I heal them. When they are seriously ill my servants bring them unguents and elixirs to cure them or ease their passing. They are taxed more lightly than any people in all of Tethera. They are safe from bandits, Northmen, Picts, other kingdoms, and even those things that go bump in the night, and believe me when I say that things that go bump in the night can be most unkind to mortals."

"They live in fear, Moriganna. They live in constant fear of falling afoul of you. Their lives, and even those of their families, are—at all times—forfeit to your whims."

"You are young and untraveled, young Llew. How much of the world have you truly seen in your scant fourteen years? I have lived for many, many centuries and I have seen it all. Most men care for little more than a full belly, a warm place to sleep, and the simple possessions they need to make life a bit easier for them than it is for the wild animals of the forest. And, of course, they have little wish to be killed by barbarians, monsters, or in the petty wars of their own petty rulers.

"If the one who brings them all that finds it necessary to hold some few accountable for their loyalty and the quality of their service, what of it? Most men do not care for shades of gray, and want no part of them. They want black and white; they want to be told to do this and not to do that. This is the only way they can be happy, for it is the only way they feel free of concerns that they might somehow err, all unknowingly."

Llew's eyes narrowed and he said, "Safety cannot come at the price of freedom. It cannot come at the price of allowing oneself to be treated as a child."

"Indeed," Moriganna regarded him coldly, "safety at the cost of your youthful and ignorant ideas of freedom may not be a price all are willing to pay, but I believe most will. Moreover, when the issue is survival at the cost of such freedom, they pay it eagerly."

His hand out of sight, Llew used a trick Afaggdu had taught him and which he had also seen Llewellyn use. He now held, still concealed, his largest hidden dagger. Magic or no, Moriganna had been mad to come here alone.

"The only thing I see the people of the five kingdoms in

danger of not surviving is the crazed schemes of you and Lord Arawen, and your endless war with each other."

Moriganna laughed unkindly and, although she could not possibly have seen it, said, "A hidden dagger, really? You think I would not have brought bodyguards with me if I had anything to fear from that?"

She suddenly looked over her shoulder and spoke to empty air. "How dare you! How dare you all! You know I am not to be disturbed when that door is closed. I should—what? He is where? He has done what? Well what are you all standing here for? Go!" she shrieked. "Hold them off just a few moments, that is all it will take. If you survive, all the better, but you all know the fate of your families should you prove craven!"

Moriganna abruptly looked back at Llew, who had been momentarily frozen in astonishment. Had Moriganna completely taken leave of her senses? Surely it was long overdue, but why now?

"Well," she said in a much calmer tone of voice, "there is some minor trouble on the home front, it seems, so I will have to do this the hard way. We will simply finish our discussion later. Now, I believe if you were a turtle I would find you much easier to carry out of here."

She waved her hand at Llew and spoke a brief series of words that, except for the word 'turtle', he knew at once he could never hope to pronounce. Nor was there time to do anything except realize that he had failed. He waited for the end but nothing seemed to happen. Taking stock, he realized that if he was now a turtle then he must be a really big turtle, for the floor was still as far below him as it had been as a man. He shrugged his shoulders. It certainly did not feel like he had a shell. No turtle then.

Moriganna looked more shocked than he was. "No, I will not have this!" she cried. Waving her hand repeatedly she called out, "Chicken, mouse, rabbit, sparrow, monkey, beetle, snail." Yet still there was no effect.

Llew's eyes hardened. Had she just tried to turn him into a snail? Bringing the dagger into plain sight, he marched toward her with malevolent intent.

Clearly panicked, she gestured again, called out something in that strange tongue and, just like that, Llew could go no further, his feet were firmly stuck to the floor.

Once again Moriganna looked over her shoulder into empty space, saying furiously, "Even if you succeeded you know better than to interrupt me again—oh!" she exclaimed. "You? But you are in my service! How dare you?"

There was a pause, which Llew used in a desperate attempt to pull his feet free from the floor but with no success.

"You are what?" Moriganna continued. "His brother? Rubbish! Taliesin is centuries old, he has no living brothers and even if you were one, this does you no good. Only by shattering the amulet I used when I sealed him into a tree, and let his daughter become a bird, can they possibly be freed—but the amulet is well beyond your reach.

"No, I certainly cannot," she continued, "and if you ever want to see him stop dropping acorns on the ground you had better either put down your weapons or go take an axe to him and put him out of his misery. Perhaps his remains would make some nice shelves for your library."

Moriganna abruptly returned her attention to Llew and a vision of pure panic blossomed on her visage when she turned her head back about and could see him.

The reason for this was that, for his own part, and while

still stuck to the stone floor, Llew had knelt while placing Cymri's amulet on the floor before him and was holding the pommel of his dagger just a short distance above it. Llew had been terribly worried he was about to do the wrong thing but the look on her face was a welcome confirmation that this was not the case. With a downward swing of the pommel he shattered the amulet into a myriad number of shards. It had always appeared to be silver but, given the shards, seemed more like some crystal in its composition.

"You have no idea what you have done," hissed Moriganna.

Llew smiled mirthlessly and said, "Oh, I think perhaps I do."

"Fool, I am not speaking of the amulet. I am speaking of breaking your oath to me. You must now be the one to kill Pendaran and it will be much more dangerous. You must make it look like an accident or else pin the blame elsewhere. Take his throne. Do it quickly and I will contact you later."

"If," drawled Llew, "you were ever under the impression that I gave an oath to you, then I assure you that either, one, you were incorrect or, two, I had my fingers crossed."

With a hiss, she turned her attention back over her shoulder again. Llew again tried to free his feet, then it occurred to him to just slip them out of his boots.

"Why, Lord Taliesin," Moriganna began, "fancy seeing you again. My, you look nice! And wearing my colors, too. Your brother was just telling me he was here to take you home—what, wait! Do not touch those chalk lines! It is a very complex spell and it is all that is keeping—"

Her voice chopped off abruptly and as it did so, she changed. Llew found himself two feet away from a seven foot tall shape-shifter as it turned its head back from looking over its shoulder to gaze directly forward and down at him.

Time seemed to slow down. *Well,* Llew thought to himself, *here we are, I know firsthand how formidable barrow warriors are and these things rip right through them. I really wanted to see more of my own story, but it would seem it ends here. I hope Llewellyn finds a way to continue to hold the kingdoms together. I hope Cymri is human again—oh gods, I hope she was not flying! If she changed back to human when I smashed the amulet—*

All this was while he drove his dagger up under the monster's chin, burying it in the roof of its mouth and pinning those horrendous fangs shut. Remembering advice Afaggdu had once given him on how the fastest way to get to the floor was to simply let himself fall, he released the dagger and did just that, rolling under a table and out from under the other side while the shape-shifter's claws closed where he had been standing a full half a second before. Springing to his stocking clad feet, Llew ran headlong for the door.

Meanwhile the beast ripped the dagger free and was able to let out its first real roar. Then it came leaping over the table for him. It was a very well made table, but it had never been intended for that kind of weight or that kind of force. It shattered into fragments and dumped the shape-shifter to the floor. Proving it had no kinship with felines of any kind, Llew's pursuer lost precious seconds regaining its feet amidst the splintered remains of the collapsed table. This gave Llew the time he needed to get to the door and close it just as the monster reached it.

The creature was too enraged to use the door handle, if it even knew how. Instead the door rumbled and shook as though it had been struck by a battering ram; Llew was tossed several feet backwards onto the floor. It was abundantly clear that one or two attempts more was all the door could withstand.

Llew picked himself up and, despite everything, could not resist shouting, "Who is there?" in Helgar's accent as he raced for the next door. Somehow the inner bar had been set to hold it shut but it smashed open as he reached it and three of King Rhodri's guardsmen came rushing in. He was taken completely by surprise when they tackled him and fell on top of him.

It took Llew several seconds to fight partially free of their clutches and, while he did so, he heard the door to the bedchamber shatter, accompanied by a terrible growl that was all the more terrifying for its immediate proximity. Thus he could do nothing other than watch as the whole thing came to its gory conclusion.

The shape-shifter sprang into the room, then pivoted and sprang again. Coming in with several others just behind the guardsmen, Princess Llewellyn reached it first and made a sweeping, spinning attack that carried her in close and brought her sword in an almost flat swing under the beast while it was still in mid-leap, then her continued rotation spun her away to one side. The creature landed with a whimper and an ungainly sprawl. Llewellyn's swing had removed both its front paws in mid-leap. King Rhodri leapt forward and pinned it to the floor with a heavy boar spear, allowing Helgar to rush up and bring down his enormous axe in a mighty swing.

Llew winced. He somewhat doubted that even a Spriggan in its giant form could have survived that final strike.

"Sorry, my lord," one of the guards offered as they let him up. "We was under orders to keep you from harm."

"Ah, there you are, sire," said King Rhodri, leaving the boar spear where he had planted it. "When we heard the commotion I was already coming to tell you that King Pendaran and his escort are at the gate requesting entrance."

Llew was still trying to absorb that when Lunid ap Rhein came hurrying in and whispered something fairly lengthy to King Rhodri.

"Ah," said King Rhodri, "it never rains but it pours. I am told there is also a young, naked, red-headed woman on the roof of the great hall who is holding on to the weather vane for dear life, while a black bird sits on it and caws at her. Apparently she is calling for help, and all the while making loud and unseemly remarks about your parentage, Prince Llew."

Llewellyn glanced at Lunid ap Rhein, "Excellent, that sounds like that would be our little troupe's bard."

To his credit, Lunid ap Rhein did not react at all save possibly for a slight reddening of his ears.

Chapter XXXVI

Gwri's Tale: The End and the Beginning

The path the shape-shifters followed led around a pair of low, almost treeless, hills, into a thick forest just beyond. They were still a small distance from the tree line when the mercenaries in front set up a clamor and kicked their horses into a gallop. Gwri strained to stand in his saddle and was rewarded with a glimpse of a few men on foot fleeing into the tree line.

"This is it," Afaggdu commented grimly. "Tell Cymri to fly high, stay safe, and keep a look out. You stay here and I will go ahead and try to make sure no hothead hurts the prince. Maybe I can save some of the others, too, but I would give long odds against it."

The arms instructor took a deep breath and let it out. "A final thing, lad, and this is an important one. I must tell you now because I might not be able to later. Stop calling yourself Gwri. Do not let anyone else call you that either—not anymore."

"What? Why not?"

"They only called you that because you were a boy with fair hair, and they thought you had no name of your own. You do have a name, and it is a good one. It was given to you before you ever came to live at Caer Mallcoedwig. It is Llew, do not forget that. Do not allow anyone to call you differently."

"But Llew is the prince we are here to rescue!"

"Aye, and I am telling you, it is not one whit less your name than it is his."

"This is insanity," he protested.

"No, it is necessity. Now then, what is your name?"

"But—"

"That is what you sit on, it is not your name. What is your name? Tell me!"

Hesitantly, almost one word at a time, the young man said, "My name is . . . Llew?"

"That is a question, not an answer. Say it as an answer."

"My name is Llew," said the one who had formerly been Gwri.

"Good, now do not, under any circumstances, regardless of what happens, who lives, or who dies, forget that."

Afaggdu nudged his horse and galloped down toward the trees. At the rate he was going, he would not get there before all of the accompanying mercenaries and shape-shifters, but he would still get there ahead of most of them.

The young man put his hand to his medallion.

"Do not trouble yourself," scoffed Cymri. "I love my uncle but he is bit thick in some ways. Just because he cannot understand my words does not mean I cannot understand his as clearly as you can. Not to worry; I will stay out of the way." With that, she sprang off his shoulder, flapping wildly and ascending very quickly.

It was getting a bit lonely where he was. It occurred to him he was not well-suited for waiting and, he reasoned, it could not be any safer to remain out here by himself, certainly not with bands of bloodthirsty Picts running about. "Besides," he told Gower, "it was probably Gwri that was supposed to wait here, but I am Llew, not Gwri. This Llew is already a different sort of fellow. This Llew would never sit back and let others take his risks for him."

After considering it a moment, he had Gower proceed to trot them down to the forest. They had only just entered the trees when he heard fighting ahead of him. There were a few yells, but it really did not sound any worse than the practice yard when there were several men going at it at once. The fighting sounds ended almost as quickly as they started. Then there was only the sound of men yelling to each other, as well as that of brush and sticks cracking underfoot, as they ran about doing something.

A moment later, the forest ahead of him was suddenly alive again with the sounds of movement and fighting, mixed with the screams of men and horses, and the wild howls of something else. It sounded as though the hunters might have become the prey—and the prince he had come to save lay somewhere in the midst of that!

He hesitated only a moment, then said aloud, "You see? There is no choice here. The one we seek is somewhere in the thick of this mess and, whoever I may be, my future most certainly depends on finding the true heir of Gwent and getting him home to his kingdom."

Although he had ostensibly been speaking to Gower, he suddenly knew full well he had actually been persuading himself. With that realization, the one now called Llew drew his sword and, together, he and Gower plunged ahead toward the heart of the conflict.

Chapter XXXVII

The King Speaks

Two weeks after arriving in the capital of Gwent, Llew stood on the highest balcony of Caerleon, sometimes called the last great castle. It was a magnificent construction, with gleaming white walls in the noonday sun, surrounded by a man-made lake. The scale was difficult to believe, the inner courtyard alone spanned several acres. Built with both defensive and aesthetic considerations in mind, it possessed a sheer overwhelming majesty. Draped in massive curtain walls, it was festooned with soaring towers and great arches. Every possible approach was designed to constrict an attacker and force him over multiple obstacles, always funneling him under and along the length of high defensive walls, and against successive barbicans, each more daunting than the one before it.

It stood guard over the town of Caerwent, a town bigger that any Llew could ever have imagined existing. Some believed it actually qualified as a full-blown city, greater even than some in ancient times. Possibly it even rivaled those of the fabled Roaming Empire itself. Sadly, now that it was become the Sunken Empire, only the people of the sea could have visited the ruins and made the comparison. Llew somehow doubted it was something that Dylan would ever be likely to discuss with him.

Besieging Caerleon would require many armies and a great fleet to interdict the river that could otherwise be used to bring in supplies from the coast. Storming it, Llew suspected, would require more armies than anyone, perhaps even the Lord of Annwyn and Moriganna together, could ever hope to raise on their own. Every tower had pennons flying.

The celebration following the news that Prince Llew had escaped the clutches of Dylan, Moriganna, and Arawen himself and returned safely with the Princess Llewellyn, long thought dead in infancy, yet actually hale and whole and a bit of a hero in her own right, had instigated celebrations that had lasted a solid week.

For that was the story that they had gone with. Prince Llew, after all, had been alive and well and right there in Caerleon nearly all of his life so far as anyone knew.

The stories about their adventures that were currently making the rounds were certainly enough to make even Helgar blush, almost. The young Northman, contrary to Llew and Llewellyn's expectations, was hugely popular among the people and was hardly allowed to pay for a meal or a drink anywhere he went. Yet Llew knew these people hated and feared Northmen in general as much as they ever had.

Hafgan had quite frequently accompanied Helgar as they made their rounds and though he had never said a word about being a Spriggan, he had told many stories of how great and fierce they were, and of their cunning king, the personal foe of all things of Arawen.

Llew and his father had spent considerable time with Hafgan trying to get the Spriggan monarch to ally with them against Arawen and Moriganna. The diminutive king had been adamant in his refusal. His own subjects, he explained, would never countenance a war on Moriganna without considerably more cause than she had given them.

On the other hand, neither would he make an alliance with mortals against the Lord of Death, preferring the freedom to move howsoever he saw fit. If they deemed it the best course for eventual success, Spriggans were prepared to wait far longer than the lives of mere mortals. And yet, Hafgan had allowed that, if his friend Llew ever found a solid plan to bring the Lord of Annwyn down, Spriggan assistance might be quite readily available.

When Llew asked him where Garl was, Hafgan had shrugged and asked, "Garl who?" Llew could only hope the dark dwarves would get good use of him in the coming century as it seemed unlikely he would be able to return to his master in the land of Annwyn any time soon. That might even be fortunate for him, depending on whether he had earned a reprieve for the little bit of help he had provided Llew in eluding Moriganna.

Shortly after that, the king of Spriggans had vanished. Presumably he was back in his own demesne by now, deep beneath the sometimes ruins of Cas-Eiddew.

Before he left, when the two of them were alone, he told Llew one more thing. "Moriganna seems to think you are some lowly born that she has forged into a weapon, albeit one that has turned in her hand. Arawen and the rest here think you are Pendaran's son and that the babe which died was only a changeling.

"Keep an open mind going forward, lad, because, whatever the truth, I know that both of those are wrong, at least in part, if not in all."

"If you were to speculate, what other possibility is there?"

Llew had asked. "I am on the edge of nothingness; surely you can advance a theory, be it right or wrong."

Hafgan had hemmed and hawed a bit before he spoke again. "Lad, our best guess—and it is only a guess—is that you may be the changeling that was meant to be substituted for Pendaran's son and somehow you lived on after the original died. That is at least possible, Caer Mallcoedwig is a magical place and that might have been enough to let a changeling babe survive, but that cannot be all of it either. There are too many holes.

"As I suggested, just keep an open mind. Be on the lookout for additional clues if you want to pursue this. Ah, and cheer up!" Hafgan advised, as he clapped Llew on the arm. "You have lots to do and too much speculating on dark mysteries will just distract you."

It was only a bit later that Llew recalled the words Oswalt ap Hire, Queen Moriganna's kennel master, had once spoken to him: 'Yet to preserve a line it is necessary to eliminate all those that merely resemble what they are supposed to be.' Mulling over this was still costing Llew a great deal of sleep.

Llew turned back to step inside the richly appointed room behind him. Llewellyn—he still had to mentally shake himself to think of her as his sister—was still talking to King Pendaran. Father . . . the other name for him was father. Llew was truly having trouble with that concept. Moriganna had trained him to be a prince and a king, not a brother, and certainly not—and he swallowed hard at the thought—a son.

Both of them looked up as he reentered and smiled at him. He could not help smiling back.

Llew had done his best to explain that he might not be who they thought he was. He had even mentioned Hafgan's inability to perceive him and the Spriggan's belief that it was because he did not know who he was. The king had punched holes in every objection. Finally, he had pointed out that even if the Spriggan was right about why he could not see Llew, it might not be because Llew did not know who he was, so much as it might be because Llew did not yet completely believe that he was who he was.

"It is hard to take in all at once, son," he had said. "But you are Llew. We needed you so badly and here you are. Dead for nearly fifteen years and—oh, you did not know? Yes, you and Llewellyn have your birthday next month, on the seventh. It is a good thing, too. I cannot have children riding around the countryside and pounding all of my enemies into submission for me. People might start to talk."

The king had laughed at that. "Where was I? Ah, the point is that even if you were not actually Llew but, as Moriganna initially believed, just a happenstance look-alike, you are still a godsend, and no less my son, however you originated. You have brought back your sister, overturned a monstrous plot, defeated the Queen of Deceit, banished the Lord of Death, saved my life, provided us with a solution to a desperate deception we could not maintain much longer, and brought back hope, for our family, for our kingdom, and for all of Tethera."

Had the king's eyes looked a little moist?

"And, let us not forget, wounded the war chief of the Picts, foiling their invasion in the process. I am so proud to have you as my son that I would not care if that witch had conjured you up out of swamp moss," he had finished.

It had taken Llew awhile to find his voice after that. "So far as I know, she can turn any creature into any other creature but I do not believe she can turn someone permanently into one specific person or she would already have done so. Certainly I never saw her do that. Even that thing she did with the shape-shifter at Caer Enion, appearing first as Addfwyn and then as herself, was more of an illusion I think. Although," he considered, "she did use a shape-shifter to do it so mayhap that had something to do with it as well."

The king shook his head, "Bad business that. For years, she must have walked freely through Caerleon while occupying a possessed shape-shifter. She could have appeared to the rest of us as anyone she liked. We know she took different forms on a regular basis so she could put her offers to Afaggdu. She also must have watched Llewellyn frequently. We are so very fortunate she never saw through Llewellyn's disguise. She could have killed any of us at any time had she cared to."

Llew had been aghast when he thought this through. "How on earth can we protect ourselves against this," he had whispered.

King Pendaran had grinned and clapped him on the shoulder. "Oh, Caerleon is quite safe now. Cymri has always had a keen fascination for the kennels and she had a thought on the problem that was quite clever. It turns out dogs are not confused by shape-shifters' ways at all. They can smell them in whatever form they take. We always wondered why they would behave so strangely at times, growling and snarling at people they should have no trouble with. Now we know the reason. One mystery solved another. In the week after we returned, we discovered two shape-shifters here. One appeared as a baker's assistant, the other as a courier.

With a rueful sigh he added, "Or possibly it was the same one twice. The things are damnably hard to kill when they choose to flee, rather than stand and fight."

"What about Gower? How are the dogs reacting to him?'" Llew had asked nervously.

"Your splendid, ah, horse?" King Pendaran had raised his eyebrows before he replied, "Oh the dogs love him. They all defer to him just as though he was their pack leader, even as the horses all seem to assume he is their herd leader. Strange days indeed, eh?"

As for the Queen of Deceit herself, she was still free in the world and, no doubt, still plotting. At least, Llew thought thankfully, she would no longer be doing it at Caerleon. Nor would she be doing it any longer at Caer Mallcoedwig. A hero had led an uprising and turned her own long suffering people against her.

Fortunately for Llew, it was this that distracted her when she was speaking to him through a possessed shape-shifter. Word came that, after she inadvertently revealed what breaking the medallion would accomplish, and Llew had done it, Taliesin regained his form and raced to confront her.

Despite his and Afaggdu's best efforts, however, she still managed to escape. While a spell filled the room with a nearly impenetrable smoke, Moriganna had shape-shifted into something dreadful. She then batted away her enemies with a massive paw and gave a great roar before launching herself to freedom from the windows and flying away into the night sky.

Llew knew he had not seen the last of her. This was a thought which was still able to shake his new found confidence whenever he considered it.

So he was stuck. How ironic his greatest desire was to roam the world just to see what was out there. Now he must at least try to be who everyone thought he was, for none would accept any substitute. Worse, he knew what was at stake. He could not abandon these people, let alone all people, to the mercy of such as Arawen, Moriganna, Goll One-Eye, Dylan, and whatever else was out there scheming against the people of Tethera. It simply was not an option for anyone resembling the kind of person he wanted to be. Of course, he had no one to blame but himself. He had been the one trying to make a future for himself, after all.

He shook himself from his recollections as there came a staccato knock at the door. Without waiting for a response, Cymri poked her head in. "Are you royals receiving at this time?" she asked pertly.

Then, without waiting for an answer she strode right in. "Your highnesses, having only just arrived from their long journey, my father, Lord Taliesin, the Chief of Bards, and my uncle, Lord Afaggdu, the Scourge of Annwyn and the Liberator of Caer Mallcoedwig."

Llew reached Afaggdu in an instant and embraced him in welcome, exclaiming, "Last I saw of you there were barrow warriors on all sides and, well, frankly I did not know if I would ever see you again."

Afaggdu harrumphed, "Those poor wights are no real problem. Too many people are in all too big a rush to smack them down quick. You just have to settle down, find your rhythm, and do not be in such a hurry. You can always wear them down over time, a piece here and a piece there. To do so, you only have to do but one thing."

"And what is that one thing? It would have been nice to know when I met up with the fellow that was carrying away Llewellyn."

Afaggdu, gave him a stern look that broke up into a grin. "You just cannot let them kill you in the meantime."

Llew mock theatrically clapped his hand to his forehead, "Oh, why did I not think of that?"

Helgar had trailed the brothers in. "I am not so sure that is the best way," he opined, "smash them up into small pieces quickly and then there is more time for other things."

"Whatever works best, for you," laughed Llew. And then, "I think there may be different methods for different people and that this is acceptable, so long as their goals are in accordance."

Taliesin raised an entire eyebrow at that. "Afaggdu might have been right about you. Your instincts are good and are just what are needed in these times. I trust you found my sword useful after I misplaced it?"

"Oh, I certainly did," exclaimed Llew. "It never even seems to need sharpening. I know you had little say in the matter, but thank you very much for the loan."

He begin to unbuckle his baldric, but Taliesin reached out and stayed his hand. "Thank you, Prince Llew, but for the time being, at least, I feel safer with it on you than on me. That may change but, for now, please consider it my investment in your future. Please tell me you will keep it within easy reach, even when bathing, unless I call for it back?"

Llew opened his mouth to protest, then thought better of it. "I will do so, friend Taliesin, and thank you."

"Ah, by not arguing with me you are showing exceptional wisdom at an early age. Perhaps I could compose a song about that—but you still have a modicum of humility and it might make you uncomfortable, so never mind for now. The sword is named Fragaroc. It has other names as well, but remember that one. Moving on, I am supposing you might have some questions for Afaggdu?"

"Very well," replied Llew, turning to his arms instructor. "All we heard was that a hero of 'horrifying visage' drove the old witch out. You can start right where I rode away from that little set-to you were having under the big tree."

"Alright then, your highness. You rode off after my former student, the one that was not what he seemed to be, and I lost all track of time. Eventually all those rotting hulks of meat were finished off, and there was naught but me and a couple of the shape-shifters left. I figured there would never be a better opportunity, so I also polished them off—stupid things are too fond of fighting to even think about running away when they could and should—and headed back to Moriganna's. With no horses left it took me a bit. Once I arrived it was not too difficult to convince all the normal folk living there that, with me leading them, and most of her mercenaries and almost all of her shape-shifters gone off and away, it was time to get rid of the old witch."

"What about the guardsmen?" Llew inquired.

"Oh, them? You think I could not handle forty lowly guardsmen on my own?"

Llew flinched and replied, "It does seem like quite a few, providing they did not all run for the hills when they saw your face again."

"Your highness should have more faith in me. I had three years to work on them. Most of them would have jumped off a cliff for me after the first year or two. Mercher was my number two."

Llew felt relieved at that news. "I am glad to hear that; none of them were really bad men. They just had the bad luck to be born in thralldom to Moriganna. I wonder what will become of them now?"

"I would say that is up to you, they were only too eager to put you on the throne when I offered them the chance."

"Me?" asked Llew. "Why me? I was not even there!"

"She made you her heir from what I heard; even used the

old blood ceremony. No way to undo that. Not to worry, I found a good steward for you and he will keep things running until you can give them some attention."

"Who would that be, Mercher again?"

"Nay, another fellow. Good man. He held everything together for years and years, kept things running and limited Moriganna's damage with her none the wiser. Now he does not have to hide. People jump to when he whistles, why yes they do."

"Really?" said Llew, slowly. "Who is this steward? He must be pretty sneaky because she would never have countenanced someone else having that much power."

"The man is brilliant. Be very glad he is on your side. He speaks quite highly of you and, what is more, Taliesin and I decided he meant it. His name is Tomos."

"Wait," Llew interjected. "Do you mean Slow Tomos?"

"Aye, that was his disguise. He pretended to be a bit addled so Moriganna would not suspect him, even if she suspected there might be someone like him. Can you imagine? Only a complete fool would not get to know the people around them well enough to see right through such a trick."

"Yes," said Llew, a bit sourly. "Only a complete fool would not."

"Where was I? Oh yes. We forced our way up to her solar pretty easily, but she was sealed behind these chalk lines that were like steel walls. Nothing we did could reach her through them. I was still debating what to do with her when Taliesin comes running up, no longer a tree, and wearing nothing but one of her banners wrapped around himself. Tal always knows what to do . . . mostly. One stroke on that harp and then he scuffed his toe through those chalk lines like they were nothing more than— hmm—lines of chalk. That ended her spell in a hurry."

"Wait," objected Llew, "how did he have that harp? From what little I knew, it was locked deep in her vaults."

"Oh, well, his harp. That harp is the same one he washed in to shore on when he was but a babe. He would have lost it long since were that easy to do, just as I did with my shield, but the harp always calls out to Tal when they are separated. It will even fly to his hand when he calls it, and it will destroy any obstacle that stands between them as it comes. He calls it Uaithne, but some believe that is actually the name of a harper who played it in ancient times, and whose very soul became embedded in its wood, where it remains unto this day.

"Where was I? Ah, so there was Moriganna defenseless before us. Sadly, both of us together and we still could not think quickly enough, or swing fast enough, to keep her from escaping. We tripped all over ourselves in that thick smoke she conjured."

"It is probably just as well, for the moment," consoled Llew. "Were she no longer in the equation, Lord Arawen would feel free to throw all of his forces against us at once. As it is, he must still tread carefully for she certainly has other schemes to fall back on."

A voice spoke from behind him. "I still look forward to the day when she reaps the rich harvest she has sown. After my beloved Arianrod died so suddenly, and of a foul disease that none have ever encountered, either before or since, we have always suspected the hand of the Lord of Death. Finding Moriganna so caught up in those events makes it seem we should, perhaps, change our focus."

Llew half turned, to see that his father and sister had finished their exchange with the bards and all four had joined them. "Nay, father, I spoke to both of them and am convinced by their hate for one another that this is a very old game between them. Whenever one of them attempts to move against Tethera, the other then moves to take advantage of the situation, spoiling the plans of the first. My feeling is that it would be very unlikely for both not to be involved, each to their own purpose, in what happened to our family when . . . mother . . .another strange word to force past his lips—was killed."

Afaggdu nodded, "Not quite fifteen and you already have those two figured out. Not too bad, Llew. I will be back later but I need to make my exit for now. My wife and children have not seen me for three years and I have some things to catch up on."

"Your wife and children?" blurted Llew, before thinking.

Fortunately, Afaggdu just laughed. "Does that surprise you lad? That I have a wife and nine children? Ask Taliesin about it; women find me irresistible. Centuries upon centuries and I have never been unmarried for more than a year. My offspring must number in the hundreds and I have lost all count of my descendants. All of it is proof positive of the power of my personal charm—and the apparent fact that, regardless of whether or not it is beauty that draws men to women, it is not beauty that draws women to men!"

With that he made a hasty exit.

Llew was startled when someone grabbed him from the side and gave him a hearty hug. "What do you think of my star pupil, father?" Cymri asked of Taliesin.

"Star pupil? Was he not your only pupil? Have you ever even had another?" Taliesin retorted.

"Now, now, father, be nice. It is not about quantity after all; it is about quality. Once it gets around that I was Prince Llew's bardic mentor my reputation will be made."

"Somehow, I doubt notoriety is going to be a problem for any of you going forward," King Pendaran remarked.

Taliesin clapped King Pendaran on the back, a shocking familiarity. "Your young warrior's instincts are good ones. You have a keeper here, Pen."

Pen? Llew rolled that around in his mind. Perhaps, to a man of Taliesin's great age, all normal men seemed somewhat like children? In any case, Llew was certainly not going to take it amiss if the king himself did not.

"Yes," replied the king, "I think we will keep him about. He seems to pull his weight. Although that young Northman he brought with him bids fair to empty all the kitchens of Caerleon!"

Llew glanced at Helgar in time to see him blushing and remarked, "Well, that is not a sight we see every day."

Llewellyn laughed, "Do not be mindful of him, Helgar. Simply remind him of his own impending marriage to Princess Bloddeuwedd—she of the white flowers."

It was true, Llew's own furious blushing easily outmatched that of Helgar.

Author's Notes

In books we find, ready-made, our lands of enchantment. Some of these lands are special just to us and perhaps a few others, while some find favor from a far greater audience. We tend to like it when others like what we like, but we should not demand that they do, nor should it even be of central importance.

Two gentlemen, as the story goes, once met in a pub and lamented that no one wrote the kind of stories they wanted to read. To redress this, they each pledged to one another that they would go forth and, separately, each would undertake to write the kind of story they would like to read. Writing the kinds of stories they could not find but that they wanted to read eventually gifted us with Narnia and Middle-Earth. I can think of no better advice for creating fiction than to write the kinds of stories you would want to read.

I am speaking of enchanted lands, however, and although I have read many, many works of imaginative fiction, many of them extremely enjoyable, only a few have introduced me to additional lands of enchantment. Among them were places with names such as Earthsea, Prydain, Pern, Amber, the World of Tiers, and Xanth. Later I discovered the Kingdoms of the West, the Land of the True Game, the world of the Pliocene Exile, Hos-Hostigos, and the Dragaeran Empire. I am certain there are others I simply can't bring to the front of my mind as I write this.

All of these lands differ in their own way, even if they all bear certain similarities to each other as well. This is appropriate as they are intended for different audiences at different ages and are written in different times with different messages to support different stories and different types of stories. Further, if any two of these enchanted lands ever became identical, then there would no longer be two, just the one. If scientists, those who tell us that our own world is but one of many, are correct then I expect the same is true of these worlds as well, but I digress.

As thrilled as I am when I realize I have found a new candidate to add to my lands of enchantment, I am always greedy enough to wish that I had still more. Although I am no J.R.R. Tolkien or C.S. Lewis, I finally decided that I had to follow their lead and create my own enchanted land.

In creating an enchanted land in which to set your story it becomes abundantly clear that you are not so free as you might have thought. The problem is that every world imaginable is going to be, in some way, derivative. Try to imagine a setting for a story that has not a single thing in it you have heard of before.

After that fails, you are faced with picking things you like, then it becomes a filtering process. Inevitably, there are going to be some resemblances to other things. I want swords and magic? Wonderful, now my work is derivative of every sword and sorcery story ever written.

You can make the conscious effort to throw out anything

that seems overly derivative (if you think you can define what that means) but this is somewhat like treading water in the middle of the ocean. The longer you must do it, the harder and harder it becomes to keep doing it . You can only hope to do it long enough to encounter a rescue ship—and that's a very long hope indeed—which in this case is a metaphor for reaching the end of the story.

I wanted what I like. Swords and horses and castles and deep intrigues and elder races and dark magic and brave companions and evil villains and noble steeds and scary monsters and, against it all, a single protagonist on his own hero's journey.

Then I needed my land of enchantment. Authors have used everything from the Earth's ancient past to alien planets, alternate realities, and the far future, and that's just as their jumping off points.

Personally, I am not a big believer in labeling people based on their genetic makeup, or where their ancestors lived but, if I were, then I would have to insist on calling myself a Celtic-American. I made the conscious decision that I wanted to do an essentially Celtic-based fantasy, utilizing elements of Celtic myth, and set in a time not entirely dissimilar from the period after the Roman legions left Briton, but without the Saxons and Angles and Normans and whoever else came calling. I really wanted to avoid King Arthur as I am tired unto death of King Arthur stories. It is no reflection on them, it is just that I've read far too many.

I wanted Celts when they dominated the British Isle and before they were relegated to the areas of modern day Scotland, Wales, and Ireland. I also wanted Picts. I freely confess that were the Picts in this tale meant to be historical representatives, I would have done them poor service—especially considering that I probably have a fair number of them as ancestors. Do not worry, should the tale continue, our heroes will eventually find there is far more to Picts than the ones they have met thus far.

At least I think they will. It's constantly amazing to me how I can outline a story, events, back-story, and sketch out the characters I want interacting within it. Then a curious thing happens which I have often heard other writers speak of but which still amazes me. Almost like a newly forged weapon that turns on its maker, they become something else. In their interactions with each other, personalities emerge and I discover that their dialog and even their goals—often the main reason for which I created them—change as they choose new goals. It sounds bizarre until you try it—but I digress, again.

Then I rediscovered how poorly documented Celtic myth is. This gave me pause for a bit until I realized that, rather than presenting a serious challenge, this was actually an opportunity that would afford me a great deal of freedom to interpret its vagaries in a way unique to my story's needs. As long as my enchanted land was internally consistent, it did not require a solid basis in this world's history, mythology, or physics. It was liberating.

Brython became the basis for the enchanted land of Tethera, a great kingdom fallen to treachery and malevolent forces where all is now crumbling and failing and only the very stoutest of hearts, the bravest of deeds, and the most steadfast of resolution might yet save the day. I had a grand tableau to work with but there was still, in my mind, a problem.

One of my favorite lands of enchantment was already based on the ancient post-Roman yet pre-Anglo-Saxon Brython of myth. Despite the many hundreds of versions of King Arthur that were already published, I had somehow gotten it into my head that an earlier writer, by using elements of Welsh myth (which itself is frequently well blended with Irish myth), had somehow claimed dibs on all of it and that anything I did might therefore be considered hopelessly derivative.

I put aside my notes and forgot about them as my life began offering quite enough drama—both then and for some time after—as I spent more than a decade wrestling with a personal tragedy. Much like Llew, I found myself, despite my best intentions, drawn into an unhappy situation that I could not resolve unaided and could not run away from. Fortunately, not unlike Llew, I found many allies along the way. Around 2005 or so I finally wrote a single chapter set in the very middle of this book. Every couple of years after that I added another chapter. I could not help myself.

Finally, my life in some semblance of order (as much as it ever seems to get, at any rate) I told myself that the work I was afraid of being compared to was over fifty years old and, moreover, no one author should or could lay claim to an entire culture's mythology, no matter how wonderful his use of it was (and is). As far as being influenced by writers that came before? Well, what writer can honestly say that he or she has not been? It was like avoiding writing pirate and buried treasure stories because of the existence of Robert Louis Stevenson's *Treasure Island*.

Then I bore down and finished the book, nearly twenty years after it was begun.

At once I began to go through again and again, scouring out any similarities that did not seem in some way connected to the source material.

Modern stories need great villains and, in mythology, who is ever a greater villain than the ruler of the underworld? Alas, poor Arawen. He is not portrayed too badly in the myths but, let us face it, he is the Lord of the Underworld and, after millennia of exposure to the Old Testament, our own culture tends to interpret that title in a very negative way. Compare how Hades and Hel—two nominally not-evil sovereign gods of the underworld in their own pantheons—are typically treated in modern culture. For a modern audience, Arawen assumes his mantle as the principle villain naturally and I make no apologies for it.

Much as I wanted to employ it, I deliberately avoided all use of a certain cauldron despite its enormous prominence in Celtic myth and the fact that a Lord of the Underworld cries out for minions that come crawling out of it from beyond death's door. I made other sacrifices, too, but I no longer regret them and feel that the work may be better for having made them.

I have tried to create a story that I hope stands on its own in our modern age, yet is grounded in the distant past, and intended to stand the test of time going forward into the future. Moreover, I have tried to create a story that, had someone else written it, I would be eager to read and, later, to reread and, still later, to read to my grandchildren when they appear on the scene—and they are old enough, of course.

Despite having aimed strictly for the kind of story I would like to read, it is my fervent hope that you enjoy it as well.

Michael Laird
Eastchester, New York

P.S. For those who have asked what has happened to

Afaggdu, I did what I felt I must. It was always my feeling that the old tales dealt roughly with him and not only in his deformities but in making him out to be a great whiner, even if he was the ugliest man in the world. When I came across the real-life Egil Skalla-Grimsson, a man who, despite being even less fortunate than the Afaggdu of legend, always managed to grip life in both hands and make his own mark, for better or for worse, I knew what I had to do. Please bear in mind that our Afaggdu is a much more even-tempered individual than Egil.

About the Author

The author thinks it a bit silly to write about himself from a third person point of view and believes he will soon cease doing so. Before doing so, he would like to point out that it seems a bit early for a bio as he is quite certain he is not even halfway done with providing content for it.

I've lived all over the world and worked in a large number of jobs ranging from lifeguard, appliance salesman, rifle range instructor, missile launch officer, assistant professor at the University of South Carolina, and captain in special ops. More recently, I have primarily worked as a contractor/consultant in fields pertaining to software development.

The Forged Prince is my first published work of fiction.

I live with my wife, Linda, in Westchester County, New York. Between us we have four grown children and expect that this may eventually lead to grandchildren (even though we are obviously much too young to be grandparents). Currently we are between dogs.

Please feel welcome to visit my sites at: http://lairdmichael.com

I can also be twittered (what a word!) with @King_of_Tethera